WHEN NIGHT BREAKS

Also by Janella Angeles

Where Dreams Descend

WHEN NIGHT BREAKS

KINGDOM OF CARDS, BOOK 2

JANELLA ANGELES

WEDNESDAY BOOKS
NEW YORK

For those who thought they'd lost their light, and kept walking
in the dark regardless

First published in the United States by Wednesday Books,
an imprint of St. Martin's Publishing Group

WHEN NIGHT BREAKS. Copyright © 2021 by Janella Angeles.
All rights reserved. Printed in the United States of America. For information, address St. Martin's Publishing Group, 120 Broadway, New York, NY 10271.

www.wednesdaybooks.com

Map and interior illustrations by Rhys Davies

Library of Congress Cataloging-in-Publication Data

Names: Angeles, Janella, author.
Title: When night breaks / Janella Angeles.
Description: First edition. | New York : Wednesday Books, 2021. |
    Series: Kingdom of cards ; book 2 | Audience: Ages 14–18.
Identifiers: LCCN 2021008132 | ISBN 9781250204325 (hardcover) |
    ISBN 9781250204349 (ebook)
Subjects: CYAC: Entertainers—Fiction. | Magicians—Fiction. | Memory—
    Fiction. | Mirrors—Fiction. | Magic—Fiction.
Classification: LCC PZ7.1.A566 Wf 2021 | DDC [Fic]—dc23
LC record available at https://lccn.loc.gov/2021008132

Our books may be purchased in bulk for promotional, educational, or business use. Please contact your local bookseller or the Macmillan Corporate and Premium Sales Department at 1-800-221-7945, extension 5442, or by email at MacmillanSpecialMarkets@macmillan.com.

First Edition: 2021

10 9 8 7 6 5 4 3 2 1

SPECTACULAR SCANDAL: A DOOMED DUO, DEMARCO DISGRACED

No one can say for certain what truly happened in Glorian during the last night of Spectaculore. Conflicting stories have cropped up from all over Soltair, ranging from one outrageous tale to the next. The facts are few, and only questions remain:

How does a star disappear into thin air?

And what does a showman's fall from grace have to do with it?

As the most notable contestant among the competing show magicians in Spectaculore, the performer known as Kallia pulled her own vanishing act after a final performance gone wrong; in her wake, a lovesick mentor whose magic is nothing more than a lie.

Once hailed as "The Daring Demarco," the story of show judge, Daron Demarco—celebrated former show magician who shares familial ties with the honorable Patrons of Great—is one woven with falsehoods.

"He never wished to use his magic, claimed to have left that life behind when he stopped performing," declared Janette Eilin— daughter of Mayor Andre Eilin of Glorian, who remains one of the many still hospitalized after Spectaculore's finale—in her exclusive correspondence with the Post. *"I should've known it was all an act." Eilin's reports further cited Demarco's abstinence from magic as "admirable and honorable" for the simple ways of Glorian. "And he took advantage of [that]," she went on to say. "Of all of us."*

Demarco still refuses to give any comment on his actions and intentions, nor on his alleged lover's disappearance on that fateful night in a once-small city. Whether he agrees to comply or not is no matter in the case of showmen and frauds.

Even in a world of illusions, the truth will come out.

—The New Crown Post

DRAMATIS PERSONAE

Kallia. . . . The Star
Jack. . . . The Master
Demarco. . . . The Magician
Vain. . . . The Headliner
Herald. . . . The Trickster
Roth. . . . The Dealer

THE FAMILIES
The Alastors ▲
The Fravardis ▣
The Vierras ★
The Ranzas ◉

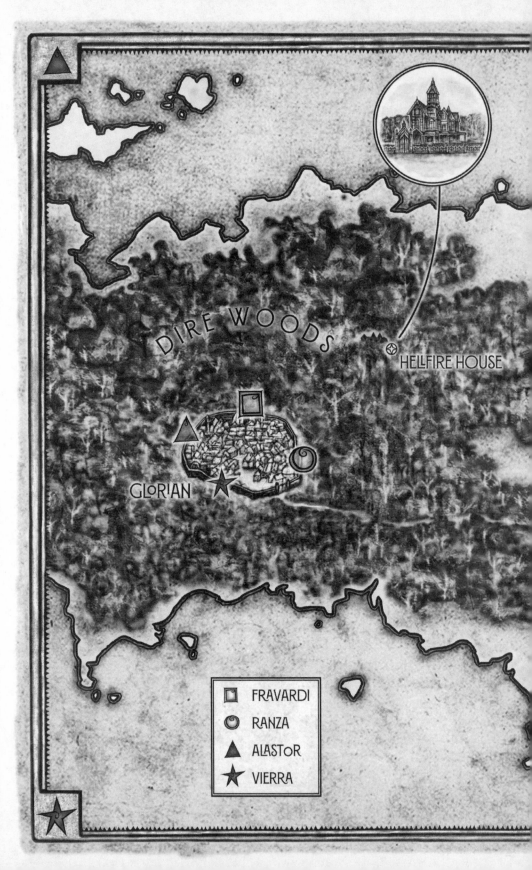

DIRE WOODS

HELLFIRE HOUSE

GLORIAN

FRAVARDI

RANZA

ALASTOR

VIERRA

SOLTAIR

NEW CROWN

TARGANA

ZAROSE GATE

DEQUE

QUEEN CASINE'S
ACADEMY

VALMONT BROTHERS
ACADEMY

PROLOGUE

The magician stared at his reflection.

His face was not as he remembered, the edges more prominent. The shadows, a shade darker across bronzed skin that had long lost its luster. His eyes, especially, looked like a stranger's. So often, he'd been told he possessed noble eyes. To which he'd laugh. There was nothing noble about him now.

And they were empty. Exhausted, like all his other reflections captured in the mirrors lining the room. Some stood on their own, others propped against easels. The interesting thing about being surrounded by mirrors was that your reflection looked a little different in each of the frames. A little wider, a touch darker; some startlingly clear, others somewhat musty. No matter their shape, they were doors all the same.

Still, no one came through.

No matter how long he stared, no one ever would.

Yet he kept coming back, unable to do what was needed.

The magician rose to his feet, flexing out his fingers on a deep breath.

He flung his fist into the first mirror before him.

No pain, no blood. Just fractures across the surface, broken so finely they appeared more like glitter than glass. He'd thrown harder punches before, taken them himself. But his fist trembled from this one. From an opponent who was nothing more than a reflection.

He shook out his wrist, the energy humming through his veins. Someone would've heard that, but he no longer cared.

Let them come. However weak he was, he was still strong enough for this.

The magician curled his fingers into another fist, destroying what he could of the mirrors around him.

ACT I

Once upon a time,

a magician fell into a world below . . .

The Dire Woods flashed by Daron's window like a nightmare he knew well. Blurs of black trees and branches jagged as thorns, bumps riddled along their path as though they were driving over scattered bones.

Only the dead could feel alive in woods like these.

Daron recalled his first trip to Glorian, how he'd tried not to pay much attention to any of it. Aunt Cata had always warned him and Eva of the woods no one dared enter, and that first carriage ride alone had only been a taste. Even in the safe confines of a coach with a map in hand, the shadow weight outside seeped through the walls. There was a reason no one was ever foolish enough to enter the Dire Woods without a sense of where they were going. Getting lost led to something slow, something suffering.

That fear was long gone after what had to be his hundredth journey through the woods.

Even with the occasional chill, he'd become numbed to the sight of trees flashing by like shadows reaching out to him. Their touch had dulled, the woods no more than a horror story. An incomplete and *immensely* infuriating one.

Hellfire House was nowhere to be found, almost as if it didn't want to be.

As if it never existed in the first place.

No matter how many times Daron shook the thought away, a slight thrum of panic remained.

No.

He couldn't entertain the idea.

It was all they had, a hope dangling on a hook already crumbling to pieces.

Daron stared hard at the words glaring at him across the seat, a bolded headline bracketed between the reader's polished sharp nails holding the paper out before her.

SPECTACULAR SCANDAL:
A DOOMED DUO, DEMARCO
DISGRACED

No one can say for certain what truly happened in Glorian during the last night of Spectaculore. Conflicting stories have cropped up from all over Soltair, ranging from one outrageous tale to the next. The facts are few, and only questions remain:

How does a star disappear into thin air?

And what does a showman's fall from grace—

"Do you really have to read *that*?" Daron turned back toward the window, his throat tight. "Right now?"

The issue lowered, and Lottie's serpentine eyes peeked over the top. "What? I'm reading quietly."

The headline taunted him. "You couldn't have picked a book?"

"This isn't some short pleasant jaunt through the park," she snapped, shaking out her paper to smooth out the crinkles. "As much as it pains me to read the *New Crown Post,* it's better to know what stories the world is believing."

Judging by the stack of issues crammed inside Lottie's emerald briefcase, there was far more coverage on him than during his performing days on stage.

"How do they even know?" Daron dragged a hand down his face. "I thought you and Erasmus arranged a deal. You've been the only eyes on the ground."

Lottie snorted. "I swear, for someone who was once in the thick of show business, you really overestimate the morality of others. I might be the only pen here now, but people talk. Letters find their way to the right and wrong hands. Your case is probably close to bursting, so it won't be long before a flood swarms in to cover this story."

Zarose. Daron hadn't opened his courier case in a while. Not since the constant telltale clicks of new letters started up again, until he finally shoved the damn thing under his bed. Just like when he'd first stopped performing, the world wanted answers. So the stream of letters kept coming.

He had no time to wade through them. His scouting trips through the Dire Woods kept him busy enough.

Every day, he searched through the dark for a glimmer of something. For the flash of a rooftop or hint of a building between the trees. He stared as though he could will them into being, though hours brought him nothing.

Finding *her,* however, was never hard. All he had to do was close his eyes.

And there she stood in that dark, just as he last remembered.

You'll be here . . .

The whisper pulled at him. Her voice from memory, or perhaps from the woods.

. . . at the end of this, right?

Daron squeezed the bridge of his nose, his stomach churning. He had to get out. Stretch his legs a bit. Breathe. Hours in the carriage sometimes passed in a blink, or dragged on like a slow death. But that was how he spent his days. Every day.

Most times he'd go alone on horseback, but today was a coach day when Lottie offered her company. Thankfully, she secured a ride for them easily. Like much of Glorian, even the coachmen scowled at Daron whenever he approached. But in the end, they took their payment with gruff silence. Coin was coin no matter who gave it.

Not that it mattered much. Daron was used to cold shoulders. Far better to be alone than in the company of those who despised him. Or just barely tolerated him.

"I'll drop you back off." He cleared his throat, knocking a fist against the roof. "I don't know why you even came with me this time."

They rarely talked. Merely occupying the same room would lead to an argument one way or another, so he was surprised the carriage hadn't caught fire yet.

"A long drive is good for the mind every now and then." Lottie gave a half-hearted shrug, watching him knock at the ceiling. "And I was curious."

His fist paused.

Curious. Coming from her, it was an omen.

"About what, exactly?" Irritation reeled through him as the driver kept on. No sign of slowing, or turning around.

Firmly situated, Lottie tossed her folded newspaper aside and crossed her arms. "You're not going to find her out here, you know."

The wind rustling the trees outside stopped.

You'll be here . . .

Daron's heart strained.

That whisper wouldn't leave. Every day, it grew louder.

"I'll drop you off," he repeated tersely.

"The driver's on *my* coin today, so I'm in charge of where we go." Sighing, Lottie straightened her newspapers into an orderly pile. "Come on, Daron. You need to stop this. You've combed through these woods for—"

"Sorry if it's not more exciting work. You're more than welcome to stay back with the others." Daron held back a scoff. It came as no surprise how easily they'd fractured almost as soon as they'd banded together. The first to drop from the group was Canary, who had no patience for hours-long rides through the woods, or for Daron. The fire-eater had never much liked him when they'd begun working together, whereas Aaros at least somewhat endured him. Though judging from the assistant's eventual absence to carry on his own lead in the city, perhaps Daron was wrong about that, too.

"If you haven't found anything remotely promising by now, you *must* move on," Lottie pressed. "You're just going in circles."

"Have you forgotten that these woods aren't normal? They're known to lie and play tricks." His nostrils flared. "You're the one who brought up that bloody club in the first place."

"And I know when to step back once a trail goes cold," she countered. "It was an interesting lead, but it's led nowhere."

Daron desperately wanted to escape this coach, even if it meant exploring the Dire Woods on foot. "That could change any day. It's fine if you don't agree."

Lottie clenched her fists. A feat, considering the length of her nails. "I could *shake* you, I swear," she huffed. "When will you realize you don't have to do this alone, and that I'm on your side? For Zarose sake, we're all on your side."

Daron gestured indifferently at the empty space around them. "Quite a team we have on our side," he said, leaning back. "Why are you even here?"

His voice was all ice, the only thing holding him together. And no one brought it out in him more than Lottie.

He still hadn't forgotten. After what she'd done, all those years ago, his body remained primed for attack just in case, waiting for the Poison of the Press to spin her web of stories. Miraculously, she'd stayed her pen against him for this long, but that wouldn't last. For people like her, it would be a shame for a good story to go to waste.

"Despite what you think, I do have a heart," Lottie said pointedly. "And I know what yours is going through. *Again.*"

Daron averted his gaze, bracing himself against his seat.

Why did she have to do this now?

"I went through it, too. I understand how lonely not knowing feels," she continued. "But you don't have to be alone for it this time. Eva wouldn't have—"

"Don't." His pulse stilled as the ice returned, the shadows swarmed.

Her name, said aloud, snapped something inside him every time.

"We have to talk about her sometime."

Even with every bump and jerk of the carriage, they were frozen. Lottie, damn near a statue on her side. He couldn't bear to even look at her now, not when Eva entered the carriage. She remained between them in every room, every conversation. A whisper, a ghost. Lottie had made her one to the world years ago when her story had gone to press, despite claiming they'd once been friends. A friend would not play up another friend's disappearance to captivate her readers. Even if it was to throw the world off to carry on searching in secrecy, she still got her money's worth. Eva was gone, and a glamorous stage tragedy filled her shoes instead.

"Is that why you're still here?" Daron asked stiffly. "To finally corner me? Get some new angle?"

Lottie's eyes slitted to dark slashes. "Is *this* your new front?" Her voice turned so cold that the ice in him faltered. "Can't confront what's wrong now, so you keep digging up the past?"

"It's no front. I just don't trust you."

He must've been out of his mind to think this time would be any different. From the moment she'd stepped into Glorian and spotted him, she'd been hungry for blood. No one changed appetites that quickly.

There was so much in her heavy glare, the harsh twist of her mouth before diffusing under a humorless laugh. "You just love making me the bad guy, don't you? It's so easy," she drawled. "When *you're* no better. And I'm done hiding it."

Daron frowned. "What did you just say?"

The passing shadows of the trees outside flickered over her face, but her eyes remained lit. Livid. "I've tried patience with you, especially now. But if you're determined to just sit in coaches thinking *that's* the best course of action, then here's some entertainment for the ride," Lottie said, nostrils flaring. "I've covered your ass from social ruin long enough, Demarco. Had my suspicions even longer. And not once did I air them out, because Eva didn't." The corner of her lip turned slightly in disgust. "Clearly in protection of *you.*"

"What the hell are you talking about?" Eva's name was no longer gentle or hesitant between them. Lottie wielded it more like a sword, a lit match held over a trail of oil. Daron could hardly summon any anger. Only confusion. "All of my secrets *have* been aired out."

It was front-page news all across Soltair. However outlandish the stories, they got one thing right: Daron was a fraud. No power to his name—not *true* magic, at least. Once, it had flowed through him. He was a born magician, after all. Same as Eva.

But what was a magician without powers? If such powers only came and went whenever they pleased? After Eva had vanished, so much else had fallen away from him. His love for magic, the stage, his grasp on his own power. Grief had hollowed him out so thoroughly, it only made sense that his magic followed suit.

Until he came to Glorian.

"You truly believe that's all there is?" Lottie tsked. "I thought you were just playing dumb and powerless."

Powerless.

His heart lurched as Kallia's face flashed before him. The pain gripping her body, her features, as she fell to the floor drenched in mirror shards.

While he rose to his feet, power flaring in his palm.

He'd replayed those last moments a million times in his head. Again and again, the melody wouldn't leave. Not until he knew every note of the music.

And the part he played in making it.

"I . . . I thought it had to be Glorian."

Eva had always brought it up. Something wasn't right about the city lost in the cursed woods, or any of its alleged mysteries. It was the only reason he'd come in the first place, with no other lead to Eva's whereabouts in sight.

"You thought." She raised a dubious brow. "Well, have you ever thought there could be more to it?"

Daron touched his temple, begging his thoughts to quiet. Every time he saw Kallia's face in the back of his mind, the knife dug deeper as he remembered her last words. Her last look.

It had always been staring him in the face, since he arrived in Glorian.

Since he'd met—

Lottie's bitter laugh sounded across from him. "If I'm right, then this began *long* before you came to this city. No surprise you're only noticing now. Too much spotlight will do that," she muttered with a shrug. "Do you really think as the Daring Demarco, you were running the show that whole time?"

"Of course not," he bit out. "Eva and I always worked—"

"Together? Is that why you're here and she's not?"

Cold blood thundered in his ears. It ripped away the numbness like a curtain drawn back, revealing more. All that he'd missed and ignored so often.

There was him, every time he took final bows at his past shows, grabbing Eva's hand so she could join him. And her fingers trembled. *Always* trembled in his hold.

Then the shadows under Kallia's eyes—he'd seen shadows like that before. Exhaustion plagued them after every performance.

Though he felt none himself.

"I didn't—" Daron couldn't move. Couldn't breathe. "I didn't know . . ."

It never would've occurred to him when that wasn't how the world worked. Magic couldn't just abandon the magician and latch onto another, prey on another.

"No, you didn't," Lottie noted with genuine dismay. "Eva never even told me outright, but I'm good at connecting dots. I remember this one time when she showed up at my apartment late one night, practically halfway to death, while you were off at a post-performance party."

Daron's chest seized once more. "How could she say nothing?"

"She didn't want you to know," she scoffed. "Didn't want your name tarnished . . . not only to protect your stage act, but because she's your sister."

"And I'm her brother," he gritted out. To hell with their stage act. "I would never want to harm her in any way."

Lottie flattened her lips, as if debating whether or not to say what she wanted to. But Daron already knew. Intent was a false shield when the harm was already done. Even if he hadn't known the whole truth, the signs had been there. Even clearer with Eva.

Those moments of irritation. Comments that sniped at his starring role before deflecting with humor. The days she didn't wish to practice with him. The long hours before their last performance when she wouldn't smile. Not until she hit the stage.

Somehow, his mind had parted with these glimpses. As if grief only wanted to hold onto the good, the happy, and never anything else.

There was so much wrong he had to make right. So much broken he needed to fix.

His temple nearly banged into the window from the rocky jerk of the coach. The motion jolted him with an icy awareness of the trees outside, the weathered velvet of the seats. Zarose, he'd almost forgotten where he was altogether.

"Don't worry Demarco, I have no plans to add more fuel to the fire." Lottie inspected her fingernails. "Lucky for you, gossip never lasts. You'll be fine not being Soltair's golden boy for now. You'll survive people hating you, losing whatever Patron privilege came with your name before everyone forgets—"

"Do you think any of that matters to me?"

His outburst shook the carriage, caused even the winds outside to fall still.

He stared hard at his palms, nausea roiling in his stomach. *These* hands, that had stolen so much. Careless. Thoughtless.

And deep down, he'd always felt something was wrong. Why else hide away after Eva had gone, from his aunt, from the stage, in the years that he'd become nothing?

Not nothing, something worse.

Daron suddenly wanted out of the carriage. He didn't care what the Dire Woods would do. He needed to stop. To breathe. To scream so loud, the woods would bend.

"If you knew . . . ," he whispered, brow furrowed. "Then why say nothing, all this time?"

There had always been that fury in Lottie's eyes. Even now, beneath her strange shadow of calm. "I couldn't be sure until I met Kallia, but she wouldn't have believed me. Nothing I said could change her opinion of you. Or keep her away," she said with a small eye roll. "But aside from that, what good would that do to hang you out to dry?"

"You could've turned me in to the Patrons."

A snort of a laugh. "I've been shouting about magician disappearances for years and it's gotten me nowhere. The *one* time I covered one as a death, they actually cared enough to show up to the 'funeral,'" she said, miming stiff quotation marks. "Now that the papers are all churning out the strangest shit I've ever seen, maybe they'll finally take notice."

Daron gave a wary nod. The stories spreading throughout Soltair *would* reach their notice, one way or another. With every terse, casual correspondence from Aunt Cata that week, it was the last worry on his mind.

"And besides, ruining you would only make you hate me more," she continued. "And I'd rather see this to the end now that we have another shot."

Daron blinked. "Another shot?"

"To do things differently." Lottie's thumb twitched, as if itching for a pen that was no longer there. "Searching in our own corners before didn't bring us any closer to answers. And now—"

Her lip quivered as she stopped, but Daron knew that hope. "You think Eva's still out there, too?"

He hadn't dared voice it before, but the thought haunted him. She and Kallia had both vanished through mirrors, so reason stood that they might've landed somewhere similar.

The possibility fired up his pulse, but Lottie didn't appear nearly as optimistic. "I don't know. We can't assume. Time matters so much in the case of a missing person, and a lot can happen in a day. For Kallia, it's been a couple weeks. For Eva . . ."

Years.

Of nothing. Silence.

"It's harder to tell when years like that pass . . ." The faraway look in her eyes cleared. "But our recent lead with Kallia is strong. So let's take it."

"With what?" Daron shook his head. "Without that club, there's nothing else."

Somehow, her smile deepened. "Just because Hellfire House was a dead end doesn't mean there's nothing. Only way to start figuring it out is by going back," she said, pounding at the ceiling above. "And finally getting out of this—"

Their carriage slammed to a stop. Daron almost flew out of his seat as Lottie buckled forward with all of her papers sliding to the floor.

"What the hell"—Disheveled, she gripped the velvet seat to push herself back up—"was *that*?"

Head ringing, Daron helped her up. A chill numbed him at the jarring stillness, the alarm in the air.

And distant shouting, outside their window. Hoarse cursing from their coachman, at someone or something.

Odd. He'd never encountered other travelers in the woods before.

Daron opened the carriage door, shaky on his feet as he leaned out. "Everything all right?"

The hulking coachman whipped his head around with a grunt.

"Delightful. Bloody white gloves and their little caravan won't get out of my way until I declare my business."

Daron's stomach dropped. "What?"

"*You* sort this out." He spat. "I'm just the reins. If I get taken in for driving some sad fool through these horrid woods day after day, I swear to Zarose . . ."

There was only muffled grumbling from there as everything inside him went cold.

White gloves.

A dull roar thundered in his ears. Before he knew it, he was suddenly out of the carriage. Lottie's faint protests faded behind as he staggered out to a blast of fresh air. The world gone quiet once his foot touched the ground.

The Dire Woods.

Never walk through it. Every warning clung hard to him as the shadows of the trees pressed harder.

Among them, a surreal line of glossy white coaches blocked their path ahead, pristine as game pieces dropped across the board.

Your magic, and mine . . .

Echoes of Kallia's voice swirled on the wind slicing through the trees. For a moment, he swore he saw her lounging atop the branches overhead, observing him hungrily like a bird watching a worm in the ground.

For a moment, he swore he was imagining those white carriages. And the person walking out.

Daron blinked hard, unsure which was the dream. Which was reality. Those were the games these woods liked to play. The kind no one could win.

When he opened his eyes, Kallia had vanished.

The white carriages remained, as did the white-gloved woman walking out from them. Palms out, ready for a fight.

Daron's fists remained at his sides as he took in every detail from afar. Even with swirls of silver, her hair was as dark as his, wrapped in an unforgivable bun. Angular spectacles framed around sharp, challenging stare. "Daron?"

Blood thundered in his ears at her voice.

She was no dream. No matter how many times he blinked, she remained standing there before him. And there was no other choice but to answer. "Aunt Cata."

The spotlight found Kallia the moment she rose to her feet.

Applause followed. So startlingly loud, she froze. Her heart pounded, every desperate beat a question. *Where, how, who?* Every time she looked out for the answer, her vision watered against the piercing light.

So bright, dizzying.

The crowd cheered on, even when she shielded her eyes.

Never in her life had she ever wanted silence more.

Pulling in a breath, she forced her gaze downward, for something still. An anchor. That was the trick to balance whenever she spun over dance floors: focusing on the dirtied tops of her shoes and the smooth polished ground.

Kallia stilled, taking in the same shade of wood. Same lines and indents.

Even the smell—that old oaken scent that chilled her every time she breathed it in before a performance.

She was back. In the theater of the Alastor Place.

The applause raged even harder. Whistling, cheering.

Kallia

Kallia

Kallia

The song of her name was intoxicating as this spotlight she'd longed for like a fire in the cold.

It took everything in her not to close her eyes and enjoy.

"Kallia."

She turned at the voice, lost in the roar of the applause.

Before it was all shattering glass—over her skin, numbing her ears against the shower of mirror shards in that endless dark. One moment in the Court of Mirrors, and the next, receiving a standing ovation on stage.

As though she'd just come off the greatest show of her life.

Kallia

Kallia

"Kallia."

Her eyes flew open to light harsh as the sun. She searched for that voice. Those footsteps.

The smallest swirl of smoke entered in one thin tendril, pluming into a dark cloud, like night vanishing the moon. In its place, a figure slowly stepped into view, taking all light with him entirely.

Kallia edged back from the darkness he brought, familiar as the silhouette—the hint of a lean muscled frame in the sharp suit she'd know anywhere. "Jack."

Not a question; a certainty.

He walked on, unfaltering. "Keep talking to me, Kallia."

While his steps grew louder, the applause fell softer. The shadow rows of velvet seats behind him parted in strange whirls of smoke at his movement. A dream coming apart the deeper he cut into it.

"What the hell is happening?" Her voice broke as the walls bled, creeping to the stage. "What are you doing to me?"

Jack paused, his dark eyes narrowing. The regal tilt of them, sharpening. "You think *I'm* doing this?"

"Wouldn't be the first time." As if she didn't know exactly what this was.

He'd gone back into her mind, as he did in Hellfire House. Soon she'd wake up recalling nothing, only to find his hand outstretched to her in concern. A hand she knew all too well. Kind and gentle at first, until it twisted.

She'd been here far too many times.

"Kallia, the longer you believe in all this, the longer it'll keep you." He dragged out a long breath, gesturing all around him. "You have to pull yourself from it *now*."

There was no choice when Jack was by her side already. Far too close, too fast, that it forced her back a half-step—

And the rest of the theater disappeared.

Quick as a candle snuffed out.

Darkness stole over the world, and cold air ruled it. Pure as ice, whipping across her skin until she shivered. There was just barely enough light in this night to look down at herself, all tatters of her red dress. Scratches and cuts scored down the split hem, with the graceful swoop of her neckline left dirtied and frayed. Absolutely destroyed.

Yet when Jack presented himself, he looked infuriatingly perfect in his sharply fitted suit. Unaffected, save for the relief relaxing his stance. "Good. You're out." The tension in his shoulders dropped a fraction. "I was worried you might—"

Her fist connected with his nose.

Bone cracked.

Jack staggered back with a shocked grunt. If it left something broken and bleeding, it still wouldn't be enough.

"Stay away from me." Seething, Kallia shook out her fingers and turned. There was nothing more to say, and she wanted nothing at all to do with him.

"Kallia, *wait*."

She kept walking. In which direction, she couldn't tell. Anywhere far from him seemed the safest option.

"Do you even know where you're going?" he called out. "You can't go off alone."

"Of course you would say that," Kallia snarled under her breath. Just like all those times he'd told her to never go to Glorian because anything else just wasn't for people like them.

"I know." There was a smile to his words, something warm beneath them. "But alas, no. At the very least, we're not that."

There was nothing assuring in the way he said it as he turned and walked on. No glance behind. No need, with no other choice but to follow like a fool.

An even bigger fool would simply stay put.

The bleak thought pushed her forward, following the man who walked through the darkness as though he knew exactly where it would take him.

The last time Daron had seen his aunt, it had been at Eva's funeral.

It was a dreadful day filled with shaky sobs and sniffles into handkerchiefs, eyes glistening all across the room. Daron's remained completely dry as he stared at the mountain of flowers atop the closed casket. A symbolic memorial, as no body had been recovered.

No one questioned where that body had gone once it passed through the mirror—where it was now or what her true name had been. As if it wasn't bloody obvious enough that this funeral was no more than a party for Soltair's latest tragedy.

No one had known it was Eva behind the mask, yet they knew every wretched detail of their last performance. The story spread like a wildfire. So sudden, Daron felt at times he was stuck in a dream for how the world had become a stranger. Believing a story, but not the truth.

He glared at the empty casket, every inch of him wanting to scream. *She's not dead.*

The look his therapist had given him when he'd said that was not the most encouraging. He knew better than to bring it up again after that. The world saw what they saw first—his assistant disappearing forever through a mirror from magic gone *horribly*, horribly wrong.

He had Lottie to thank for that. Whether or not she had become friends with Eva in earnest, she was the Poison of the Press first. Her coverage reached everyone before Daron had even reached his home, more isolated than ever. Losing his mind to a different story no one would ever believe.

She's alive.

Out there.

Not dead.

Daron was a man of logic, not impulse. And for him, the story had not ended that night.

His aunt, of all people, *had* to believe him.

When the room shifted around him, gone quiet and still, Daron knew she had arrived. A distinct chill hit the air, right on cue with the curious whispers behind handkerchiefs. The way the ground slightly shook at the orderly march of boots told him she'd brought the cavalry. The Patrons rarely made appearances as a unit for such occasions, certainly not with Head Patron Cataline Edgard.

Daron knew she would come. He'd expected it.

What surprised him was the white-gloved hand landing on his shoulder from behind. A touch of greeting, a gentle squeeze. Aunt Cata so rarely ever indulged in warm gestures, that Daron almost forgot to react.

She saved him the trouble by lowering into the seat beside him. From the way she perched at the edge, she wasn't staying long. Always serving Soltair, without complaint.

Surely this had to be a case no stranger than what she'd come across. His aunt was always the first to question everything, to press hard until the desired result came about. And most of all, she knew him as only family could. No one else would believe him but her.

Shoulders tense, she stared straight ahead at the casket, ignoring the curious glances. As the seats around them creaked, Daron knew he only had so much time before she fled to avoid the crowds. A silent getaway.

"I can't fix this."

Her soft words halted his thoughts. Even as she stared stoically at the casket, her eyes as dry as Daron's.

"Aunt Cata." He spoke quickly under his breath. "I need to talk—"

"What you need is to stay away from this sort of life," she snapped, fury hiding behind her lips. "I warned you both, and now she's gone."

Daron felt himself beginning to sink.

Gone. Such a hopeless word. A lonely word, which the whole world but him believed. Anything he said otherwise sounded like a story he told himself.

What if they were right?

The memory carved into his stomach now as he sat across from Aunt Cata in the carriage back to Glorian. For once, he wouldn't have minded riding back with Lottie. Already, he missed having the room to exhale and stretch his legs. Even just the freedom to lose his gaze in the window.

This vehicle left no room for distraction. Ever practical and efficient, the Patrons' compact carriages prioritized fast transportation, not luxury.

Their silence burned between them as they drove on together, every soft, uneasy bump of the ride sending a jolt up Daron's spine. Like he was suddenly a little boy again, ordered to her study for making a mess with Eva.

Sitting across from her now, he felt just as small.

"These woods are dangerous," Aunt Cata finally noted aloud. Nothing cut through silence more starkly than her clipped tone. "It's troubling how it's grown since I last came to this side of the island." Her frown deepened at the window as the passing shadows outside flickered about her face. "And from the sounds of it, you've been riding through here frequently."

That edge in her voice always sharpened whenever she reprimanded, but this was no scolding. No time for excuses.

Daron blinked slowly. "How did you know I'd be out here?"

"Already looking for a way to escape?" Her gaze slitted behind her slim spectacles. "And before you try switching the subject, you don't get to ask the questions here. *I* do. It's all I've done these past years."

There was never any yelling to her anger, which made it all the worse. "Aunt Cata, I can explain—"

"Explain?" The carriage hit a hard, violent bump, but she remained unmoved. "Maybe you can also explain why you haven't bothered to write me back even just once?"

The worry lines creased over her brow.

He'd put them there, carved them deeper.

"Not heard a single thing from you in over a year." Aunt Cata seethed. "The only reason I knew you were alive was because your courier case was still accepting letters. And of course, the press." She slightly turned her nose up, as though some offensive scent entered the space. "The papers seem to be the only things willing to talk, nowadays."

Daron's jaw clenched. He had no good answers, all selfish. If no one would believe him after Eva, he seemed better off alone. No one could see him, or see what he'd become. What he'd lost.

"I'm sorry," he said quietly. His heart pounded mercilessly against his chest. "After Eva . . . I needed time alone."

"And I gave it to you, Daron. I gave you time, I gave you space—" Her throat bobbed hard. "You wouldn't visit me, wouldn't write to me, and *still*, I kept trying."

Her voice never broke. Nothing about her ever did.

Remember to eat something green once in a while.

Don't party too hard on an empty stomach.

Please write back.

Her letters flew to the forefront of his mind, each line skewering him. She'd always had a subtle heart, kept behind iron-forged bars. It's not that she never showed warmth, it just wasn't often. Like rations, doled out in the times when it was most needed, not when he would've liked.

The first time he'd broken his arm after he fell from a tree—a tree which, a day later, had mysteriously been chopped down to a stumpy trunk.

When he'd gone to bed far too drunk after a night out with some Valmonts boys, only to remember in flashes his aunt sleeping in an armchair right by his bed, bucket in hand.

Those were never just moments, but pieces that only connected for him now. Far too late.

He didn't even have to question the disappointment spiking in her eyes.

He truly was a piece of shit.

"I'm sorry." Daron couldn't say it enough. Didn't know how many times it would take. "You don't deserve that. I should've done things differently."

A quiet fell over them. Even the motion of the carriage had smoothed its course, a sign they were nearing the city on the worn paths many have traveled before. The trip back was usually much quicker, but Daron swore he'd never experienced a longer carriage ride in his life.

Tell her, Eva's voice taunted in his ear. *Tell her everything.*

Daron turned his back to the window. The woods would not sway him, no matter how it tried. "I'm so sorry."

"You already said that." With a sigh, Aunt Cata placed her gloved hand on his carefully. The gesture, once again, gave him pause. "It's past, now. Driving it to the ground will not change it. Better to forget and move forward."

Daron didn't want to forget. He couldn't. Every time he saw her worry lines and shadows beneath them, he'd remember. Every hurt in every unanswered letter.

"No more silence between us." She capped the solemn order with a gentle pat. "We start over."

He nodded without argument. The weight of all that was unsaid dragged down everything inside him. The unspoken wrath, days of worrying, heaps of disappointment and frustration masked behind her work. She could curse him sideways right now and he wouldn't stop her.

But Aunt Cata never was one to indulge in such reactions. She expressed her emotions by putting them aside, and moving on.

Tell her. Eva's voice still teased as their carriage rolled through the Glorian gates.

About Kallia and the show, about his magic and the mirrors. About how she'd vanish, same as Eva. Lottie had been right to assume the

Patrons would take notice of the papers. He just couldn't be too sure what she believed.

"Aunt Cata," Daron began as the carriage slowed to a stop. "What you saw in the papers—"

"—is among the many reasons why we're here." Tightening her gloves across her fingers, she smoothly maneuvered her way out of the cramped carriage. "We'll chat more later, but there's business to take care of. Come along."

She disembarked without another word, leaving Daron nearly speechless. He'd never been asked to tag along on Patron business, almost thought he'd heard her wrong until she popped her scowling face back into view. "Just because I forgive you doesn't mean I've forgotten your tendency to run at the first chance."

Her sharp, expectant tone triggered some muscle memory that had him out of his seat and on the street in a blink.

Frantic, his eyes darted all about them. A line of other small white carriages continued long after theirs against the curb.

Just like the sight of white coats and gloves, patrolling everywhere he turned.

Daron's pulse spiked. "What's going on?"

"That's what we're here to find out," Aunt Cata said brusquely before a Patron flanked her side with a leather-bound clipboard. While continuing down the street, they conversed in hushed tones, far too soft for Daron to catch a word as he followed.

The Glorian surrounding him now was different from the one he'd left before his ride. Amidst the curious chatter, there was a quietness about the streets, as quiet as the time he'd first arrived in the city covered in ice.

People paused near the foreign row of Patron carriages conquering the length of the curb. Faces peered in windows, between the cracks of closed curtains, observing the new arrivals.

Lottie had been right. Nothing killed an old headline better than a new one. People forgot just as swiftly as they condemned.

Without asking, Daron already knew where they were heading.

After any event, Aunt Cata always prioritized interviewing those directly affected, collecting firsthand accounts herself. Her Patrons assessed the situation from the ground, but she went straight to the heart.

Chaos echoed throughout the hospital halls from the moment they entered. The sharp screech of metal and shouts only grew louder as they moved through the patients' quarters—rows of seemingly peaceful beds to the one closed off by a thrashing sheer curtain at the end.

"*Paper,*" a voice croaked. "No, get *off* me—I need paper!"

"Father, please—we must get you cleaned up . . ."

Daron followed his aunt toward the violent clang. A tin pitcher of water was knocked over. A hiss of a curse following after.

To the sides, attendants overseeing patients straightened instantly at Aunt Cata's emergence. Even the visitors sitting by bedsides kept watch.

At the flash of ruby-red hair, Daron stiffened, and accidentally met Canary's gaze for a tense moment. She and a few other Conquerors sat beside Juno, the tattooed performer who still had not risen. Much like the other magicians lying in the pair of beds across from hers, it was a troubling sight. Not much had changed over the past few weeks. No difference, no progress.

The fire-eater broke eye contact almost immediately, always doing her best to avoid him. He'd gotten used to such cold shoulders in Glorian. For someone who played with fire, hers was by far the iciest.

It hardly mattered to Daron now with the scene ahead. Tools and water puddles and pieces of paper were scattered on the floor like a trail. A man thrashed under hands trying to settle him, his restless white-gray hair smeared with bits of black tufting out. His eyes were wild, somehow bloodshot and drowsy and alert at once before closing in pure exhaustion.

Mayor Eilin.

The change in him was startling. He'd known the mayor best in a top hat and pressed suit with the collar buttoned high to the neck, disapproval ruling his manner. The man who'd fought him and Kallia during the competition every step of the way.

Hardly any of that existed in the patient before him.

Aunt Cata assessed the situation with a steely air, taking in the resting mayor as though he might rise in attack at any moment. She'd subdued wilder perpetrators before with just the touch of her hand, a last resort to prevent further harm.

As the group approached, Janette sprang away from her father, looking just as harried. "Excuse me, but this is a private—"

"I'm Head Patron Cataline Edgard," said Aunt Cata, smoothing the palms of her white gloves on full display. "My team and I have only just arrived. You summoned us."

"Oh—" Janette's hard expression cracked under a break of tears. "Oh thank Zarose you're here." That softness sharpened right back up as she spotted Daron among the group. "No one requested your presence."

The words stung in his chest.

He was saved the grace of having to respond when Aunt Cata cleared her throat. "I insisted he stay by me today. I hope you understand." The way she shifted position subtly shielded him. "He won't interfere."

"Fine." Nostrils flared, Janette sharpened her focus back toward the bed. "Thank you for coming so quickly. He only just woke this morning, has been out for a little over a week."

"I understand that he was attacked?"

"Knocked out cold." The girl's jaw clenched. "It's all over the papers by now, isn't it?"

"There's a lot that's in the papers right now. It's hard to find the truth of it."

"You want the real story, then?" Janette scoffed, resting her hands on her hips. "He was attacked by some mad magician who brought down the last night of our show. I worried he might never wake up."

"Wait." Blinking, Aunt Cata held up a hand. "Tell me more about this . . . mad magician?"

Daron had some choice words for him. The magician hadn't been in their presence for long, but he'd brought disaster as soon as he'd descended upon the ballroom like some nightmare. With Daron's face, no less. So many theatrical accounts of the night circulated throughout Soltair. Rarely did they speak of the nameless magician who'd brought down Spectaculore.

Jack.

Daron would never forget the way Kallia had whispered it, like it was less a name and more a warning.

". . . he and Kallia knew each other somehow. Zarose knows why he showed up—probably to help her win that stupid competition." Janette's tongue clicked hard against her teeth. "In any case, he hit my father like some cheat brawler and would've destroyed a lot more given the chance, so I expect there to be consequences."

"Consequences come once the perpetrator is caught." Aunt Cata nodded to the Patron beside her taking notes. "Since we have no name, would you describe what he looked like, Miss Eilin?"

"Tall, light-brown skin, dressed fine as a gentleman, dark eyes. Almost *too* handsome, if you ask me, though I guess that's typical with magicians of his kind." She chewed on the inside of her lip. "And then . . . he wore these odd rings."

"Rings?"

"Yes, but they covered something. Some marks . . . it all happened so fast, I didn't get a look." Janette's frown deepened. "I swear, my father had said something about the . . ."

Aunt Cata tilted her head. "Yes?"

The girl blinked. "Nothing. Just old families, you probably wouldn't—"

"Janette, *don't.*"

A raspy voice sounded, before a rustling of blankets and the squeak of metal springs as Mayor Eilin roused himself back up. "You don't know what you're saying. Or what they'll do to you. To us all."

Terror clung to his voice, so much that even as it made no sense, it chilled Daron.

"*Who?*" Janette went to Mayor Eilin's side, her hand going by his. "It's all right, Father. You're safe now."

When the man only shook his head harder, Aunt Cata straightened back her shoulders. "Mayor Eilin, please." Her voice reached out gently. "My team and I were summoned. I'm only here to help—"

"I don't believe you." Eilin glared out the window overlooking a collection of gabled roofs in sight. "I don't believe any of this. Not anymore." When he looked down at his palm, the dark ink smudges against the side, he perked up. "Where's the paper I asked for?"

Janette sighed. "We'll give you more, *after* you finish speaking with the Head Patron."

"But I need to get it down now, before it all goes . . ." The mayor's gaze wandered to the floor where some scribbled papers had fallen hastily, before there was a pause. "Ah, Demarco. Is that you?"

Daron's throat went dry, more from the uncharacteristic sunniness than the recoginition.

"Excellent timing." The mayor continued humming to himself. "Saves me the trouble."

Curious, Aunt Cata immediately stepped aside to give him full view of Daron. Not that Janette even cared, by this point. "What business do you have with him?"

The mayor tipped his head back with a light chuckle. "Wouldn't you like to know? Wouldn't we all?" With a small, tired smile, he patted his daughter's hand. "You don't remember, but you will. It's not our faults we've forgotten."

"That ball was utter madness, Father." Janette pulled the blanket back over his feet. "I can't imagine how anyone—"

"No, I'm not talking about that night." The mayor's brow furrowed. "This goes far beyond that night. Years before it."

Silence pulled at the air between them, every wordless second its own tense heartbeat.

"Father . . ." She regarded him unsurely, delicately. "You're not making any sense."

"I'm seeing clearer than I have in a long time. Like a weight that was pressing down on me from somewhere, now gone. No clouds, no blocks.

I remember—" He sighed harshly, examining the planes of his fingers. "That young magician in the dark suit, with triangles on his knuckles, I *know* him. We all do."

Daron hadn't even realized he'd pressed forward until Aunt Cata urged him back with her shoulder. Were it anyone else, he would've knocked them over without hesitation.

I know him.

Which meant the man knew more, knew where Kallia could be.

A lead.

Finally.

"I'm afraid we'll have to talk another time, Head Patron." Janette lifted her shoulder with an apology. "I think what my father probably needs most right now is some rest."

Mayor Eilin shoved the sheet blanket off him. "No, I don't need rest. I need to get it all out before it goes away." He glanced frantically at Daron, then to Aunt Cata. "Head Patron Edgard, I've had all sorts of questions in the back of my head that surely you'd know the answers to. Patrons, and all."

Cata's "We know much, Mayor Eilin, but not everything."

"Isn't that the irony of this city, too? We're even more in the dark. Shoved in it, if you ask me." He raised a brow at her, turning it on all of them. "Because why is this city no more than just a wild rumor and speculation? Unremembered, unknown to so many. Lost, when there's not even much found about it in the first place."

A prickle of awareness ran through Daron. He'd wondered all of this before. Not too long ago. The riddle of Glorian wasn't just for those outside the city looking in, but for those within the walls, too. Rumors spread fast, but this silence had endured. It bred stories and theories that became like a mask. And somehow, all of Soltair had just accepted it as that.

How can a city disappear when it stood around them?

"No guesses as to why?" the mayor posed, watching them carefully. "Not even you, Head Patron?"

In an interview, stilted silence from Aunt Cata was rare. She always had a ready answer, or at the very least, a response to keep the victim at ease. Somehow in all of this, Mayor Eilin had turned the tables on them all.

Janette finally broke the silence with a nervous, shaky laugh. "That's quite enough." Her cheeks flushed pink. "We can reschedule this so I can ring the nurse—"

"Janette, you've known for a long time that something has not been right. We all have." Mayor Eilin picked up his daughter's hand again, placing it against his head. "Someone has stolen from us, right *here*. Again and again."

She pulled back from his hold. "Father, *please*."

"You know I'm right. You don't remember yet, but you will."

That line again hung over them all, more ominous than ever. Something warred behind Janette's eyes, slowly watering to the edges as she withdrew from the bed. "I-I need to step out for a moment, but please keep him here." Without looking at anyone, she gestured for a nurse, her face crumpling. "However well he says he feels, he clearly needs some rest now."

The sight of Janette's shaking shoulders on her way out left a hollow feeling inside Daron. He didn't know who he felt more for, the girl or her father who solemnly looked at the spot where she'd just been holding his hand.

Daron recognized the sort of loss that shadowed over the mayor's face. If his own daughter didn't believe him, no one would. He knew that feeling well.

"The truth can be so large, not everyone is ready to hear it." The mayor let out a low sigh. "Wouldn't you agree, Head Patron?"

Aunt Cata let out a tense hum of a sound, neither in agreement nor disagreement. Furtively, she examined the other Patrons' notes before they exchanged glances and hushed whispers with one another.

Daron's pulse quickened at the slightest tug from his sleeve.

"Be careful with whom you trust, Demarco," the mayor whispered in a low, gravelly voice. "You've been looking for answers ever since you arrived. Far more than that, too."

Daron gave a jerky nod.

The mayor bore a smile of relief. "They wanted me to pass along some advice," he said. "It's hard to find a single thing when the game board's been wiped clean, even harder when you're on the wrong game board altogether."

"Who's *they*—" Daron's pulse skipped as his fist clenched tightly. "What are you talking about?"

"Look for the gate, and you'll finally find her."

Daron's heart went still.

Kallia.

He pressed closer to the bed. "What did you say?"

"Daron?"

His aunt's voice fell to the side as he shook her hand off him. "*What* gate?"

"You know it." Mayor Eilin spoke quickly, holding up the black-stained sides of his hands. "I tried drawing you the path, to find the way in to get below the surface. It's closer than you think—*wait*—" His eyes began drifting, his speech slowing. Slurring. "Lose yourself . . . where those dare not . . . get lost . . ."

No, no, no. In a burst of panic, Daron shot forward, close to shaking the man back awake by the shoulders.

Not until he noticed his aunt's hand on Mayor Eilin's. Her cold stare intent, focused. "That's enough for now. You should rest."

"One magician can enter . . . only one can . . ."

"What are you *doing*?" Daron seethed, ready to tear her hand away before someone grabbed him back by the elbows.

Daron struggled hard, slamming his shoes to the ground. "Eilin!" he shouted. *Please.* Just a moment more. A question. "Is she safe?"

He had to know.

He didn't want to wonder anymore, to imagine the worst. Whatever the answer, he had to know that.

His chest nearly caved when the mayor finally faded, sleep thickening his voice. "Don't . . . let them . . . take . . ."

As Kallia and Jack walked, the memories kept following her in the dark.

Like beasts tracking prey in her periphery, the illusions rose from the shadows, begging for her attention. Tugging at every familiar sensation.

Dark-rose carpets sprouted beneath her feet while the delicate music of clinking utensils and teacups of the Prima Cafe swirled around her. Soft, cool satins and velvet brushed up against her like when she'd browse through Ira's dress shop. Bursts of laughter and too-warm air found her in a heady blend of sweat, perfumes, and liquor from the Conquering Circus tents.

"It's not real."

Jack reminded her every time she stood still for too long or slowed even a little. Because despite everything, for a torturous second, she believed in them. Even as she knew better.

Just like the others they came across.

The first magician who had attacked earlier was far from the last. There were more. A faraway voice, jaunty whistling, faint steps that were neither hers nor Jack's. Occasionally she'd catch their forms staggering in the distance. Ghosts drifting past.

Kallia knew better than to run to them now. There was no reaching someone lost in their own world, and the knot in her stomach sank like a stone each time they crossed paths with one.

All it took was one look to drown.

And there were so many others drowning around them. Without Jack, she'd no doubt be among them, wading blissfully through the dark as though it were light.

Kallia hated it. This was a different kind of dark, and walking with him in it made her a fool. But at least she was still walking. A fool, but a surviving one.

"When will this end?" She seethed. They must've walked the length of a city five times over, and yet Jack continued looking out into the darkness ahead of them. As though waiting for something to rise from it. "You said this would end eventually."

"And it will. Eventually."

Kallia glared daggers into the back of his head before down at her feet.

It didn't escape her, the way he walked too calmly. With every step came a potential trap, and she couldn't begin to comprehend how his gait remained so unbothered. "They're not following you," she observed. "Why?"

"Who?"

"The horde of flying snakes behind us." He was just being insufferable now. "The illusions, or magician traps—whatever you called them. If they're all around us, why aren't they pulling at you?"

"Who says they're not?" Jack countered. "I know this world better than you, and it loves to prey on new souls."

This world. That phrase still bit at her like an unhealed scar. "What is this world, exactly?"

Predictably, he laughed. "You mean you actually *want* to talk to me?"

"Don't flatter yourself," she said in a droll tone. "Everything is a lie with you, but I'm curious to hear what stories you're going to spin for me now."

"What's the point if you won't believe me?"

"Why should that bother you?"

The chill returned in the air between them. A tense second of silence.

"It wasn't all lies, Kallia."

Her muscles went rigid as she looked down at her feet, focusing on her steps. "It certainly wasn't all truth, either. But you knew that."

There was so much Kallia wanted to know, so many questions. And with Jack, she'd have to choose them carefully. Like her, he would never answer anything that revealed too much of himself or give another too much of an upper hand. The rest did not matter if she could confirm one thing for certain.

It's not gone forever.

It was not the first time he'd said so, and the possibility of it being a lie terrified her. If she ever hoped to somehow get out of here, she'd need her power. All of it, if she ever hoped to make it past Jack.

"I did tell you before, mirrors are like windows. Like coins and cards, there are two sides. The world we see—where life is true and fleeting and mortal," Jack said before raising a hand around them. "And the one we don't. The other side, beneath the surface. A world below."

"A world below." Every piece of his answer chilled her. "And what's the difference?"

A hesitant pause carried into his next breath. "Power."

It's not gone forever.

Kallia squeezed her fist tight, no magic behind the warmth clenched under her fingers at all. Just anger. And the slightest, most foolish bit of hope.

"And how does one go about hiding an entire world?" Kallia mused. "Strange to have never heard about any of this until now. First devils, now this? I'm surprised Patrons haven't fallen from the sky from the lunacy of it all."

"Your magicians in white gloves have only just touched the surface of magic." An amused smile tilted his lips. "Though it's really not hard to figure out what's always been in front of you." He sent her a sideways glance. "When Zarose closed that gate, what do you think was on the other side?"

Kallia's brow crinkled in earnest. *Zarose Gate.* It had its place on the map, yet always felt like a legend at the core. Every time she'd stare at the map of Soltair in her past studies, that point of reference was all she'd known of Zarose Gate, aside from stories. "That's all the way on the eastern part of Soltair."

At that, Jack drawled out a laugh. "Some Patrons claiming a pile of rocks on a map as the legend is only believable if the people buy it. Doesn't make it the truth."

"And why would *they* lie about it?" Kallia had never crossed paths with the Patrons herself, but she'd always understood them to be the peace and order of magicians. Demarco had hardly ever spoken of his aunt, but there was a distinct respect in his voice whenever he did. Those who wore the white gloves could not afford to get their hands dirty.

As if hearing her every thought, Jack paused just to throw her an incredulous look. "Apologies if this may come as a shock to you, but I'm not the only liar in this world. Everyone lies. Sometimes they have to, sometimes they want to. But good or bad, we *all* lie—especially when it comes to power."

Jack walked on before she could pick at his words, but even she was not so naive as to deny them. She'd told her own share of lies, never one so large as this. Another side worth hiding. A world below.

Once upon a time, a magician fell into a world below . . .

It all snapped into place, Erasmus's voice spinning the start of the story. A tale that began long ago, one that built the world she knew and the magicians that inhabited it. A world brimming with so much power, it would've consumed everything, had Zarose not shut its jaws.

It's not gone forever.

"You said my magic would come back." There was no sneaking around it anymore. She needed to know once and for all.

Jack paused, waiting for her. "It's not gone."

"Well it's not entirely there, either." No matter how much steel she forged into her voice, it always bent. *"How?"*

It couldn't be a question of *if*. In a world like this, she needed everything if she stood even the slightest chance of leaving it.

"I can't say for sure, it's never happened to me. I've always been powerful."

"Lucky for you." She growled.

"No, what I mean is . . ." Jack trailed off, looking off into the distance as if his eye had just caught something. "Magic is not the same on every side. It might take a magician time to acclimate, or it could take just one step in and it's there."

"One step where?" Kallia set her gaze out, following his line of vision. Expecting darkness.

Instead, she found the moon, a murky distant light in the ceiling above. The soft glow of the trees and plants of all shapes and sizes around her was brighter, filling out the vast room cased in old glass.

Warm night air washed over her, sweet and familiar with wild, sprawling growth all around.

Should I have gotten you something bigger than a greenhouse?

Kallia blinked, surprised at how her eyes stung with warmth. How a place could make her want to stop, just to remember. To wait for Demarco to arrive and complete the picture.

Her pulse quickened at the sound of footsteps.

"This isn't your greenhouse." Curiously, Jack walked through, every plant and pot dissolving in his path. The deeper he stepped into the scene, the more it disappeared.

Kallia swallowed hard as she wrenched her gaze away. The desperation to stay gripped her hard, but she fought that false promise. It wasn't real, none of this was.

Not real.

She was only convinced when Jack shook her out of it. The greenhouse, gone. The illusion, vanished. Once more, they were standing in the dark. The loss, as overwhelming as a death that she had to shut her eyes for a moment before firmly fixing her stare back to the ground, hoping for the end as she walked past him.

Only Jack didn't move to follow her. Hadn't moved at all.

Perhaps he wasn't so impervious to the traps after all. Panic spiked in Kallia as she uttered his name, especially when his shoulders hiked up. "It's here."

Lights played across his face, forcing Kallia to spin around.

Her breath caught hard in her throat at the sparkling lights that nearly blinded her.

A mirage. It had to be. Like some grand trick, where there was only barren wasteland ahead was suddenly blocked by glowing gates, wrought-iron and bent into all manner of rectangular shapes.

Cards.

She drew back at the familiar sight. Her pulse quickened once more. *It couldn't be.*

Those gates. Her vision narrowed on them. They glinted and glowed, but it was less like a dream. More a nightmare.

And Jack didn't even try waking her from it.

"These . . ." Kallia took in all that she could of the wall, of the entrance. "These are the gates to Glorian."

Jack's reaction to the arrival was stoic, as if staring into the face of an old friend. Or an enemy. "Not the Glorian you know."

Daron had been escorted out before in the past. From parties or clubs where brawls broke out when the drink poured too freely and guests grew too rowdy. The ever-sober corner of his brain knew never to fight the hands of guards dragging him out if he partly deserved it.

From the hospital to his hotel room, Daron struggled against the Patrons every step of the way.

The fog of rage had blackened out most of it. He only knew from the harsh bruising grips on his arms still steadying him, his heart racing from thrashing in their hold. One moment he was being pulled away from his aunt in the hospital, and the next, he was shoved toward the door to his hotel room.

"You need to calm down, Demarco," muttered a stern-faced Patron. "Get some rest."

That only enraged Daron more. "I don't follow your orders," he seethed. "What the hell is going on here? I need to talk to my—"

"There's a lot of ground to cover, so you'll most likely be able to reach her by the day's end," the other Patron supplied, setting back her shoulders. "Until then, it might be in your best interest to stay put."

Stay put.

He'd done nothing wrong, other than let a lead slip right through his fingers.

Look for the gate, and you'll find her.

How could Aunt Cata have silenced the mayor like that? The way she'd done so, without any hesitation at all, sat so uneasily inside him. It was never the way of the Patrons to enforce magic upon another without magic. Especially one who posed no threat.

He'd been so close. To something, *anything.*

The Patrons weren't leaving until he marched right into his room, so he slammed the door in their faces, immediately pressing his ear to the surface for a few beats but the doorknob was already stiff when he tried twisting it.

They'd locked him in.

Daron gave one last kick to the door before thinking through all his options. The last thing he wanted to use was magic, if there was any left in him. He could scream until other hotel guests were disturbed enough to get him out, climb out the window and scale the ledge because surely—

"Zarose, are we bloody stuck here now, too?"

Daron whirled around, slamming back-first into the door at the sight of two intruders casually in his common room area—Aaros splayed across the couch, Lottie perched comfortably on the arm of it as she read through her notebook. Both settled as though they'd been waiting for a while.

"Why . . ." Daron could hardly string a coherent thought. "How did you get in here?"

Aaros raised a hand. "Thief."

Lottie closed her notebook and arched her brow at Daron. "You look like hell," she said. "We got a quick tip that something happened at the hospital. Though it looks more like you came back from a wrestling pen."

"You got a *tip*?" Daron deadpanned. "You have informants slinking around the city now?"

"Even I'm not that nefarious." She shook her head as if offended by the idea. "Let's just say the circus is always watching. And they seemed worried."

Canary. She'd been at the hospital, but surely couldn't have relayed the information so quickly. The mere idea of her worrying over anything concerning Daron, enough to inform Lottie and Aaros, was laughable. "And what did these ears hear, exactly?"

"You tell us." She glimpsed past his shoulder, down to the door, which was most likely still as locked as when he'd kicked it. "Given that we're all stuck with you."

Reluctant at first, he paced about the room to unclench every muscle in him before the words all came back to him. And the line that haunted him, still.

Look for the gate, and you'll finally find her.

He'd been *so* close. If it were anyone else, they might've thought it pure nonsense. But to Daron, those words were light, even if the whole picture was not yet complete. The man had even claimed to have drawn him a map, for Zarose sake, and Daron hadn't even been able to secure solid evidence of that. By now, everything surrounding the mayor's hospital bed was no doubt in the possession of the Patrons. Just like all of Glorian.

"Mayor Eilin . . . who would've thought?" Aaros blew out a low whistle, a confused laugh rolling out after. "I knew the man was traditionally backward, but this sounds like he's going a whole other direction entirely."

"Don't knock it just yet. We're either dealing with madness or truth." Lottie tapped her pen against her mouth,. "There's a fine line between both."

"Don't tell me you're *actually* entertaining this?" Aaros tipped his head toward the window with a groan. "There are so many other pressing issues. We've got Patrons running around *everywhere* now, and if we don't get them out of the way, they'll stomp all over the Alastor Place."

"As if you haven't already swept through that building four times over," Lottie said. "And since nothing else has popped up, I don't want to waste time on another dead end."

Aaros's lips screwed tightly, a rare expression from the usual grin. Just as Daron had taken to the Dire Woods, Aaros had taken charge of the Alastor Place. The ballroom, in particular, had been left in shambles after the last night of Spectaculore. Rather than let the ruins rot as they had before, Aaros was among the group sorting the building back to rights. He'd thrown himself into the work, hoping something might surface from the destruction.

"Well at least I found *something*," Aaros fumed, digging into his pocket. "That's more than either of you can say."

His hand emerged with a crinkled cloth, a battered rose with ever-falling petals stitched across the other side. It was a strange bit of fabric, but undeniably Kallia's. She'd never gone anywhere without it. The cloth never left Aaros's pocket, since its discovery beneath shards of mirror. Every time it was in sight, Daron remembered when Kallia had last held it, for luck or comfort, just before they took the floor together and performed their last act.

Looking at it was as painful as it was hopeful.

"You found that scrap ages ago. It's hers, but tells us nothing about *where* she is." Lottie tilted her head in challenge, waiting for a rebuttal. "Logic over sentiment, boys. Consider yourself lucky you found it before the Patrons did."

"You wish to play the logic game, when you're suggesting we listen to a man who just woke up from a coma?" Aaros folded the cloth within his fist. "This is ridiculous."

"Any more ridiculous than your boss disappearing through a bloody mirror?" Lottie fire back. "Because if *that's* the baseline, then nothing's off the table."

"So you believe all the rest, then?" Daron leaned against the wall. "All that talk about memory?"

Aaros barked out a laugh, *"No!"* just as Lottie shrugged with, "Well, why not?"

Doubt trickled in freely, Daron couldn't help it. The idea was so outlandish, it sounded like something out of a dark, strange nightmare. Surely if something like that were even possible, he would've heard about it. But he'd never known any magician with the power to mess with memories. A magician with such skills was impossible, danger-ous. And if that were the case, that meant everything else the mayor had said was just as false.

Look for the gate, and you'll find her.

It's much closer than you think.

The words all rang in Daron's head, louder and louder.

". . . really, Aaros, *you* are the local among us. Have you never ques-tioned anything?" Lottie snapped. At the silence, she sent a withering glare to Daron next. "Wait, am I the only one who's asked about this so far? *You* came here to learn more about this place, after all."

Daron's face went hot. "It was not exactly research I was trying to advertise at the time."

Back when he'd been trying to investigate Eva's disappearance in connection to the strangeness in Glorian. Back when his purpose in the city had been to play a role.

He'd enjoyed playing the role a little too much, dropping his search day by day. His focus, elsewhere. On someone else entirely.

Daron was not proud of it, and the judgement spearing through Lottie's tone was more than a little deserved.

"The incompetence, I swear." She huffed, tilting her head up at the ceiling as if in prayer. "Tell me everything you know, assistant. About your life here, the city, some morsel of truth to prove the mayor wrong since you insist it."

"How is any of *this* relevant, for Zarose sake?" Aaros bit out.

"It could lead to nothing, or to something. Never hurts to explore a question sitting right in front of you," Lottie said, her eyes narrowing. "Or do you simply have no answer for it?"

"No, I . . ." Aaros's brows raised, defensive at first. Faltering, the next. "Those . . . those were vague questions—"

"Who's your family, would they know?"

"Didn't have much family growing up," he said, scratching the back of his head. "Ira looked out for me, though she doesn't like to admit it."

"Ira?" Daron and Lottie repeated in unison.

"Older than old seamstress over in the Ranza Fold. A bit of a nightmare to everyone, loves *me* to pieces though." The faint smile on his face fell as fast as it had appeared. "And Kallia. She took to Kallia real well, too."

A stillness filled the room whenever her name emerged.

How she would laugh, if she could see them all right now.

"Older than old, you say?" Lottie cleared her throat. "Perhaps she'll remember something useful, then."

"There's nothing to remember. Nothing off, nothing strange." Aaros shook his head. "This is pointless."

"There's always something to remember. Or there should be," she fired back. "Do you remember the last mayor before Eilin? Any unrest? The last time any real crime crossed these city streets? Petty thievery not included."

Aaros didn't even have it in him to look offended. Only confused. "I don't know what exactly it is you're looking for. Before Spectaculore, Glorian's always been peaceful."

"That's not how cities work. Nothing is ever always peaceful," Lottie stressed. "Either that's the lie you've always told yourself, or have been told all along. You've really never questioned a single thing about the world you've lived in, even once?"

"Do you?"

"All the time. Especially now," Lottie answered soberly. "Why do you think I do what I do for a living?"

"Because you like to question everything?"

"So why do you feel the need to question nothing?"

Daron was tempted to step between them at that point, but Aaros had already risen from his seat. He didn't glance in either of their ways, though in passing, he was noticeably shaken as he strode away. The Patrons must've left their watch by then, for Aaros had already slammed the door behind him before Daron could utter a warning.

The silence lingering afterward pressed from all sides.

"You knew." Daron inhaled deeply before setting his sharp stare on the woman across from him. "You asked him all those questions, knowing he wouldn't be able to answer them."

Lottie pressed her lips tight. "I didn't need to be convinced. You and I have both known something about this city is not right. This only just confirmed those suspicions."

"So you believe him? The mayor?"

"Why not?" She raised a definitive brow at him. "You were so ready to believe him at his word about a map. Why not believe this as well?"

A fair point. He couldn't pick and choose what was truth and what was madness. It was either entirely one or entirely the other. "I just don't see how it all connects. Especially to Kallia, it doesn't make sense."

"Perhaps the reason is in why dear old Cataline went all rogue." Lottie tapped her fingers against her chin. "The Patrons would never act unless there's a threat. Or unless something of what the mayor said *was* the threat."

Daron swallowed hard at the idea, so against everything he knew his aunt to be. "These are all hypotheticals."

"For now. We need answers." She crossed her legs, assessing him intently. "And you're going to get them."

"Me?" He grimaced. "I'm the last person she's going to want to see."

"Of course not, you're family. Play that card hard while you still can."

Nothing about this turn in the conversation sat well with Daron. "If you remember not too long ago, she had me forcibly hauled off the premises and out of her sight," he said. "She would never just tell me anything."

"Obviously, it wouldn't be that easy. You'll need to be a little more artful than that."

"No, I mean we have not spoken in almost two years. My aunt would never just trust me implicitly with her dark secrets."

"So you were a terrible nephew for a short time." She shrugged. "Put on your best apology face and change that. Grovel. You're still important to her in ways the rest of us could never be—so you have the advantage," she said. "How else do you think I've kept Erasmus Rayne on a string all these years?"

"Do you really want me to answer that?"

Her expression slitted. "He loved me. Might love me still, but the dent I left in his little heart is the kind that'll never go away. Love is a scar like that. And pressing on it can come in handy sometimes."

The lengths Lottie would go to for her work shouldn't have surprised Daron in the slightest. For whatever heart she may have possessed, she'd still always be the Poison of the Press. "Do you love him back, though?"

Lottie tilted her head to the side, as if the question were new to her ears. "Not the point," she said in such a carefree manner, resuming her shrewd assessment.

"Love is a way in. Use it."

Kallia's jaw hung at the pretend city before her eyes.

It wore the bones of the Glorian she knew, but the flesh stretched over it was not the same. She knew that much just from looking beyond the gates—the lights flashing and colors dancing across her vision, raucous laughter mingling with music echoing in the air, mocking her from afar.

"Is this a joke?" Kallia's scoff rasped in her throat. Her first arrival in Glorian, which already felt like ages ago, had welcomed her with nothing but silence. Scornful looks and ice in the air so biting, not even her cloak could shield her from it.

Nothing of that world existed in this one.

As expected, Jack was the picture of calm rolling back his shoulders. "It's just an illusion."

"*Just?*" She had never seen one on such a large scale, with so much life and detail in it even from a faraway glance. Standing just outside the gate, the familiar shapes of spires and roofs peeking beyond the gate tops. All of it overwhelmed her. A *city*. Even she couldn't fathom re-creating such a feat, and maintaining it as a living, breathing place at that. The choice, above all, haunted her more than anything. "Why Glorian?"

"You'd have to ask the magician behind the illusion." He assessed the city with not nearly as much awe. "Of all the places, who knows why he chose to bring this one to life."

That immediately edged her curiosity. "Who is it?"

It shouldn't have surprised her, the silence that met her question. Just when she thought she'd calmed, the spark of rage lit inside her again. *Jack.*

"Let's keep moving," he said, the city flashing before them. "Knowledge comes at a price, behind those gates. And the less you can claim to know, the better."

Every curse imaginable flashed through Kallia's head. She could wring his neck. Her fingers clawed with the temptation, but she needed him alive more than she wanted him dead.

"Do you honestly believe that, or do you think I'm just stupid?" she hissed, keeping at his side. "In case you haven't noticed, that philosophy hasn't exactly worked out so well for you, either."

Clearly, from the way he watched the city—like some ghost he thought he'd long since banished—returning was the last thing he imagined would happen. The fact that it did, against every secret and lie told, was as unnerving as it was satisfying. He might've been the Master of Hellfire House before, in control of every part of the show. But this world beyond the mirror had shown it would not be controlled.

A resigned sigh slipped under his breath. "The magician behind the city goes by the Dealer. If you find him, or he finds you, a deal will be struck whether you intended to enter one or not."

Kallia crossed her arms tightly. "I don't make deals with strangers I've only just met."

"You don't?" At his pause, she felt his eyes briefly run over her before their gazes touched. The way they had, that night they'd first met years ago.

How would you like to know more?

It was all she'd ever craved, and one look had told her Jack could give it to her. She said yes to the stranger, and he delivered on all that he'd promised.

In the end, she'd gotten exactly what she wanted: *more*.

More than she'd expected, and far more than she bargained for.

"I'm a fast learner." Icily, she drew back her shoulders and kept walking. The closer they reached this Glorian, the more people there would be. No more alone time with Jack, which she could not wait for. "Sounds like you and the Dealer aren't friends, all things considered."

"The Dealer doesn't have friends. He has favorites."

Kallia didn't know what to do with that information, with *anything* Jack dispensed even though that's what she wanted. With all the sides to his words, there was no telling which way they truly fell.

Still, it was rare to see Jack wary of anybody. That, alone, drew her attention.

"And let me guess, you're not one of them?" She tilted her head, studying him. "Yet you're suggesting we go through?"

With a humorless snort, Jack gestured to the surrounding darkness at their backs. "Given the options, would you rather return to *that*?" He turned on his heel with a grim shrug, as though what lay ahead was no more appealing. "It's a power-hungry city, but you'd at least be safe from what lies out there."

Kallia shivered at the thought of walking out into the shadowy, wind-ridden path again, her memories stretched thin while she stared hard at her shoes to keep from drowning.

She'd have a much better chance leaving this world altogether in the place where she'd have her head on her shoulders. Where her magic would come back.

There was not much else left to lose.

She didn't look back as she stepped right up to the threshold. The air around her quieted, tightening as though she were walking onstage for the first time. That held breath, before the spotlight hit.

The streets glowed. That was her first observation when her feet touched the flattened cobblestones that radiated different colors with every step. Like coals simmering under the stones, a burning rainbow. Devilish red to lush orange to petal pink, and the air about them even mirrored the shades of the streets in the faintest hues. Like breathing in the very colors themselves.

Power. She felt it on those streets, in the air.

She didn't even check to see if Jack followed. She began to relax on a deep inhale, waiting for that flame to rush beneath her skin, restored.

Patiently, she waited.

And waited.

"How do you feel?"

Her eyes snapped open when she felt him come up behind her. His question, a mockery more than anything. Even when she tried to pull on her power, there was that tug of pain. Resistance. As though her heart were fighting against her.

Nothing.

Warmth stung, blurred her vision. She'd throw herself to the devils first before showing any of it.

"You lied," she fumed, slowly whirling around. "You told me it would—"

Kallia's heart stuttered to a stop, felt the world go with it.

Jack's face scrunched harder in confusion. He spoke in mumbles she could hardly hear, a dull echo, slow as the crawl of night. She didn't care to decipher.

The gate they'd just entered was gone.

Gone.

It was a sight straight from her memory. She didn't remember seeing a wall while walking around the outskirts of this city, but it rose around her now. And it sealed at the point of entry in smooth, untouched stone.

Just like before, when Glorian had become a cage.

"Where is it?" Hands shaking, Kallia didn't have the heart to bring them up to the wall. She knew what it felt like, that panic would consume her the moment she pressed at the stone.

"Where is what?"

Something about Jack's tone snapped her back, the daze cleared from her mind. Startling clarity rushed through her as she took in

Jack's stance—crossed arms, the dubious arch of his brow—and the realization slammed into her.

He lied.

Jack *always* lied.

One moment he stood watching her warily, and the next he was on the ground. Kallia heaved in a breath, her hands searing to shove him back down again. "I'm *so* stupid."

Jack lied. The one warning she knew for certain, and she'd chosen to believe. The foolish mouse, following the crumbs straight into the trap.

Now she had no power and no way out.

"You mean you actually *want* to go back out there?" Jack remained on the ground, propped up on his elbows. "What is this about—"

"Fuck off, Jack."

Kallia couldn't take another lie from him, couldn't think as she turned and ran. Through raucous groups, between the ever-beating traffic of carriages and cyclists. The chaos of the streets provided the perfect cover to hide. Color and magic burst in every direction. It would be impossible to find her. Already, she breathed easier as Jack's desperate calls faded from her ears.

But there was color, so much of it.

After walking in darkness for so long, every shade and hue felt like a new discovery. Every detail, a dream. Lip tints that sparkled and gilded eye paints that swirled across the face, noble coats that seemed lined with starlight, and ruched gowns layered in impossible jewel-bright shadows. No proper coats or furs, for the air swept over them like a hot summer night, burning with both sweetness and smoke at each inhale.

So many gowns pulled hard at her envy, especially as she'd never felt more out of place in her ripped dress. No finesse, no flair. By some miracle, no one took notice of her disheveled state. They were lost in the revelry, drunk on each other.

It was a wonder this city was still standing with its entire populace dancing and swaying over the cobblestones.

Kallia veered away from stumblers taking down victims unfortunate enough to be in their path of fire. A trio of ladies arm-in-arm knocked into a line of gentlemen who fell over like empty bottles. No fury, from the roars of laughter bursting from each party. Nearly everyone Kallia walked past strode blissfully clumsy, and she hissed each time the swift, gem-encrusted carriages darted through streams of people, fast as bullets. No one else seemed concerned, or worried about anything else other than their own enjoyment.

She wished for more eyes to take it all in, her gaze snagging on everything in its path. Every sensation pulled and invited her to join. To walk down the streets she'd ventured down countless times.

Except this was not Glorian. Just its skeleton doused in celebration like oil and flame in this strange, new city. The Conquering Circus had brought life to the streets she'd known—but what took over these streets now felt far beyond life. It was utter pandemonium.

She had to take as much advantage of it as she could. Even with a good head start, she wouldn't underestimate Jack. Each time she shot glances over her shoulder, she kept waiting for his shadow to appear among this explosion of color.

Hopefully the world was as much a minefield of distractions for him as it was for her. Beyond the volume of color, shows went on in every direction. From packed sidewalks to gatherings right in the middle of the road. A girl shuffling a deck of cards before sending them flying up like birds in formation. A pair of musicians playing from glowing flutes that somehow produced the sound of an entire orchestra bursting all around them. A couple of men partnered up beside them, executing grand lifts and tosses in the air, spins so fast they almost blurred.

Such overwhelming impossibility. A competition of every sense and sight. She couldn't even dare dream up such extravagant acts, such demanding choreography that her bones tensed at the thought of trying them on her own.

It hardly even bothered her when the few bystanders that did take notice of her presence whispered and pointed her way. Some threw glances as they continued down sidewalks. She was just as fascinated by them.

Who were these people?

"They're real."

Kallia whirled around at the raised voice. Not Jack's, but another. A dark-skinned boy no older than her, watching her as he leaned against a lamppost lit with ever-changing colors. The sleek gold-framed spectacles over the bridge of his nose glinted beneath the radiance, as did the amused smile he wore. "Sorry. You just look as though you're wading through a dreamland. Which I guess is true, depending on who you ask."

"Excuse me?" After hours of speaking only to Jack, with the music and laughter blaring in her ears right after, simple conversation with another threw her off. "What are you talking about—what's real?"

He pushed off the lamppost—pausing for a group of giggling ladies chased by a devilishly masked figure—before nearing Kallia. "Everyone you see here. Of course, there are harmless illusions among us. Friends, lovers, spectators, stage candy . . . you can build it all here," he said, flaunting his hands about him. "Every illusion is tied to a magician."

Illusions. With an illusion of a city, a city full of them made a perfect kind of sense. It became all the more clear as she peered closer at those who passed, some moving through the crowds as though they breathed a different air. Some expressions were filled with emptiness, while others overcompensated in attire far too outrageous. Though in a world such as this, discerning the illusions from the magicians was no easy distinction. Even when she'd known only illusions for so much of her life.

She gave the boy a closer look, unsure what to make of him. He had a strange and carefree way about him, with a rare clarity in his eyes. Absent in so many around her. "And what are you, magician or illusion?"

The stranger barked out a laugh. "Buy me a drink first before getting so personal." He caught his breath, throwing a hand over his chest. "Alas, I got here the same way you did, fell through the cracks of a mirror right into this performers' paradise."

Kallia's guard went up at the casualness with which he said it all. Falling into mirrors was no normal practice, and yet magicians seemed

to be performing every ten paces she stepped. Surely such a phenome-
non could not go without notice in her world. Though in a world well-
hidden, as Jack claimed, anything could happen.

"You're really not from around here, are you?"

The boy continued assessing her curiously, as though she were a
rarity. But the slight drawl of pity was not lost on her.

Her fists tightened. "What makes you say that?"

"For starters, your dress isn't even *artfully* torn, it's just . . . something the style houses here would have the biggest fuss about." He
grimaced. "Most of all, you've got that look about you. Freshly fallen.
Like all of this is somehow new to you." He cocked an eyebrow at her.
"Fun and games get old pretty fast once you've been here long enough."

Though right now, he was looking at her like she was a new game.
Her naïveté, a rarity. Kallia didn't want any part of it.

"Fascinating." As she continued checking the crowds for Jack's
figure, it was only a matter of time before he found her. Movement was
her one safety. "Excuse me, but I must be off."

The dismissal in her tone did not deter him from following. "These
streets are not exactly kind to newcomers. Would you like a companion?"

"Nope."

He rested both hands over his heart, wounded, before delivering a
gallant bow. "I'm Herald."

Kallia offered nothing in return, wary to give anyone anything
in this world. "You can stop following me." She craned her head over
those all around her. "I'm meeting with a friend just around the corner
who will be very—"

"*Worried?*" Herald laughed, keeping pace with her. "Ah, you see,
that's where you expose yourself, lovely mortal. Friends don't exist in
this world when there's so little spotlight to go around. Here, everyone
is out for themselves. So if you have a '*friend*,'"—he used his fingers for
air quotes—"Then you best be careful."

Once, Kallia would've agreed with him completely. A single beam
of spotlight meant there was only enough room for one on stage, and

she had been prepared to do whatever it took to get it. All of the applause for her. She'd never had to share it with anybody before Glorian.

One glance around showed her she was not alone.

"Though you mortals value such frivolities, yes? Your loves and your losses, those memories you hold as dear?" Herald's sigh was drenched in pity. "What sort of friends could you have like that here?"

He was lucky she didn't punch him in the face. It probably would've entertained him more, and she wasn't giving him a morsel of her temper.

Mortal. He uttered it in the way someone would speak of a poor, defenseless creature.

As though he were something else entirely, beyond the constraints of mortality.

"I'm meeting with the Dealer, actually." Kallia shrugged back her shoulders. All ice. "And he'll be expecting me alone."

It was the first excuse that came to mind, and sometimes lying was just as powerful as magic. Even more so. In a stark blink, fear surfaced in his eyes. "Damn, are you really?" His throat bobbed. "Shit, mortal. If you have to be friends with anyone, that's the one."

With a tight smile, Kallia walked more surely as if she knew exactly where she was going. "And he doesn't like to be kept waiting."

"That's for sure. The last person to keep him waiting—I don't even want to think what's become of that unfortunate soul now." Herald shuddered. "Never piss off a magician who's made deals with the devils . . ."

Kallia nodded, despite the chill prickling up her spine at the thought of those barren shadows beyond these gates, where half-dead magicians wandered freely into traps. A force like that would accept no compromise, no negotiation.

Unless the magician on the other end of the deal was more powerful, more terrible, than them. With the way the mentioned stilled the air wherever she went, she could believe it.

Kallia had to ask. The question was poised right on her tongue, before everything came to a sudden stop. All thought, gone.

There, in the crowd, waited a figure in dark clothes against the chaos of color. His skin appeared almost golden brown from the lights flashing around him, and the rest was just as familiar: broad shoulders she'd coasted with her hands, disheveled hair she ran his fingers through too many times. Just as he was doing now, before noticing her as well.

Demarco.

ove is a way in. Use it.

L It didn't sit right with Daron, but he still found himself pacing back and forth in front of Aunt Cata's hotel room hours later. All mental rehearsal, as he didn't trust the words to flow naturally without practice. Even when he was young, his iron-eyed aunt always left him a babbling mess where any argument crumbled like sand between his fingers.

He couldn't afford that when he needed answers.

A curse erupted from Daron when the door suddenly opened at his back. His aunt's arched brow met him on the other side. "Were you ever going to knock, or simply pace yourself into the floor?"

Cavalier was not in her nature, and the tight smile pressed against her lips could not look more out of place. "Aunt Cata," Daron whispered sharply. "What the hell is going on?"

A hint of rage goes a long way, Lottie had said.

His was hardly a hint. Everything boiled back to the surface in his blood: every trace of Kallia gone, every lead a dead end, and the *one* moment a glimmer of something finally found its way to him—his aunt silenced it.

Rage was an understatement.

Her face fell at the sight of it. "Better come in, then. And close the door behind you."

With a resigned sigh, she walked back inside toward a desk already piled high with papers and work. So calm, so composed as only Head Patron could be. Whereas he was walking on fire the instant he stepped through. "What you did at the hospital—the way you used your power against him . . ."

She blinked long and hard before lowering into her seat. "It's not what it looks like."

"Oh, really?"

His nerves were so set on edge, he couldn't sit. He paced the long of her desk where an orderly chaos strewn with papers resided. Some flat-pressed in neat piles, others just crumpled bulletins and crinkled newspaper pages.

The map.

The thought struck his pulse, but a quick cursory glance showed nothing.

It had to be there somewhere. The map to Kallia.

"What am I supposed to think?" Daron wrenched his eyes away before it gave her reason to toss everything out altogether. "The mayor has no magic, and yet you broke your code. You used yours against him—"

"To protect you."

"*Excuse* me?"

"I watched you, Daron." Aunt Cata began wrangling her scattered work, any reason to keep busy. To keep any hint of emotion from her face. "If the mayor had told you to walk off the rooftop, you would've begged him to pick a building. You hung onto every word he said like it would save your very life. Or someone else's."

Kallia. Every pained beat of his heart held her name. *Kallia, Kallia, Kallia.*

"I can only surmise what truly happened here, for the news is so all over the place." She leveled him with a pointed look, finally setting the papers aside. "But when I talk to you, it seems as though I've walked into a story that's only half-truth, half-lie. And that whatever the whole truth of it is, broke you."

His gaze dropped from hers at the warning hot pressure behind it. He couldn't. Not now, not in front of her. "It would seem we're all dealing in half-lies and half-truths. I don't for a second believe you put down the mayor just for my well-being."

"You don't think I care for you?"

"I think it's your job to care for a lot of other things."

The most imperceptible flinch shook her, twisting him hard in the gut. There was love in his aunt's heart, he knew. Deep, but there.

It still didn't change what she'd done. When the mayor began speaking, she could've simply removed Daron from the premises and left the man alone to calm down. Silencing him altogether was a choice.

"I am your aunt, Daron. But I am also Head Patron," she stressed. "I have a job to do here, and not many trustworthy pieces to work with. Only my instincts."

"Why not ask me about it, then?" Daron ground out. "You've had numerous opportunities."

She exhaled a slow, sad breath as she sat back. Her ungloved hands clasped over her lap. "We haven't spoken in years. A reunion is no place for an interrogation." Aunt Cata gestured to the chair across from hers. "But I hoped you would open up to me yourself. With the truth."

Daron wasn't sure what the truth was anymore, no more than the rest of Soltair did. Everything had twisted into such a dream, escalating the longer he was lost to it. No one wanted it to end more than Daron. To know what it all meant without the lies clouding it all.

"Only if you promise the same," he said.

Aunt Cata crossed her arms. "This isn't a negotiation."

"Hasn't it always been?"

Deep in thought, a long, hard look of concentration simmered in her stare. "Fine. Deal."

Daron took the seat across from her, and when the first word broke, the rest fell. Every thread unraveled from the story beneath sensationalized headlines and rumors, about a show that was not what it had promised to be, and a city somehow lost to those living within it. Of chaos lurking within its shadows, and the powerful girl he'd met while trapped behind its gates.

And magic.

Nothing more than illusion in his veins, for the longest time. The largest lie. The truth of it was plastered all over the papers, and the world hated him for it.

The whole time, his aunt listened with a mask hard as stone, carved without judgement. Her Patron face when approaching every case, no matter how far-fetched it may seem.

As he reached the end, the very last words hovered between them. A tightrope pulled taut from one end to the other from his very ribs. The only sensation in him was the thud of his pulse. Once again, he was a little boy before her, fearing disapproval. Hoping she could stay by his side while he fixed the mess he'd made. It had taken him this long to realize that Lottie was absolutely right. He couldn't face this alone. Not again.

The whole time, he'd dreaded her anger. At the very least, shock.

Not indifference. Nor a silence running on far longer than it should've, winding him so tight he felt ready to break into pieces as he watched her closer. "You don't . . . seem surprised by any of this."

Something awful settled in his stomach as she finally lifted her gaze to his, alert and unblinking. "The range of possibilities in the papers prepared me for anything, but it's not my job to be surprised," she said. "It's my job to know, to anticipate."

"So you knew?" The walls around him pressed in, dizzying him, but his temper jolted him back with scalding clarity. "You knew *all* this time?"

"About the predatory nature of your power? I had my suspicions, but they really formed when I'd begun reading back issues of the *Soltair Source*." When Aunt Cata pressed forward, her stare softened as it locked with his. "You were very close to this girl, yes?"

Kallia's laughter rang in his ears.

The shape of her smile pressed against his neck like a secret, the arch of her brow when she was right about something.

The way her hands cupped the back of his neck, bringing their faces closer.

Not touching, just close.

Together.

"What does that matter?" His chest ached, his voice low and hoarse.

"You can never see anything clearly when you're too close," she said, glancing over her desk. "And you're not the only one, Daron. With power gone wrong. Compromised."

Daron swallowed hard. *Compromised.* Giving it a name made it no less chilling, only more unnatural. All his life, he'd only known magic to be two things: born and acquired. Magic never abandoned the magician, nor compromised them. "What does that mean?"

Her fingers clenched tigher over the table. "Have you bothered reading *any* of my letters?" Quickly, she held up a hand. "Never mind. It's bad enough everything went unanswered."

"Of course I read them." He couldn't tell if that made him a worse person for reading them all anyway without any reply.

The surprise that had been missing from her face arrived at that. "Then you know what's kept me from checking up on you sooner?"

"The eastern border, right?" Every letter he'd read and reread returned to the back of his mind. "You were taking on strange cases out there, but nothing you don't normally handle."

From her tone, it hadn't seemed out of the ordinary.

The shadows crossing her face spoke otherwise.

"We've seen strange cases over the most recent years, did what we could to quell them before a summons came from Valmonts," she started. "Initially we thought it was just some boys wreaking havoc among their classmates, but their hospital wing was overrun with magicians who were bed-ridden and could hardly move. Not even to perform a trick, they burned out so easily. I'd never seen so many all at once. We figured it had to be some disease." Her brow creased as she stared straight ahead, nowhere in particular. "Until I caught sight of the remaining students on their way to class. All energetic, practically glowing." Her eyes finally returned to his, troubled and worn. "The math was simple from there. For every magician with the strength of ten men, there was always one with hardly enough energy to rise."

Kallia.

The dagger in Daron twisted. When he'd last seen her in the Court of Mirrors, she'd struggled. The way she'd fallen to the ground and clutched at her body, as if a poison had taken over. The whole time he'd thought it had been the other magician, Jack.

He'd been the poison, all along. "How many cases of this have you seen?"

"This year alone, there've been a handful," she answer. "Among a family in New Crown, a couple in Deque. And now yourself." She turned her glance toward the window. "We treated each situation on a case-by-case basis, thinking no connection to it because magic never turned against the magician. We never thought it possible."

Until it was. A terrifying uncertainty, like not being able to trust the hand that picked up the knife wouldn't plunge it right into your very own gut.

To hear his affliction was more common than he'd thought was like a quarter-comfort. Part relief, and even more dread. "You've kept this from all of Soltair?" He blinked hard at the realization. "All this time, you've *known* something was wrong and said nothing. Just waited for the next magician to steal power and another to lose it."

For what reason? If he'd known magic had become like this for some, perhaps his fear wouldn't have isolated him. Perhaps he would've known to stay away from magicians altogether. Perhaps Eva and Kallia would've still been here.

"These are not decisions we make lightly, Daron. We can't stir everyone up in a mass of panic without any hard knowledge or solution to back it up." Her jaw worked to a sharp edge. "Unlike your friends at the papers, we need all the answers first before making declarations."

"Well, clearly you haven't found much in silence," he pressed. "You work for the people, and the people deserve the truth."

"The truth will turn people into monsters, Daron." Aunt Cata squared him with narrowed eyes. "Once others believe magic is unstable, fear will grow. Misinformation spreads faster than knowledge, and people will take to it first. Information like this *must* be certain when shared."

The longer they waited for certainty, the more harm would come to others left unaware. "Then tell me, how long have you known about this, only to convince yourself that lying to the public is the best option?"

"We're not lying."

It was not an answer, and it didn't sit right with him. If they could comfortably justify this, what else they were hiding?

A dark thought tapped at the back of his skull.

"This is not how I wanted one of our first conversations in so long to go." Aunt Cata squeezed the bridge of her nose. "I'm—"

"Why did you *really* silence the mayor?"

She stilled in her longest pause yet, and he wished so badly for a better answer to come. Not more lies, more secrets.

Finally, Aunt Cata stood as if unable to hold herself calm any longer. She paced to the window, as if the chair had been constraining her all this time. "It's complicated, Daron. But I did not lie. I am protecting you, because I know what you *really* came here for." Crossing her arms, she watched him from afar. "Go on. He drew quite a few that are on the top, just turn it over."

When she gestured at the pile of papers sitting on her desk, Daron tensed at that crumpled sheet of paper on top like some trick was upon him.

The mayor's map to show him where to go.

Wasting no time, he carefully lifted it though it could crumble to dust at any moment, his heart pounding when he turned it around.

On the other side lay a nightmare.

A violent mass of black scribbles and scratches.

A darkness, staring him in the face.

Frantic, he grabbed the others in the pile and tossed them over, finding the same image on every one. Nightmare after nightmare after nightmare. "What did you do to them?"

"I only picked them up from the floor," Aunt Cata said evenly. "But there's your map. Satisfied?"

No. Blood roared in his ears the longer he stared at the strange drawings that told him nothing. No path, no map.

Another dead end.

"Then why—" Daron's hand crumpled into a fist over the table. "If it was all just pure nonsense, why silence him from saying more?"

Turning her heel on him, her spine straightened entirely. He thought she'd fight him more on it, but her lips pressed into a hard, resigned line. A deep exhale. "I guess there's no use hiding it all things considered. You won't be leaving until you get your answers. Not that they matter at all."

Of course they did, but her defeat was so easy he felt no relief that she was giving in. Telling him everything. "Why would you say that?"

"Because by the time we're gone, none of you will remember any of this."

Demarco.

Each time she blinked, Kallia expected him to disappear.

Her heart raced at that familiar rhythm when she caught a glimpse of his face, the hard side of his profile.

Here. He was here.

The shock struck her with such force, she almost missed the way he turned back into the crowd as if intending to vanish completely.

No.

Get to him.

Kallia forced her way across the busy street, no apologies or niceties in between elbowing through magicians and illusions who grumbled after her. Twisting around daring performances and elaborate costumes. Avoiding collision with fast glittering carriages as much as folks carrying towers of frilly ribboned boxes as tall as tiered cakes.

Had she been at full power, she would've cut through this crowd like an axe splitting wood. Without, she just concentrated on the back of his head, narrowed in predatory focus.

He shouldn't have come. That was the first thing she'd say to him. He should've stayed exactly where he was, with everyone else.

Typical Demarco. Chivalrous idiot to the end.

Kallia stamped down the stupid flutter in her stomach, the heat rising behind her eyes.

Get to him.

Her thoughts drummed, again and again.

Just get to him.

"Slow down there, mortal."

The harsh yank at her elbow stopped her, and her stomach plummeted. Kallia never stopped watching Demarco, growing farther and farther from her as she thrashed in Herald's grip. "Don't touch me! Get your hands off—"

"What exactly are you chasing?"

"None of your damn business," she snarled, released a moment later. But that was all it took.

Demarco was gone.

A pressure built deep in her throat, tight as a fist.

Gone.

"It wasn't real, whatever you saw."

"You don't know what I saw." Kallia's vision wavered violently at the words. The way clarity doused her like ice water.

Gone.

As swiftly as he'd appeared.

"I saw *you*, taking off like a starving lion that's just spotted its meal. Please feel free to thank me for the two carriages I had to stop from crushing you into the cobblestones." The pity as Herald observed her was somehow even worse than his amusement. She couldn't bear it from a stranger.

Kallia's lips pressed into a hard line. "I thought such tricks of the mind were only reserved for those wandering beyond the gate." Another lie from Jack no doubt.

"Just the dangerous kind," Herald clarified. "It's a brief price to pay when coming to a new side. Breathing in a new air, adjusting to a new rhythm. Sometimes you'll feel things, see things—those ghosts of your mortal life, just illusion playing with memory. Eventually they'll stop bothering you, but ultimately, they're harmless."

She wished that were true. Illusions were far from harmless. She knew firsthand the pain they caused without drawing a drop of blood. They were knives, piercing the most vulnerable places. Waiting to stab you when you least expected it.

The pain had not dulled in the slightest. It was even sharper, rawer.

"Whatever fragment you were chasing couldn't have been that awful." Herald's tone lightened, more than eager to switch the subject. "It led you right to the Dealer's doorstep."

Kallia snapped back, finally registering the familiar rise of buildings sharpening overhead, the music returning to her ears. Lights flashed like stars, scattered over the streets against lines of lamps glowing a vivid green-blue that guided drunken partiers to the source of the ground-shaking beat. A moving line snaked down the sidewalk, right through the ornate doors of the dark beast of a building ahead.

The Alastor Place.

Kallia had visited often enough to regard it as an old friend. The ruined, quiet corner of Glorian. So familiar, she half-expected to see Erasmus Rayne strutting out with judges at his heel, or labor magicians filing in and out with their tools and supplies to raise the broken stage from the dead.

This Alastor Place was alive. A glory. No longer wrapped in shadows and cobwebs, the outsides were awash in illumination. Posters encased within gilded frames at the entrance showcased captivating illustrations: a group of red-suited men sword fighting across tightropes, a musical genius whose melodies spun memories and inspired madness, a host of the most peculiar animals led by a leather-clad tamer on a throne of snakes. So many more, but of them all, one poster's frame glinted brightly with lights, caging the image of sleek and powerful silhouettes hanging off glittering hoops in the air.

"Diamond Rings." Herald gave a small snort over Kallia's shoulder. "Their nights are always chaos."

Breathless, Kallia studied them all. "Who are they? Entertainers?"

"Headliners. Best gig in town, to live in this joint with a guaranteed notoriety and stage time. You don't have to scavenge the streets for a morsel of applause or relevance." He tilted his head up to take in the grandness of the Alastor Place, before his brow quirked. "Though *you* should already know that, being friends and all with the boss man. Right?"

Kallia's face burned under the lights. Any more lies would make her look pathetic, so she didn't even answer. It had gotten her this far.

Right on the doorstep of the king of this court.

The Dealer.

Not exactly her option of choice, but the most promising lead to finding a way out of here. And from how Jack described him, an enemy of her enemy could only be an ally.

She braved the steps of the Alastor Place as though she were wrapped in her finest wear, not the tatters and tears from disaster. The sound of footsteps followed behind to no surprise, but Kallia turned sharply anyway. "I must've missed the part where I invited you to escort me in."

"Invited?" Herald appeared far too amused as he held the door open for her. "Why, I'm here to enjoy the show."

A small pang went through her. Not by any haunting illusion this time—only the sight of him standing gallantly by the door, a noble gesture made wicked by the glint in his eye, conjured no illusion. Though it was all too familiar.

Small moments came back to her—that sharp elbow looping with hers whenever they strutted out together. How he would always be the first to open a door, out of politeness but also for the opportunity to dip a hand in an unguarded pocket.

Perhaps that was why she couldn't shake him even when she'd wanted to. There was something about him. Something undeniable that reminded her of Aaros.

Without him by her side in a new world—a new game—was like taking the stage all on her own. The act, incomplete.

No. Kallia's throat tightened as she passed Herald without a word, hardening her features into a mask. She'd taken the stage alone before. She could damn well do so again.

❃   ❃   ❃

Grand as the outside of the Alastor Place was, the inside existed on a different realm. The last time Kallia had walked down these carpeted floors was the last night of Spectaculore. She'd never been more swept away by the party winding through the halls, every inch glittering from ceiling to floor like an old polished diamond.

Now, she was utterly drowning.

Every part of the Alastor Place dripped with decadence. Velvet filtered her vision, satin soaked in the air. Lush black curtains that shone teal in the small flames flickering off silver-rusted candle vines that twisted across the walls, styled more like tentacles frozen in time. The icy chandeliers fixed to the ceilings remained grand as ever, sparkling coldly despite the heat of the party and its guests streaming from all directions.

It was all an illusion, she kept reminding herself. The whole city was.

Yet whoever conjured it into this dream crafted each space with such detail and intricacy, a labor of love for a city she'd thought had been forgotten by all.

The Dealer, whoever he was, grew into even more of a curiosity, the deeper she fell into this world.

As the familiar doors of the Court of Mirrors loomed ahead, lights shining through with every partier passing in and out, Kallia tensed.

The last time she'd entered, she had never left.

"See, I'm not the only one who can spot a mortal a mile away."

Kallia tore her focus from the doors and onto the departing guests who slowed by her and Herald in passing, whispering among each other. Kallia's insides tightened when one even perched some ocular accessary on the bridge of her nose, though they were no more than a few feet apart.

Herald snorted. "Your costume is a bit of a giveaway."

Kallia didn't bother looking down, unable to shake the unease of the word he kept throwing around like confetti. "If I'm so mortal, what does that make you all, then?"

"Something we all become in time, the longer we remain. More than just magicians." He pushed the doors wide open with a triumphant grin. "Here, we're like gods."

If the pounding music and shaking walls had been the warning hints of smoke, the blaze was the Court of Mirrors.

The dark ballroom stretched out like a glittering circus wrapped in mirrors, rows upon rows running across the walls. Within the frames, the surfaces appeared slightly aglow with faintly moving images. Kallia couldn't make them out from where she stood, but the rest of the room was enough of a show for the eyes. Bright lights shined upon round red-glassed tables, occupied by patrons enjoying their drinks and those with heads bent over card games and rolled dice. Shouts of outrage layered over raucous victory, the music of winning and losing playing as one.

The scene was so reminiscent of Hellfire House, Kallia half-expected to see Jack waiting at the bar that snaked around the tables. Just the thought made her tense, alert—

Until fluid movements snagged her attention.

The shadowed silhouettes of ladies, descending from the ceiling.

One after the other, they fell. Not to their deaths, but above the heads of their audience, limbs braced along the curves of large glittering hoops hanging suspended by chains that lifted them from high above. Like birds gliding on a wind, the performers rose and fell at varying heights, striking their poses with fearless grace to the sultry music pulsing in the air.

The poster from outside lit up in the back of Kallia's mind.

The Diamond Rings.

At their entry, the crowd roared their approval. Games were abandoned, drinks left untouched. All to watch the performers lowering like a troupe of black widows coming in for the kill—

Before a dagger speared through the air, deep into the chest of one girl.

Kallia's blood went cold as the body fell. A few screams erupted. Nothing made her sicker than the resounding laughter from the boorish group of drunken magicians a few tables away. Among them, one had his foot stepped on the seat of his chair, chest puffed out with a knife in hand as if ready to take aim again.

Vision searing red, Kallia pressed forward.

Only to be tugged by the back of her dress.

"Not much you can do, mortal. It's just a bunch of idiots getting their kicks," Herald said, shaking his head. "They hit an illusion. It'll be fine."

"Fine?" Snarling in a breath, Kallia searched the floors for where the stabbed performer had fallen. She should've known when there was no thud of a body, or even the hoop that held her.

Still, illusion or not, it wasn't fine by her. It was easy for cowards to feel brave with the cover of the audience, and the fact that no one lifted a damn finger to stop a thing had Kallia grinding her teeth.

She threw a sharp elbow back, but Herald artfully dodged it. "Trust me, you do not throw yourself in their line of fire."

"If you don't let go," Kallia warned, wriggling like a cat caught by its scruff, "I'll throw *you* into their pathetic line of fire."

"I wasn't talking about—"

A desperate scream ripped through the air.

The room went dark.

Kallia stilled as shrieks burst around them, before the light finally returned in a gradual rise over the tables. The silhouetted forms of the Diamond Rings sat within their hoops, all lined up in a row over the party of magicians who had been laughing earlier. Among them, one was missing. The bold gentleman who'd taken aim.

The stark beam of the spotlight exposed how he trembled, dangling one-handed from a large glittering hoop like bait on a hook.

His whitening knuckles strained between the pair of heeled boots of the new masked performer above him.

"Look what got on my hoop," she drawled in disgust, as if noticing a stain against her costume: an ink green confection of lace and feathers pluming down the back like a dark bird of prey ready to take flight. From her apparatus high in the air, she certainly looked the part. No mercy, as she inched her heels ever so closely to the hanging magician's hand.

Laughter built among the crowd, drawing the air tight in anticipation.

"You want to play with weaponry?" The dark bird crooked a finger to the rest of the Diamond Rings dangling around her. "Then let's play."

The ladies howled in approval, the crowd echoing it.

"Let me down!" the magician cried out. From the tight fit of his suit, it was painful watching him hold himself up by one hand. "Please, Vain, let me down—"

"Begging." She tilted her head, cocked her hip. "And you even said *please.*"

More chuckles from the tables. Not even the slightest alarm as seated figures leaned back farther into their chairs, watching the show go on.

"You're free to fall. Though at this height, it won't be pretty. And my ring knows better than to save vermin," the dark bird went on, inspecting her fingers fashioned more like claws from their glowing tips. *"Or,* as you've shown quite a taste for target practice tonight, you can stay put where you are and we'll fulfill your every wish. Lucky you."

Sweating, the man heaved out a sharp gasp as he did his very best to avoid looking down. "Bitch," he spat.

The dark bird smiled wider. "We aim to please."

With the snap of her fingers, the chandeliers overhead glittered and spun, sending colors all across the room from the walls to the floors. A lively beat started up again from the corners of the room, building and building like a thunderstorm overhead as the air vibrated. The ground rumbled.

And knives lifted off place settings across multiple tables.

At the high-pitched whistle, the Diamond Rings soared down to retrieve them. By some miracles, the chains hooked to their hoops did not tangle as they flew in slow, vulture-like circles around the magician holding on for dear life.

Armed with weapons and vengeful smiles, they themselves looked like knives in flight. Every head in the room was tipped skyward, and a few even shot up to their feet at the hoarse shriek of the first knife thrown. The magician thrashed out of harm's way, jolting the hoop into a wild spin.

The dark bird miraculously kept her balance, both hands effortlessly maintaining their hold at the curve by her head. Unbothered, unruffled. Like the kind of performer who could take a twenty-foot drop with a landing graceful as a swan's. As the lights struck her, she shrugged innocently before grazing the heel of her boot over the magician's straining knuckles.

The crowd went wild, one word on their lips.

Vain

Vain

Vain

It was a melody that kept going, a song the girl was used to hearing from her triumphant grin as she stretched a leg high to dodge the path of one knife.

Kallia followed the lethal harmony of the hoops, entranced.

"Close your jaw, mortal." Herald raised an amused brow at her. "Though if you like what you see, I could introduce you."

"You *know* them?" All too soon, the group finished torturing their victim once they ran out of knives. When they deposited the now deathly pale gentleman back to his table, he slid right beneath the table before he even hit his seat.

Incredible.

"Oh, everyone knows all the Dealer's headliners," he said with a slight eye roll. "You won't be mooning over them for long. Bunch of divas on a power trip, all of them."

"You don't sound bitter at all," Kallia murmured, observing as the performers assumed different positions for a new set. "And they're *all* magicians, working for the Dealer?"

Kallia didn't know why she asked. In a world of magicians, of course they were. But from just one performance alone, she wanted to know all she could about who they were, how they got there. What it took to get a stage just like theirs.

"Yes. I mean, they do use some illusions for show, which most folk find tasteless. Like an act that's all props, no talent," Herald commented. "But it's a choice. And regardless, they put on a good show."

"Oh, be still my heart."

At the sly voice, Kallia whirled around.

The dark bird waited behind them, arms crossed as though ready to fight. The sheen of sweat across her brow was all she carried back from her performance. No exhaustion or fatigue. It was unfair how a knife fight in the air left her black hair in perfect form, sheared smooth and short to her ears, with an elegant swoop framing a delicate bejeweled face. Dark green gems studded across her eyes, over the golden skin of her brow. A mask, hiding absolutely nothing.

"Look what the dinky old mirror shop finally dragged in," Vain said, breathless with adrenaline. "Enjoy the show, Herald?"

He took an exaggeratedly long pause. "Say that I didn't . . . how badly will you ladies hurt me?"

The corners of her lips curled up. "Just enough to change your answer." Her stare slipped over Kallia and narrowed. "Well, isn't *this* quite a find."

Kallia wasn't quite sure how to take that, but she straightened back her shoulders, chin tipped up. "Good work up there," she said, hiding her laugh behind a grin. "If only the target practice could go on longer."

"If only."

A tense silence followed forcing Kallia to swallow back her laugh. Vain just stood back and observed her like everyone did—as if her newness were a stench. But Vain's assessment was a touch more searing over Kallia. "The least he could've done was get you cleaned up a little."

Kallia's nostrils flared a bit. She could practically feel the shards of glass still tangled in her hair, especially as she stood by Vain, who looked every part the polished black diamond.

"*Ladies.*" Herald stepped between them, gently pressing at their arms. "It's too early for claws."

"Stay in your corner, mirror boy." Vain tilted her head. "If new arrivals can't take a little bite, better to find out now then later."

"Is *this* what you call bite?" Kallia said through a clenched smile.

Vain snorted. "Lucky for you, this is only a taste."

And to think, Kallia had been about ready to bow down to this girl and the rest of the Diamond Rings like everyone else in the room. Not even the mayor had been half as scathing when they'd first met in Glorian.

"Let me guess, you marched right in here to demand an audience with the Dealer." the Diamond Ring drawled, bemused. "Tough luck. All of the pieces have not been assembled yet. And I'm afraid, Herald, there's still one—"

He lifted a knowing hand. "Just wait for it."

On cue, the doors burst open as though by a gust of wind. Only a few spectators turned at the interruption, though no one appeared alarmed in the slightest at the circle of strange figures walking in. Strange, for they donned top hats and sophisticated dark suits but possessed no faces. No flesh.

Kallia frowned as they approached, nearing close enough that she could make out the top hats sitting atop gathered smoke. Faceless. Nightmares in the guise of gentlemen, from their velvet gloves atop canes to the silky cravats at their necks.

They had to be illusions. They were too unnerving not to be, especially as they herded someone within their ring as if guiding a prisoner to their cell.

As Kallia squinted, struggling to see who was trapped within, Vain laughed again. "You needed the help of lower devils, mirror boy?"

"They're the only ones powerful enough to probably hold him." Herald sighed sharply. "And I did my share, it's not like I came here empty-handed."

Kallia stopped searching.

His grip remained on her arm. The moment she looked down at it, her heart stilled at what had been there all along. A familiar row of sinister shapes marked across his knuckles.

Black triangles.

Kallia pulled back, her gaze darting between them and the shadow gentlemen—whoever they'd entrapped in their circle. "What the . . . ?"

In the space between the top hats, her eyes locked with brown so dark, it was near black.

Jack.

Something in her snapped. Cracked.

"Don't come near me." Kallia backed away, fists balled at her sides. She had to get out of there. Especially when she swore she saw the ice in Vain's mask thaw with what might've been a sliver of pity.

Run.

"Don't make this any harder, Kallia. It's not worth it." Herald made no attempt to restrain her again, which meant running would lead nowhere. Especially as he knew her name when she'd never once given it.

The trap had been all around her, and she'd walked right into it.

"Let him out," Herald called out with the crook of a finger, and the shadow gentlemen broke formation. No belligerence in their stance, not that there was any need when their prisoner walked out without a fight was telling enough. If even Jack saw no point in trying to get past them, then they were forces worth fearing.

Once their gazes met, there was no letting go. Whatever question seared behind her eyes, there was no answer in his. Only a whisper of worry, the slightest crack in those pools of dark ice.

"So *this* is the great and powerful Jack . . . ," Vain murmured. Her heels clicked slowly as she waltzed right up to him. Whatever venom she'd bottled for Kallia, she'd stored a surplus just for him as she looked him up and down. "Pity. From what I've heard and seen, I figured you would be more fearsome in person."

Jack blinked, the worry gone from his eyes. All stone now. "I didn't realize the Dealer got his sideshows to field guests for him."

Applause shattered the air behind them, causing Vain's knife of a smile to sharpen. "Do we look like a sideshow to you?"

She tilted her head at the Diamond Rings still performing behind her before crossing her arms. Kallia's pulse raced at the marks branded across her long fingers: black triangles that moved as she tapped her glowing green nails.

All of them bore black triangles.

A warning. An omen. Kallia knew what those marks meant in Glorian.

Here, they could mean anything.

"As much as I'd *love* to stay and watch this tragedy unfold, we've got another set to prepare for later." Vain was the first to draw away with a soft laugh, stopping only to pat Kallia on the arm. "Though a word of advice, it might be best to look away from the mirrors for now. Wouldn't want your head to explode."

Kallia's skin prickled as she took the bait, unable to help herself.

And she froze.

Now that the Diamond Rings had left their stage, the walls of the Court of Mirrors came fully alive. It was the grandest collection of mirrors—ornate frames large and small, fitted like a spectacular glassy puzzle—all alight, reflecting other moving images that could not be. Reflections of faces peering forward to straighten their ties or apply a touch more rouge to their cheeks. Some young partygoers striking poses with a ruffle of their skirts or the smooth buttoning of suit jackets. Private moments, intimate ones. Windows into different lives, scattered across the walls.

Many of which glowed with Kallia's face.

It was like watching herself in many dreams. There she was, trying on dresses in Ira's shop, avoiding her own reflection. Another, just a hint of her face as she pulled a velvet curtain over the surface. One displayed her face hardened in concentration while she levitated the dagger onstage, and a sliver of her laughing in the Prima Cafe with her friends. A captured moment of her descending the steps into a party in the same scarlet gown that hung mostly in tatters over her now.

Fleeting moments, all around. Jack appeared in some, too—but the one that stood out most was a group of mirrors piecing together a vision of Kallia, holding his face close. A word on her lips, a breath falling from his.

"You deserve more than this, firecrown."

Kallia couldn't tell where his faint words echoed from.

From her head, or the mirrors.

"More than him, more than this place and its people . . ."

Her stomach churned harder at a bitter answering laugh so much like hers. At their faces surrounding them, memories replaying to the delight of the audience now turning to the walls like a new show had begun.

Theirs.

"About time you've arrived."

The stranger's voice forced Kallia to spin around. Behind her stood a complete stranger grinning too warmly, too widely, clasping his hands together. "The mirrors do not do you justice, my dear."

Kallia could hardly speak or do much more than take him in. His richly embroidered suit was more subtle than those she'd seen tonight, overwhelming more in presence than appearance. Burly build, silver peppered into near-black hair slicked back like a curved cap against his scalp. Outside a neatly trimmed beard, the smooth brown skin gave him a youthful air, but there were creases and lines weathering his face. Nothing about him rang with a memory, except his eyes. There was something familiar there. Peculiar.

"Are you the Dealer?" Kallia was amazed she could talk at all. From the way the others edged back from him subtly, as though moving aside for a king, he had to be.

Which was why she forced herself to keep still as the man's large outstretched hand hovered by her cheek.

"I'm far more than that, Kallia." He chuckled. "As are you."

The loud snap of his fingers gusted cold air around them. Smoke filled their surroundings, the feel of a velvet glove on her shoulder.

A shadow gentleman, at her back.

"Save yourself first, Kallia . . ."

The faint words echoed all around the Court of Mirrors. Or perhaps they rose straight from memory. She could no longer discern between the two as her mind spun, and her body shook. Not in pain, but with the sheer emptiness filling her. As though she were dissolving.

Disappearing.

Her panicked stare found Jack, held by a devil behind him as well. She didn't know why, what she hoped to find, but desperately, she looked for something. Anything.

"That's the only way out."

And then nothing, as everything went black.

Wake up.

All Kallia wanted was to find herself beneath the sheer canopy of her bed in the Prima. Or the aged ceilings laced in cobwebs of the Ranza Estate, her head resting against Demarco's chest. Something she knew. Familiar.

The ache for it was too much. She could almost feel the warmth against her cheeks. The smell of fire, the sound of it softly crackling. No more applause or music from the Court of Mirrors closing in around her like a cage.

Until laughter and the clinking of glasses reeled through the air.

"Cheater!"

Kallia winced at the shout, the pang in her chest. Dread flowed back into her veins as her eyes blinked open.

Everyone that had been around her remained in place, except for the Court of Mirrors. Instead of dark, booze-stained beneath their feet was all marble pearlescent tiling streaked with gold. As jarring a shift as the whole room now around them.

Without moving a step, they somehow now resided in an area swathed in green, meandering into different sections—what appeared to be a long window to the far end overlooking a view of flashing lights, a fire burning atop a large gold dish hanging from the ceiling, and velvet chairs and tables spaced across the room. Some empty, others occupying no more than a few people casually lounging back.

Nearest to them, one card game occurred between a small group by the fire. Or perhaps ended, from the way one young man with deep purple hair sat back and sulked.

"I didn't even have to try to cheat." His opponent triumphantly threw his cards down. "Stick to making music, maestro. Your lovesick devotees will thank you."

"At least I *have* devotees." The purple-haired gentleman's posh accent dragged out the last note—cut off the moment he noticed the sudden arrivals. The others straightened in their seats as well, laughter dying instantly. Even those sitting in the tables farther back stopped what they were doing to catch a look.

Kallia nearly startled at the arm looping within hers, the too-strong hit of cologne warming the air. The Dealer reassured her with a pat on the elbow. "Carry on," he said, beaming out at them in curiosity. "We're just passing through."

"With new meat, apparently?" the man with purple hair asked, brow raised.

They all had their brows arched high, it seemed.

"If you're worried already, children, then perhaps you should spend less time in the Green Room and keep practicing." The Dealer let out a rueful snort, nodding at Herald and the devils to follow. "And no interruptions."

Kallia could barely catch their reactions, she and Jack were led so swiftly into the next room. But she'd seen enough, felt the tension roiling in the air. Whatever lay behind their close watch was not curiosity, but a watchfulness.

The look predators wore when unsure of what had just strolled into their domain. A fellow threat, or their next feast.

"The vultures are in fine form tonight, Roth," Herald muttered as he closed the doors behind them.

"Headliners are always bored on nights that aren't theirs." With a shrug, the Dealer strode deeper into the room. Far more intimate than the immense lounge outside, but still carrying its own grand air. The spacious study was fortified by walls wrapped in a thick black material ridged like the skin of a snake. Candle sconces dotted every corner, melded into the shape of hands with claws. The only furniture in sight was the black wooden desk that dominated the room on wooden paws, as if any moment now they would start prowling about.

The Dealer took his time making his way behind it, humming a pleasant tune under his breath. "Don't let him out of your sight."

A sudden grunt with a hard slam shook the room, forcing Kallia back, her pulse racing. The two devils accompanying their party shoved Jack into the wall, holding back his arms. While he didn't struggle, he was absolutely fuming from every sharp intake of breath.

"Roth—call them off," Jack hissed, face pressed to the wall. "I wasn't doing *anything*."

Her jaw nearly dropped.

The devils only tightened their hold on him. Any more force, and they could easily dislocate both his shoulders if they wanted to.

Kallia never thought such a sight was even possible: Jack, apprehended. Overpowered.

It was far too good to be true. She was almost convinced it was an illusion.

"Oh, but you've done enough." Lighting a pipe from across the desk, the Dealer let out a slow reel of smoke in a misty coil that trailed all the way to Jack. "Call it a necessary precaution, as you've clearly developed *such* a disappointing penchant for lying and trickery we never saw coming," he tutted, waving him away. "Take him outside for now, but keep a close watch. I'll deal with him later."

His tone, the way Herald nodded swiftly and strode toward the door with the devils following suit, carried an ominous note.

"Wait." Jack turned, eyes wide. Reaching. "Kallia—"

"You've done enough harm." The man rested the pipe on an elaborate tray that hadn't been there before. "And clearly, she agrees." For the first time, Jack didn't make it easy. Even against devils dragging him out, he refused to go quietly without one last look back. At Kallia.

That mask he firmly wore had crumbled, and only searing panic lay beneath. As though there was so much he wanted to do, to say to her in that moment.

He'd had more than enough. Enough moments, enough time. He was only trying to save himself now. Like always.

Her insides unclenched when the devils finally pushed him right out the door with Herald. As the doors swung closed, a few heads of the other people lounging outside leaned over and peeked in to see what they could.

Before the door finally shut, leaving Kallia with the Dealer.

Alone.

The room fell silent, save for the crackling of the fireplace and the weary sigh that followed.

"Apologies, my dear. I imagined our first meeting would be far more regal than that." The Dealer gave a sheepish laugh, gentle as a knife slicing into soft flesh. He lowered into a grand seat she swore had not been behind the desk before, crooking a finger upward that lifted a full wineglass seamlessly from the surface of the table. "Would you like one, too?"

She certainly could use one right now, but she didn't trust it. Didn't trust *him*, or anything around her.

Even with Jack gone, it still didn't mean she was safe.

Every so often she glanced at the door, not far from where she stood. The fact that this man didn't mind her walking about freely or had none of his devils stay by to keep her in check told her she wouldn't make it far even if she tried. Especially with all those people waiting outside.

And her magic, being what it was.

Kallia pressed her teeth together until her jaw went numb. The surge of helplessness, constant and never-ending, ran through her like bile.

A wineglass suddenly emerged on her side of the table, and she glared even harder at it. "I didn't say I wanted one."

The Dealer snorted in genuine amusement. "Then let me offer it. I can only guess what lies that beast has told all your life. *Jack*." He spat out the name, tapped the pipe against his lips before taking another inhale. "We never saw it coming. He'd been so obedient and loyal before. What *have* you done with him?"

He chuckled once again.

It took everything in Kallia not to throw her wineglass right in his face. "I didn't *do* anything, nor did I make him."

All she wanted was to know what the hell was going on, but that slow tide of anger rose within her. The idea that she deserved even a morsel of blame for the things Jack had done, the life she'd lived in a gilded cage and all that came with it, enraged her. Especially when presented as a joke.

"If someone wants to make terrible decisions, that is their terrible choice," she seethed through gritted teeth. She couldn't influence Jack, any more than she could manipulate the skies. "No one else's."

"True, very true. But depending on how you can use it, you really shouldn't underestimate your power, my dear," he added, setting his pipe down in favor of his wine. "It's impressive that he even cares at all. Didn't think him capable of that, either."

Kallia's nostrils flared. If he was testing her, studying her reactions to see beyond them, she wanted to move on. And yet, part of her couldn't deny the relief of being in a world that for once saw Jack exactly as she did. A monster of a magician. A liar.

And right now, he wasn't holding all the strings over her head. The very person puppeteering this world sat right in front of her, offering her food and drink.

Whatever his interest might be, she could use that.

"Please sit." At the Dealer's nod, velvet brushed the backs of Kallia's legs. A lush, turquoise chair waited behind her where there hadn't been one before. "I'm sure you must have many questions. And you're no doubt famished after your journey."

Lowering into her seat, Kallia was certain her stomach had never felt emptier. Though in a matter of seconds, platters of all kinds began rising to the top of his desk—a tray of mini high-tiered cakes frosted like art, a crystal bowl of steaming jade-green rice, a large roasted chicken rubbed in some scarlet-gold spice, mounds of golden toasted breads molded into towers with butter dripping down its sides, and even more delights just as grand. Almost too beautiful to consume.

"I know it's not much—given our meager table settings—but please, help yourself. Feel at home." He waved a hand all across the feast, wafting all the smells toward him. "Don't worry, our food and drink don't curse or poison or entrap in any way. I know mortals can get so paranoid about such rumors, but those are old tales. When it comes to such delights, we only aim to enjoy."

Savory scents swirled all about her, yet Kallia kept her hands firmly in her lap. It felt all *too* inviting, too much like forbidden fruit for the taking. Especially when it came from someone with a penchant for dealmaking.

Kallia observed the man as he took one last draw from his pipe before tucking it away. The claws of smoke held over him like a mask, muddling his features slightly.

Once it cleared, those brown eyes pierced through.

Familiarity struck her again. And it didn't end there. Not with the slight roundness of his nose. The confident air he radiated, that expectant gaze that only grew more bemused the longer their silent staring match continued.

"You know," he drawled, leaning forward, "most people can barely look me in the eye for more than a moment."

"Out of fear?"

"Something like that. When you come to rule or achieve any bit of fame, it comes with intimidation." He reached over to grab a small soft ball of pink dough from a bowl that he popped into his mouth. "That's not foreign to you, I'm sure."

No. Kallia relished the way her competitors could throw taunts at her in a group, but could hardly face her directly. As if there was something within them, within *her*, they couldn't bear to see.

"I still can't believe it."

Kallia blinked, uneasy with how he watched her over the rim of his cup. "What?"

"You look . . ." He appeared as though he wanted to say more, the thought close to leaving his lips before he shook his head. "You really don't know who I am, do you?"

"I know you're the Dealer." Kallia blinked, crossing her arms. "That's it."

"Ah, yes, that name. Makes me sound so ominous." He gave a frivolous wave of his hand, though from the curl of his lips, he relished the infamy. "What else have they said about me?"

He hungered to know, much like someone who enjoyed hearing himself talk.

Oh yes. She knew exactly how to talk to men like this.

"That you're the magician behind this impressive city. Such a remarkable likeness to the Glorian I know." Kallia softened under wistful admiration well. A smile here, a little sigh there. Even without magic, charm worked just as dangerously. "Like walking through a dream."

"You truly like it?"

For some reason, her approval mattered to him. Interesting. And even better. "Absolutely," she said, coyly turning away to hide her troubled expression. "It's . . . all so overwhelming. I know nothing of you, when you obviously know everything about me."

Not just knowing, *watching*. The mirrors on the walls filled with her face—images of herself she would never forget, completely unaware. The one useful habit she'd taken away from Jack was staying wary near mirrors. If she hadn't, Zarose knew how much more this world would've witnessed.

The Dealer clasped his hands together eagerly. "*Everyone* knows who you are, my dear. The Court of Mirrors is the most popular joint in my Glorian, after all. My people love seeing glimpses of reality on the true side. And the show you and your lot have been putting on has kept us all on our toes to be sure," he said, buzzing with excitement. "So much drama, so unpredictable! You, my dear, are infamous without even having set foot in my city until now." He raised his glass to her. "Quite a feat."

Kallia lifted her drink similarly, her smile stiffening. His fascination with reality—*her* reality—chilled her. All this time, the game she thought she'd entered in Spectaculore had been far from the only show happening.

It explained so much of her welcome. Those eyes and whispers following her since she stepped through the gates, the way Herald had tracked her down so easily. And fooled her, as well.

"I didn't realize my life had become your entertainment." Kallia pressed back into her seat, jaw clenched. "If I did, perhaps I would've started smiling more."

His laughter boomed like a rumble of thunder. "Smiles or not, you still have many admirers, and, of course, the scathing haters—which is the truest badge of honor in the business." He winked. "I certainly had to deal with a fair share of them, back in my day. And look at me now."

"Yes, impressive." The leader of a city, the man behind an illusion so vast, she never dreamed such a trick could be possible. That such a magician could exist.

With the casual lift of her glass, Kallia swirled the dark wine within. "If you've been watching me all this time, it's only polite to at least get your name in return," she said. "Aside from the Dealer, that is."

"Yes, it's about time we've stopped acting like strangers. A bit silly, all things considered." He brought his drink to his lips in a short sip. A wink. "Rothmos Alastor, but you can call me Roth."

It was a miracle Kallia didn't shatter the wine glass in her grip.

Alastor.

She should've known.

How simple. How *infuriatingly* obvious. They were in the Alastor Place, after all, filled with people with black triangles branded across their fingers. Those pieces had all been before her, but she never imagined an *actual* Alastor could be behind them. Or that any would still be living.

In her world, at least.

"How nice. You clearly recognize the name." Roth unfolded a cloth napkin over his lap. "That was more than I expected, given how often the true side forgets."

"Glorian remembers the Alastor name, all right." Kallia tapped her nails against the desk surface, recalling the power the family still had over Glorian. The way the mere whisper of the name could send a chill through any room.

"Can't say I'm shocked it's not in an accurate light. History is only one side of the story, after all." Roth dipped one of the serving spoons deeper into a dish filled with a creamy stew with flecks of gold. "And that history only lives on with those left standing to give it. Which leaves so many tales half-told."

With Glorian, the biggest one of all. Ever since she first stepped foot through the gates, she'd noticed the way the city was shrouded in shadows. From its ruin to its past, no one ever minded the questions. Especially those who lived within it. Even Aaros, sharp as a knife's edge, went about his days wearing a blindfold like everyone else.

"You wish to know the other half, don't you?" Roth's gaze stayed on her, all searing intent. "I can see it in you, that anger. That burning to know. It's absolutely cruel that Jack chose to keep you in the dark. All this time."

He was right, and she didn't like how easily he saw it.

Because it meant he could use it: her desire to know, to understand, after a life of questions unanswered. A life with everything, and nothing at all.

"I fail to see how any of this is relevant to me." Kallia traced a finger around the rim of her cup. "Or why I should trust you if I couldn't even trust Jack."

On a conceding breath, Roth steepled his fingers. "Ah, but I'm nothing like Jack. I'm a magician, and a man of my word. And the first thing you should know about me is that I would never lie to family."

Kallia stilled.

She heard wrong. She had to.

Family.

It hung between them, a ghost of a word. For a moment she felt nothing, and then everything. Like falling into ice and fire, every part of her burning. Numb.

He was mistaken. Strange men always said strange things. Especially when they were desperate.

"That's not possible," Kallia started, treading calmly. "I've never had family. I was found—"

"In the dark woods one day, only to be raised by some mysterious benefactor who provided you with *everything* you could ever need?" His brow curved up slowly. "Yes, I know the story. Crafted it myself. Rest assured, I always take care of my own. Even from this side."

Kallia plunged back into fire. Ice.

Ice, fire.

Breathe, she reminded herself. She had to.

She grasped at what she could remember: scattered memories of Sire that were scarce, but real. The way he'd kept to himself, always hunched against the tall back of his chair or just about to ascend the stairs to his room. Rare glimpses revealed wrinkles upon his face, sometimes the occasional word or two, but not much more. Even his own domain, up until he passed away.

It had been odd, but it had been all she'd known. And when you knew nothing else, you didn't think to question.

Now the questions squeezed her by the throat.

"You wouldn't be the first to live among illusions, my dear," Roth said. "Some are easier to cast than others from here. And depending on the make of them, they truly can provide a much kinder life."

"Kinder?" She couldn't believe her ears. Her grip tightened on the edge of the desk. It was a miracle it hadn't flipped over yet. "What's so kind about throwing me in a box, all from the comfort of your throne?"

Her heart stilled for a beat when that twinkle in his eye disappeared, darkened. "And what exactly was this box but a life of luxury, well-enjoyed? A string of tutors who taught you the basics of magic? A roof over your head, food in your stomach, clothes for your closet?" He listed every item without hesitation. "Most people happily walk through life on far less. Don't act as though you suffered worse when you were provided privilege and power from the moment you were born."

Heat lanced across her cheeks the longer his shrewd assessment of her lasted. "My dear, I did what I could to keep you safe in that house. So you could grow stronger, more powerful, in peace. I never had any of that," he said, absently taking in his plate. "You call it a box, but they would've had you in a much smaller one. Why, you'd still be in that sad girl's academy out east, had I not pulled all the strings to break you out."

Kallia shook her head at the idea, the pure lunacy of it. She had no recollection of this. Any of it. "You have the wrong person. I've never stepped foot in Queen Casine's. Never gone that far in Soltair, ever."

"Is *that* what you remember?"

The words left behind ice. The reminder that Jack was on the other side of that door, his fingers marked by the same black triangles on the magician before her.

"Fight me all you want, but you're here now. So you might as well listen." His lips none of the jovial smiles from before, long past pleasantries. "I'm the only one who's willing to tell you the truth, Kallia."

He was willing to tell her a lot. But from a stranger, the truth could be anything.

"No. This is ridiculous." Kallia finally pushed back from her seat. If he saw no wrong in pulling strings over her head her whole life, she needed no further reason to leave.

On a halfway turn toward the door, she froze.

It was gone. Lost in the thick of black scales as though the serpent of the walls slithered right over it.

Her entire chest seized as she threw a glare over her shoulder. "Whatever you want, if you don't let me out, I'll—"

"*Scream?*" Roth cocked his head. "And who would come, even if they could hear it?"

The churning in her stomach intensified as he continued licking at his sugared fingers after biting into a glistening pastry. "You could try letting yourself out, too. I'm not stopping you." He shrugged. "It's all just magic, in the end."

Not to her, but he knew that.

He knew *everything*.

Kallia bit the inside of her cheeks to keep the pain in one place, to stop it from reaching the backs of her eyes. She would rather taste her own blood than cry. Blood, she could hide. Tears, she couldn't. Though her fear was enough to mask everything well, lifting the hairs on her skin.

"Don't look at me as though I would ever dare hurt you, my dear." Roth chortled, too good-naturedly for the circumstances. "You are blood, after all. And we're all that's left of the family, unfortunately."

"I want proof."

"Any proof is long gone. Though you look a hell of a lot like your mother."

His certainty nauseated her. She pressed two fingers to the side of her throbbing temple, closing her eyes.

This wasn't real. She wasn't an Alastor.

She *wasn't*.

"Your reaction, I suppose, is not entirely unwarranted. With the lies you've been fed from Jack, from the true side even, it's difficult to believe in anything." Roth released a dark sigh. "But if you think I'm bad, just look at those in your world, the one you left behind. Your Soltair, your Glorian . . . it's not real."

J ack was tired of waiting.

Of watching, and being watched.

The eyes that followed had not left since they'd dragged him back into the Green Room. A smart move on Roth's part. A viper pit of magicians and devils might pose enough of a challenge to keep him back.

Still, no one dared lift a hand against him.

The collection of headliners scattered about had clearly heard about him. Among them, he recognized no one—all different faces from the last time he'd resided in the other side. Roth rarely kept performers up in the high nest forever. For the Dealer, talent was as fleeting as life. A prop with shine that dulled over time, and inevitably lost its luster. Its novelty.

It was likely the only reason saving Jack from being ripped apart right now.

The dagger looks that stabbed across his back were as sharp with envy as they were with fear. When it came down to it, they left him be. And Jack preferred it.

Alone, he paced by the far end window, taking in the spectacular view offered from the jewel of the Alastor Place. The Green Room overlooked the Court of Mirrors in full swing, lost in a song and applause with no end. The glass thrummed against the rippling music—all dark, heavy beats and loud strings harmonizing like wolves howling at the moon.

The same headliners from earlier were still at it. Magicians and illusions draped along glittering hoops that spun beneath the spotlight. In the center rose their leader in green. The vicious one with the claws about ready to scratch Jack's face off. Not everyone was terrified of him, at least, though it seemed little would terrify her—all winks and blown kisses for the crowd, while fire slowly blazed around her.

The whole group formed a dazzling spectacle worthy of the Alastor Place. The Dealer's chosen headliners were not favorites for nothing.

Though not even their next trick could compete with all that the glass reflected behind him. The occupants of the Green Room, waiting and watching at his back.

And the shape of those doors to the study, as still as the moment they'd closed.

Jack tensed whenever light flickered beneath the crease from the other side.

What was happening in there?

The thought made him ill. It was convenient enough that she already wanted nothing to do with him. The Dealer would press on that wound. Control the pain. Use what little she knew against all that she didn't.

If Roth told her . . .

Hell, he should've turned around and fucking left when he had the chance.

There would be no getting past the shadow servants by the doors now. Another reason not to look. Roth could order them to jump from the window to slaughter all of those partying below for his own amusement, and they would crash through the glass without question or guilt. Just obedience.

Jack understood the cost too well.

And like everyone, he wasn't dumb enough to try fighting through them. They weren't simple one-note illusions. Their thoughts were the thoughts of the devils, all of one mind and power with many forms.

While they kept their eerie watch by the door, silent and still, it was all in lethal patience. Waiting to strike down any threat, if necessary.

If only he could.

"Care for a drink?"

The nearby voice was a shock, as was the offering: a half-filled crystal glass wrapped in dark-skinned fingers marked with black triangles.

Lifting his gaze, Jack relished the slight flinch the young man—the wily one with the spectacles who'd brought Kallia in. He didn't seem like the performing headliner type, but those black triangles did not lie. Anyone working under Roth received the prestigious marks, a warning to others as much as to the beholder. No magic could get rid of them, not even with the skinning or burning of flesh. Jack tried it all.

They would only disappear at Roth's release.

For Jack to think hiding them under a mask was any freedom at all was only the first of many mistakes he'd made on the true side.

Jack took the drink, the cold of it comforting in his hands. An unexpected kindness. Bold of the boy, to be so near Jack when no one else dared.

A bold fool, but clearly not a stupid one.

Before taking a sip, Jack eyed him. "What for?"

The young man grinned and lifted his own glass. "Everyone deserves one last hurrah. Even you."

Perhaps he *was* stupid.

"Is that so?" With the slow raise of his brow, Jack tilted his head. "You're presumptuous for a headliner."

A cackle erupted. "Oh, I'm no headliner. The real magic is *behind* the scenes . . ." He gave a smug half-shrug. "I'm like you, I guess."

Jack highly doubted that and had no trouble hiding it.

The boy pushed up his spectacles casually, though they hadn't slipped down his nose even a little. "I have my uses. Though unlike you, I delivered quickly. So I'm here to stick around."

"That's really up to the Dealer, I'm afraid."

His eyes narrowed. "Yes. And it's clear Roth wasn't pleased to see you." Through his superior airs, he pressed up the thin gold frames. A nervous habit.

Always the first things Jack took stock of when encountering strangers.

"I wasn't counting on it." Jack dragged his gaze back to the window's view, the madness playing out below. "And how do you suspect he'll try torturing me to oblivion? By making me play his personal lackey—*oh*, that's right . . ."

The boy's mouth pinched. "Some of us need to work to keep moving up. Not all of us get to enjoy breaks when you've got to make do to survive."

"I'm aware." Jack understood far too well that surviving wasn't always honorable. There was strategy and luck in it, more cowardice than courage in most cases. He certainly didn't anticipate how his plans would turn. Especially where Kallia was concerned.

"You've got a funny way of showing it." The boy took a quick sip. "That mortal was due here long, long ago. And it's not as though you can pretend you couldn't find her."

"Do you see me trying?" The mirrors all over the walls below still flashed faintly with reflections of other people, other places. No one could've hidden away from them forever. Certainly not Kallia.

His eyes flicked to the corner, back to those doors.

"You know, once she and Roth are done in there, he'll move right on to you." He tipped his glass back with another cavalier sip. "And from what I can tell, he likely won't be as nice."

No. Roth was going to try every trick in the book to tear Jack apart. To make sure it hurt.

It would be interesting to see him try.

"You're so confident in his plans?" Jack asked. "If they don't work, who's to stop me from coming for the first person to piss me right off?"

He was slightly mollified when the boy stiffened for a breath. "No one is indestructible. Not even you."

The words gave Jack pause, lit his blood on fire.

"Might want to drink up, if it's your last."

The boy left soon after, and only then did Jack drain the glass dry. Wintery, potent. Not that it ever did the trick; it took far more to knock him out. And even far more to destroy him.

If a show was what they wanted, that's exactly what they'd get.

t's not real.

Cold sweat broke out across the back of Kallia's neck. She was grateful to be sitting and gripped the desk firmly, a needed anchor when her heart galloped harshly in her chest. "What the hell are you talking about?"

It's not real.

Those were damned words.

She couldn't show Roth the power they had over her, but the wound was just as fresh when remembered. Rawer than memory. Learning that her friends and tutors at Hellfire House, her time spent with Jack—knowing him, trusting him—had been nothing but illusions nearly shattered her.

The thought it could all be happening again terrified her.

"I think perhaps *you* can answer that better than me," Roth countered with the wave of his hand. All the food that had filled the space between them disappeared, the scents ripped from the air.

Without the colorful confections surrounding him, that devilish smile gracing his mouth, Roth appeared every bit the magician the city parted crowds for. The Dealer. The Alastor.

"What can you recall of your Glorian?" he posed, as one would issue a challenge. "What is remembered by its people?"

Glorian is a city built on cards.

That had stuck with Kallia, ever since the mayor said it across a dinner table a while back. The irony in it was just the truth. How fragile a city could be when made of cards.

"Odd, how there's *nothing* to remember, right?" Roth appeared a little too satisfied by her silence. "With you, it's far more understandable, given your life of lies. But to the rest—how can that be? To live in a city, yet not know it."

"What's your point to this?" Kallia bristled. "I'm well aware something isn't right in that city."

"Oh, Kallia, it's not just the city. It's everything, and everyone," he said, a sugar-coated smile of pity. "Forgetting history is never an accident. And you can thank your Patrons for that."

Her blood like iced. "The *Patrons*?"

Jack had insinuated something similar, and this only added to the madness. The Patrons were servants of the people, the ones who stepped in whenever magic posed a threat. Though Demarco had avoided the subject altogether, there was no denying his respect for them regardless. The respect *everyone* had for them, for keeping order between those with power and those without.

Kallia's eyes narrowed. It had to be some sort of test—a blatant lie, to see how easily she could fall for it. "And why would the Patrons, of all people, want to do a horrific thing like that?"

"Because despite popular belief, Patrons are still people at the end of the day," he said. "Anyone with even a smidge of authority, a taste of power, will do anything to stay in control."

"How are you no different, then?"

"I never claimed to be." All cooled triumph, without shame. "I know who I am, as do my people. And I do my best to do right by them," he said, inspecting his fingernails. "That's a lot more than those in your world can say. They'd rather erase disaster than face it head on."

Kallia bit the inside of her lower lip, all to keep herself from clutching her chest. The more she let it rile her up, the truer it would feel.

And if that last night of Spectaculore was as disastrous as memory served, then the Patrons wouldn't need any formal summons to swarm Glorian to assert order.

They would be there already.

The faint roll of laughter and calls for more bottles seeped through the doors. A world without care, just a step away when she felt hers breaking on the surface.

"Erase what exactly?" Kallia knew firsthand what it was to not remember. The effort it took to keep such a ruse in place. And the toll.

"The reason why *any* of us are here in the first place." Roth threw out his hands like a true showman, before setting his head at a curious tilt her way. "You truly *do* look an awful lot like her. Your mother."

Zarose.

The comment came without warning, unexpected as a slap. "My mother?"

Kallia had never uttered the words before. The strange aftertaste of them carried a bitterness so unfamiliar, she wasn't so sure she wanted more of it.

Not that Roth noticed, as he gave a solemn nod. "She was a distant cousin—there was a whole brood of us back then, like a pack of wolves. A bunch of terrors, we all were." There was uncharacteristic tenderness in the way his eyes closed for a fleeting beat, before he blinked hard to wipe it away. "Don't worry, I'm not here to go all soft on you with family talk. I'm not the sort, and I have a feeling you're not, either."

The relief coursing through her was a balm to her nerves. Kallia had never cared much for family before. She owed nothing to people she'd never met, halfway wondered if she hadn't just fallen from the sky one day. It was more preferable than wondering why she'd been left to a stranger's care in Hellfire House.

"Why bring it up, then?" Kallia straightened in her seat, dead-eyed. "How is any of that relevant?"

"Because we're blood, you and I. The last ones standing."

A chill skipped across her spine.

It struck her then that she'd met no other Alastors except the one before her. And there was no other indication that any were around.

"What happened to them?"

Silence stretched raw with a tension that thickened the air. Even the noises of revelry outside softened to it.

Roth focused back on his glass again, either contemplating his words or another refill. "I can't tell how long it's been. I don't even know what a day feels like anymore," he confessed. "Live long enough here, and the memories start growing hazy. I hardly even remember what sunshine feels like. No matter how many perfumes or ointments promise the sensation, it's never the same."

Given the luxury of this study, of the entire gilded palace of a city itself, how strange for its king to yearn for such simplicity.

Except it wasn't all that unbelievable. That pang of longing hit Kallia every time she'd sit atop her greenhouse, the sunrise illuminating a faraway Glorian in the distance.

Those had been her daydreams. The luxury of something lost, or never experienced.

"Glorian has changed since I last stepped foot in it, from what the mirrors have shown." The lines of Roth's lips grew tense. Troubled. "It's so cold now. So orderly and quiet."

"That's how it's always been, for as long as I've known." Kallia gave a half-shrug. "No shows, no magic."

In spite of that, she'd still wanted to go. No matter how often Jack refused, how unremarkable it seemed from the strange tales alone, it only heightened her imagination.

The last thing she expected was a city wrapped in ice, in more ways than one.

"Figures." Roth shuddered, as though in agreement. "Our mirrors only wake for magic. I truly thought the city had fully burned to the ground, after everything."

Kallia's brow creased. Something about the story felt familiar, some piece of it falling into place.

It brought her back to that first time she walked through the broken Court of Mirrors, overrun by crashed chandeliers and blackened shards of glass and ghosts who had been silenced underneath it all. Even the

Ranza Estate had had its share of wreckage. And still, these ruined places and pieces remained, telling a story others could only speculate about.

Kallia pressed forward slightly. "What caused it?"

"What else but a party?" A whisper of a smile graced his lips. "The first of its kind, and the wildest celebration I've ever attended. It ran all across the streets of the city." The excitement in his tone ran heavy with fond remembrance. "Night after night, countless party after party with spectacles every hour and dueling illusions in each corner. An opulent ball today, an intriguing menagerie tomorrow. Unlike *any* event I've ever attended."

Given the current state of the city under his thumb, the idea of anything more extravagant alarmed her. Maybe during Spectaculore, but any wildness earlier than that seemed inconceivable. As if Mayor Eilin, a man who balked at Kallia's attire alone, would ever stand for it.

"There was purpose to it, mind you," Roth added. "The Show of Hands was slated to be our newest tradition in Glorian: the greatest showcase of all time where those with power could perform, and those without could enjoy." Roth's fond smile lingered at the edges. "Until it arrived."

Kallia's stomach tightened.

"Completely out of nowhere," he elaborated, blinking slowly. "The few of us thought it was all some prank, but we found it standing right there in the woods, outside our gates. I'll never forget the details of the frame. Lines of beauty and ruin, carved across its edges like a curse."

There was fear in his voice. And perhaps, a little awe.

"I was lucky that was all I saw," he said, the blood draining from his face. "There was a scream before the first body dropped. Followed by more, and *more*. It took everything, and—"

His breath hitched slightly, his gaze lost to the memory.

"The rest is all fractured from then on. I remember fire, then nothing. Darkness. Swore I'd died in that wreckage." Roth pressed two fingers to the bridge of his nose. "I sometimes wish that were true."

Rothmos Alastor was a liar.

It was the first point Aunt Cata made abundantly clear, and she wouldn't let Daron forget it. Not that he could. After all those days of the competition spent in the Alastor Place, not once did he hear an actual name behind it. A person, a figurehead.

Someone his aunt despised from just a name alone.

"The Alastors were never perfect, but that man was something else. And he always knew exactly what he was doing." Aunt Cata let out a sharp sigh, jaw clenched as she peered out the window of her room. "Left a trail of bodies and nearly destroyed an entire city just to get what he wanted."

Daron hadn't budged an inch from where he sat, too frozen to even move a fraction.

Of all the tales he expected his aunt to tell, it certainly wasn't this: a story of a Glorian that had been standing before he'd even been born—of a bustling city coursing with magic, overseen by families whose names and symbols marked each fold.

And the story of how that Glorian fell.

They were the answers Daron would've killed for when he first arrived in the city to judge Spectaculore. Not just answers, but confirmation. All this time, just as Eva had suspected, something strange and dark had always been at work here.

That their aunt played such a role in it was the last thing he saw coming.

"What's worse is we had some warning of it before it all happened," Aunt Cata ground out. "From *him*."

Daron blinked. "The man told you of his plans all along?"

"Not in those exact terms," she muttered, her lips tense. "The week before, I remember my superiors had received a letter, a formal city request to hold a celebration engaging in high levels of magic. Normally, New Crown sent us those whenever they put on particularly risky spectacles drawing large crowds, but it was a first from Glorian."

"The Show of Hands," Daron recalled the name, still stunned by the picture Aunt Cata had painted. Days upon days of magicians performing across the city on all manner of stages. Just imagining such a nonstop show exhausted him.

Aunt Cata nodded. "The Patrons have always been there to step in when needed. But back then, we were far more lenient. If a city sent a courtesy letter with advance notice, then we could track any damage. All incidental, nothing worth our intervention." On an inhale, she turned from the window. "Every city has its thorns, and the dynamics between the families in Glorian were always fraught. Because entertainment has the tendency to exclude, the Show of Hands sounded like an opportunity for all to enjoy. Those without magic, and those *with* magic."

Regret thickened her voice, and she cleared her throat with a prim, shaky cough. "As you know now, that's not at all what took place."

Daron nodded, letting the understatement linger in the air. Aunt Cata hadn't provided too many details on what she'd seen, not as a means of secrecy. The more the story unfolded, the more her face broke from its careful hold.

"Why, then, design such an elaborate charade if that was never his intent?" Every question left on a held breath. He'd never tread with more caution than now. "What exactly did he want out of it?"

"The Alastors were known for collecting and recruiting magicians, rather than being magicians themselves." Aunt Cata's nostrils flared. "And Roth wanted to change that."

Daron scratched at his brow. "What about acquired magic?"

"For some, acquired magic is never enough in this world." Her shrug was paired with the small shake of her head. "And he certainly tried that path, but not everyone has the blood for it."

All those days he'd spent scouring the mayor's library to no avail flashed in the back of his mind. He'd never uncovered anything of use or far back enough to tell him much about Glorian or whatever happened behind its gates.

All this time, those pieces had been with the Patrons.

Bystanders.

Nothing could be further from the truth. All of them were in on it, pulling every secret string behind the curtains. Hiding events that would've made history and headlines for years to come. The fall and destruction of a city was not the kind of story that died quietly.

It only made it that much more disturbing, how easily they'd pulled it off.

Because by the time we're gone, none of you will remember any of this.

Aunt Cata's words kept whispering back to him like an omen. Part of him had hoped he'd simply misunderstood. Memory magic on such a vast scope as this was unheard of. Impossible. At least, that was what he'd always been led to believe, like everyone else.

What else was lie, dressed up as fact?

Daron forced himself to sit back, the picture of calm while his heart quaked beneath his chest. Memory magic on such a vast scope was unheard of. Though if anyone had the power to pull memories with the resources to hush it all up, it would be the Patrons.

Run. His pulse kicked up a desperate beat. If anyone had the power to dig into minds with the resources to hush it up, it would be the Patrons. And being related to Aunt Cata guaranteed no mercy. Daron knew his aunt too well for that.

He just needed her to keep talking, because he *needed* to understand. Every ugly, dark thread that had long been hidden away connected to something greater in all of this.

And he was so close, he could taste it.

Look for the gate, and you'll finally find her.

Every muscle in Daron tensed, drawn tight as the nerves coiling beneath his skin. "What gate, Aunt Cata?"

The utter calm he projected astounded even him. Especially when that controlled armor of hers chipped away in her face, past the point to take anything back. "Zarose Gate."

His gut tightened in response.

Not only because it was so simple, but so *impossible.*

The site of Zarose Gate was located all the way across Soltair, about a week-long trip from here with even the fastest horses. Like every other magician growing up, he'd visited the legendary birthplace of magic. He walked where Zarose had stepped when he rose as the first magician, before closing the gate to keep power from drowning their world altogether. For such a grand legend, the sacred stage for it was no more than a vast, rocky crag. So many in the past had attempted to dig through the blockage to no avail, a true iron seal thrown in place by Zarose himself.

Or so the story went.

"Where is the gate, *really*?" His pulse thundered. "Because something tells me it sure as hell isn't the one on the map."

Everything in his life he thought he'd known so well, solid as a stone in his hand, now fell fast as sand between his fingers at just the slightest pressure. After all he'd heard today, he didn't trust anything in Soltair to be solid anymore.

Her resounding silence was as good a confirmation as any, gone on a stretch too long before she tilted her head. "I've already said plenty. There's no reason for you to know any more than that."

You'll be here . . .

All Daron could hear now was Kallia, growing louder. Closer.

. . . at the end of this.

The possibility squeezed at his heart until it grew numb. "Please."

"I won't say it again, Daron." A warning growl lay low in her voice. "You don't understand the full dangers of this situation, and I hope you never will. We haven't protected Soltair all these years just to see it crumble again."

Heat flashed across Daron's cheeks. She hadn't used that tone with him since he was much, much younger, and those same old boyish nerves kicked into gear. The urge to hide, after he'd angered her for some sort of trouble.

The feeling died as quickly as it sprang. He was not a child who didn't understand. He saw too clearly, and he was not going to take any scolding from his aunt, who was in no position to judge.

"Lying to the people to cover what you don't want them to know is *not* protection," Daron ground out. The way it all sounded when he spoke it out loud sent more nausea down his throat. "Erasing what happened is not a solution. That's an avalanche just waiting to collapse."

"Would you rather our world collapse, then?" Aunt Cata stressed, her nostrils flaring. "We take no pleasure in deceit, but we can't take any chances."

Daron shook his head. It was chilling, the madness and logic of it all. All to keep the gate everyone knew about a secret. No secret could be worth so much trouble. "What is so wrong with it?"

Aunt Cata frowned, deep in thought. "Truthfully, no one knows. We're only meant to guard it, to ensure no one opens or tries to open it ever again."

"So, not even you know?"

"Our orders are to guard that gate using any means necessary. Now you know why," she snapped. "How Alastor figured how to find that gate or what he did to it, but it created all manner of cracks and holes in our world. For magic and magicians," she said. "But he never succeeded in opening it completely. Otherwise we'd be living in a much different world."

A stale victory, for if what happened then still affected them now, there was no knowing what more would grow from the cracks and holes left behind.

"No, but at least now we know how to stop the fire before it starts. Before one fool's decision devastates so many," she said, eyes closed. "In all my years as a Patron, I've never seen a city bleed like that."

Zarose. Daron almost couldn't bear to listen any longer. To see Aunt Cata like this, hurting from a memory he had the luxury of never knowing. There was no agreeing with it, but it was a luxury all the same to live in ignorance. A luxury his aunt would never know.

All his life, he thought she'd kept herself like a wall of stone to remain impenetrable as a fortress. Though maybe wearing such armor wasn't to protect herself from war. Perhaps it was all to keep the war inside from getting out.

Daron stared at her hand across from him, gloveless, which was rare. Elegant yet weathered hands of tawny-brown skin, a mere shade paler than his. When he was much younger, he always dreaded holding that hand on outings, for he'd always found it to be too cold.

He wished for nothing more than to take her hand now, knowing she would only pull away the moment he reached for it.

The silence weighed over them heavily, before Daron pressed forward, hesitant. "Did you ever find him?"

He was grateful to see movement as she shook her head instantly. "It was difficult identifying the dead by face, but their hands were all marked. It was how we figured he was targeting the families. Half circles on both hands that came together as one, stars inked into palms, squares stamped on the tops of hands, and triangles across the knuckles—his *own* family and recruits, even," she said, her lips flattening in a grim line. "We searched everyone bearing dark triangles, but if he was lost to that wreckage like the rest of them, then at least those families can rest peacefully."

The image forced Daron to straighten immediately. *Dark triangles.* The detail pulled at his chest, the mayor's words returning.

I know him. We all do.

"Aunt Cata," he started, carefully. "I've seen marks like that on someone before."

She turned her hawkish gaze on him. "Yes, that mad magician. I caught that."

Daron nodded, his heart close to bursting from his chest. Even though Lottie wanted none of the Patrons' help in their search, everything was different now. His aunt knew what the rest of the world did not. She would bring them no dead ends. "What the mayor said was true," he added. "On the last night of Spectaculore, there was a man who—"

"Yes, we know," Aunt Cata cut in swiftly. "Many reports have already confirmed the presence of an unknown magician matching his description. We're already on it so worry. You won't have to be too concerned about it soon enough."

The reassurance felt hollow. He'd hoped, in vain, to convince her otherwise, but it was hard to change a person when they firmly believed they were right.

A quick three-beat knock sounded at the door.

With a small gasp, all the life slammed back into Aunt Cata as she shot up from her seat, springing into action. "That would be my team lead." She rushed across the room, fixing back her hair in the process. "I'll be debriefing for much of the evening, but if you're—"

"Does it matter if I say no?" Daron rose slowly, watching her fret. "If I don't want to forget?"

His aunt stilled in place, her hand just about to reach for the white coat on the wall hook. He wondered if she might lie again. Or just leave cold, no explanation.

"I must do what I came here to do, Daron. And now you understand why." Aunt Cata took her coat off its hook, slipping her arms through the pristine white sleeves. "From what it sounds like, Spectaculore was a mess. And it'll only get worse."

Erased.

Forgotten.

"Is that what you call it?" Daron laughed bitterly. Forgetting Spectaculore meant forgetting everything it brought him. The people he'd grown close to, the city routes he could walk in his sleep. The good days, the bad days, and the nights that made him feel alive.

And Kallia.

His eyes closed, as though he could hold onto every moment, every memory.

"If this is your solution, then why tell me?" he asked, his breath ragged in quiet desperation. "Why not just take everything now and be done with it?"

The truth will turn people into monsters.

This one certainly would, and he'd make sure of it. That sliver of sadness in his aunt was all the sign he needed to know she wouldn't go through with it. Not now, not with him. Even she still had enough of a heart to hesitate.

"You could shout it out the window right now, and you'd still be competing with every other headline flooding the world."

The back of Daron's neck prickled at Aunt Cata's too-calm voice as she pulled out the white gloves from her pocket. "As soon as our affairs here are in order, we'll begin. It's a painless process, and everything will return to normal soon after. You'll see," she continued, her gloves firmly on as she reached for the door. "Once we leave, it'll be like none of this ever happened."

11

Without anything to keep the time, Kallia tapped softly at the stem of her wineglass, if only to give herself something to do.

She would've felt worse if the man didn't love the sound of his own voice so much, especially when it came to detailing his own suffering.

How they fight bares their weakness; what they say shows their downfall.

One of Sanja's lessons, from long ago. Regardless of the illusion, Kallia valued everything she'd learned from her old tutor. In fact, she appreciated all of her teachers, in whatever form they came. Because even without magic, they'd armed her with a collection of unseen weapons.

So Kallia listened, and waited.

Watchful as a bird, she listened until she noticed.

For someone who mourned his fragmented memory, all the pieces Roth glossed over against the parts he recounted to such a vivid degree told another story beneath the story.

Kallia remained as rapt with attention as an audience member, waiting to see what it was.

"It felt like death, ten times over." Roth frowned into his still-empty cup, letting it hover just by his lips.

"Such a rare kind of blistering pain no magician could survive. And yet somehow, I awoke here, bleeding in the darkness."

"How terrible." Kallia lifted a hand to her mouth, widening her eyes above it in shock while covering a short yawn.

All she cared to know more about was the mirror. A terror beyond any beast imaginable. Kallia would've preferred walking through glass, if given the choice. But if that object had forced Roth's entry into this world, as she suspected, then it must have the ability to work the opposite way around, too.

She kept that card close to her chest. There was no greater weapon than knowing exactly what someone wanted.

"It truly was. Until the devils found me."

Kallia stilled, just as she had when Jack mentioned it. As a child, they'd never frightened her. Devils who danced below the surface had always been just a silly myth.

One walk outside these walls in that dark sea of dead-eyed magicians was all it took for that fear to finally take.

"You have nothing to fear, my dear." Roth noticed her pause, her shiver. The fool could slip back so seamlessly into the fox when something caught its interest. "They can't hurt you in my city. Not under my watch."

Depending on a stranger's benevolence for safety wasn't all too reassuring, either. "Until today, they were just ridiculous lies tutors would tell me any time I burned their hair by accident."

Roth dragged out a laugh. "Contrary to parenting beliefs, they do not eat those who misbehave. But those old stories left out quite a bit." He winked. "I was hardly conscious enough to make any judgements when they took me in, but for whatever reason, they saved me from becoming a corpse in the cold." Deep in thought, he murmured, "Powerful yes, but not always so monstrous as we were led to believe."

Kallia's brow furrowed slightly, remembering the magician that had attacked her out beyond the gates, one of many still out there. "What about what they do beyond the gates, then? Outside of these walls?"

"Our arrangement with them is not perfect, I admit. But it's fair, given the circumstances," he said. "Technically, *this* is their world. They were here first. We've all just merely landed at their feet. And once we kept on coming, it was clear we needed some rules established. Boundaries set."

"Magicians own the city," Kallia said in slow understanding. "Devils take the rest."

"Exactly." Roth nodded, his smile dimming. "There's no way of knowing where or when magicians will arrive to these parts, so the onus is on them to make the journey to our little oasis. And occasionally, some magicians will get lost on that journey and never make it."

Though crestfallen, he spoke as though it were inevitable, unable to be helped. And maybe it was. Maybe not every magician could be saved in a world like this, when it wasn't theirs to begin with.

Kallia hated to admit that not even she could've made it to the city on her own. Not without her power. So many times, the intricate traps had been laid out before her and she'd been *so* close to falling.

Except Jack wouldn't let her.

He'd guided her, pulled her out of every snare that snapped its jaws open for her. Even when she didn't ask for it, when he didn't have to.

It was a haunting thought, how many times he'd saved her.

"Even still, we've had our truces in between. The devils who follow me are but little shades they've loaned me to uphold our city. Obedient servants, utterly speechless." Roth grinned, as though relieved. "While they enjoy the shows we put on like an audience from afar."

Kallia tensed. "They watch?"

Roth nodded. "Zarose may have locked them in, but they still have their fun wherever their limited reach allows on the true side," he said. "Those harmless little whispers in your ear, through a mirror, maybe as you dream. They may not have our flair for spectacle, but they enjoy playing games and tricks just as we do."

Everything he'd listed set Kallia on edge, and the game finally became clear. The first was Spectaculore, which had been far from harmless. Though the threshold varied for most. After living among them for however long he'd been on this other side, Roth had developed some understanding with these beings. A fondness reserved for the wild stray animals who calmed under his palm.

"But again, not to worry." Roth clasped his hands together at her hesitation. "The devils don't hunt in the city. Outside is the only gray area, but no one here needs to truly fear that. As long as they do their part and perform, it's not the worst hand to be dealt. Stages galore and shows with no end, a spotlight that never dies. Endless applause, wherever you go."

Performer's paradise. That was exactly the world that glimmered behind Roth's eyes, every time he lit up.

A world that seemed right out of her dreams. It was almost too easy to envision her very own poster lined in lights. Her own dressing room lined with flowers and furs where she'd get ready to earn the endless applause that would meet her every night.

It was all around her, that dream, begging her to take it.

"I can't." Kallia's jaw tensed. "I don't belong here."

Roth appeared confused. "Why not?"

So many reasons, but power rose above the rest.

It wasn't a mask she could fake or pretend with everyone watching. To make it here would be an impossible act, in this sea of stars and performing magicians who currently held more magic in their fingernails than she had in her entire body.

Without light, she was no star.

And that wasn't what she'd come here for.

Kallia looked down at her fingers, tapping them softly against the desk's edge. "And what if someone wishes to leave?"

She almost felt sorry for asking from the way his face fell. As if the thought had only just occurred to him. It only further proved that as much as Kallia would've preferred holding this card to herself a little longer, it would've done little good. A king would see no reason to leave his kingdom.

If she wanted to find a way out, she had to ask for it herself.

"Beyond the city?" he asked, head tilted. "Usually no one ever chooses to go back out—"

"Back to the true side," she said firmly. "A mirror brought you here, same as it did to me. Surely there's a way to go back."

After a brief stretch of silence, deep in thought, Roth looked toward his empty glass. "It's not quite the same as you think," he said. "Leaving is much harder than arriving. And there's only so much we can do on this side." Roth sighed. "We can watch and send illusions out through mirrors, though most times, they weaken all too easily and never last. The devils like to play their little games and small tricks, but despite their power, even that is a great effort for them." He steepled his fingers together, resting them beneath his chin. "Just as Zarose did before, the only way magicians can return is through Zarose Gate. And I'm afraid that wouldn't be wise here."

"How come?" The answer was so obvious, right there in the legend that had been staring them all in the face. "Have you even tried?"

"My dear, what do you think brought me here in the first place?"

Kallia's stomach began to sink.

"Because you see, that mirror that brought me here—that tore down a whole world behind me and ripped everything I knew to shreds— that was no mirror at all. Not one you'd want to meet your reflection in, anyway," Roth added. "*That* was Zarose Gate."

Kallia froze in her seat, blood thundering in her ears.

"So you see why that is not an option." He inhaled sharply. "It never occurred to me that the gate we've all learned about was not a location, but something that could be called. In the presence of enough power, enough to blur the lines of the world." Roth shook his head. "And bring so much terror with it."

Regret ran deep in his voice, that fall of Glorian back in his frown again. When Kallia had first seen this city of illusion, the level of detail and intricacy unnerved her. It was like walking through her home where everything was opposite. A ghost town forged entirely out of lights.

Maybe all the lights were to drive out the ghosts that still haunted Roth.

"Why bring me here if there's no way out?"

"I didn't bring you here. You brought yourself, remember?" he pointed out. "Yes, those Patrons have a habit of hiding a lot. Not sure why, but all I can say is after I arrived here, others followed here on their own. Who knows what other strangeness the gate might've brought, but if you knew nothing about it until now, then the Patrons are certainly doing their job well."

Kallia clenched her fingers to stop them from shaking. She couldn't help but think of the Patrons in Glorian now, her Glorian, around everyone she left behind.

Doing their job well.

She had to find the gate, and she had to get out. *Now.*

"There has to be some way around it," Kallia said. "Something that was designed as a gate in nature *is* a gate. One way or another."

If Zarose had done it before, then it *could* be done.

"A double-edged sword like that is not something you want to face." Roth frowned, pensive. "You can't win against a mirror where you meet death in the reflection."

Kallia thought back to the last time she'd seen her reflection, in the Court of Mirrors of the Glorian she knew. Her form, fractured until shattering to nothing but pieces on the floor.

"You can if you break it."

She could feel her heart pounding against her chest as the words flew from her lips. Nothing emboldened her more than when Roth's eyes widened in almost comical shock, unblinking. "Not me," he said, shaking his head in wonder. "The mirrors favor *you,* Kallia."

Her blood turned cold at the way he watched her now, as if only just realizing something in the puzzle pieces fitting right behind his eyes. "What do you mean?"

"They always have," he went on, breathless. "At first I thought it was because you were an Alastor. And a born magician, at that. But once those mirrors were able to find you again, they couldn't stop following. That's how you know a magician holds something extraordinary, if even glass bends to them."

A shiver went through Kallia at the thought of the Court of Mirrors, the ways in which her face fit the frame of one mirror or spanned the length of many sitting next to each other.

"What an irony." Roth held his chin in a pensive grasp. "That what started with me would end with you."

There was such certainty in his voice that it made Kallia lightheaded for an abrupt second. A moment she desperately needed for the clarity. To remember what she'd already forgotten so quickly.

"No, I . . ." Her heart began racing. Maybe it had never stopped since the moment she sat down. "I can't do it."

The words hurt, burning in her throat.

But it was the truth.

Before, she had the power to perform. She had the power to do everything. To break and shatter in a single snap, to own the stage in just one step.

Now that power had gone so dark, she didn't know if it would ever come back.

Roth watched her intently. "I understand if you're scared," he said gently. "You don't have to make a decision—"

"No, I . . ." Kallia gritted her teeth to keep her jaw from trembling. "My power."

That hollowness in her chest rang sharper. Absence, worse than any pain she'd known. The part Demarco played in it left her emptier, because even if he didn't mean to, she wasn't sure if she could forgive what he'd taken. Her anchor, her power.

When Kallia couldn't trust her world and the people around her, at least she had her power. At least she'd known what she was capable of, and that would never change. Magic was her first love, after all. The first to give her fire and make her come alive.

If it was all gone for good, she didn't know what she would do.

She wanted to leave.

She wanted her power.

She wanted too much, as she always did.

"Ah, yes." Roth gave a solemn nod of understanding. "I see now, and I saw then. That Demarco fellow made off with some of your magic. I'm quite sorry for that."

Kallia didn't know how else to respond to that, other than a weak nod.

"He didn't know, if that's any consolation. The effects of the gate, I'm afraid," Roth continued, unsmiling. "Magic turning on its head for some magicians, pulling from another."

Another nod. There was no comfort in the explanation. What happened had happened, and that didn't change what she was now: without what she needed to get what she wanted.

"Chin up, my dear. All is not lost, and you did nothing wrong," he said, rising from his chair. "Power *always* returns, especially at the source."

It still didn't answer the question that had been weighing on the back of her mind all this time. "If it's so difficult to leave this side, how did Jack get out?"

The flicker of hope on his face darkened at the name. The mood of the room, changed.

"I figured he would've told you already." He laughed to himself a little as he walked around the desk. "Though I guess he's not one for words, with how he's kept you away. Away from me."

The possession beneath his tone unsettled her.

Without warning, he gave a sudden clap of his hands thunderous enough to make her shoot up from her seat.

The walls that forged the study dissolved all around them, as though they had been nothing but sheer curtains all along. A dramatic reveal, even for the magicians still lounging across tables and couches on the other side. They perked up instantly for the new show, murmuring among themselves and gathering their drinks to catch a closer look.

First, Herald strode through to join Roth at his side.

Then Jack was dragged in by the arms, two devils still at his side, bringing him to center stage.

For once, he did not look up to meet Kallia's gaze. He only stared down at the ground, as though he knew exactly what was coming.

"How was he?" Roth asked.

"Civil," replied Herald.

For some reason, Roth appeared mildly surprised at that, before turning his steely gaze on Jack. "You *really* thought you could play your own games with me and win?" he tutted. "Is that what the true side taught you?"

When Jack gave no answer, Roth let out a laugh. "Not much for talk these days, I heard," he said. "How cruel of you to keep so many secrets."

He snapped his fingers.

In an instant, the two devils in the room somehow became five. Whether they split or others emerged into being, Kallia wasn't sure. But their intent was clear from the predatory way they circled Jack.

Kallia's heart raced. She wasn't sure how to feel. Alarm, excitement, the two were entwined in her veins. "What are you going to do with him?"

"Whatever you'd like." An arm drew over her shoulders. Roth, grinning cheerily, brought her closer as if showing off a new toy. "Any special requests?"

Kallia was reluctant to answer, bloodlust colliding with a stream of panic. "I thought no one could fight the devils."

"I don't normally set them on anyone. That would be a most unfair match," he said with a seething gleam in his eye. "Though Jack is a rare case. And now that I have the chance, I can't help but be curious."

"About what?"

Roth's eyes remained on the fight brewing before them. "How fast it would take to kill a monster."

Of all things, fear iced Kallia's breath. Before she could answer, Roth decided for her with another snap of his fingers.

Followed by the harsh rip of bones, the thud of a body.

And Jack's head, rolling at her feet.

Beyond the gates stood a girl who looked familiar, even with her back turned. There was something about her height, the dark hair cascading past her shoulders. His heart pounded when he called out a name, but couldn't hear it.

What was he saying?

Whatever name he called again and again, it couldn't be her, for she didn't turn. Almost like she couldn't hear him, only kept walking into the forest until she disappeared within its shadows.

Daron rushed to follow, his steps slower than stone. When he finally managed to get through the gate, there was nothing but the darkness of trees surrounding him. Overhead, all around him. Everywhere.

He was so close. *So,* so close.

The name was back on the tip of his tongue like a melody, finally coming back to his ears.

Before the ground swallowed him whole, devouring his screams.

Daron awoke, gasping in breaths. As it had nearly every night. This one was the worst.

Kallia.

He remembered. Just like he remembered all the rest, all there and untouched. Such a devastating relief. He'd almost been too nervous to fall asleep, unsure if Aunt Cata would send the Patrons in secret to finish the job on her behalf sooner than she'd planned.

Not knowing when or how, only that it was inevitable, was the horror of it all.

He needed to warn the others. To get out of this city.

Under the dark curtains of the early morning sky, he walked out of the Prima to inquire about carriages out of Glorian, hoping he could pay one of the riders extra to keep one on reserve for when the time came. But when he arrived, the stables were barred off, no attendants present. Not even as he waited for over an hour, before giving up entirely when he noticed flocks of people making their way to the entry gates.

Only to discover they were flanked with half a dozen Patrons.

They stood at attention on each end of the gate, not at all perturbed by the passersby nearing them. Not even by Erasmus Rayne, whose face flushed with fury as he yelled in the face of one of them. "What do you mean we can't leave—didn't we just go through this already?"

"It's only a precaution, sir," one of the Patrons answered sternly. "Head Patron Edgard insists on a brief lockdown while she personally investigates the situation at hand further."

"By Zarose, the show is already over!" Erasmus spat out a cold laugh, looking around as if someone might groan with him. "What situation is there?"

"Oh, just the missing magicians, the hospitalized ones, and the terrible press every strange occurrence has wrought." Canary sidled up beside him, smiling sweetly at the Patrons. "Did I get that right?"

The Patrons' resounding silence seemed a good enough answer as any.

"Well in that case, this is *quite* the overreaction, if you ask me." Erasmus was practically frothing at the mouth, looking out into the curious crowd gathered all around them. "Demarco!"

Before Daron could dissolve into the crowd, the proprietor clawed a hand onto him with a commiserating scowl. "Can you believe this inconvenience? We've got to make a brief stop in Deque next week to scope out another potential venue for another show. Do you think they even care one bit about the business of others?"

Daron doubted it. The last thing the Patrons could be bothered with was a showman frustrated over not getting his way.

"Speaking of, how is your dear aunt?" Erasmus murmured under his breath with the slippery rise of his brow. "Would you mind slipping in a good word for us to loosen the reins? For old times' sake?"

The man was utterly shameless. Since the show's end, it was the first time Erasmus had interacted with him. The scandal of a fraudulent judge was not in fashion to associate with, and his Conquering Circus agreed. Among them, only Canary could stand to look Daron in the eye whenever they passed in the streets. Always in a glare, nothing more.

Her acknowledgement now was a step up to civil indifference, at least. Still more preferable than Erasmus's aggressive attentions.

Daron begrudgingly met the man's waiting stare. "In case you haven't noticed, Rayne, I'm not exempt from the lockdown, either."

It felt like retaliation. Aunt Cata had known the first thing he would do was attempt to leave, sneak away while he still could.

Though maybe this was how they always handled such situations. Herding in everyone as soon as they could, right underneath Aunt Cata's palm until she had everything sorted to her liking.

"Too true." Erasmus clapped a hand over his shoulder. "After your past transgressions, I don't think I'd want you on the loose, either."

He laughed in jest, and it speared nausea down Daron's gut.

"Don't worry, Demarco, you don't need to fear my ire. I understand your place better than you think. Yes, we're in the industry of magic and entertainment, but ultimately, we're in the business of selling dreams and lies." Erasmus winked. "The better the salesman, the better chance of survival."

The attempt at camaraderie didn't soothe Daron in any way. If anything, it made him feel worse, to be placed on a greasy pedestal alongside this ringmaster.

On a scoff, Canary looked about ready to punch both of them in the faces. "Well, don't you two make the brightest pair, then." She shoved against Daron's shoulder as she passed them to join the rest of the crowd.

"Don't take it personally," Erasmus said. "My girls have a hard time separating feelings from business. All those emotions, you know?"

All too eagerly, Daron withdrew from the proprietor's grip with a forced grin before filing out of the grumbling crowd that had begun to disperse around the gate. Only when he was sure no one followed him did he dig into his jacket pocket for the note he'd felt Canary slip in there, bearing one instruction.

Meet us in the tents.

The roaring applause drowned out Kallia's screams.

Laughter exploded. Fists rose high.

Endless shaken bottles popped, releasing the spray of fizz everywhere like glittering liquid confetti.

A few droplets hit her cheeks. She couldn't move as more showered. All she could manage was shutting her eyes so tightly, every part of her shook.

His head was still lying there. Seared in her memory.

Jack.

The ringing intensified in the back of her head to a point of numbness.

Roth held her tight against him, his body rumbling with amusement deep within. Just being this close nauseated her, but she needed the anchor. He was all that kept her from falling over and retching out everything boiling in her throat.

She never wanted to open her eyes ever again.

"Is that really the best you can do?"

Kallia froze.

Impossible.

As she woke, the bile immediately returned.

The air had gone hot with bloodlust, smoke swirling with sweat. Dim lighting revealed the gathering around the ring of devils, even rowdier than before. Some watched on wide-eyed, while others hollered for death on drunken breaths.

In the center of it all, as if he'd been there all along, stood Jack.

"Well, that was disappointing." Roth released a glum sigh of annoyance. "I thought that might leave a scar, at least."

The cold dug into Kallia so hard, she couldn't breathe.

She'd seen his head fall. Heard every wretched snap and thud of his body. When he dropped to the floor, the world had rejoiced.

What the *fuck* was happening?

She couldn't even blink. The only other person in the room not cheering appeared to be Herald, standing on Roth's other side. He kept shooting glances her way, far more entertained by her reaction than the show taking place. Once their gazes caught, he gave a knowing *told-you-so* waggle of his brow.

Before, when she'd run through the streets earlier, he told her she'd imagined it all. That she would *keep* imagining, and there was nothing to be done about it. Was that what this was? She'd chased Demarco in the crowd, only to watch Jack have his head ripped off as easily as a doll's. Just a hallucination, completely normal.

Or had all of that been a lie, as well?

"No mercy!" Roth's screams joined the other cutthroat calls in the audience. "Throw everything you've got at him!"

Kallia tore herself from the viselike grip of his arm. "What the hell is going on here?" Fury slammed in every breath. "What is this?"

Roth finally turned to her, his expression the picture of surprise. "You poor, poor dear. Such a shame how the deceptions never end with that one."

His dismay rang false and struck a harsh chord in her. He was well aware how she'd been thrown in the dark too many times, but perhaps he didn't care as he claimed. The man gloried more in the shock and savagery surrounding them, taking it all in. This was a show he'd long been waiting for.

"Let's give it another round," crowed Roth in a booming voice. *"Again!"*

Kallia cringed at the explosive cries of approval and delighted gasps as all heads turned to the center of the room. In unison, the devils assumed defensive stances around their quarry.

Jack rolled his eyes for a long moment before unbuttoning his jacket. It earned a few catcalls and whistles as he tossed it aside.

"By all means, let's not displease the Dealer." Ice rose in his tone while he folded back the sleeves of his shirt to his forearms. "No matter how many times he gets it wrong."

Only Kallia could see how Roth tightened his fist by his side. "Everything must come to an end, Jack. Even you," he said. "How I can't wait to explore all of the creative ways it could take to find out just how . . ."

Jack scoffed. "You really think the end scares me?"

"You truly believe you're indestructible?" A chilling promise lay in Roth's smile, invigorated by the challenge in front of him. "Every magician has his weaknesses and every illusion carries flaws. A creature who's of both is bound to have his downfall."

The blood drained from Kallia's face faster than she could stop it.

"Luckily, this creature feels perfectly fine." The promise in Jack's grin was just as chilling. "Though I can't help but wonder why *you* aren't fighting me yourself?"

The drop of silence froze everyone in the room and struck a nerve in Roth. His eye twitched, jaw clenched so sharply it almost appeared broken.

"Don't forget that I *made* you, boy," he seethed, lifting his hand. "Which means I can have you unmade just the same."

At the snap of Roth's fingers, the next round began.

The devils charged in a frontline of smoke, and Jack met them head-on. Shadows trailed from his feet like a blaze of black fire so impossibly fast, one would miss him in a blink.

One darkness against another, they collided. It was a miracle the floor hadn't cracked beneath their feet from the violent impact shaking the room. Some magicians fell over, most screamed and jeered even louder.

Kallia remained completely still, composed, through every brutal slam of her heart to her chest.

Impossible, it drummed harder each time. *Impossible, impossible, impossible.*

An arm slithered around her shoulders with a conspiratorial squeeze. "What you're seeing now, Kallia, is a battle of the ages no one has seen before. A true fight for supremacy between the monsters and the monstrous." Roth spoke close to her ear. "The illusion versus the devils that made him."

Her stomach dropped hard. And still, she showed nothing in her face.

Impossible.

She held onto the word, and it gnawed at every part of her. She searched all her memories of him, looking for some sign or moment. An answer.

Life at Hellfire House had been all just an act. Littered with cut scenes and grand props and ever-changing players, she saw the signs for what they were now. While Jack existed as the only constant in it all. The one real thing about that place, just as she was to him.

It's impressive he even cares at all.

She glared hard into the fray at the center, expecting Jack to meet her halfway. A look, a sign, anything. He'd been so desperate to catch her attention earlier.

Now, he was fixed on the devils alone. As they raised a sinister wall of jagged black arrows, he vanished and reappeared all over the room. From behind the devil to the top of a table, sliding down the bar while the arrows turned and followed his every direction.

Without warning, they shot him down.

Her nostrils flared as she watched him bat away a few from his face, spearing right through his hands instead. Every inch of his torso, entirely impaled, in a manner no one could survive. The blood loss alone would be devastating.

The way he ripped out the arrows by the handful without so much as a wince was not half as terrifying as the sight of his shirt: still white and pristine as ever.

In all of her memories with him, she never once saw blood. No cuts or bruises or injury, despite the fights he'd often need to break up in Hellfire House between club patrons who'd had a bit too much to drink. A small scar lay across his eyebrow, a designed imperfection to sell the act. Any time she noticed it felt like trouble.

As Jack tore out the last of the arrows from his body, only then did he look up as though he heard the call of his name.

When his eyes finally found hers, there was quiet.

No violence, no fury. Not even an apology.

Everything was there, all the signs she hadn't seen before. The one word she'd shoved into the far corners of her mind, hoping it could never fool her again.

"Illusions can't become magicians," Kallia bit out. "They're made *from* magic."

That was always the tell. Like clay, magic was an element that could be molded. It couldn't simply move around and form itself into any shape it wanted. The purpose of illusions on stages such as these were all for show, nothing with intent.

She heard how naive she sounded to her own ears, reflected in Roth's gentle smile. "That's what I thought, too," he said. "But not all magic is the—"

The crowd shoved them both back. A few elbows caught Kallia by the side, then in the gut as everyone parted for the fight moving outward into the lounge area.

More devils appeared, as if more had flown in out of nowhere or the two had split themselves again and again for reinforcements. The floor between the adversaries was flooded entirely with smoke. It was mesmerizing how they maneuvered around each other—fast as lightning, shadows trailing at their feet. As intricate as a dance.

Kallia had seen smoke like that before at Jack's feet. Every time he had visited her in Glorian like a nightmare rising, it went unquestioned. Just like everything about his power, inevitable and nothing more.

Whatever expression overtook her face, Roth delivered a gentle pat on her shoulder as though she needed soothing. "You have nothing to worry about, my dear. He may be powerful, but he can't hurt you anymore," he said. "No matter how strong, the lone wolf rarely survives against the pack. We'll find a way to get rid of him eventually."

It didn't seem likely. Jack proved he was unstoppable against the devils, which meant he could most likely take out every magician in the room in one go. *"How?"*

They turned at the excited surge of screams.

All of the devils held Jack by each limb while he thrashed in their hold. A beast caught in the trap, but still standing. Still thrumming with power.

The pulse of the room peaked and waited for the next violent act. The next piece to break.

"Does it please you to see this, Kallia?" Roth watched with pride. "There's nothing more satisfying than to see someone who wronged get exactly what they deserve. When trust is broken, it is our right to break them back."

As he spoke, the devils weren't quick with their punishment this time. They waited for no command, but pulled slowly at every limb. Thrashing to pull free only made it worse, so Jack held still. Waiting. Kallia felt all her joints lock up just watching it. For a moment, she thought she saw a flicker of pain cross Jack's face as his shoulder looked close to dislocating. Both of them.

Did he even *feel* pain?

Whether or not he did, the crowd went wild and begged for more.

"You've been at his mercy for so long. Now, it's about time he's finally at yours."

From his encouraging smile, expectant and waiting, this was a gift. One designed perfectly for Kallia to give the final order of violence that would be hers to enjoy. It might not kill him, or it could just be enough to take him apart like slaughtered meat. Jack's life, whatever life was in him, had been placed in her hands.

And just as he'd done to her, she could do whatever she wanted with it.

She'd been waiting for this moment, longer than she'd ever known.

It's impressive that he even cares at all.

If that were true, they wouldn't be here. In a room thick with blood-thirst, calling to Kallia. Every moment in Hellfire House returned, every memory forgotten and twisted away, every doubt he lodged at her in Glorian. Every lie he'd ever told and secret withheld, to keep her away from this—this world of more power and even more liars waiting for the next kill.

It wasn't all lies, Kallia.

If that were true, then she could use that.

Kallia watched the scene a moment more, letting it burn in her memory before looping her elbow within Roth's with a conspiratorial smile of her own. "Stop the fight."

Every part of her wanted to take the words back, to choose fury and be done with him. Even Roth's face scrunched, hoping he might've misheard her. "What was that?"

He wanted her to change her answer. She could hear it in his voice, in the curses that erupted from the crowd when the fight came to a halt.

There were other ways to have him at her mercy, and Kallia wouldn't waste them.

"Don't worry." She spoke in that same gentle voice, sweetened with pity. "He'll get exactly what he deserves."

14

Hardly anyone wandered by the Alastor Fold anymore. The cursed corner of Glorian once more, it had slipped back into the ominous shadows, preferring the solitude after some days in the sun. Balance restored, in an odd sort of way.

The only mark of change was the Conquering Circus tents still parked outside the Alastor Place like an immovable, dark-striped serpent. The tents lay dormant as the sector itself, but the whispers of music and laughter ringing within betrayed the hidden life inside.

Daron entered on a deep, wary breath, greeted by a sight as icy as he'd anticipated.

Music continued reeling from the corners, but his presence brought a noticeable pause. Performers he noticed from past circus nights in the city streets shot him looks of confusion, distrust. A pair of dark-haired twins he'd met once stretched on the ground in mirroring movements, breaking formation at his arrival. He'd remembered how one of them excitedly asked if he was the Daring Demarco, the way many of his admirers used to.

They all looked ready to claw his eyes out right about now.

"What are you doing here, showman?" a lady with knives asked.

Her fingertips danced along the handles sheathed along her belt. "Who said you could come in here and—"

"Knives away, Camilla."

A wall of patchwork curtain to the back end of the room slid open, revealing Canary on the other side. Not at all surprised to see Daron there, nor her fellow Conquerors watching him like target practice. "We've got things to discuss, so leave him be."

Without another word, she jutted her chin at him to follow her. It was a slow, tense trail, bypassing the one with the knives and the twins on the ground watching him like vultures. Only when he reached Canary did Daron let out a full breath. "Thank you."

"You're lucky the one with the lion decided to take her out for a walk right now."

He blinked as she kept on walking, expecting him to follow. "Why did you ask me to come here?"

"The others insisted there are new developments, and I was feeling hospitable," she said over her shoulder. "Given how the Patrons have descended like a swarm of bees, I'd say places to gather without drawing notice are scarce."

"I thought . . ." Before she slipped through another set of curtains, Daron stopped her gently by the arm. "I thought you didn't want to help."

Canary didn't immediately recoil from him, but he withdrew anyway. Which was clearly the right decision, as she met his gaze head-on. "Look, I don't know you, Demarco. But I know your kind," she said, flexing her fingers. "My performers and I, we all fight for a moment in a light that can't really see us. Something which you pompous showmen have never known, and never will."

Her jaw clenched sharply, cutting shame right through him.

But they were words he needed to hear, so he listened.

"And on top of using your light to lie to the world, you lied to my friend. She trusted you more than anyone, and now she's gone." Canary's face crumpled for a harsh second as she gritted her teeth. "Why *would* I ever want to help you?"

It was the very question he grappled with, for Aaros and Lottie. Now Canary. He wasn't there to fight or defend himself. He was simply there to do better. "I . . . I really don't know."

An insult must've been ready on her tongue to fire off, but something in her faltered slightly. "I saw you in the hospital the other day."

Ah, that's why he was there. Daron dug his hands into his pockets. "I know. The two intruders in my room told me a bird sent them."

Her snort was perhaps the warmest noise to have come from her. "Your aunt seems as delightful as a tombstone."

"She has her moments." His smile went bitter at the weight pressing hard on his heart. A shadow now hovered over their relationship, something he couldn't see past in her, and all the things she wouldn't hesitate to do. "There's . . . a lot I never knew about her. So much wrong I'm only just learning now."

No matter what, there would still be love. As her nephew, that could never change. She would always be his aunt who had looked after him and Eva all their lives.

But she would also be this, too.

"Don't blame yourself for having a screwed up family, Demarco. There's a lot we don't see until it's too late. And from what I saw . . ." Canary cocked her head. "Looks like you could use all the help you can get."

She slipped through the curtains. A wordless command for Daron to follow, and he breathed a little easier as he did, grateful for the invitation.

He almost walked face-first into a rack of clothes, the room was so crowded with costumes, boxes, and mannequins. Closed off from the main entrance, the space must've been a changing room that had become a place for overflow storage. They navigated around towers of boxes and junk toward the center where a pair of familiar silhouettes waited—Aaros and Lottie, gathered around a makeshift bed of two mismatched love seats pushed together.

A scowling older woman sat atop it, blankets bundled around her as she restlessly tapped at the deck in her hand.

"Ridiculous," she grumbled at her captors. "I'm dizzy, children. Not dying."

"Dizzy is not ideal, either." Aaros leaned back against a few stacked crates. "Just trying to make you more cozy, Ira."

So this was the famous Ira. The seamstress. Daron had never encountered her before in all his time in Glorian, nor seen her among the audience of Spectaculore. Not that she seemed the type to enjoy a spectacle. She looked like she could hardly tolerate being in a circus tent.

"Cozy, indeed." Lottie frowned at their tight surroundings. "Though a far cry better than that wooden cot at your shop."

"Sorry I wasn't born in a pot of gold, de la Rosa." Canary emerged from the back with a scoff, bracing her elbows over the top of an empty standing crate. "Remind me again why I need to sacrifice my favorite furniture rather than turn her over to the professionals?"

"Look, firebird, if you really must know—" Ira's eyes flared, dimming briefly when they latched onto Daron as she deftly shuffled the deck of cards between her hands. Her technique was impressive and sly. And the deck itself was unlike any numbered cards Daron had seen, flashing hints of familiar symbols at the edges before disappearing into the fold.

"You don't know who you can trust in this town anymore . . . ," the woman continued, drawing her gaze carefully back down at her lap. "And I'd rather not follow in Mister Mayor's footsteps, the poor sod. It's either bed rest on my terms, or *theirs*."

The Patrons. Daron swallowed hard as the mayor's cries returned. His desperate words and hoarse pleas.

The cold slide of Aunt Cata's gloveless hand upon his arm.

Her worry was warranted. There was no trusting anyone in Glorian, especially not the ones who claimed to be there to save it.

"So, you brought the young Patron boy to keep me company?" Ira's shuffling remained uninterrupted, even as she shook her head on a disappointed sigh. "You've got honest eyes and a strong jaw. Of course she took to you."

The knot tightened like stone inside him.

"You *and* your tricks," she added, until the rush of cards ceased. The deck, now split evenly in each hand. "At Casine's, one of the first lessons they teach us is to be careful, for true power only favors a few. And there will always be those who want to take it. I can only assume they preached the opposite at Valmonts. Is that right, young Demarco?"

Guilt knifed deeper through his ribs, and he took it. Silently. While Daron was sure he'd never met Ira before, she certainly knew much about him. And Kallia.

Clearing her throat, Lottie took stock of everyone gathered. "Look, we didn't all gather here to put Demarco on some bloody trial."

"Says you." Ira arched a weathered brow. "I'm not chummy with the Patron boy. How can you be so certain there aren't any strings on him, either?"

Daron pushed down every rising instinct to apologize, to clarify, to express every mistake he needed to right. That wasn't what they were looking for, not that it would matter. There was only one person who deserved to hear everything, and she was not there.

"That won't be a problem, seamstress." Canary's hand clapped hard upon Daron's shoulder. "If any strings emerge, he'll have a hell of a time trying to get out of this city in one piece."

Not just him. They all would.

A fresh wave of dread crashed through him. Everything Aunt Cata had told him, he could all too easily envision now: everyone in this room, back to complete strangers at the very beginning. Forgetting days as though they never existed. Not even a force like the Conquering Circus would be enough to stop it. In a few days' time, no one would.

"I'm *not* a Patron," Daron stressed, his breath calm. "And I'm not asking anyone to trust me. Zarose knows I've done more wrong than right. But I fear for what's happening around us—and *will* happen, sooner or later—if we do nothing."

The air cracked under a stilted silence. "What do you mean *will* happen?" Lottie perched herself atop an armrest with a troubled frown. "I take it the family card worked."

Too well.

He relayed all he could remember. All the details of the Patrons' involvement—from hidden histories and marred memories, to conspiracies and cover-ups that manipulated their world in invisible ways. From the truth of Zarose Gate to the truth about Glorian, and the mission to bury both no matter how it fractured a people. It all cobbled together in a tale too unbelievable to forget that turned everyone motionless as statues. At one point, Ira stopped shuffling her cards altogether.

Through every revelation, no one appeared more ill than Aaros.

"So what the mayor said, it's all . . ." The tower of crates toppled behind him as he staggered back a step, blinking slowly. "They can't just . . . do that to us—how can this be?"

"You tell us, assistant," Lottie said quietly. "You're the one who's actually lived in this place for years."

Aaros's head creaked in a nod. "I-I don't know. No one knows what they can't remember. But I wasn't involved in any of that, for Zarose sake. I don't think—" The question hung as he dug a hand through his hair. "Ira's been here longer. Maybe . . ."

Daron had never seen the assistant more shattered, not since those first days following Kallia's disappearance. His eyes watered at the edges in doubt, processing a truth as immense as the lie. This was the side Aunt Cata never saw in her work. The truth of how taking, even a little bit, broke more than it fixed.

"No need to get all sniffly, boy. It was long before your time."

Everyone stilled as the sharp shuffling of cards resumed.

"Wait—" Canary almost choked on a breath. "How do *you* remember?"

"I've been feeling strange for a while . . . and nothing ever made sense until now. Even when it's just bits and pieces, coming together." She went quiet for a few beats, staring straight ahead. "You feel nothing when you forget, but everything starts hitting you when you're free to remember."

"And what do you remember?" Lottie pressed. "Anything that could help?"

"You're a little leech, aren't you?" Ira snapped self-righteously, turning on all of them. "How do I know you all won't send me away? Or that the Patron boy's loyalties won't drive him back to auntie dearest?"

"I'm not on her side in *any* of this." Family or not, Daron knew exactly where he stood. "Nothing leaves this tent."

Everyone slowly nodded, except Ira. "All right then, Demarco. Let's see if your intentions are true." She studied him. "Give me a number below sixty."

Over her head, Daron's confusion paralleled the rest of the group's. "Why?"

"If you want me to play, then you have to play, too." Undeterred, she stacked her deck altogether. "A number, please."

Young miss, just who do you think you are?

Number twenty-four.

The memory slammed into him. His chest seized at her voice, spinning back into his ears as though it never left. "Twenty-four."

A short *hmph* sounded from Ira as she began patiently counting out cards. One by one, they dropped facedown over her lap in ordered chaos. "Memory is a funny thing. A strong element that's surprisingly malleable." She spoke as the cards continued to fall. "We forget, and don't question why. I can only assume he saw it as a mercy, every time he came into the city and left behind his trail of nothing."

"Who?" Patrons never traveled alone, especially not for an undertaking such as this. "Was my aunt there?"

Reaching what he could only assume was the twenty-fourth card, the seamstress tapped the edges of what remained in the deck. "Tell me when to stop."

Without warning, she tossed cards over her shoulder, one smacking Aaros square in the face. "Am I missing something? What are you *doing?*"

"Something I've only just started remembering." Ira continued, all focus. "Playing cards is no random game. It's not by chance you receive your hand, it's by fate. From the simplest deck to the rarest." She cocked her head at Daron as she kept on throwing over her shoulder. "Demarco?"

The thinner the deck started to grow, the more panic pulled at him. "St-stop."

Once she did, she lifted her cooled gaze. Tit for tat. "From what I can remember, your Head Patron was nowhere near him. In fact, there were no Patrons at all." Her brow hardened. "Not a white glove in sight."

Impossible. The strangest cold swept down his spine.

"That can't be," he swore. "My aunt told me everything herself. Patrons are the only magicians with the means to sweep through a city the way they did."

"This is their first time on the ground here in a while, is it not?" Ira asked, pressing a finger to her temple. "There's still much to chip away in here—as will most likely happen for you too, Aaros. And many more in this sorry town."

Aaros brought a fist beneath his chin, the rose-stitched handkerchief peeking out between his fingers. Kallia used to grip it tight in a similar manner. For strength, comfort. As if it could anchor her in a turbulent sea pulling her under. No one needed it more than her assistant, still holding on.

"All I can glean from your story of Glorian, Demarco, is fire. No one here likes it much, which makes it a fear running deep here," Ira said. "Even if the story isn't ringing any bells yet, I feel pieces coming back together. Memory will return if left unblocked . . ." She tapped at the top of her lips. "And someone *has* been keeping it that way, continuing what your Patrons first started. Or at least, that's how it seems."

Her words tangled everything Daron thought he'd discovered. Everything Aunt Cata had told him. From her lips, she sounded convinced that the one time they pulled the memories from the city had been enough. It had lasted Glorian this long, and now as if the timing could not be more perfect, they were due for another coating.

"How is that possible?" The horror on Canary's face deepened. "There's no way one magician could do that all on his own without a ring of Patrons to help."

"Depends on the magician, then. And if they're as desperate to quiet history."

Just one night of it.

Twisted as it was, Daron recognized the logic of the Patrons. Their duty was in preserving Soltair from the ones with magic to those without. To them, erasing all knowledge of Rothmos Alastor summoning Zarose Gate was justified to prevent another incident from occurring. Daron couldn't fathom how or *why* anyone else would carry on such a responsibility alone.

And from the looks of it, neither could Ira. Under a hard swallow, she placed the first card facedown on her lap. "This represents what you seek," she explained. "Now, for what you'll find . . ."

Daron didn't like this, more a crucible than a game. Dealing in hypotheticals and certain uncertainties with fate was dangerous magic to be playing with. Fate never asked to be bothered with, and when she was, she rarely ever responded kindly.

Placing down the second card, Ira stared hard at her scar-ridden palms. "For the longest time, I thought he was only a dream I kept having. He'd walk past my shop on a rare and quiet day, and everything would just . . . fall quiet and blur after that," she said, her frown deepening. "I thought I was going mad, but Eilin knows of him, too."

The lines were crossing so quickly, Daron couldn't keep them straight anymore. "This magician you saw outside your shop?"

"The face is still vague, but he fits." Ira nodded. "I only know he wasn't a Patron because that young man looked exactly the opposite— suit black as ink, with the knuckles of his fingers wrapped in dark metal."

I know him. They all did, it seemed. And there was no coincidence about it.

Daron's pulse sped until it crashed. "Are you sure?"

No other magician had power that could rival the Patrons, but then again, it was clear from the way he'd descended upon the ball that Jack was no ordinary magician.

Ira's brow raised, glancing at them all. "I take it you've all met him, too?"

"At the ball, he took Kallia," Daron bit out, recalling that fear in her when she'd first confided in him about her life before Glorian, with Jack. And his unnatural arrival at the ball, bringing the monsters in the mirrors with him. "She's gone *because* of him."

"Is that so?"

"Ira," Aaros scoffed. "Please—"

"Please what? Are you so sure that everything you think you know is exactly what it seems?" The seamstress's voice rose to an edge. "That girl is full is secrets and sides you probably never saw. She *loves* power. And if hers is supposedly gone, how can you be so sure she didn't choose to follow this magician again just to get it all back?"

Because Daron knew Kallia. He knew she'd been running from this magician even before the show started. And a magician powerful as that could not have been easy to outrun.

Not when such power had drawn them together in the first place.

Daron stiffened. The last time he'd seen them, the two had been standing close by the mirror. No force, no forceful arms pushing her through the glass. Just a soft look in her eyes. No panic, no fear. Choice.

"Maybe *I'm* wrong then, if you're so sure." Ira clasped her hands together. "From what it sounds like, Eilin remembers far more than I do. He'd be your best bet at more answers than questions, and he clearly knows how to get to where you want."

Lose yourself where those dare not get lost . . .

Where? Daron never once imagined he'd want alone time with the mayor, but now, he was desperate.

The man had already hinted at Kallia and Zarose Gate. The rest was all still a riddle.

"It's impossible to even be in the same room with him, now." Daron gritted his teeth. "Too many Patrons watching him. And me."

"Everyone needs to blink eventually. Just seize that moment when it comes." When Ira finally flipped over a chosen card, she chuckled deeply at it. "What you seek, Demarco, is the Crown Jewel of Flames."

Daron wasn't sure what was so funny about it. Warily, he studied the card's design: a glittering onyx crown, surrounded by black triangles. The shapes were a sign of the Alastors. The marks inked on Jack's knuckles.

That was no coincidence there. It had to be in some connection between the magician and a man like Rothmos Alastor. Maybe he was even an Alastor himself.

"And now, for what you'll find . . ." Ira trailed off.

Daron wasn't sure he even wanted to know, until the pads of Ira's fingers hovered over the last card, froze like the rest of her.

"Where in the world did you get *that*?"

A cold shift hit the room. Daron straightened instinctively in pre-guilt, only to find he was not the target of the woman's intense stare.

"What's the matter?" Aaros stepped back, pressing at the front of his shirt and his pants. "What's on me?"

"Not on you, foolish boy. In your hand."

"It's a *handkerchief*?" His head flinched back slightly, gaze dropping to his fist. "And it's not mine, it's Kallia's. I found it around the area where she disappeared."

"Hmm. Poor frayed scrap looks like some cat had quite a time with it." She snapped a finger in demand. She assessed the embroidered flower stem stitched over it. Nearly headless, with all the petals that had fallen. "Doesn't explain why she'd have it. I could've sworn she wasn't an academy girl."

"No, she had tutors." Daron's brows knitted together. "She's never gone beyond the Dire Woods in her entire life."

"You're not going to find one of these growing on a tree out in those woods."

Everyone pressed in closer as the seamstress unfolded the crinkled cloth over her palm, inspecting it. "I would know, because I have one just like it," she murmured, pensive. "All the girls at Queen Casine's receive a rose cloth upon entry."

Queen Casine's? Daron shifted on his feet, unable to recall if Eva ever possessed such an item. Then again, she had hated the academy. For Aunt Cata's sake, Eva had grinned through her years of study, but it wouldn't shock him one bit if she'd destroyed the rose cloth on sight.

But Kallia?

"It can't be."

Ira arched a displeased brow. "You calling me a liar, golden boy?"

"How can *you* be too sure when your memories have been scrambled like eggs?" Canary snatched the fabric for a closer look herself. "I burned mine before dropping out of the academy," she said. "And it looked nothing like this."

"You really think someone who sews for a living wouldn't take her fabrics and cloths seriously? If you hadn't turned it to ash first, birdie, perhaps you would've seen it's no ordinary rose. Like an illusion tied to its magician, this sort of embroidery breathes at the touch of magic. As long as that thread of power remains."

"It looks quite dead, actually," Lottie remarked off-handedly, and had the decency to appear somewhat chagrined from all the glares. "Sorry, but look at the petals."

The longer Daron did, the more he noticed the slight drift in the tips of the leaves at the stem, a subtle brush against the petals below it, nearly drifting off the edge.

So many fallen petals.

"Dying . . ." Canary cocked her head at the rose still living on the cloth. "But *not* dead."

They all startled at the sudden whoop from Aaros as he snagged back the rose cloth with a victory wave in the air. "*Not dead*—we'll take it!"

Ira rolled her eyes. Lottie contemplated. And Canary looked conflicted as Aaros's cheered relentlessly in the background. Daron pressed a hand to his stomach, relief slamming into him.

Alive. The confirmation felt like a miracle.

"Not dead, but still weak."

Deep in thought, Ira's stern expression had not shifted as she tapped a finger against her chin. "And, in case you've already forgotten, she's also not who she seems. Or at least, not what she told you."

"Why must you ruin the moment, Ira?" groaned Aaros, an attempt to keep the mood light.

Daron chewed at his inner cheek. Whether or not Kallia truly had been an academy girl shouldn't have mattered. But with the gates to Glorian closed, and Queen Casine's all the way across Soltair, it couldn't tell them much. Only that there was a lot he didn't know, a lot she'd kept from them all.

"Better to question now than wish you did later," the seamstress muttered. "I'm not saying *don't* search for the girl. But too many lies have led to this point, and we all know trouble has been following her since she entered this city. Can't be too careful."

As she finally flipped Daron's last card, she stilled.

It set his nerves on edge. His gaze dropped to a card bearing no suits or numbers. Just an image, turned upside down. A group of solid black silhouettes against the stark white shadows in the shape of a top-hatted gentleman, mixed with those who took more beastly forms.

"What is it?" Aaros ducked his head in close like everyone else around.

"It's nonsense." Ira snatched it away and hastily gathered all the fallen cards. "Never you mind. My memory can't remember this silly game anyway."

Ice traveled up Daron's spine to the back of his neck as the woman shuffled more aggressively. The two cards drawn for him, now lost and devoured by the deck. "It doesn't sound like nonsense."

"Nor like some silly game," Lottie noted, crossing her arms. "What does the card mean?"

"I don't know. I've never pulled it before."

"Why start lying now, seamstress?" Canary raised a brow. "You've never held back before."

"I'm not lying, red," Ira shot back. "I've never drawn that card because cards of the Unknown suit in a Glorian deck are not easily found. They find you." She continued splitting and folding the deck back into each other seamlessly. "I've had this deck for ages. Probably the last of its kind for obvious reasons, but discontinued for others."

"Why discontinued?" Aaros watched the rapid movement between her fingers. "They're . . . just cards."

"And we all thought Glorian was just a city." She lifted her shoulders in a shrug. "Not everything can be easily cleaned up. And even objects left behind as simple as cards can open up a world of questions."

"So what did that card mean?" Daron pressed. He couldn't accept nonsense as an answer. He wasn't even a believer in fates determined by cards, but Ira's reaction held him by the neck, and it wouldn't let go until he knew why.

In response, Ira fanned out her freshly reordered deck before him. "Choose again."

When he did and flipped over his choice, she hissed out a curse at the card bearing the same black shadow against the stark white background.

"Cards of the Unknown suit, in particular, are rare," she whispered. "No matter how the deck is rearranged or if every card falls face up, you won't be able to find it yourself. But if a card like this keeps finding your hand, it wants you to listen." The omen hung so heavily in the air as she nodded at him. "That one is The Devils. Inverted."

Daron hadn't heard the term spoken with such severity in so long, probably not since he and Eva were much younger and prone to misbehavior. The way Ira looked at him now made him feel about as old. The same way Aunt Cata had always regarded him, if he was in trouble or soon to be.

"The Devils, in general, represent desire that comes with a cost. Upright indicates power and might. Turned around, it can be loss and deception. Death." A dark sigh drew from her as she plucked the card from his hold. "You go searching for the Crown Jewel of Flames, Demarco, and that's exactly what you'll find."

There was no greater dissatisfaction than a thirst for blood left un-
quenched.

Kallia knew the risks. If all of the headliners had already despised
her on sight before, she'd now just ruined their night of fun. And she
would eventually have to pay. Having Roth's arm looped within hers
all the way out of the Green Room did not make her untouchable. Far
from it. If anything, it made her even more of a target. And without
power, that much easier to hunt.

She needed a predator of her own.

"A bodyguard? What for?" Roth scoffed as they walked down the
halls of the Alastor Place to her bedroom. A pair of shadow servants
trailed at their backs, and Jack's even quieter footsteps followed somewhere behind. "My dear, you're an *Alastor*."

"I know how the others look at me," Kallia said. "I wouldn't be surprised if one of them tried stabbing me in my sleep tonight."

"My headliners? Oh, they're just jealous little things. Harmless." He
ticked his tongue against his teeth and gave a frivolous wave of his hand.
"They like to play their games with each other, but that's really all it is."

Either the man was acting deliberately obtuse, or knew exactly what
was happening right under his nose. No one stayed on top without

pushing others to the bottom, especially in a ring of performers all fighting for fame and favor. It was only a matter of time before they descended upon her. Because in any game, nothing united rivals more than a common enemy.

It was Spectaculore all over again, except the players of this game were far from incompetent. They were the best of the best on this board, and they wouldn't let her forget it.

"Come now, don't be paranoid. We're all one big family, really." Roth clasped his hands together. "But if it makes you feel any better, we can all enjoy a grand meal together tomorrow. Make some introductions, smooth over any bad blood, go over event plans and such—they'll love you, I'm sure."

Kallia smiled, absolutely certain a formal introduction and food would not fix anything. "You're right, thank you."

"And besides, what better way to pair you up than to bring you right into the fold? Like I said, you'll have your pick of the best to train with." He beamed. "And then you'll be back to your old self. Your magic *will* return."

Her stomach soured. The idea sounded as disastrous as when he'd first brought it up, but there was no convincing him otherwise. "In the meantime, I'd still like a guard of my choosing," she said with a sigh. "Until my powers come back, of course. I'll only feel completely safe with security that's even more powerful than the devils."

If Jack were listening in, which she did not doubt, she could only imagine what he was making of this. Not that there was another choice aside from being torn to pieces.

"So you'd place your safety in him?" Roth balked. "After what you just saw?"

The fight with the devils told her all she needed to know about Jack's ability. As well as everyone else in that room who would dare challenge it.

"He won't hurt me. As you said, he *cares* for me." Kallia shrugged, shooting an icy glance over her shoulder. "It would be fun to see just how much. After everything he's put me through."

And everything he'd kept.

Vengeance came naturally to her. There was nothing fake in that, just as there was nothing more satisfying than the thought of holding the most powerful being in this world in the palm of her hand. More powerful than the devils. Than the Dealer, even.

Perhaps that was why Roth hesitated and pressed so much, to a point where Kallia was worried he might see through it all, and refuse.

They came to a stop by a door at the end of the hall, where Roth paused in consideration while seconds dropped like hours.

Kallia held her breath the whole time, an unbearable tightness in her chest. It killed her, how much patience she needed to get a fool's approval. To wait for his permission, like a bloody child who didn't know any better for herself.

"*Huh*," uttered Roth. His brow quirked in deliberation. Amusement. "An interesting proposal, indeed. Not quite what I pictured for his sad, quick ending . . . but perhaps you know his wounds better than any of us." He nodded slowly. "He's all yours. But if he for one moment disobeys—"

"I'll let you handle it," she reassured. "By that point, I'll have had my fun."

"Good girl." He patted her elbow proudly in passing. Before excusing himself for the night, he turned a slow heel on Jack with the shake of his head. "The illusion and the magician." He chuckled. "Even beasts get what they want. Though probably not in the way that you hoped."

Red drenched every inch of Kallia's room. Scarlet curtains draped over the walls in lush waves, highlighting the grand four-poster bed of sheer canopy with roses scattered among the gauze. Windows as tall as the towering vanity mirror rose at the sides, brushed gold with specks of crushed rubies all along the frame. In the center hung an elaborate chandelier in the shape of a pointed starburst suspended in the air. In another world, another time, Kallia would've sighed over such a room. A bold, lush lair. Fit for a queen.

An Alastor.

Kallia's jaw clenched at the sound of Jack closing the door then. The tension in the air pressed hard, but she waited. Listened for the whisper of Roth's footsteps outside, fading in the distance away from her room.

The block of ice in her chest melted a fraction. Raking a hand through her hair, she released a long, deep breath. The first time she felt able to do so.

"So . . ."

The ice returned as she turned to Jack, dragging his feet over the carpet almost sheepishly. Hands shoved into his pockets. As if the magician who fought as viciously as a devil had been all in her imagination.

Not a magician.

"Kallia." Uncertainty carved across his brow. "Fire—"

Firecrown.

The name was a lie, a slap in the face.

Kallia snapped. One moment she glared at him from across the room, and the next, she shoved him right against the wall. Every curse she knew seared behind her teeth: *"How?"*

She didn't know what possessed her when she'd seen him take a beating from the devils—hell, his fucking *head* had been ripped off, and he still stood now. Any power she dared reach for next would be a raindrop against a fire. She knew this, and he knew this.

Yet Jack stayed pressed against the wall, as if she held all the tools to end him. "I'm sorry."

"Sorry?" The first time was a rarity, the next was a joke. She couldn't tell if she was shaking from laughter, or rage. "For which part now? This list keeps growing, Jack," she bit out. "That's not even your real name, is it?"

Jack's nostrils flared. "It's the name I was given, so of course it is," he said. "Roth didn't think too hard. It's a common enough name."

Another mask to hide what was beneath. A secret.

An illusion.

With more power than any magician alive.

Her hands curled into fists against his chest. It rose and fell. All hard, cold muscle. No heartbeat. She'd noticed that, once, when he'd haunted her in Glorian. Smoke trailed from his steps, his touch. He'd found her in mirrors and shadows, arrived at the ball with a face that was not his own. So many more signs had been there.

She released him with an irritated breath. "I should've just let them keep fighting you."

"You still could." Jack leaned back against the wall, arms crossed. Deceptively casual. "Not even *I* know what it takes to fully destroy me. But I'm sure Roth would love to solve the mystery with you."

"Maybe I will, then," Kallia muttered. "At least the man gave me answers."

Jack stilled for a tense breath. "And you believed them? All of them?"

"Of course not, you idiot."

Answers yielded clarity. Roth's only shoved more weight on her shoulders, pushing her to one direction: the one he wanted her to follow. The one side to the story he told, where he had everything to gain.

"You think I haven't learned by now?" Kallia scoffed. "Because of experience, I'm not entirely brainless."

Despite the jab, the smallest smile curled on Jack's face. She wanted to smack it right off, before it fell entirely on its own. "Careful."

She followed where his gaze drifted past her shoulder, finding nothing but the closed door. Then a hint of movement beneath the crease.

A shadow walking, waiting.

"I know a place." Jack nodded to the window. "We can talk and we won't—"

"What makes you think I want to talk or go anywhere with you alone?" Her head tilted as she glared. "Because *that* always ends well."

He stopped midstep, his expression unreadable. "I'm not going to hurt you," he said. "I never wanted to hurt—"

"It doesn't matter what you never meant to do. You did it all, anyway."

Jack never hurt in the obvious ways. That didn't excuse the hurt he had inflicted, the scars left behind however unseen. She would make sure he saw them, lest *he* dare forget.

Silence had never been so loud. Not between them. Jack, at least, had the grace to hold her gaze for every tense breath they shared. For all he hid from her, he never looked away to hide what he could. "I did."

For some reason, the admission hit harder than the apology.

"Hurt me, if you wish. However you want," he continued. "After all, I technically serve *you* now. So you can do with me what you like."

Bodyguard. It was the first role that had come to mind, and the irony was laughable. Jack was only ever capable of protecting himself. Any kindness, otherwise, was an accident.

"Don't patronize me." Kallia swallowed hard. "We both know you can turn the tables to your favor when it suits you."

"Ah, but look around." A harsh laugh fell from Jack as he strode to the nearest window and pulled back the curtain. "There's no other side of the table for me to turn to."

The solemn realization gave her pause. To her, he was always Jack. The magician with everything, and more. The Master of the House whom many feared but hardly knew. Without any house to his name, no riches, no illusions at his beck and call—he had nothing left but the power at his fingertips.

At the soft click of the window handle, the pulsing beats of the street party below streamed in. A slight breeze brushed at his hair as he peered out the window frame. "Ah, yes. We're just beneath it."

It was the first time she'd seen the odd grin cross his face. "Beneath what?"

He made a swift jump to the window ledge, holding onto the frame with one hand outstretched to her. "One of the rare places where we won't be disturbed."

The seconds dragged as she stared at his hand, struck by how different it appeared without those black brass knuckles. Like someone else's hand reaching for her. She knew better than to take it.

Kallia jumped on her own, keeping close to the ledge. Back already turned, Jack led the way over the eave, his hand always hovering out behind should she wish to take it.

She never did. Never needed to.

Ridges marked the back of the roof like footholds, and she was grateful there was no rain to coat the surfaces slick. Still, though they were more than five stories up in the air, the climb was not as risky as one would imagine were they to look up at the Alastor Place from below.

"Where are we going?" she hissed through a pant.

Jack made the trip with ease, as though he could climb these steps blindfolded. "You had your place in your greenhouse. This, here, was mine."

Still a few paces behind, Kallia already braced herself. Knowing Jack's tastes, especially on this other side where the impossible thrived, anything could've waited ahead. The city had already exhausted her eyes so much so far. There was hardly any wonder left in her for one more spectacle.

Once at the top, Kallia copied the way Jack had swung himself onto the flat surface. Her heart pattered as she rose slowly to her feet and blinked hard all around her.

There was nothing.

Just a small flat expanse of roof covered by an old rug, frayed and flattened smooth from use. An ordinary spot for stargazing, only there were no stars to this night. No moon, no clouds. Nothing in the dark above their heads.

"No one really cares to enjoy the rooftops here." Jack ambled over to the center of the rug, taking it all in with a pleased breath. "They're a reminder of the truth."

"The truth?"

"That no matter how much shine there is, this world is still just a shade of yours." He gestured out to the building tops of this Glorian, all sparkling illumination to rival the sky. "It's all trickery down here. Sugar-coated truth. Most would rather get lost in lies than face reality, however much they enjoy it from afar." He rocked back on his heels. "That's probably why I enjoyed this so much. It's quiet. Honest."

Fascinated, Kallia kept to the outskirts of the rug as he lowered himself into a seated position, long legs stretched out before him. She'd never seen him sit on *any* ground, let alone unbutton his jacket then toss it to the side.

He didn't gesture for her to join; the invitation was clear should she wish to take it.

Her presence could've been entirely forgotten from the way he looked out across the city the way one would at a sunrise. Just like how she always searched over the Dire Woods for Glorian.

"For some reason, I often found myself coming here," he said quietly, gaze straight ahead. "Even I knew it was a good place to hide."

From what? Someone as powerful as Jack had no reason to hide. Nothing to fear.

"Never thought you'd be here as well, one day." He paused for a beat that went on too long. "You were never supposed to come here."

Her scowl iced at his statement. "Where was I supposed to be, then?" she snapped. "At Hellfire House? Standing in one place for the rest of my days?"

His side profile turned. Just the corner of his eye felt as intense as his full stare. "Standing still isn't so bad."

"If it's a choice."

For someone who called her *firecrown,* how he ever believed she'd be satisfied with such a life astounded her. The bird's name was one she'd worn proudly before, a perfect fit for a rare creature of flight. But rather than let her go, Jack had kept her in Hellfire House. In the palm of his hand.

Kallia pressed her lips tight. "A cage can be pretty and filled with everything one could ever want. But in the end, it's still a cage," she said. "The illusion of power, of a life."

This very rooftop was proof that Jack understood the difference. Even more than the magicians lost to this city around them.

"I'd hoped it could be enough," Jack mused, deep in thought. "But perhaps cages are all I'm used to now, I don't see bars anymore. Only . . . safety."

"Safety from what?"

"Standing still *here.*" He thrust both hands out to the world at their feet. Another grand cage.

For Kallia, at least. "You could leave at any time, couldn't you?"

Envy speared deep into her bones as she spoke. "You did before, probably still can again."

His silence was telling, louder than all the sounds of revelry reaching them. He'd thought about this. Probably since they started walking outside of these gates.

And still, he was here: sitting on the roof beside her under a starless sky.

"Want to know why Roth created me in the first place?" he asked, staring ahead for a long beat. "I was made to find you."

Kallia's heart pounded, knocking against her chest. "I don't understand how that's even possible."

"It's not. Or it shouldn't be," he said all too simply. "Roth found out the hard way that no magicians could leave unless it's through Zarose Gate . . ." No further explanation was needed, from the way both of them shuddered. "And illusions were not an option, either. They can exist on both sides because they're really nothing but figments of magic and memory. But ultimately, they are temporary. Weak."

Kallia frowned. However cruel, the truth of it remained. It was why boorish magicians like the one at the Diamond Rings' show threw daggers into the act, fearing no consequence. Or why the illusions of Hellfire House changed so frequently around her. From Sanja to Mistress Verónn, and all the names and faces she couldn't recall—a new part was always cast to make up for the absence.

And Mari.

A twinge went through Kallia. She recalled flashes of fear in the girl's eyes as they neared the edge of the Dire Woods, and then nothing. No one.

"And Sire?" asked Kallia. "How could *he* be an illusion? He brought me up himself, raised me for years."

"Did he, or was he just simply there?" Jack raised a brow, his suspicions confirmed when she averted his stare. "The more you know an illusion is indicative of how much it took to conjure them. For magicians, creating a prop is easy. Sculpting a puppet to play a role—takes slightly more finesse. But to forge one that can dance and sing and walk without its strings . . . that takes much more power. More effort."

Kallia paced slowly down the edge of the carpet. If she stood still any longer, she might entertain the idea of sitting down next to him. "And that's you?"

"Roth didn't want any more puppets." A humorless chuckle. "He needed a puppeteer."

The moment the sadness of his tone registered, she stopped at her next step. A warning, waiting in the chill of the air.

Jack *always* lied, and could be lying again. The only difference was, she knew the worst of it. Should she fall down that same path again, there was no one to blame but herself.

Celebration echoed from the streets. A burst of piercing screams and bells ringing hard, competing with the nothingness above. The quiet of the night.

Head tipped backward, Jack took it all in. "It's not a true sky, you know."

Kallia's eyes narrowed. If nothing about the other side was true, why would the sky be any different? "Without stars, I figured."

"It's not as simple as a night without stars." He snorted. "Those are the devils up there."

"*What?*" Her pulse started. Panic gripped. "Why the hell are we out here, then?"

"Don't worry, they're so far up because they're too many. Like a swarm of bees."

Repulsed by the image, she choked back a cough. "Don't *worry*? If devils can fill an entire sky, then they could—" The possibilities were endless. When Roth mentioned these forces were watching, she never pictured this. A canvas of eyes, draped overhead.

While people partied riotously below without a care.

The music raged on, accompanied by hoots and whistles so obnoxious, Kallia pressed at her temple. "Do they even realize?"

"Why do you think they're dancing like it's the end of the world?" His shoulder raised in a half-shrug. "The end of this one could come at any time . . . but any type of revelry pleases the devils, gives them a taste of that magic they so crave. And if the devils are pleased, Roth is pleased."

"So the parties never stop," she trailed off with a bleak nod. It had only been her first night in the city, and already, she saw it for the dreams it offered. Endless, spectacular dreams no one wished to wake up from, like a song with no end.

"The parties, the entertainment, whatever power is used to fire up these streets . . ." Jack cast a downward nod. "Magic begets magic. And devils love the taste of it too much to pick away at a field that happily grows it. Even if they don't realize it."

Roth failed to mention that. Many things, in fact. It didn't fit his picture of paradise, the pieces that truly allowed him to thrive. The devils, as well.

"Is that how they made you?"

The set of Jack's shoulders straightened. His posture, too perfect. Tense. "Roth always felt there might be a way to blend illusion and magician," he said. "After all the deals he struck with devils, asking them to give up any magic, for a feat that might not even work, was a risk. Even for him."

Roth's brown eyes flashed every time Kallia blinked. They blazed with challenge, thrived on chance. No one earned a name like the Dealer without eyes like that.

"The devils agreed to one—a perfect, obedient servant," he drawled. "Though Roth would ask for an army if he could."

Relief coursed through her. No other illusions like him lurked on either side of the gate. A power like that existing for many was a war waiting to happen.

But to be the only one—the only one of *anything*—

Kallia chased the feeling away by clearing her throat. "If they brought you here, I'm surprised they didn't try their hand at more."

"One was enough." The somber line of Jack's smile, hard as glass, needled at her.

"Roth never went a day without reminding me of the sacrifice the devils made, wasting so much magic on me. If I didn't come out perfect, I would've been in trouble."

At the harshness of his laugh, the way it went on for a little too long, her brow creased. "That wouldn't have been your fault."

"No one likes to be wrong. But when they are, there's always someone else to blame." He loosened the small buttons at his neck. "Thankfully, I emerged exactly as I am. I trained, I learned. I punished when I was asked, answered when questioned, but most importantly, I obeyed at all times."

"Even if you didn't want to?" The knot at Kallia's throat tightened. It was no secret that Roth was the kind of man who sent others to get their hands dirty for him. A cleaner conscience that way, at the expense of others. "You had all the power to stop it, didn't you?"

"Didn't mean I could use it." A muscle ticked in his jaw. "What I wanted didn't matter. I think they all figured I'd be empty as a shell. An illusion."

Everything he'd said called to everything she'd felt.

For her, there was nothing worse he could ever do to her that he hadn't already done. He'd opened the cage and locked her in, forged friends and memories she'd soon forget, fed her lies until she was full of them, and more. So much more.

We're not so different, you and I.

The truth scared her far more now than it ever had then.

"The timing, at least, was perfect. Not too long after the devils delivered me, the last illusion in Hellfire House was about to fade," Jack continued. "I had my instructions, knew your face from the mirrors, and how best to lead you through them. Make you want them."

The calculation of it all. So cold, so callous.

Except none of those things had happened. Nothing even remotely close. "So you *could* choose, then?"

It was a long while before Jack rose to his feet. Too restless to sit still, to stay grounded. "It didn't hit me or anyone else, until I crossed over, what might change once I reached that true side." Some memory lay behind his wistful expression. "Because as soon as I left and walked out through the Dire Woods, my first thought was not of you."

Kallia blinked. "What was it?"

"I was so damn cold, and I just wanted a drink."

He said it so plainly, soft-spoken and unlike him, that the pressure in her chest built into a laugh she couldn't hold back. So loud, even Jack whipped around with such alarm, one would've thought he'd heard a scream.

"A drink?" Kallia only laughed harder until tears found the corners of her eyes.

Far too many beats later, his expression remained sharp with regret and unsmiling as ever. "Keep cackling and they'll figure out where we are."

She gasped in a breath, then another. "Of all the things you could want for yourself in the world, you chose a *drink*?"

"Why is that so funny?" Jack bristled defensively. "There are always fancy bottles all over the place here, and Roth never allowed me to have any. Just to serve them." His bitter frown deepened. "Not that I could ask, even if some part of me wanted to."

Kallia clamped her lips shut at the soft realization dawning on her. Every memory of Jack, more often than not, included him with a drink in his hand. Sometimes he'd sip at it, other times it remained untouched. That never made any sense to her, but now it did.

Her shaking soon fell to tremors as she gathered herself together. She hadn't laughed like that in ages, and the dizziness got to her. She could barely recall the last time she'd shared anything with Jack not coated in sarcasm or disgust.

I was made to find you.

The drop of the cold reminder was all it took. The slap in the face to wake her up, to never let her forget. "You still managed to complete the job. By finding me."

Jack was not her friend. Never had been, either. He was nothing more than a means to an end to her. And to him, she was just an order. Those lines were still drawn between them.

Jack had done everything to keep her away, for it meant never returning himself.

No wonder Roth hated him as much as he did. The last deal you ever want going bad is one made with the devils.

"What was your reason with me, then?" Kallia's glare was unwavering. She deserved that at least. "You could've let me go off on my own. You didn't have to keep me in that house and play that whole charade with me. You very well could've left me on my own somewhere else."

"Alone, with no family? Nothing?" He grimaced, as though the idea offended him. "He would've found you, eventually. The mirrors would've found you."

"Not good enough." A being with such immense power had little room for excuse. "You kept me from mirrors easily enough, you could've hidden me wherever I landed. Maybe set me up in some town far away, sent me to an academy, left me in the care of some lonely folks whose memories you've stirred to oblivion."

So many lives stretched out before her, so many options and far easier ruses. That Jack chose a life at Hellfire House, the hardest of them all, went against everything she knew of him. He never wasted an effort, and never decided on anything without thinking five steps ahead. At one point, he must've predicted the entire act would crash all around him, one way or another.

"It's because you chose to stay."

His voice sounded so near, Kallia turned and found Jack sitting beside her now. She didn't even startle at his proximity. "What?"

"When we first met, I gave you a choice," he said quietly. "To go elsewhere, or stay."

That night unraveled behind her eyes. How ready she'd been to leave, to be free from a house that had held her all her life. And how quickly it had all changed, the moment Jack closed a hand over her fist, and offered her more.

"I don't know why I even asked, back then. I don't even know what I was saying that night, it wasn't . . . part of my plan." He cast the briefest sideways glance at her. "None of this was."

She hadn't known that. It changed much, and nothing at all. The intent was no matter, for it led to everything else regardless. He could've stopped the show at any time, inserted her into a new life rather than insert new people into hers.

She would drive herself mad, thinking of all the things he could've done. And how one choice on her part might've changed the course of it all.

"Be that as it may, it didn't stop you from doing what you did." Her trust bruised so easily now, so quickly, after being thrown against the wall too many times. "You can't expect me to start trusting everything you say now, after something like that."

Jack's nostrils flared for a hard second, but he nodded. "Why keep me around, then?"

She had her reasons, but those seemed flimsy in comparison now to all the reasons to turn him away. To have a power like his at her side could be the difference between her finally returning home or staying locked on this other side. There was risk in it, like every step forward in this world and everything else.

"I don't know when my magic will come back at full strength. If it ever will." Kallia swallowed hard. She hadn't voiced the worry yet, but it was every bit as terrifying out loud as it was in her head. "And in a world like this, that just won't work in my favor."

"No. It certainly won't." His words held a small smile to them, even if he bore none on his face at his next assurance. "And your power *will* return. Even if you're without, I remain as much at your mercy as you are at mine."

Such a ridiculous statement. Kallia rolled her eyes and pushed herself to her feet. "If that were the case, I'd throw you off this roof right now."

Jack gave it some thought and shrugged. "You can, you know. I'd survive it."

"Don't give me ideas."

Her snort went unreturned as his stare fell down to his pocket, fixated. Some mental debate went on in his head, before he eventually dug inside. "Here. Take them."

His hand reemerged, outstretched and inviting.

And the black brass knuckles waited in his palm.

It was the first time she'd seen them not over his fingers. No point in it, she supposed, when there was nothing left to mask. Just a weapon, now. "You want me to *hit* you?"

"You could." Jack didn't sound opposed to the idea. He dangled the dark row of rings over one finger. "But that's not why I want you to have these."

Of all he could've given her, this felt the most like forbidden fruit. Because of the way it called to her. Because it was his. "I don't need gestures, or anything of yours for that matter."

"These are as much mine as they are yours." His chest rose and fell as he drew the black brass knuckles close to him. "I never take without putting it somewhere else. Every memory I've taken from you . . . echoes in its weight."

Her heart strained.

Memories.

He twisted at them so effortlessly, she assumed they were all lost for good. A rose ripped from a garden, discarded soon after.

The brass knuckles dropped into her palm with a cold weight, heavier than they looked. It was a wonder he once wore them every day. "Why would you give this me?"

Jack dug his hands into his pockets, gaze cast down at the weathered rug they stood upon. "I can't take back what I've done, but I can give back what I've taken."

There was a ringing in her ears. Her whole body tensed. Blood simmered.

"Doesn't erase what never should've been touched in the first place." She glared. "Giving back what's already mine is not some grand gift."

It felt dangerous, holding them. Any memories he took were ones she didn't want to see. Zarose only knew what horrors made the weight of them so cold.

"Then at least you can see them for yourself, if you want." Jack sighed. "At least you have the choice."

They were following him. Daron was sure of it.

Over the past few days, it was more than obvious. The way the Patrons hushed whenever he passed, the hint of white always in the corner of his vision. More so than usual. On his walks, he took note of the two always stationed by the gates, the few patrolling along the city wall, and some simply walking through the streets at any given time. Their watch held an orderly rhythm over Glorian. The ones that followed him from afar, no matter how they tried to hide it, disturbed that clockwork melody. Aunt Cata might as well have been breathing down his neck now with every defeated step into the Prima Café.

"They know." With a frustrated sigh, Daron pulled out a chair besides Aaros and Lottie. "I was tailed halfway across the city, right after trying the hospital again."

"And I'm assuming that try was a fail," Aaros supplied, dropping a lump of brown sugar into his tea. "Again."

Daron simmered in his seat. Unhelpful, but not wrong. Their discussion with Ira confirmed that much more how he needed to speak with the mayor again. Without his aunt or any Patrons present, which was an impossible order now. Every morning and afternoon, when looped by the hospital for any opening at all, there were only more obstacles. From the Patrons passing through the building to the one stationed right by Mayor Eilin in his bed.

"That's not suspicious," Lottie murmured into a sip of her tea. "You don't give someone a watchdog unless it's to see who comes to them."

Aunt Cata's instincts never failed. Already, she was a few steps ahead, anticipating his moves. "My aunt knew I would try to talk to Eilin again."

"Of course she knew." A scoff burst from her. "She didn't become Head of the Patrons by accident."

"Then how do we get past her? Or any of them?"

Out loud, it sounded more like a joke. They were a scant band of fighters against an army of many. The only magician among them was Canary. Daron hardly counted, with the unpredictability of his magic. Though he feared it might become necessary, with however little time they had left until Aunt Cata raised the signal to the Patrons. A fresh new coat of paint to mask everything beneath.

"Let's pray they find something more scintillating to focus on." Aaros lifted his empty cup over his head to grab the waiter's attention. "Shouldn't be too hard. We've made so little progress, we're practically going backward."

"Don't insult the one thing we know absolutely for certain." Under the table, Lottie nudged at Daron with her heel. "Dare's got devils and death hanging over his head."

Daron aimlessly stirred at his coffee as the two snickered together. The Devils card haunted him more than he wanted to admit. He rarely trusted in cards to spell out fates, never enjoyed the ways such games guided decisions more than determined them.

But the seamstress's reaction was enough to make him question.

"It was nothing but a game," he muttered. "Probably to scare me off. It's no secret that she doesn't like me."

"Don't worry, Demarco. She doesn't like anyone."

"Speak for yourself." Aaros dug a hand in his pocket, unearthing that tattered rose cloth out of habit now. With every glance, Daron hoped to suddenly find the rose in full bloom, but the petals remained fallen. A glimmer of life.

Still holding on, wherever she may be.

"We need to keep going," Daron said, jaw set. "No matter what the cards say, we can't just stop."

"Oh yes, we can."

There was a flash of ruby hair before the table rumbled. The force of Canary's arrival toppled a half-full water glass, but her eyes glinted too brightly to care. "I know what to do."

"Does it involve getting me another glass of water?" Aaros scowled up at her as he dabbed his napkin to dry his setting.

"The opposite, actually." Canary grinned without apology and stole a chair from a neighboring table. "This strategy of laying low with private meetings has been a great bonding experience for us all, but it's not moving the needle. Nothing will just fall in our laps. *We* need to make something happen."

"Of course. Because were such a force to be reckoned with." Lottie waved both hands over them, as if she needn't say more. "Unless someone here has experience taking down established institutions, doesn't seem like we'll be making waves any time soon."

"Pessimism will get you nowhere." Canary snatched a tea cookie off Lottie's plate, too quick to get properly swatted away. "It all came to me after what the seamstress said. If we stay quiet and cautious, we're making it easy for the white gloves to roll all over us. Did you see how quickly they took over this city?"

Because the people saw nothing wrong in it, only due diligence. They trusted in the Patrons as much as the Patrons trusted no one to question their ways when all would soon be forgotten.

"So what are you suggesting?" Daron pressed forward. "We might not be a force, but we could be a minor inconvenience at best."

"You all seem to forget that I have a circus." With a sharp huff, Canary popped the cookie in her mouth. "So let's give the Patrons a nightmare to clean up. Let's raise some hell and set this city on fire."

The crunch was all that could be heard amid the stunned silence across the table.

If Lottie's brows arched any higher, they'd disappear. "Not sure I quite remember Ira suggesting that, but even I draw the line at arson and murder."

Aaros raised his hand in agreement.

"No one is going to die." Canary yawned with a shrug. "Just think of it as . . . a little well-timed chaos. A show that goes so gloriously wrong."

There was both relish and readiness in her voice, amped enough to take to the streets now if need be. It piqued Daron's interest. A quiet, deliberate plan of attack was more his style, but chaos was Canary's specialty. And if anyone could orchestrate it well, it was the Conquering Circus.

"Didn't we *just* survive one?" Aaros's brow crinkled. "I'm sure nobody wants a repeat."

"Sure they do." A strange light of realization entered Lottie. "Everyone loves a good show."

"And no one looks away from a bad one." Especially not the Patrons. Daron propped his chin under his fist, shifting toward Canary. "You think you could clear the hospital, buy me some time with the mayor?"

"Every Patron on the street will have no choice but to come running to shut us down." Her chuckle rasped up her throat. "You'll have enough time to throw a tea party with him."

Could it work? For a while, Glorian had become such a tricky game board. One wrong move could set him back, though no strategy at all could ever guarantee a clean victory. Not on a game board that was already broken. If the old rules no longer applied, then there was no need to play by them.

"My aunt, though." His frown weighed down heavier. "She *will* figure us out in the end."

"By that point, it won't matter." The fire-eater raised her chin, all smug as she tossed her long red hair past her shoulder. "I suspect they'll be a bit preoccupied trying to stop the ship from drowning first before targeting who's responsible."

A perfect distraction.

"Zarose help us." Chuckling, Aaros reached into his coat pocket. Not for the rose cloth, but a small metal flask he emptied into the last dregs of his tea before raising the cup in a toast. "To weaponizing mayhem."

No one clinked glasses with him. Instead, Lottie bounced in her seat with a notebook already miraculously in hand. "All right, how do we even begin constructing a show of that scope?" she started, her pen flying across a fresh page. "Do we get the word out about it now? Where should it—"

Canary plucked the pen right out of her hand. "Not so fast, poison, this is *my* domain. Leave all the planning to me, and just arrive on show night."

Lottie's fingers twitched at the loss of her weapon. "And when will that be, exactly?"

"Who knows . . ." With an impish giggle, the fire-eater twirled the pen over her knuckles. "It'll be a *surprise*."

"An event this important should not be left up to surprise," Lottie replied, her death glare simmering. "If we don't know specifics, how can we be sure this will work?"

"And that Rayne will even be on board, no questions asked?" Daron added, as worried. If not more. They only had one chance to genuinely throw the Patrons off guard without warning.

"Don't worry about him. The man would slap his name on a funeral if you pitched it to him as a show." Canary shook her head. "As long as he can get up on his little stage, he won't ask questions. Leave everything to me."

Lottie sat back, looking skeptical as ever, but Daron felt his lips tug upwards at the corners. Strange, the hope that came at the promise of disaster. That lightness stirring inside, no longer satisfied with waiting for answers to arrive.

It was about damn time they demanded the answers for themselves.

"As long as you don't *actually* destroy this town." Aaros waggled a finger in Canary's face. "People still live behind those gates, you know."

"I'll be gentle with her," she reassured with a snort. "She's withstood much worse. What's one more disaster behind her walls?"

17

Kallia couldn't sleep when the bed felt nothing like her own.

Her silk sheets itched against her every time she turned away from her bedside table. Her lush-cloud of a pillow demanded more fluffing. She felt too hot, too cold. Her body begged for sleep, for dreams.

All night, her eyes wandered back to the small table.

The black brass knuckles watched her from the dark. Thick black curves of cold metal, frozen with stolen pain and memories best left forgotten.

Kallia entertained the idea of shoving them under her bed. Hell, throwing them out the window sounded appealing. But every time she reached over, she pulled back.

The thought of touching them again, even for that, unnerved her.

"*Ridiculous,*" Kallia hissed. She shot a glare straight at the door, through the lock, hoping Jack might feel it.

Before he'd taken off for the night, he promised to stay somewhat close. Certainly not stationed in her *own* room, but not too far away, either. Not if the bodyguard act were to be believed.

Kallia couldn't ignore the practical advantages. It meant having his magic—*some* kind of power, at least—and all that came with it. No one would dare bother her with him at her back.

It also meant staying close together at all times. He would have to escort her from room to room, accompany her on walks. Keep a steady watch on her through meals and parties. Dutiful, obedient, always at her side.

The more the ruse came to life in her mind, the more she regretted suggesting it in the first place.

Sleep was her only breathing space alone. The most time she would have to herself in this world.

And even *that* was ruined.

Kallia threw her head back into the pillow with a frustrated growl. The bastard had to have known what giving her those brass knuckles would do. Before, she'd accepted the memories he'd taken were simply lost. Just collateral damage in a convenient, cruel means to an end that left him unscathed. Disposing of the evidence should've been just as easy as well.

And yet he'd held onto them. As if for the day when they might be returned.

It never occurred to her that they could be, though that still didn't make it honorable. Maybe he saw a step in it, but she saw no great leap. Just an empty gesture. They were *hers*, after all. Not his.

Perhaps that's what made it so frightening.

The candle lights around her flickered before flaring to life as she rose, forcing herself to sit up against the headboard. Rubbing and dragging her hands down her face, she couldn't stop her sideways glance to the object.

At least you have the choice.

Any choice of hers was gone if she felt even a splinter of fear. The chill of nerves up her spine, that flutter of doubt in her chest, even the grating itch from avoidance—there was only ever one way to make it stop. Pretending only prolonged it.

A pang of curiosity existed as well. If she could stomp that out, all the better.

Without thinking too hard, Kallia snatched the brass knuckles. Muscles tense, she weighed them in her palms, deciding which hand to crown before sliding them on her left.

Her fingers curled into a fist to stop her from tearing them off too soon while she waited for sensation to take. Some strange feeling to unfurl. Jack hadn't described what would happen if she decided to wear them, so the silence disappointed her. Surely a flash of familiar, or an image would take shape.

Though if Jack had worn them every day, there had to be some trick to them. Not at all something that unlocked at will without permission.

Kallia let out a deep sigh, relaxing the tension in her shoulders. Nothing would come to her if she didn't welcome it inside.

When Kallia finally closed her eyes, she heard it.

An echo.

Soft as a faraway bell. A warmth unfurled in her chest as she followed the gentle sound, growing louder. Clearer.

Before her own scream thundered in her ears.

And flashes like lightning struck between them.

Her, running through the doors of Hellfire House, where the vast front lawn met the hard soil of the Dire Woods.

Her, in a different dress, curiously walking along the forest's edge.

Then jokingly hopping near the rocky path as if challenged to a dare.

One, where she had just tripped before a shadow rose over her. A few times, when she finally looked back, her mouth falling open in disbelief. The word on her lips, always the same: *Jack.*

His name was a question. A scream.

A whisper, then a laugh.

The dream took her through. Strangers she'd never seen before danced across her vision. Above them soared the blurred faces of patrons from the club. Grins widening madly and top hats falling like rain. The recollections shifted from stranger to Jack, to her *and* Jack. So many to choose from, passing her by.

The clearest one came at the knock on a door.

At the sound, the lines of a room sharpened on command. Oddly familiar, with the shapes of the windows showing the night—

Jack crossed the moonlight-streaked floor to answer the knocking on the door. Persistent as a drum.

Who was on that other side?

Not a friend, from the strained breath that rattled out of him. He pressed his brow against the frame, lost in thought, before he reached for the door handle.

Kallia squinted as the door swung slightly ajar. It was still too dark to fully make out the figure on the other side, until she caught that first wink of glitter from a show costume. Black hair shining in waves past her shoulder. A wicked red smile that blazed fresh from a performance.

It was her.

A little bemused, Jack tilted his head. "Ah, firecrown. What brings you to my—" He cut deadly when the Kallia before him answered by lifting her hand. The shape of them was off in the fingers, with odd streaks running down to her wrist. "Is that blood?"

"See, this is what happens when you decide to leave right after my act," she huffed. "You miss the brawls."

"Brawls?" His next breath burst in a low growl. The door swung wide after him as he stalked back into his room with the smooth wave of his fingers lighting every candle in the room. "What the hell happened?"

"Just rich fools being rude fools." Kallia wasted no time strutting in and making herself comfortable. She perched herself on the large cushioned armrest of the soft by the fireplace. Legs crossed, bloodied fist held aloft. "I might've thrown a punch or two, as well."

"You sound pleased with yourself."

"Anyone stupid enough to steal a kiss deserves all the damage I inflict."

Before she'd even finished her sentence, Jack had already turned toward the direction of the door, a look of murder storming over his face.

A long-gloved hand stopped him from behind.

"It's fine." Kallia reeled him back in, slightly amused. "I took care of it. Trust me, his nose looks worse than my hand."

Jack's frown hardened as he glanced down at the hand splayed by his chest. "While I don't doubt that at all . . ." He stepped out from under her arm, placing it back on her lap. "I don't tolerate that sort of behavior in my club, and everyone knows it."

"I can assure you, he more than knows that now. Same with everyone else." She lifted her injured hand with a hopeless shrug. "A little help?"

When he took a closer look, a slight hiss came through his teeth. "What happened, did you punch a knife?" He grimaced. "You should've fixed yourself up earlier."

"Bones are a more complicated puzzle, you know that." She lightly kicked him in the shin from where she sat while wearing a pout. *"Please?"*

Please.

With his own quiet plea, he tipped his head back in deliberation. There was no denying the mischief in the pair of eyes before him.

"All right, give it here." Jack relented, cradling her injured hand in one of his while his free hand hovered over hers. "Hold still, it'll hurt."

"I don't need the warning." The girl yawned, masking the small intake of breath. The bloodstains faded from her skin as though absorbing back into the veins. A soothing, calm minute of silence—before the quick little crunch that evened out her fingers.

Kallia jerked, but made no sound. Even as the angry swelling around her fingers had begun to lessen, her expression remained every bit as closed. Only her eyes had turned glassier, just a little.

"I just set your bone back into place," he said, applying the finishing touches. "You don't have to pretend like it doesn't hurt."

"It was only a pinch." She exhaled at the immediate relief once her palm fell to his.

"You would sooner die than shed a tear." A quiet laugh rolled in his voice. He bent each finger gently, experimentally. "How does that feel?"

Kallia was too preoccupied by the room to answer. "So these are your chambers . . ." She took in every wall, traced each window. "It might be the only place in the House I've never seen. Sire never let me in, and now you, too."

Jack raised a brow. "I like my privacy."

"You like hiding." After finishing her exploration of the room, her gaze dropped to their hands. "I wish you didn't."

The silence seared in the space between them. Neither of them breathed, just as neither of them pulled away. As if allowing something to grow for a moment.

Just a moment.

"It's late." Jack eased her off the armrest to her feet and firmly let go with a step back. "You must be exhausted."

Jack had barely pivoted toward the door before Kallia stopped him again. This time she stepped closer, tracing her newly healed hand up the path of buttons on his casual shirt. A slow, leisurely journey that paused where the buttons were left undone at his collarbone.

"I'm not tired." She lifted her gaze to his in question.

There came no answer as he refused to look back. The wind howled outside the window, trees shaking and clouds drifting, while they stood frozen for the first time.

Or maybe they'd already been here before, and just hadn't known. It could've been either. It was all so familiar, and new.

Complicated.

The shadows deepened beneath Jack's eyes. As if *he* were the tired one among them, fighting sleep when it would be all too easy to fall right now. "You should go to your room."

Kallia stayed, head tilted in earnest. "Aren't you curious?"

"About what?"

"I think you know."

Yes. The word breathed around them in sighs and echoes. *Yes, yes, yes.*

Jack's face stayed closed as a fist. Unyielding. "Curiosity like that makes people go places they cannot come back from."

"That's no reason to not try," Kallia countered. "We've been in this place together for a while now, just circling each other. Knowing each other, and learning more." She walked her fingers up the collar buttons closest to his throat. "I want *more*."

More.

It was the thing that came to Kallia in pieces, but never the whole. Never everything. And she no longer wished to choose what to keep and what had to wait in order to get what she wanted. She wanted it all.

And he wanted something, too. Every time he looked at her.

The candlelight flickered hard around them, the dark keeping the light on its toes. Jack drew back all the more quickly. "That's not what this is about, Kallia," he said slowly. "Or what it's supposed to be."

"Then what is it *supposed* to be, Jack?" For every step backward, Kallia followed. A give and take that formed the dance they knew so well. "Because I don't even think *you* know."

The air between them was charged, the tension so thick that neither of them hardly breathed. Kallia did a much better job at hiding it. Jack, not so much with the strain in his jaw. "I'm not—" he began a thought that quickly died. "I just know this wouldn't work."

"How do you know this already?" she demanded. "We've done nothing."

It didn't feel like nothing. It never did. And when the challenge in her voice dared him to finally stop thinking, to take, he addressed the taunt by taking.

After another sharp look up at the ceiling—either a curse or a prayer on his lips—he stepped forward and took her face between his hands.

The shock on her face was almost insulting. She didn't think he would do it, didn't realize how it would feel to be too close. He was always far too careful, too reserved to get too close to fire.

His touch felt anything but careful, and their lips hadn't even met yet. His hand slid slowly behind her neck, coarse fingers that pressed into the skin there. The brass knuckles, holding her closer with the slightest force and bite of pain.

Her head tipped back, waiting.

"Kallia." His dark eyes, this close, held a certain light to them. She'd never noticed it before and wanted to remember it. To capture and bottle it for later.

Jack's lips coasted over her hair, pausing just over her ear.

"Sleep," he said.

Kallia blinked hard in confusion.

"I healed your hand, and that is all," he whispered, watching her slowly drift away. Her body, slackening against him. "This conversation never happened. The adrenaline from the show exhausted you, and you went to bed right after I fixed your hand. That is all."

That is all.

That is all.

That is—

Red exploded in her vision when Kallia awoke.

Gasping, she clutched at her chest. Took in the scores of red across the walls and curtains and ceiling overhead.

The color anchored her. Always had, which made the room the only thing she liked about the Alastor Place. Her heart drummed hard as she finally caught her breath when the dream began to fade. So vivid and sharp in some places, fuzzy in others.

A bloody hand.

The slow trail up a path of buttons.

She was too dizzy to chase the rest of it, but more would come back.

Clawing at the silky sheets damp with her sweat, she shuddered in relief when her fingers flexed out and formed fists with soft, little pops at the knuckles.

She found the oddest indents marking the skin around them. For a few seconds she grazed over them in question, sharply curious before her eyelids began blinking slower, and slower. Fighting to stay open.

Before finally, she succumbed to sleep.

The party never stopped in a city that never slept. Though most of the magicians had turned in for the night, the streets still celebrated. The drinks still poured. Heels clacked like horse hooves against the cobblestone, while far more people loudly succumbed to the dirty, sticky ground with their bare feet and sweet sighs of relief.

Jack snorted from the comfort of his roof. Resting on his back, both hands pillowed his head as he listened to the stragglers still roaming the streets. No night was ever peaceful when those on the streets fell into cursing matches or belted out drunken songs that nowhere near matched the melody playing on.

It was the strange sort of music no one should miss, but Jack always found the oddest comfort in it. Hellfire House could never achieve quite the same symphony of chaos, though there were some nights when it had come close.

And now he was back.

You truly believe you're indestructible?

Any comfort he'd found earlier withered the instant he stared up at the sweeping darkness. It was better to be alone for this. This way, he felt more like an offering of bait splayed out on the roof, waiting.

Every magician has his weaknesses.

He waited for a whisper, a pull.

A thought not his own.

Jack waited for all of it in those hours beneath that dark, for something that might or might not come. Like a guessing game that only ended when the coin decided which side to fall on. There was always more terror in that uncertainty.

That uncertainty that had haunted him, ever since he left.

Every illusion carries flaws.

Jack was still waiting by the time more people had risen to explore the city again. The savory scents of street foods drifted all the way up to him, while a fresh, fast-paced melody started up in the air like the echo of a rooster's crow marking the new day.

At that, his eyes finally shut for a moment but found no sleep. Always beyond the reach of dreams.

Nothing had arrived, but there was hardly any relief in it.

Even a creature of both has his downfall.

Jack looked back up at the darkness over him, wondering if all this time, the devils within had been waiting for him as well.

Can the Conquering Circus Actually Conquer Again?

In an interesting turn of events, rumors have sparked that the not-so-quiet city of Glorian is once again playing stage to what is allegedly billed to be a glorious show by its current entertainers in residence, the Conquering Circus. Riding the aftermath of their disastrous competition debut, Spectaculore, who knows if this spectacle will actually promise wonderment, or once more end in unexpected dangers.

Acclaimed show mastermind leading the Conquering Circus, Erasmus Rayne, insists the whispers of this new show is "nothing at all like Spectaculore" and will be "unlike anything Soltair has ever seen—in only the best of ways." However true that may be, vague details invite more speculation.

For such a fall from entertainment grace with their failure to secure a headlining act, it's clear the Conquering Circus will need more than a few crowd-pleasing tricks to prove themselves as the Conquerors, or else become the Conquered—

"How the hell did they get this out so fast?"

Lottie snatched the paper right out of Daron's hands before handing it over to Canary. "Need something to catch the bird droppings with in the tents?"

"Even bird shit deserves better." Canary took one look at the headline and burned the issue in her fist. In seconds, nothing but smoke and ash swirled around them. "Never much liked the *New Crown Post*."

That pleased Lottie. Daron, not so much, as he waved a hand about to clear the air. "Thanks," he muttered. "Not like I paid for that or anything."

"Don't waste coin reading garbage, Demarco," Lottie advised, shaking her head. "Waste it on the *Soltair Source* instead."

"That doesn't sound like a conflict of interest at all." Though Daron could admit, it was damn near impressive how well Lottie had kept her word. With each passing day, he woke up bracing himself for the streets to be buzzing with issues of the *Soltair Source* chronicling details of their search. It had all the makings of an exciting story; the steady stream of letters pooling in his courier case still begged for a comment or updates after Kallia's disappearance, and the aftermath of Spectaculore.

Miraculously, none of it had made front page news. Not when readers were already itching for the next fresh story. Another mysterious show, on the horizon.

"Look, I've written nothing remotely juicy in weeks." Lottie let out a groan, rife with agony. "The self-restraint is killing me, so you owe me. Especially if you're supporting my competition."

As if she hadn't been reading stacks of other issues not too long ago. Daron shot her a pointed stare once they stepped off the sidewalk toward the Alastor Place. "Weren't you the one who suggested reading what the public is believing? To see what's actually taking, if any of what we're doing is working?"

"Of course it's working," Canary said, leading them through the circus tents. "Like I said, I know how to work a crowd."

It had only taken days for Glorian to begin whispering of a new show in the streets. A welcome change of pace. After the dreadful silence since the end of Spectaculore, the emergence of this show with no name sparked a strange new light in the city. They no longer talked of the missing showgirl or her fraud of a mentor, nor the disastrous last night that ended in a ballroom of smashed mirrors.

Like bugs swarming to sugared water, the buzz spread swiftly as wildfire over the city. "Spectators never change." With an edge of glee, Canary observed all those around them without breaking her stride. "Always eager to find their next talking point or hit of entertainment. Must be nice to be sitting safely in those cushy seats."

From the newfound fervor in Glorian, Daron still couldn't fully tell if the crowd hoped for a genuine spectacle, or another disaster. There were moments when even he fell for the mystique a little, from the barest scraps Canary would tease. He was surprised she'd even brought them through the tents with all her secrecy. Not even Aaros had been invited to catch a glimpse of the inner-workings of the false show.

For a false show, the Conquerors still prepared like no other.

On their way through the flaps of the circus tents, it was all madness and preparation on the other side. Contortionists and aerialists stretched together in a line, legs splayed in effortless splits as they glided their reach from the back leg to the front. Birds of all colors flew overhead, with one girl across the tent snapping and whistling out a language only they could understand. The twins Daron recognized before cursed after them for the mess the birds had made on their thin mats, which they grudgingly dragged through another set of door flaps leading to a completely different section of the interconnecting tents.

Everyone seemed to thrive on the chaos, welcoming the work toward something, rather than dwell on all that had happened before.

Daron welcomed the distraction as well.

Amid the commotion, a Conqueror pulled Canary aside for a quick word, which ended in the sharpest curse and panicked glare.

"You're kidding me—where's Aya? How does one lose a lion?"

"She's a cat." The Conqueror gave an exasperated shrug.

"You better pray she's not hungry." Squeezing the bridge of her nose, Canary glanced briefly at Lottie and Daron. "Stay put. You do not want to play hide-and-seek with a man-eating lion."

"Does she really eat men?"

"Would you like to find out, Demarco?" Brows arched, Canary backed away to join in the whistling and high-pitched kissy noises of a small group that swiftly disappeared through another set of tent flaps. More strange sounds to add to the ever-growing cacophony of the Conquering Circus.

Daron jerked once his back found the wooden edge—a long plain table covered in all manner of props. A few masks studded with multicolored pearls, jars of glitter in all shades and shines, a stack of wooden cups beside bottles both empty and half-full. So many more objects littered the surface, a maelstrom of color as unruly as the tent itself.

"You know she would've loved this."

Lottie sidled up next to him until they both leaned against a table covered in all manner of props. It was rare that Lottie ever caught him alone, aside from their last carriage ride through the Dire Woods. Even rarer, how he didn't mind it now.

"She would've." Overlooking the chaos, Daron could've sworn he heard Kallia's laugh in the midst of it. And another's. "They both would've."

Her hand paused over one of the props, a fake flower in full bloom that appeared more real than any he'd ever seen in any garden.

"Do you think . . . ," he began, his breath hitching on a hope he'd never uttered once before. "What do you think the odds are that Eva's still out there, too? That maybe both of them . . ."

He'd never asked the question out loud. Kallia was their focus, the strongest chance they had with all the evidence gathered, and timing on their side.

Whereas Eva had been gone for years, now. Either by force or by choice, there was a far better chance neither of them would never find the truth.

After a long pause, Lottie sighed against the table. "I've wondered that. Now more than ever." Her absent gaze drifted across the tent that stood far less rowdy than before. A few Conquerors packed up, departing in small groups as dusk dimmed the fabric of the tent overhead.

"When I'm on a story, I've always trusted my gut. Most times, I'm right. But then there are the times when I'm wrong, when even *I've* wondered how true a feeling may be. Is my intuition alive because deep down it's true, or only because I wish it to be?"

The fear was mutual. It pricked at him in every glimmer of pity in the eyes that followed him, in all the well-meaning condolences after Eva's disappearance that made him want to shatter every window in his house. He learned to shut them out and play the mourning magician, certain that she could be found if he only searched hard enough. If he only followed that heartbeat echoing deep in his bones, all the way to where she had to be.

Only now, he questioned whose heartbeat he actually heard: hers, or his own beating louder all along?

"How can you tell the difference?" Daron swallowed hard, the world gone much darker and quieter around them.

"If only I knew. It would make my job a lot easier knowing how the story ends every time one comes my way." Lottie blew out a low breath. "But alas, no attempt is in vain. It means we're trying. When we don't have those answers, we make them. We build stories and find paths to take us in any direction." She blinked slowly. "It keeps us moving forward, the hope that something might lead somewhere."

Might. The past couple of weeks had been for the sake of might— following leads that might lead somewhere, asking questions that might get them the answers they wanted. Wanting was not enough to make something true, not even with all the magic in the world.

Daron dug his heel into the hard-packed dirt. "Sounds like we're only fooling ourselves, then."

"You're only a fool when you give up too early." She pushed off from the table, dusting off her hands. "Especially after all of this effort, might as well see it through. What's the harm in a little possibility?"

Where's your sense of imagination, Dare?

Daron tensed as the memory washed over him. The tent fell completely silent. The walls, slowly closing in, as he remembered winding down that night with Eva after one of their shows with a usual card game. One of the last conversations they'd ever shared, her words unfurling like a riddle of a prophecy.

"What's wrong?"

The poke in the shoulder snapped him back. "Nothing, I just . . . Eva used to say that."

Her face cracked under a snort. "That thief."

Whatever small smile started on his lips drifted. The last time he'd spoken of her, really spoken about her, was with Kallia. And just like then, he felt that pinch of pain transformed into a searing burn. Guilt.

For so long, he'd blamed Lottie. When all along, he'd been the reason Eva became a ghost in the first place.

"We could've been looking for her together, earlier. We could've found something much sooner." His nostrils flared as he inhaled. "If only I had just—"

"Don't go down that bottomless hole of what could've been, you'll find nothing there. Trust me." She folded her arms. "Don't blame yourself for something that cannot be changed. We're looking now. And in my opinion, we have far more to work with."

"A lot more questions, too."

"They're more promising than you think." Lottie shrugged, staring straight ahead. "More questions mean something's still happening, that you're getting—"

A crackling explosion boomed outside the tent.

Then another, and another.

As they grew louder and louder, his pulse thundered. He shared a wary glance with Lottie before they sprang for the exit at a cautious pace. The Conquerors' domain breathed with an unnatural quiet without any of its members in sight. Hardly any lanterns lit, they hoped every next set of tent flaps they encountered would be their last.

When it was, Daron almost didn't trust it as he gulped in a cold breath and found nothing but night.

A faint flicker of color rippled through the sky. Like a bright purple comet, it surged high, disappearing for a blink before breaking apart in spirals and sparks.

Fireworks. They shot up in the air in quick succession, one after the other.

When a fast and steady beat thrummed distantly beneath the explosion, Daron knew. Just as Lottie knew, as their heads remained tipped toward the sky painted in Conquering Circus purple.

And the show had just begun.

19

Even in sleep, he haunted her.

The moment she closed her eyes, Demarco was there. He looked just as she last saw him, mere steps away with his back to her.

The dream was good to her, which meant it could not be trusted. It became clearer the more she called his name, and the way he did not turn.

It wasn't until she started walking toward him that he showed any sign of life, and began walking away.

Demarco.

Her heart lurched as her shout was met with silence.

So she broke into a run. So fast, she tripped to the ground and skinned her knees, but kept going. Desperate to beat the distance and catch up.

Yet the distance between them rapidly grew, as if every step she took added five more to her path.

Demarco.

Every time she called out his name, it was a whisper now.

Her throat burned from her quieting screams because it wasn't fair. How every time she ran, it only made her slower. How every move she made fed the distance.

Please turn.

If only she could see his face.

If only he could see *her.*

Every muscle in her tensed when Demarco paused abruptly, as if he could hear her. Somehow.

When he turned, she caught a horrifying flash of black bleeding eyes, before the world suddenly plunged into darkness just as cold.

Kallia startled awake, shouting his name.

She forced herself upright, shoving away the tangle of silk and plush pillows before clutching at her chest. Beneath her hand, her heart drummed at such a painful tempo, realizing a dream was just a dream.

Drawing in a shaky breath, Kallia pressed hard at her eyelids, the soreness of them. Massaging them brought no relief when she discovered the short dry streaks that had trailed from the corners.

She used the heel of her palms to rub them away. Only when all evidence was gone did her breaths start to even. Dreams, even the worst ones, were nothing to cry over.

Though if tears were to fall, then at least they fell in private.

Kallia forced herself to drink in a breath, stretching out her arms and spine for that long-awaited crack of bones that never came. A sinfully comfortable bed would do that, even after a terrible bout of sleep that took her for a few hours.

There was nothing well-rested about her when she stood, her toes sinking into the plush carpet. Next to them, she found the black brass knuckles basking in the candlelight.

Kallia watched them like she would a spider, moments before ending it with her shoe.

Never again. She no longer feared the object, at least. Now she despised it and wished she'd never taken it in the first place.

Jack.

All that she'd seen came crashing back. Everything she'd said to him, how they'd moved around each other, and how she'd touched him. It all now sat proud as a memory refreshed, bursting with the fullest color.

Why had he wanted her to forget?

She was glad she had no answer, especially when a quick knock came from the door.

She kicked the brass knuckles under her bed and shoved away everything that came with it.

When Kallia reached the door, she dragged her hands down her flushed cheeks before squaring back her shoulders. The icy picture of composure.

Her expression cracked almost instantly at the sight of Herald on the other side of the door, greeting her by taking another bite of the too-red apple that matched his spectacles. "You look well-rested."

"What do *you* want?" Kallia fumed.

She hadn't forgotten. He'd hunted and herded her in the city streets, and somehow, he had the nerve to look offended. "Oh, come now, showgirl. No hard feelings. Can't blame a magician just doing his job, can you?" he implored with the tilt of his head. "I apologize for the deception, but I come in peace now."

Now. How temporary and changeable and entirely expected.

"Goodbye." Kallia reached over to slam the door, stopped only by the flash of folded gold trapped between his fingers.

"It wouldn't be wise to ignore a message or its messenger around here," Herald warned. Once satisfied by her rapt attention, he presented her with the gold note stamped with a solitary black triangle in the palm of his hand. Wings as sheer as a dragonfly's rose from the gold of the paper, fluttering open before her eyes.

Once you're fully rested, please join the headliners and me to dine in the Green Room. We still have much to discuss and much to prepare for. —R

Kallia frowned. She recalled nothing in her conversation with Roth about preparations for anything. Before she had a chance to reread, the winged note crumbled suddenly in the air. Nothing but gold foil dust, falling to the ground.

"Messy little bastards, aren't they?"

Whirling around, Kallia found Herald somehow in front of her grand wardrobe, throwing both doors wide open. "If you're going to be dining with headliners, then you're going to have to look as good as them . . ." He took another bite of apple, sending a pitiful glance over his shoulder. "And certainly better than *that*."

He was lucky her powers weren't at full strength at the moment. She would've ended him where he stood. "I did not invite you in here. Get *out*."

For his convenience, Kallia sharply pulled back the door she'd almost closed.

Until it swiftly flew shut on its own.

"So commanding, you truly *are* an Alastor." Herald lifted a hand over his chest, bearing an expression of astonishment that dropped with the pursed line of his lips. "Look, showgirl, Roth only told me to deliver the message. I'm just here to help you."

He proceeded to dig through her wardrobe, slinging garment after garment over his shoulder. A ridiculously impossible amount considering the wardrobe. For its moderate size, it could've been an endless abyss from the heaps of clothes he kept yanking off the row of hangers inside.

"I don't want your help." She stomped over the mountain of clothes. "Get out—"

A testy hand met her face. "If I don't help you, then someone from the style houses will be in to doll you up. And most of them are mean as piss if you don't fit their beauty quota." He stopped to look her up and down in consideration. "Did you just wake up or something?"

She resisted the urge to cover herself. "Yes."

"Looking like *that*?"

Zarose, she was going to kill him.

"I'm joking, of course. A natural look has its moments." Shrugging, Herald finished off his apple. Vanishing away the core in a flash, he gave a definitive nod at his latest wardrobe find. "Yes, *here's* a winner!"

"What the hell is going on?" came a sharp demand from the door, now opened.

Jack stood waiting within the frame, his expression dark as a storm. Possibly because he appeared as exhausted as her—or from the way his face became like stone upon noticing the intruder. "Why are *you* here?"

Nothing was more gratifying than the way Herald stiffened ever so slightly.

"Why weren't *you,* bodyguard?" he shot back with the strained, impetuous lift of his chin. "Off wandering when she's got a date with headliners? The showgirl is going to need all the bodyguarding she can get."

All irritation froze to ice when Jack's eyes locked with hers then. How different they looked to her now, after one night. Not at all like the stranger's who smiled gently at her in the memory, conflicted and warm, though nothing came of it.

More.

Kallia gritted her teeth in disgust. With an eye roll more for herself, she aimed it straight at Jack. "Be late again, and I'll tell Roth I want you torn limb from limb instead. Got it?"

Her voice cut harshly enough that it earned a snicker from Herald, while Jack blinked. "It . . . it won't happen again."

"It better not." Cruelty was not a difficult mask to wear. Sometimes she enjoyed it, when it was deserved. But it felt like a prop mask more than ever, though he caught on quickly with a mask of his own: his head bowed in subservience before he stood off to the side in watchful silence.

"What an obedient accessory." Herald cooed in approval.

Kallia smiled, more at the thought of how easily Jack could crush him with a snap. But just as he showed restraint, so did she. Sparing him was meant to be in punishment, so they had to sell it. *She* had to sell it, using every vicious bone in her body.

"After last night, I'm surprised Roth even let you keep your monster. With all of that power on a leash?" Herald nodded back with an incredulous shudder. "You're not worried he might go all devil on you one day?"

The fool was either trying to get a rise out of Kallia, or obtain some knowledge. Or both.

Kallia snatched the outfit from his hands and turned to the wardrobe mirrors. "Oh, he would never hurt me. That's the beauty of it." Resting the soft gown over her, she admired the fabric. "It's others who should be worried, if they get in my way or annoy the hell out of me."

With a glance at the mirror, Kallia maintained her cooled smile. Herald pushed his spectacles higher up his nose. Back toward the wall, a sliver of a smirk showed even from Jack's bowed head.

"Those poor, potential enemies of yours." Herald's grin grew noticeably warmer from the one he'd first walked in wearing. "So glad we're such good friends already. Aren't we, showgirl?"

Kallia's brows crinkled in mock confusion. "And here I thought friends *didn't* exist in a world like this," she reminded him. His own words that she would never forget now. "Too cutthroat for such foolery, right?"

Strangely, that brought out a semblance of a smile, as if she'd just told something remarkably endearing.

"Gorgeous." Grinning, Herald spared Kallia a sweeping sideways glance as they walked on. "They'll hate you even more for it."

Kallia took the compliment in stride. She wore a flattering jade-green gown that darkened along the tulip hem at her back. A lovely number, but the softness stopped there. The golden tips of her velvet black slippers were pointed so sharply, they could impale with a kick. Even her request for her usual red lip color was denied when Herald painted a thick, bold sweep across her lips, mirroring the thick flares of ink past her lash line.

A casual look, according to Herald.

Kallia had never worn anything finer.

As they continued through the halls of the Alastor Place, almost everyone she passed glanced in her direction. Waitstaff whispered behind hands. Some stragglers from the party the night before almost approached, before backing off upon recognizing who walked behind them. For a moment, the atmosphere of it all transported Kallia back to Hellfire House—among sweaty masked patrons whose boisterous laughter died on their lips upon catching sight of the Master of the House. Only now, his notoriety only intensified. Especially after a fight with the devils that left him with hardly a scratch.

"Wild, how the world watches, appreciating my artistry." Herald raked in an excited breath, his arm still looped within hers. The moment Kallia allowed it, he never let go. "A promising preview, before the main event."

The headliners. Their show posters flashed in the back of her mind, as did the harsh, shadowy faces jeering at Jack's fight to go on to the death. "What are they like?"

"Awful." An amused sound erupted from the back of Herald's throat. "Unfortunately, they are quite clever. Most of them. No one gets to the top of the ladder without brains . . . unless you're one of the Red Death Dukes, I guess. Those idiots are all mean muscle and maybe *some* magic."

Kallia raised a brow. "Or maybe that's just what they want you to think?"

"Maybe. They play dumb acrobatic hunks a little too convincingly. You should see what Filip d'Chane can achieve with just a tightrope on one of their show nights."

"Sounds delightful," Kallia deadpanned.

"Always gets someone in the crowd fainting." He shook his head as they turned past a corner. "They're a big team, so they rarely all show up together, but perhaps not today. I'm willing to bet all of the headliners will be in attendance just to get a good look at you."

Good. Kallia was counting on it, as she was there to do the same. The closer they approached the Green Room, the more it felt like waltzing back into those early days of Spectaculore. Observing the field, assessing her competition. Granted, she'd been up against brainless oafs with the odds in their favor—and still, she'd stepped on them all. Even with the show going up in flames.

In Glorian, there had been no question who was the best. Whereas in a world like this, *everyone* was.

Kallia gritted her teeth as faraway laughter and utensils clinking met her ears. Somehow the dimly lit lounge that made up the Green Room from the night before had the transformed green-glass cage of a pavilion just ahead. Large enough to host a sweeping restaurant but serving only a single table in the center.

It was a feast for the senses. Laughter reeled around the table from the seated guests leaning back in chairs so thick, they were more like oversized pillows. The circular table spun slowly, stacked with mountains of food divided into sections that anyone could reach for, no matter where they sat. Glittering pastries and intricately carved bread loaves, thin meats and fish flesh frying over heated rocks, fruits that were somehow grown in the shape of birds perched over bowls of sauces and creams.

It was a carousel of delights, enjoyed by all of those sitting along the edges.

All of whom immediately turned her way upon arrival.

The laughter died. The looks flashed from disapproval to envy to amusement.

"Well, well, well . . ." A burly young man in a burgundy smoking lounge jacket stood with a glass mug of orange juice. "Someone is looking quite fancy today."

Chuckles rippled around the table. In a sweeping glance, Kallia felt her gown tighten.

All of the headliners donned some form of sleepwear—long night-gowns with silk trains and lush robes lined with furs, a few even showed up in long rumpled shirts with nothing underneath but long socks and jewel-toned slippers. Hardly anyone wore a speck of makeup, or did so minimally for the earliness of the day. All comfortable and casually luxurious.

All observing her like she'd just waltzed into war wearing nothing at all.

Grinning, Kallia dug her nails into Herald's wrist. "You barged into my room to doll me up for *this*?"

"I'm trying to help you," he gasped as she pressed harder, breaking skin. "You dropped in like an absolute mess yesterday. Here's your second chance to finally show them you can look just as fearsome."

"If I throw you out the window, is that fearsome enough?"

A soft snort sounded behind, and Kallia was about ready to kick Jack in the knees, too.

"Trust me, you'll thank me later." Herald gently pulled off Kallia's grip, leaving a trail of vicious crescent indents over his skin. "If you want them to like you—or at the very least, take you seriously—you don't want to be looking as though you just rolled out of bed. I saw that look on you, and it was not impressive in the least."

"As if I care whether they like me or not," she seethed, already knowing they didn't. Not even fashion would change that. "I don't need to impress them."

"No, but you might be glad you did."

Herald drew away with a knowing raise of his brow, exiting back through the doors. Abandoning her.

There was no fleeing with him. Whether he'd set her up for humiliation or genuinely tried giving her some edge, it would look worse for Kallia to turn around now and run. Not that she ever entertained the idea.

While Jack said nothing, silent as a servant, she caught something in his lowered gaze. That gleam of challenge.

So what are you waiting for?

"Come along," Kallia ordered as she turned, chin tipped high. She would've walked in no differently if Herald had wrapped her in a stained napkin.

No one offered her a seat as she approached, not that she expected them to. Instead, most opted to observe what she might do, while others resumed their conversations among themselves over drinks and fine pastries.

In truth, Kallia wasn't too upset to find most of the table full and well-occupied. One cocky magician with purple locks smirked as he showed his bored neighbors piles of scribbled music sheets that eventually found their way to the floor. A ginger-haired woman wrapped in silks and feathers bickered with a man who tried stealing a kiss. A section of rowdy boys wearing matching dark red robes emblazoned with skulls at the back balanced tea cups and glasses atop one of their heads. They all guffawed in marvel at the towering disaster—before a thrown green slipper knocked it down.

The one who'd sneered at Kallia before thrust a hand out, freezing every object in place before they shattered to the ground. "Damn it, Vain."

"It wasn't me." The drawl came from the opposite end of the table where Vain sat by two other girls.

Naturally, the only free chair in the room remained right beside Vain.

Once the realization dawned on them both, the displeasure was mutual.

"*That's* . . . ," Vain murmured into a sip of her tea, pointedly staring. "That's a look."

Kallia beamed graciously as she sat down. "Thank you so much. Yours, too."

One of the Diamond Rings pressed a fist to her mouth and coughed—or snorted—while Vain rolled her eyes. She was one of the rare disheveled few at the table who appeared to be wearing the first thing she could grab, which somehow worked even more to her favor. The wrinkled gentleman's shirt was long enough on her that she could cross her legs without baring much, highlighting slightly bruised yet smooth skin. As well as the single bare foot by her other slippered one.

"You know Filip is never going to give it back to you," teased a brown-skinned girl with bouncy curls sitting on Vain's other side in a sheer light-pink robe rimmed with feathers.

"He can keep it." Vain stabbed at a piece of fruit. "Red Death Dukes need more variety, anyway."

"Just let them be who they want to be, darling," trilled the other Diamond Ring, a round-cheeked girl with long, braided, silver-blond hair, wearing a dark-purple nightgown gem-studded like stars. Of the three, she smiled the most, and was the first of anyone to look kindly in Kallia's direction all day. "Hello there, I'm Ruthless. Love the black lip."

"Th-thank you." Kallia blinked at the sweetness of her voice. "I'm—"

"I know," she said eagerly through a too-wide grin. "I watched the show in the mirrors—kept me on the edge the whole time! And you were just *brilliant*."

Mouth parted, Kallia wasn't entirely sure what to say to that.

"Brilliant?" Vain scoffed. "The mirrors watched her when she got to the city. That's not talent."

"Why were *you* watching, then?" Ruthless shot her a knowing smirk, to which the other Diamond Ring beside her laughed. "Kallia had more talent in a single eyelash than anyone else in that competition."

Vain shrugged before popping a small ball of fruit in her mouth. "And I believe the key word, here, is *had*."

The reminder always pressed hard. Even harder because everyone knew. They knew her secrets, her shame, in a way that stripped her to just skin every time she walked into a room filled with people.

"Don't listen to her, darling," Ruthless whispered. "She criticizes everyone."

"Yes, call it a coping mechanism for someone plagued with the inability to work on herself." The girl in pink ducked from the block of cheese that came flying at her head with a shriek. "Don't you *dare* get grease on this robe, Vain. It's new."

"You probably have five more just like it in your closet, Malice."

"Not in this shade."

Kallia dragged a finger over her empty plate, observing the piece of jewelry the leader toyed with at her neck. It was the exact same necklace they all wore: a simple chain holding a sparkling ring, very much like the hoops they performed with. Vain, Malice, and Ruthless.

The names of nightmares. The Diamond Rings.

For some reason, Kallia expected there to be more in the group from their show, though they must've integrated more illusions than she realized.

Still, these three possessed the mighty stage presence of a group of ten.

Just like everyone else in the room. From one glimpse down, each performer promised a different show, a different spectacle for the world to enjoy.

"Heard we missed a good fight yesterday." Vain lowered her cup to the table, lifting her gaze past Kallia's shoulder. "Pity."

Kallia didn't need to turn to know Jack stood behind her. He was probably the only reason why Vain hadn't yet attempted even harsher insults. Why no one at the table had even dared attack her on sight.

"You really need a bodyguard with you everywhere?"

"That *is* the point of them," Kallia muttered with the snap of her fingers. "Thanks for reminding me."

Vain's feral smile tensed while Kallia's rose when Jack leaned over on command. "Fill the plate," she ordered.

If she didn't throw some menial task on him, the others would get suspicious. Especially if she simply ignored him, even if it would be easier that way. Too many people were watching. Not only taking stock of her, but Jack as well.

For once she was grateful for Jack's presence—the one familiar face among strangers—as well as his service. The table was overwhelming enough on its own with its rotating plate of overwhelming delights, both strange and delicious. Even the teas appeared otherworldly in small glass pots sporting such baffling flavors: crushed jasmine butterfly wings, morning gold mint flowers, essence of the drinker's favorite color.

Jack set the filled plate in front of her, which she spared a bored glance before waving him away. "Now go. I don't want you hovering over me."

Ordering him around, talking down to him like an untrained dog, was not remotely close to a satisfying revenge when it was all part of a role. All meant to dehumanize and ridicule him for the amusement of others.

Proud as she knew Jack to be, he took it all. Impressively. He played his part far better than she did, accepting the dismissal with a terse nod before taking his place against the wall. Just close enough to keep watch, and run to her side if she ever needed him again.

What a good dog." Vain chewed with a smirk.

Biting her tongue, Kallia absently scraped her fork against whatever sat on her plate. Her frown deepened at the selection. He could've chosen random items, but everything he collected appeared to resemble some of her favorites: some odd bread braid drizzled in chocolate, fruit sliced like petals strung together like flowers, candied-bacon wrapped in cheese.

"Don't worry, darling," Ruthless insisted with a lilt of concern. "It's all really as delicious as it looks."

"It would be a shame, otherwise." Malice blew out a snort and began viciously ripping into a pastry. "There's enough in this world that's screwed up. No need to ruin food—"

Vain coughed hard.

The two girls straightened in their seats and turned back to their plates.

Kallia drew in a tense breath, and said nothing. She reached for one of the mini teapots just to give her hands something to do. To look busy. There was so much cold to this world. She longed for warmth. She longed for the mornings she remembered. Those days when she'd sneak away to the Conquering Circus tents for some bitter hot tea and cards, those hours in the Prima Cafe with Aaros. Or sitting beneath the sunlight, across the table from—

Kallia glanced up, and she nearly dropped the steaming pot she held.

Demarco sat casually beside her, his face covered by an issue of the *Soltair Source* while he sipped at his coffee. As if that stopped people from recognizing him. She knew it was him simply by his hands, the warm brown shade of his skin skin even darker against the pale text-ridden paper.

Kallia's vision wavered suddenly, especially when his long fingers started tapping absently along the edges as he read, following the beat of some song in his head.

The blood rushed from her face as she peered all around, the head-liners of the Green Room still in place. Unaware of the new guest who had just descended in their midst as if plucked right from the Prima Café.

The issue crinkled as Demarco folded it back together, struck by her—the same surprise flaring in his dark eyes, as if he'd been waiting for her to arrive all this time.

"Ah, there you are," he said, his lips curling at the edges. "Ready to go?"

Kallia blinked rapidly, her vision wavering abruptly. Something inside her cracked, waiting for him to disappear. Begging.

Because this wasn't real. He wasn't here, even as he sat before her.

Because leaving this place would never be as simple as saying yes, taking his hand, and going for a walk back to Glorian with him.

"Um, can I help you?"

Kallia jerked. The room violently snapped into place, and there was Vain. Brows raised, sitting where Demarco had just been. A seat he'd never occupied in the first place.

"Nothing," Kallia bristled with a slow shake of her head. Pathetic, the way it all threw her off. One glance of him, a version of him that wasn't even real, and she crumbled.

Vain assessed her with a birdlike tilt of her head. "Pity," she said softly. "I think the new girl can't keep up, Roth."

"Settle down, Vain."

The deep voice slithered into Kallia's ears before triangle-marked hands found her shoulders from behind. As he smiled down at her, she could almost forget he was the same magician who'd unleashed brutality in this very room.

Kallia mustered up the purest smile she could for him. "It's all in good fun."

"That's the spirit. A little poison every day is good for the soul, makes us stronger." Roth winked with such playfulness, she could almost forget he was the same magician who'd unleashed brutality in this very room.

"This city looks good on you, my dear." He took in her appearance with beaming pride. "Glad you could join us all. There's so much to prepare for."

An omen sat behind those words, but Kallia nodded.

The moment Roth entered the scene, he became the star of the room. And he basked in that fact, as he raised a chair from the ground beside Kallia and sat down like a king before taking his throne.

"My powerful, powerful friends, as you've noticed, we have a new addition to our group who I think needs no introduction." Roth smiled down at Kallia, lifting a finger for her to stand. "We've all seen the mirrors, and Kallia here is quite the star in her own right."

"Sure." One of the Red Death Dukes to the far side of the table laughed. "Then why does she need a bodyguard, for Zarose sake?"

The entire table tittered. Some glanced Kallia's way, hunting for a reaction.

She gave them none, didn't have to. Roth set his head at a humorless tilt. "Would any of you like to take a walk outside?"

A cold descended over the table, a quiet so confusing and chilling that Kallia shivered. Even the Diamond Rings popped their heads up at the question.

When no one answered, Roth smiled graciously. "No takers, then? Good," he said, glancing around the table. "A lot of you wear some of the sharpest claws out there to get to where you are, so I won't waste my breath on asking for any niceties. But Kallia is of my own flesh and blood. An Alastor. And you will all treat her as you would anyone else at this table. Am I making myself clear?"

The headliners remained quiet, though Kallia heard Vain snort softly.

"It *is* my greatest hope that someone might take her under their wing. Get a star back to lighting up the stage." His stare traced the faces of those present, already weighing the options without Kallia's opinion.

Not that it mattered, even if she snapped out loud. The last thing Kallia wanted was to train with these magicians. Maybe Ruthless, but even that was a stretch. One snake in the pit choosing not to bear its fangs could very well still bite.

Any scrap of kindness had to be questioned. Any time she put her magic in hands beyond her own, she'd lost so much. Jack, Demarco—even if he'd never intended it. She never wanted to be in such a position again. The possibility of losing any more, without knowing, was more terrifying than seeing it taken before her very eyes.

But *Zarose*, Kallia wanted it all back.

She would do anything to get her powers, even if that meant playing with snakes.

"Though on top of that, there is a matter of great importance I also wanted to bring to the board for a vote, which I hope might spark all of your interests," Roth announced with a gleam in his eye. "A new show in the works."

New seized everyone's interests immediately. They broke out of their ice as excited murmurs rippled over the table. Something new, after all, was something different.

"What kind of show?" one magician asked on an eager breath. "Who will be in it?"

"Everyone," Roth promised warmly. "Think of it . . . like a showcase. A magnificent pageant where all have the chance to show off their skills, their artistry, their power. All across the city, *everyone* will have a chance at the spotlight."

A few of the delighted gasps sank into curses and groans.

"Well that doesn't sound fair." Filip scoffed, his brow hardened in confusion. "The Red Death Dukes do not risk their lives shirtless for every performance just to share a stage with commoners. The natural order has already placed them where they belong." He received a few hoots from his team members, as if he'd just delivered the most inspiring adage. "You've already got the best acts in town for your show sitting right here, Roth. And the table is full."

Zarose. And Kallia thought the magicians in Spectaculore were unbearable.

"You're correct, of course. I choose only the best, just like I keep only the best." The Dealer paced around, tapping a finger against his lip. "But what if I told you that the best is not all there is, that there's so much more we all deserve? More stages, more audiences, *more* than this city."

Every headliner, including Kallia, sported similarly confused expressions. Even Jack from his place at the wall, bowed head and all, bore the hint of a scowl.

Still, the air tightened with a hunger.

"What could possibly have more than our side of the world?" stammered one of the magicians. "We have everything."

"We have a corner. A powerful one, but a corner nonetheless." With a solemn nod, Roth clasped his firmly hands together. "And it's about time we've finally shown the rest of the house what we've got, what we can do, by rejoining the true side."

Silence dropped over the room.

Under the table, Kallia dug her nails over her knee. Her pulse thundered.

Everything Roth told her the night before shuffled back into her mind at lethal speed. Glorian, the destruction, the deaths. All of which had arrived from the show he'd just described. Another Show of Hands.

She fought every urge to look back at Jack. He'd seen this coming. He'd warned her, and still, Kallia felt like she might be sick in her seat.

There was only one way a magician could cross from one side to the next.

"You always said that wasn't possible." One of the Diamond Rings spoke. So softly, Kallia couldn't discern which one, from the ringing in her ears clouding everything.

"I lied," Roth replied. No hint of shame. "It was safer that way for everyone. Zarose Gate was a cautionary tale. It wasn't possible because before, it was dangerous—"

"It's *still* dangerous," Kallia finally bit out, raising her gaze. Daring him to deny it. "No one can cross through Zarose Gate if it'll annihilate everything else. You saw it yourself, how could you even suggest it?"

The silence fell longer, colder, which made Kallia realize she'd forgotten her mask. That sweet icy composure. It was clear no one spoke back to Roth like that, questioning his intelligence so harshly.

Which made it all the more chilling when Roth's response held no anger. Only pure understanding in the way he nodded. "I know, my dear. I thought the exact same," he countered. "It wasn't an easy decision to come down to, but I do believe there is another way—and you helped me put it all together with how the pieces fit."

That was certainly not how Kallia remembered it. "What pieces?"

"One I'd forgotten, overlooked," he said pensively. "Someone who I think may be able to help you break through the surface that's divided both sides."

She tore through every word she recalled from their conversation, and there was nothing of this there. Nothing that sounded even remotely like this.

"You and I are the last Alastors, Kallia. We were spared for a reason." His eyes twinkled, glistening at the edges. "And I think it's because *we* can make a different ending, together. A better one, that can get you home."

Her nostrils flared. It was everything she wanted to believe, spun into one thought that lured her closer. As if the choice were hers.

That was the danger, in someone who didn't need to rule by force. Not if they had the power to turn any want into a weakness.

"Her?" Vain cut in with a scoff. "What exactly can she do? She has no power."

Unlike me, the unspoken thought trailed after. The stab of annoyance woke Kallia up. Unsurprising that of all the things this girl was concerned about, it was wrapped in comparison. Jealousy. These headliners cared about nothing else but their own reflections.

"Not for long." Roth's jaw clenched, far sterner with Vain than he had been toward Kallia. *"Everyone's* powers are in flux when they first arrive, that's how it always is in a new world. And you all were no different." He cast his steely gaze on all of them. "Don't forget just how easy it can be to go back."

Everyone stilled at the chilling note. Even Kallia shivered, unsure if he meant removing their seat from the table, or letting a devil have its way with their magic. If these people were even aware of how quickly it could all be taken away by what awaited outside their city gates.

Roth held them on some leash, regardless.

"Alas, power always returns because magic makes the magician." A triumphant note marched back into the Dealer's voice as he gave a decisive nod. "And once it does, our show will well be underway. And all will be—"

"With all due respect," the raspy magician with a face riddled in scratches and tattoos cut in. "But why would any of us even *want* to go back?"

It was the question on every headliner's mind, from the way they all pressed forward. Intrigued, confused. Too hesitant to share too much of both.

"The true side is for the weak. It's boring," the magician continued, chewing at the toothpick between his teeth as he propped the heels of his boots on the table. "Hardly anyone there gives show magicians the respect we truly deserve. Not like here."

Kallia's jaw nearly dropped at how many male magicians in the group raised their fists high in agreement. As if they weren't well aware how cushy they had it on *both* sides.

The sight alone almost made her flip the table. Especially when Roth nodded slowly in sympathy, understanding the shared plight.

"Then why not take this chance to prove it to them, Baranum?" he asked the magician, posing the same question to the rest. "You all have risen higher than those on the true side who believed you would amount to nothing. Those who never gave you the proper recognition, who claimed you weren't memorable enough for the spotlight or didn't fit their vision of power."

Hardly anyone breathed when Roth nodded at each of them, acknowledging every story they came from. Every rock bottom they had to claw their way up and out of.

All with that blaze of challenge on his face. Mesmerizing, and ter-rifying.

"However, their loss was *your* gain," Roth stressed. "It's unpre-dictable, how we fell through the pesky little cracks of the mirrors by chance. And even then, how quickly the world forgets about you when you disappear. How little the mortal side tends to remember," he said, smiling as if something amused him. "But I know there's nothing chance about it at all. The mirrors called to *you*, because you were des-tined to fall. To rise in this city, to sit right at this table."

A sniffle sounded somewhere along the table. Kallia wouldn't be surprised if she looked around, there'd be tears glistening at the cor-ners of many eyes.

"The mirrors saw what I see. Your potential, your talent, your power—under my watch, they will never go to waste," he said. "Not here, and certainly not on the true side."

The pride in his promise tugged a cord in Kallia. The words were ones she'd always wanted to hear, touching every want and dream and hope right to her very core. They were powerful words. Dangerous ones.

The words to make a follower of anyone.

Satisfied by what he saw in the room now, Roth smiled. "We will all show them," he went on. "And the only way to get there is by putting on a grand show. The more magic, the better. So it requires the full participation of the city."

This time, no protests. Absolute silence.

Roth paced around the table long enough that he finally reached his seat. "And of course, this all cannot be possible without the full support of my headliners. Your opinions matter so much, and your minds will make this show the greatness I know it can be."

Without even ordering a vote, each performer lifted their hand. One by one, around the table, ending with all of the Diamond Rings. And Kallia, raising hers tentatively. Unsure what might happen other-wise.

A unanimous vote.

"Splendid!" Roth clasped his hands together in gratitude as a renewed excitement sparked in the air around them. "We are in full agreement."

As he triumphantly held up a flute of green-tinted champagne that had seemingly come out of nowhere, Kallia glanced down to find the same drink suddenly by her plate, and all the place settings in sight. The delightful discovery was all the signal everyone needed to answer Roth's toast.

"And tonight"—the Dealer threw back the whole drink in one swallow—"we announce our plan, and seal our vote with a duel!"

Without hesitation, every headliner erupted in cheers. The Diamond Rings clinked their glasses together with howls loud enough for the moon. Once Filip sent his flute shattering to the ground, the other Red Death Dukes followed with boorish shouts of approval. One celebratory drink was not enough, and soon the others demanded more.

Kallia quietly swallowed down her own drink as the madness descended.

A perfect distraction.

Jack had the same idea. From the corner of her eye, she watched him slowly push off the wall and inch toward the exit, sparing a glance at—

"Exciting isn't it, my dear?"

Roth stepped right in her line of vision.

Kallia sat up straighter. She should've guessed he'd never let her out of his sight.

"Yes, exciting," she repeated half-heartedly. "Forgive my interruption from earlier. I must've forgotten the part in our conversation last night where something of this magnitude was decided."

She had a few more choice words, but they were too improper to utter out loud.

"Why, you were the muse for the idea, my dear," he declared as if it were obvious. "The endeavor is a risky one, I know. But I would've never dreamed of it again until you arrived. Nor would I ever have thought it a good plan in the first place until I realized you would not be doing this alone. There is another who will help you."

It was either a lie or the truth. At this point, she wasn't sure which one she wanted it to be. "Who?"

"It's heartening, how eager you are. But we have plenty of time to get to that later." Roth patted her on the cheek like a child to its doll. "Now, have you ever dueled with illusions before?"

Kallia knew if she pushed, he would take note of it. And her position was already precarious enough.

In a manner fitting of the fools around her, she beamed at his attention. His affection. "Can't say that I have."

"Then you are in for a *treat*! My philosophy is that dry business must end in sport," he went on, rubbing his hands together in relish. "And there's no violence allowed in my town, unless it has an audience."

"To the death?"

A disturbing laugh rumbled from deep in his chest. "Oh, that would be something, wouldn't it? Alas, it is all in good fun." The twinkle in his eye made it sound every bit as ominous. "They range from drawn out and brutal to some of the most magnificent rapid-fire spectacles you'll ever see. A great way to find new talent or cull old talent, depending on who wins. Occasionally I show mercy; other times, I give the crowd the choice. And the whole city shows up because no one can ever predict when they'll happen or what will happen." His eyes flitted warmly past Kallia's shoulder. "That is, unless you're in the ring with our very own Queen of the Diamond Rings. A fight like that always ends the same."

With the smug toss of her short locks, Vain preened. "In tears and annihilation."

Figures she would be the most cutthroat of them all.

And she wore the bloody crown proudly with a pout as she said, "Winning all the time is truly a curse. No one ever wants to play with me."

"A true challenger will come soon enough. Maybe even tonight." With a wink for them both, Roth shot back to his feet to address the room once more. "Since tonight would've been a show night for the Red Death Dukes, the gents have the floor on this one."

A round of hoots came from the red-robed team who pounded at their chests with primal joy.

"So what will it be, a traditional headliner duel?" Roth posed. "A fight with someone in the crowd, perhaps?"

"Like we would ever waste a fight with a random loser in the crowd," hollered one of the magicians, who was met with whoops and slapped hands behind him. "We're keeping it classic. A headliner duel."

An intrigued wave of *oob*s swept over the room as the selection process began. Most magicians flexed their fingers, cracked their knuckles. Even Vain had begun praying under her breath for the chance to knock their teeth out. Bloodthirst, even thicker than from Jack's fight last night, drenched the air once more. All were ready, and looking for a fight.

"We're dueling the fancy new meat."

A swift cold punch of silence.

"*Without* her bodyguard."

Kallia barely flinched. The searing weight of Jack's eyes on the back of her head was somehow heavier than the weight of the entire red army now sneering at her from across the table.

Her slow answering smile held a million curses behind it. Even more, as the wave of chuckles and low whistles across the table rolled in. A disappointed curse from Vain.

And the sharp click of the tongue from Roth. "Nice try, boys," he said, shaking his head slowly. "You all heard what I said—"

"Yes, which was to treat her like we'd treat anyone else at this table," Filip pointed out. "Which means she's a headliner."

"I'm touched," Kallia shot back, though it was by no means a compliment from the way he'd spat it out.

Of them all, only Roth appeared deeply unamused. "While I appreciate your attentiveness and effort to be inclusive, gentlemen, my Kallia has never dueled before. She's fragile and delicate and not at all ready yet. I would hate to see her get hurt."

My Kallia.

She nearly gagged. After hours of knowing her, he already threw such a claim. Even though she could've been no more than a piece of fruit on the table, from the way he spoke of her, already treating her like a shiny toy not to be touched.

She almost welcomed the chance to break, just to spite him.

"Oh, with all due respect, we don't want to hurt her. We want to help." An angelic light entered Filip's demeanor. "We just figured . . . none of us knew how to duel. *I* certainly didn't, until someone plucked me from the crowd and threw me into the ring."

The words were so sugar-coated, Kallia had to cut in, raising finger in confusion. "But I thought only random losers occupied the crowd."

A headliner sitting across took a strained sip of their tea, while one of the Diamond Rings nearly spit hers out on a laugh.

Filip's stare darkened, but his smile remained every bit as golden as ever. "Maybe a fight will do you some good," he said, lifting his gaze to Roth alone. "Just think, if she's desperate enough, perhaps those powers will finally come out to save her."

20

Daron and Lottie hastened to the center of Glorian, and they weren't the only ones. A large crowd had already begun forming throughout the streets, excited whispers and curious murmurs rippling all about. After weeks of solemn quiet since Spectaculore's end, Daron half wondered if they'd traveled back in time to when the show had only first begun.

They wove their way through the crowd, searching for Aaros or Canary among the faces. Careful not to cross any of the Patrons' paths, or worse, his aunt. The benefit of a crowd was the hiding place it provided. No one glared or recognized him as he moved, all too transfixed by what was happening in the middle of Glorian. Erasmus stood, with Canary beside him, over what looked to be a curious gathering of strings all twisted together before flaring out to the ground.

Daron looked down at his feet, realizing the wires ran along the ground beneath the people's feet. He didn't dare touch it, afraid of what he might set off.

Perhaps it was a good idea that Canary had kept them so in the dark after all. The most amusing part was the familiar grip that clasped over his shoulder.

"Daron." Aunt Cata turned him slightly, her mouth a stern flat line. "What's going on?"

It was the first time he'd seen her since their last talk in her room, and she seemed just as displeased now as she did then.

"They're putting on a show, I guess." He dug his hands into his pockets. "I really know about as much as you. They've kept us all in the dark about everything."

Softly, Lottie coughed from the side, covering a laugh. The jab was not lost on Aunt Cata. She knew when he lied. She'd watched him grow up in his prime lying years as a boy, so adept to the ways his face tucked away his secrets.

"Don't worry, Auntie, it's just a show."

It was only a matter of time before Aaros emerged from the crowd to join them. He even dared to wink at the Head of the Patrons. "No harm ever came from a night of some good, clean fun."

Daron bit back his laugh at his aunt's unamused scowl that never left her. She signaled for two Patrons to follow her into the clusters of spectators toward the front. On a quick glance, Daron noted a few Patrons sprinkled throughout the vicinity, as well as those on the edges to contain them if things got too rowdy.

"Welcome, everyone!" Erasmus crowed to the delight of the applause showering around him. "It has been quite some time since we gathered like this. Who else has been restless for a little excitement?"

Beside him, Canary stood out with her ruby hair that blazed even in the darkness. Her look of pleasure could only mean Erasmus had absolutely no idea what was in store.

"We thought it would be a grand idea to surprise you all tonight," the proprietor went on. "Because what better way to liven things up than with a show?" With a cheeky wink, he added, "Let's give all of Soltair something to talk about, again."

"I can't believe you were married to him." Aaros stood between her and the man up front.

"There's a reason it didn't last long." Lottie turned to Daron, speaking under her breath. "You ready to run, Demarco? Once things go upside down, you better be off faster than a pistol shot."

"And what will you be doing?"

The words had only just left his mouth as the roar tore across the sky. The air stilled entirely, stunning all of Glorian into a waiting silence. Even Erasmus.

"Committing to the chaos," Lottie said, letting out a high-pitched scream. *"Fire!"*

No fire to be seen, but it was as if the world alone conjured it. Everyone in the crowd scrambled in every direction, especially when a loud, heavy tolling began to sound in the distance. Bells. Daron couldn't be sure if it was the ones that tolled in dread at the Alastor Place, but no one could sense the difference. People knew all too well what the ringing of bells meant.

Once Daron slipped through the panicked mass, he looked back at the city center. Aunt Cata cupped her hands around her mouth to bring order, completely missing how Canary stumbled into Erasmus, who let the sparkling stick drop on the raised braid of twined wires.

As soon as the flame touched even one end, it spread to all the others, engulfing the entire braid to ash before tiny flames followed the paths of the wires they had originated from, running throughout the center.

Just like that, sparks flew beneath the people's feet in a series of cracks and pops. Whatever was packed into those lines, they were now erupting into sparks and smoke across the entire town center. It didn't appear as though anyone was getting seriously injured by the fireworks, so minor that they were perhaps just mere annoyances, but the panic ratcheted up the reactions tenfold. It felt less like a show gone wrong and more like an attack. "This is your chance, judge, take it!" Aaros said as both he and Lottie shoved Daron in the shoulder. "Go now!"

Daron stumbled face-first into the white uniformed back. The Patron who had been trying to calm the crowd turned at the interruption, his eyes tightening in recognition.

Shit.

Just as instantly, Aaros fell gracelessly in between them with a hysterical sob. "Help me, my foot is on fire!"

It wasn't, but Daron surged forward, Lottie at his side. As the chaos heightened around the crowd, more Patrons responded and abandoned their posts.

"One shot, Demarco. And not much time." Lottie panted, out of breath. When they reached the hospital building, he was more than surprised that she waited outside. "Report back in one piece, will you?"

Daron had never navigated this building at nighttime, though everything looked even more eerie than usual. The white cabinets of supplies shining in slices of moonlight from the windows, interrupted by bursts of colorful fractured light from the town center. The vast rows of beds, neatly made. A few scattered beds were filled, though the patients must have been under some intense nightly tonic to be sleeping through the racket bursting just outside the windows. The muffled shouts and sounds of chaos brewing below. It was a dead time for the hospital, which was not something Daron was used to seeing.

As soon as he reached the mayor's section, he ripped open the curtain.

The same eerie drawings, like the one Daron had gotten from his aunt, covered the floors. Janette sitting in the chair beside the hospital bed, watching quietly as her father stood by the window as the chaos unfolded below.

"Let me guess, this is all your doing?" Janette nodded listlessly toward the window. "As if the first show didn't do enough damage already?"

Daron tensed. It slowly dawned on him how much he regarded Glorian as a stage when, for those who'd never left the city, it was a home. A strange and twisted home, but for many, it was all they knew. All they were made to know.

A home that was more fragile than they ever realized, all falling apart outside their window.

Daron didn't know what else to say. "I'm sorry."

"I really shouldn't be surprised. I knew you'd turn up, one way or another." Janette blew out a tired sigh as she slowly rose from her seat. "And I have a feeling he did, too."

Daron's pulse leaped as he followed her line of vision to the window, noticing the mayor's silhouette for the first time hidden by the curtains, overlooking the scene below. Every bright flash of light shadowed his motionless form, which was much smaller than Daron remembered.

"He hasn't spoken a word since he last saw you," she said so matter-of-factly, pushing aside some fallen papers with her heel. "He's my father, and he won't even speak to me. Just . . . *this*." She threw out her hands toward the mess of drawings, pooled like a gathering darkness at their feet.

"At first I figured he was punishing us with silence because we all thought him mad. But I think it was because we weren't listening."

"So you believe him now?" Daron prompted. By now, she had to admit there was something wrong with Glorian. Something missing, all this time.

Her laugh was sad. "I'm not sure what's real anymore, Demarco. About this place, about anything."

With that, she took her leave, drifting out of the room as solemnly as a ghost. It unnerved Daron to see her go so quietly, leaving a trail of unease in her wake.

"Daron Demarco, I wondered when you would be back for a visit."

The mayor had turned from his place against the mirror, peering at him with his head tilted in the dark. As light burst behind him, he became like a silhouetted figure of shadow against the night.

"I don't have much time, Eilin," he said, staving off the chill from his bones as he crossed the room. "I need to know. What you said the other day—"

"If I was speaking pure nonsense?" the mayor asked. "You wouldn't have come to me if you thought that, would you?"

Daron looked down. Even if he didn't think it could be true, he'd come anyway. For any lead, anything. "I hoped it would be."

"Ah, hope and desperation. A grand combination when looking for answers," the mayor said, raking a hand through his hair though tufts of it still stuck out in odd places.

"I don't have much time," Daron stressed.

"Clearly. You're all having quite the party out there." Mayor Eilin's frown was hesitant, unsure. "Normally I would be the first to shut it all down, but I've found that I have had a change of heart since coming to."

Daron clenched his teeth until his gums numbed. "You told me to look for the gate, and I'd find Kallia. Find her where?"

"On the other side." The man smiled, as if recalling some joke in his head. "You already know how to get there. You're just looking for confirmation."

"Zarose Gate is not an option." Any answer besides that. After what Aunt Cata told him, he had no clue where to even go looking if the Zarose Gate across Soltair was just a pile of rocks.

"There is another way." The mayor watched him, head tilted. "The surface is closer than you think."

"Get lost where those do not dare," Daron said quietly. "I thought you were talking about—"

"My map, did you find it?" The mayor looked out the window.

"Yes, but what does that mean?" Daron so badly wanted to wring the answers from the riddles. "That's not helpful at all."

"Isn't it? There is only one place in all of Soltair where one dares not get lost," the mayor said pointedly, gesturing for Daron to join him by the window.

The hospital building was at a high enough vantage point that one could view a majority of Glorian and the streets snaking in between.

A city now drowning in smoke. Like a dark cloud had descended upon the deserted streets, brightened by patches of small flames and sparks flaring at random. They bore just enough light to illuminate the few forms ducking through alleyways, clutching lampposts, as Patrons scrambled to extinguish the ever-growing fires threading throughout Glorian.

It was disaster and celebration all in one, as bursts of reds, blues, and purples showered over every building within the walls of Glorian and the rustling dark woods that stood outside, watching on as if in a world apart from theirs.

He looked down at the paper, the same angry writhing scribbles overtaking every sheet of paper around him.

"We've always been taught to never venture inside alone." Mayor Eilin tilted his head, curious as a bird. "Yet we never learn what happens if we do."

Daron's insides clenched. "But you know?"

"I know only they told me." He pressed his weathered fingers to the glass. "Go into the woods where the devils reach through the cracks, and they'll welcome you with open arms. And only then will you find what you're looking for."

21

The possibility of power was too much to pass up. So after much consideration, Roth concluded that Kallia could reasonably learn how to duel in a day.

He offered her journals brimming with notes from past matches, access to the training grounds and the headliners' gymnasium, and most importantly, private training from his most vicious, undefeated dueling champion.

"You better have a high tolerance for pain," Vain said as she led them down the endless staircase of the Alastor Place. "Filip *loves* a screamer."

Kallia smiled tightly. The headliner wanted about as much to do with Kallia as Kallia did with her. That was mutual, at least, but unavoidable. In the end, the Dealer always got his way because no one refused his wishes.

For once, Kallia hardly minded it. Vain's ability was undeniable, that was more than clear the first time she watched the Diamond Rings perform. If there was even the slightest chance any of this could bring her closer to her own magic, Kallia would do anything. No matter how many venomous insults it took.

It was a shame the other Diamond Rings didn't join, as the tension between the pair could split cleanly through glass. Especially with Jack always following behind, quiet as a ghost.

It took everything in Kallia not to explode as they all walked down the stairs of the Alastor Place. There was just so much to discuss. So much to consider. With Roth's new plans, Kallia felt close to bursting from all of this madness.

Just madness after madness after madness.

Once the meal had wrapped up, she spared Jack no more than a wordless glance before Vain yanked her out of the Green Room to train for tonight. Everything else would have to wait.

When they reached the first floor after far too many stairs, the headliner showed them out through a side door of the main building. A long alleyway awaited just outside. And across, a discreet door into the next building over.

A thrill went through Kallia at all the possibilities of where it might lead. With so much noise, so many people pulling her every which way, she craved the cold, undisturbed floor of an empty stage. Or maybe a spacious gymnasium with enough room to stretch alone, far away from the others. It's all she fantasized about when Vain ordered that they have privacy, going no farther unless Jack waited outside the building like a dog.

Kallia allowed it. Less bodies equaled more space. Less distractions, more concentration.

The building they finally entered alone left Kallia staring in horror.

"You want to train me *here*?" She gaped at the darkened room overflowing with endless rows of mirrors and empty frames. Everywhere. Almost as overwhelming as the Court of Mirrors, yet smaller in scale. Tighter.

This had to be a joke.

She waited for Vain to laugh and lead them through another door, but the girl glided through the racks of mirrors before throwing her coat over the long front counter where a lantern glowed. Decidedly, not a joke.

"There's no way we can duel here." Kallia stiffly navigated between frames, her gait careful. "Everything is so . . . breakable."

"We're not dueling in here." A scoff rolled from the back of the headliner's throat. "We're not dueling at all. You're definitely not ready for that."

Not ready. So many people had thrown that at her already, and she couldn't even argue it.

"Then what are we even doing here?" The words snapped out of Kallia. "Unless you want more reasons to look at yourself."

"How do you think she ended up with a name like Vain?"

A head popped up from behind the front counter, before the rest of the figure stood. With a cheeky smile, Herald waved at them both with the rag in his hand. "Welcome to *my* domain, showgirl."

"Zarose, how many jobs do you have?" Kallia glanced around, incredulous. "You sell mirrors, too?"

"Restore them," Herald corrected, caressing the empty carved wooden frame by the wall near him. "As it turns out, mirrors break a lot around here. And someone has to take care of them."

An odd tenderness lay in his voice, as if they were pets and not the windows this world regularly spied through.

"Yes, in this dark, sad little cave," Vain said, inspecting her nails. "Thought I'd have the place to myself. Should've known you'd be here, mirror boy."

"Still doesn't explain why *we're* still here." Kallia glared.

"Even I know the answer to that." Chuckling, Herald rested his elbows against the counter. "Heard the muscles-for-brains brigade wants to kick your ass tonight. What a way to make friends, showgirl."

Unsurprising, how fast the news had already spread. Even on the true side, gossip was a beast that moved quickly.

"Exactly. And guess who has the impossible task of making sure she doesn't embarrass herself?" Vain's eyes flew right back on Kallia. "You're not ready to duel. So I've brought you here for a lesson that's . . . a bit more at your level."

"How thoughtful." Kallia seethed. "And this is helpful, how?"

"Have you ever reflected on your past performances? Not to bask in the highlights, but to look at them with a critical eye?" The headliner raised a brow. "Examining your missteps? Honing in on your weaknesses or potential mistakes? Regrets?"

All the time.

Whenever Kallia finished a performance, it replayed scene by scene a hundred times in her head like a lullaby before bed. The times when something went wrong, however, it stayed in her mind all night. Haunting her, sometimes for weeks. And the only way to combat it and finally find some rest was by shoving all doubt away. That way, nothing could touch her. "I never have any regrets on the stage."

With a hum, Vain trailed a finger along a nearby mirror's edge. "Pity. The best sort of regrets are the ones you can learn from," she said. "If you regret nothing from before, how will you do better next time?"

With that, the headliner strutted off to the far end of the store, all with the silent expectation for Kallia to follow.

"I'd go if I were you." Herald whistled in low amusement as he wiped down the counter. "She spends a little too much time around here when she's not performing, and she's no fun when she's prickly."

"What's back there?"

"More mirrors." He shrugged. "Don't worry, if she wanted to drop an attack on you and fistfight to the death, she'd want a live audience for that."

That was reassuring. From how insistent Vain had been to keep Jack outside, that was Kallia's first thought. But at that point, pure curiosity drove her to follow, if only to see what a headliner did in a tiny shop of mirrors when she had a whole court of them at her disposal.

Herald's whistling was barely audible by the time Kallia reached the other end of the store where Vain waited, tapping her fingers against an oval mirror framed in copper swirls. Not the least bit surprised Kallia had come.

"Closer," she said, shifting so that both their silhouettes dominated the frame. "One thing most people don't understand about dueling, same with magic, is that all the power in the world won't make you the best fighter. It's *how* you use it—for yourself, against the other—that makes you powerful."

When she pressed at one of the swirls of the frame, their forms disappeared from the reflection. As did the empty store, the rows of mirrors across the walls behind them. All of it, swept under the darkness, until the hints of an image rose from it.

"They rarely showed this to the court. The angle was off." Vain traced her fingertip along the frame, clearing the glass's focus. "It's a miracle there were some mirrors in the paneling of the theater to pick this up."

Kallia blinked as glimmers of a bright stage solidified in the reflection, taken from the viewpoint of the mezzanine above while a show went on.

On stage, a performer in an ink-blue dress sipped from a glass of water, before promptly smashing it into the ground.

A wall of fire grew behind her as music rose from the aisles where circus performers slowly streamed in.

Her first act in Spectaculore.

This performer, kicking down the stool across the stage, was her.

Unlike with the black brass knuckles, the memory didn't assault her with sensation. Just a strange awareness from watching a moment she recalled well, playing out through a different lens. The longing to go back to it all gripped between every bone.

She remembered that hush, before the Conquering Circus came in with their music. That joy, as they joined her.

And that power, like she held all the best cards in her hands.

Kallia had never felt more alive, more exhilarated, and more certain in that moment that she was exactly where she needed to be.

"There's your misstep."

The smile dropped at Vain's discontented hum at the scene, watching as the performer in blue screamed before falling straight into the arms of her assistant below.

Aaros. The relief coursing through, just from seeing him, was overwhelming.

"It wasn't a misstep," she remarked as the shadowed audience began clapping. Her first proper moment of applause. "I remember the stage shook, as if there was a quake."

"Devils. Like cats, innocently playing with their food." Vain's gaze lingered on the reflection, the standing ovation that followed. "Still, it's no excuse. Imagine if that shirtless boy hadn't been there to catch you. What would you have done, then?"

Kallia's mind blanked. "I would've landed just fine if it came down to it," she said. "You can't judge me for something that didn't happen. It's irrelevant."

"Not having a ready answer means you probably would've done *nothing*."

The scene glowed with glorious applause that went on and on, but every part of her shook with fury. Despite the slip, it had been one of her proudest moments. One of her best memories of Glorian.

The headliner's scrutiny continued, picking at it with venom.

"Look here, now." Vain tapped against the frame so that the performance restarted at the beginning. "When you're first walking out, look at how you linger a moment too long on your audience, as if pleased with yourself. You're thinking of the applause instead of setting up the act. Yes, you've got the circus up your sleeve later, but you should . . ."

Kallia was gone before the next insult arrived.

What an absolute waste of time.

"Excuse me, where do you think you're going?" Vain snapped from behind.

The nerve of her, to act so bothered.

"To actually *practice*," Kallia shot back without turning or any care for the creaking mirrors she bumped into. "Because we clearly have different ideas about what that means."

She was done reliving memories. Done looking into mirrors filled with pieces of her life all for the enjoyment of others. Performing that night had been one of her proudest moments. Still one of her best memories of Glorian, despite the slip.

If someone took glee in ripping it apart, she didn't have to stand there and watch.

Kallia stormed out from the back of the shop, greeted by the sight of Herald sitting casually atop the counter and clapping.

"You deserve exemplary marks for that lesson." He saluted as she passed. "Well done."

"Oh, shut *up*, Herald," came a sniping response from afar.

A bell shook above her head as Kallia burst through the front door. The stillness of the shop was lost in the clamor of the streets. From the darkness of frames and glass, there was movement. Lights. Music. Oddly scented smoke pouring through—

"What happened in there?"

For once, Kallia knew the hand at her elbow without flinging her fist behind out of habit. For her and Jack, that was progress.

Her blood still boiled as she inhaled deeply. As if that did anything to calm her. "Do *you* know how to duel?"

As if knowing even the slightest annoyance could set her off, Jack gently pulled her back from the curb, facing her to him. "I never dueled myself, but I watched." His face became unreadable. "They can get pretty rough."

"So I've gathered." Not like Vain's method would've prepared her for any of that. "Will you show me, then?"

"You should really back out."

Kallia was a breath away from tearing out her hair. "I don't exactly have that option." Throwing off his hand, she stepped back. "Unless I want to look completely spineless."

"You could *end up* spineless if you go forward with it," he said, his jaw set. "It might be easier if I make those idiots—"

"Don't you dare." The thought of Jack fighting that battle sent premature embarrassment burning through her already. It was bad enough the bodyguard act wasn't entirely an act. That she needed him far more than she was willing to admit.

Even worse was knowing that long ago, Jack would've happily encouraged her to take on the challenge, back when *she* was the headliner. The star of Hellfire House. Every night, he'd witnessed her at her most powerful, her most intimidating every time she descended on that chandelier and made the crowd below beg for more.

That magician felt like a stranger now. A costume that no longer fit, when it had been her only scrap of clothing.

"Stop giving me excuses." Kallia gritted her teeth to keep from trembling. "Will you teach me or not?

"You actually *want* me to?"

Kallia stilled at his outburst.

Her heart, cold as stone.

She wasn't at all pressed up against him, not even close. But their breaths still mirrored each other, rising and falling. Angry, confused.

Kallia, more so than anyone, at herself.

Every promise she'd made to herself slammed back into her. Jack was never her teacher; she knew magic before they even met. Hers was already a storm, long before he stepped into Hellfire House.

All he did was show her the ways power could be more.

And he'd shattered that trust. For now, there was some hold to it, pieced together out of necessity. But trust in pieces would always be easier to break again.

She'd nearly forgotten. Somehow *he'd* remembered.

"You're right." Kallia blinked, her breaths slowing. "Never mind."

The awkward tension to the air now drained all the fury out of her, until she was empty. Uncomfortably hollow.

"What happened in there?" Jack asked, more gingerly now. Trying again.

It was a nice attempt. Somehow, though he'd barely left her side all day, they hadn't been able to really speak one word to another. A true one, at least. Without masks or gritted smiles hiding insults behind compliments.

As if Kallia needed any more reason to feel foolish.

All she wanted, desperately, was a friend. Someone to confide in without fearing where the secret would go, someone to lean on in a way that felt nothing like weakness.

She longed for *her* friends. For Aaros and Canary, all of the Conquering Circus. Hell, she'd take Ira.

And Demarco.

If he were here, she knew exactly what he would do.

He would simply hold her hand, take her on a walk, and ask her to tell him everything.

"Kallia?" Jack's eyes grew more concerned, probably from whatever flickered over her expression. He was no friend. That word would never fit him in the way she knew it. But he was somehow still there, the only one from her life before at her side. Even when she'd given him every reason not to be. Even when he could leave whenever he wanted to, he chose to stay.

"What's wrong?" he pressed.

"The mortal had a little diva fit and ran away, that's what's wrong."

Vain stood behind them, hip cocked. Arms crossed. Kallia almost sprang away from Jack, but there was more than enough distance between them. Nothing compromising about their position in the slightest.

"Did you do something to her in there?" Jack's voice hardened as he stepped toward Vain. "She won't tell me—"

"Relax, club keeper. It was just a little spat," Vain muttered to diffuse the tension. Or just Jack's wrath. She seemed softer now, in the way only ice could be. "I lost my temper, she lost hers. She could've slapped me but stormed off in a huff instead, and I stopped myself from throwing a mirror at her head. That's what I call growth."

"Is that supposed to be some kind of apology?" A laugh nearly loosed from Kallia. Were it not for the triangles on full display across Vain's fingers, the girl wouldn't be standing here now. She would've gleefully left without a word, only to show up later at the duel in the front row, popcorn in hand.

Though she still showed up, just as Kallia stayed. That had to count for something.

"What do I have to be sorry for, hurting your feelings?" The venom returned in the headliner's smile. "But if you want to train, then we will train. Don't say I didn't warn you."

The skies were still dark with devils as the day stretched on.

Most would consider it an omen. Kallia certainly did. Every time she glanced up, reaching for a glimmer of afternoon light, there was none. A never-ending night.

Just another normal day for the people of the city, swaying or bobbing across the colorful streets. When Kallia had first arrived then, she barely took anything in, all the ways this illusion Glorian compared to the ordinary one she knew.

There was comfort in how little they resembled each other on the surface. Turning down familiar paths or pausing at street corners that were not rife with sad memories. No ghosts, only wonderment.

One sideways glimpse of Jack's face told how he felt the opposite.

"Hurry up." Vain groaned every time they slowed behind her. "If you lose me, you lose me."

Despite the threat, Vain continued hurriedly pointing out different areas of the city as if out of habit.

Deeper into the flashing labyrinth of this Glorian, it became even more sumptuous as a feast. The names etched in Kallia's mind, the folds named after the old families, who wore new titles now. Instead of the Fravardi Fold, there vibrant fashion spas and style houses appeared busy as beehives from all the magicians walking in and out, all around, in all manner of outrageous clothing. Dresses with fabric that floated over bodies like smoke, slick suits with the fronts that closed at a collection of long beastly teeth instead of buttons.

In the ashes of the Vierra Fold rose the sparkling marvel houses. An impossible amount of bakeries and smoking food dens lined the sidewalks, all serving up dishes and flavors to appeal to every single taste bud of the tongue. One bar boasted that they served cocktails of dreams mixed to the drinker's liking, while another poured nightmares for those seeking more of a thrill with their spirits.

The Alastor Fold, of course, was revered as the hub of entertainment.

Leaving one unclaimed, of which Kallia knew the name. It didn't surprise her with so much the city had to offer; all of the sectors bled into one another. So much so that the Ranza Fold had become a corner primarily absorbed by the marvel and style houses.

They couldn't do away with its main house, though. They hadn't throughout the other folds. And as soon as Vain began leading them down one specific sidewalk, Kallia's nerves hummed with anticipation.

The Ranza Estate.

Her body knew this route, all the steps it took to get there.

Like in the Glorian she knew, the path to the Ranza Estate quieted, riddled more with windswept leaves than people milling about. In her mind, she could already see the house within reach. It would probably wear a different color, no doubt, but the familiar silhouette would be as good as seeing an old friend. She could easily fill in the bright tiled roof. The sun-kissed exterior, the grand shape of—

Kallia's eyes flew open as she tripped.

The charred hunk of wood caught her foot and she skittered forward, where more scorched marks and ash lay.

Pulse thudding, she squinted out into the distance.

And her heart sank.

All that was left was crushed rubble and charred wood, half-formed crumbling walls and collapsed chunks of roof, split beams cloaked in tattered curtains, leaning high over the ground. A few rooms were barely left standing, roofless and bare. A building so beyond recognition, it bore more resemblance to a burnt skeleton than a home.

Stunned, Kallia stepped over a ravaged chunk of wall that would've formed the main entry hall.

She had no words left. For any of this.

"What happened here?" Jack asked, walking out from under one of the split beams.

"You mean you don't feel right at home?" The wall beneath Vain's feet crumbled as she hopped to the ground. "Your makers made this happen. This dump's always been like this since even before *I* got here."

Jack tracked the headliner circling him. "I thought the deal was that devils weren't allowed in the city."

"Your devil brethren are what allow the city to be in the first place. We're all well aware of what they can do outside of the gates." Vain threw her hands out and gave a little twirl. "This is the fun little reminder of what they could do inside."

What for? It made no sense to threaten those within this Glorian. Everyone seemed content with their way of life. A cutthroat hierarchy formed the social structure, but those were small dramas and petty rivalries. Nothing worth the devils' punishment.

"I know, it's an ugly little scorch mark, isn't it?" The headliner paused beneath a charred entryway where no door stood. "Not sure what even used to be here, but no amount of glamor or magic can revive it. So it shall remain hopelessly ugly forever."

Kallia felt her jaw tick. "Why did you bring us here, then?"

"Nobody ever really ventures through these parts anymore." Vain walked toward her, kicking all the rubble and debris in her way. "Which makes it the perfect place to practice where no one will walk by and catch secondhand embarrassment from your dueling."

It was like building an immunity to a poison with her. Her insults inflicted no pain for Kallia. Not like seeing the Ranza Estate in such a state. It had been neglected on the true side, too, until she and Demarco had begun spending their days within it.

And now, there were only bones. Some more formed, but all bones nonetheless.

"Does *he* really need to be here?" Vain padded alongside Kallia, nodding for her to follow out back. Clearer grounds awaited them, conveniently far from view of the street.

"He stays." Without looking, Kallia knew Jack trailed behind. Just as Kallia knew how uneasy he made Vain. Despite their temporary truce, the headliner could just as simply throw her to the wolves once her back was turned. "Unless you have stage fright."

Vain growled. "Don't move," she ordered, striding a few steps farther so that they stood across from each other. "I have two rules when it comes to dueling illusions. What do you think the first is?"

It felt like a trick question demanding a headliner's answer. "Win?"

She shook her head and glanced down, dragging her foot along the dirt in a large circle around her. "First rule is there *are* rules, and you need to know them well."

Once she completed the circle, Kallia found the same shape surrounding her, perfectly mirroring the one across.

"You do not leave your space for whatever reason. Stay in your circle, or you lose by default." Vain flicked a finger upward, sending a burnt hunk of wood floating between them. "And this is our anchor."

Kallia raised a brow but kept silent.

"It's the object we transform and keep transforming into the illusions," she went on. "A trick is always strongest if it's grounded in something real, manipulated rather than conjured out of nothing."

Suddenly, the burnt wood broke apart in midair—each hovering piece, slowly reflamed into spikes of fire at the drumming of Vain's fingers. The searing concentration in her eyes as she thrust her hands forward without warning.

Kallia froze.

Her heart sprinted, breath shortened.

Magic makes the magician.

The fire flew faster, closer.

She had to duck away. She couldn't stop it. Couldn't do *anything*, for there was nothing in her. Just a shattering pulse.

The heat spun toward her, but her bones were solid stone. She braced herself for the pain—waiting and waiting and waiting—but the hit never arrived.

"What the hell was that?"

Kallia opened her eyes, expecting the full burn of Vain's wrath.

But Jack was already there, nose to nose with the Diamond Ring as he sent the burning spikes to the ground

"Interference." A muscle corded in his neck. "Didn't realize all of the headliners were sadistic little cheaters."

"You got me. Sadistic to the core." Vain smirked right in his face. The only touch of nerves that rose to the surface was in the twitch of her eye at their proximity. "Call off your brute, mortal. He's not needed in this capacity. How are you supposed to duel if he won't even let you?"

Kallia's pulse still raced. The brightness of the flames blazed before her every time she blinked, but something gripped her—she didn't know what it was, why she froze.

She wasted no time roughly pulling Jack back and shoving him off to the side. "Don't you *ever* do that again."

Jack frowned, but he said nothing. He was better at this than she was. The whole ruse was all such a front in her head, the shock of him playing the part felt like a punch to the throat. There was no pretend to her rage, but it fed their story well. The charade.

Nothing more than her acting like she had any semblance of control and power, when she had so little of either.

"Now, care to explain why you didn't even *try* to react?" Vain squared Kallia with a sharp look. "What, were you scared? Don't be—"

"I'm not scared of you." Kallia didn't need it shoved back in her face. She wanted to reach for anger. For fury. For all the emotions that were easier to hold than this thing, rotting her from the inside.

Magic wasn't easy, but it was also something she'd never hesitated at. She never felt more in her element than during a trick, the moment when the music of magic swept ease and adrenaline over her. That second of freefall, before flying. Kallia only knew she was great because of the greatness magic made her feel—not just in terms of power, but in harmony with herself and everything around her.

Without that, Kallia was lost. And that was even worse than being in the dark.

"Not of me. Of messing up." Vain let out a snort. "I mean *you*. Don't be scared of getting it wrong or looking bad when you try—that's the point of practice. The more you fall, the less it hurts," she said. "And if you don't fall even once, you'll always be scared of it."

"You don't know me," Kallia bit out. "I'm not some fragile, careful—"

"Then prove it."

In a blink, the burning wooden spikes flared up between them again.

They darted at Kallia without warning.

Don't freeze.

She breathed.

Don't freeze.

She raised her hands at the tug inside, pulling back.

Don't—

At the small explosion, Kallia lowered her hands and looked down. No more spikes, just splinters blown everywhere by her feet.

No sight had ever been more beautiful; she could've cried from the triumph alone.

"See, they're still there. Not entirely useless," Vain muttered with a smug tilt of her head. "Oh, and I won."

Heat prickled beneath Kallia's skin. "What?"

The Diamond Ring's downward nod, not at the splintered burnt wood, was only victorious once her gaze reached Kallia's feet. She'd edged slightly just out of circle.

"*Stay* in your circle," she repeated. "Now, try to keep the illusion going this time."

A jagged fist-sized rock floated between them.

And they began again.

22

It was like walking out of a dream, when he exited the hospital building. And the first to wake him up the moment he stepped over the threshold was Lottie and the chaos that still wrapped around Glorian.

"Daron?" Lottie prompted. As if she'd asked him multiple times, with no response. "Where are you going? What happened?"

He could've asked the same of her, from her disheveled appearance. The dark knot of her hair flew apart in wild tendrils. Her prim tweed jacket, now dirtied and soot-smudged as her face. Somehow, she'd even managed to lose a shoe in the fray. No blood at least, which was about all he needed to see. "He told me nonsense."

"No, he didn't."

The mayor's drawings scratched in the back of his mind. If she knew where he was heading, she would stop him. Or worse, she would follow. "I don't know when I'm coming back, Lottie."

Lottie stared at him long and hard, and as another firework burst into the night, he thought he saw a glimmer of a tear at the edge of her eyes. "Be the one who comes back, please."

His throat knotted, and before he knew it, he had pulled her into a hug. Weeks ago, this seemed impossible. But now, he finally understood why Eva had befriended her.

Daron drew away without saying goodbye, because it was easier that way. Because at least that wasn't the last word said between them.

As he ventured through the town center, he marveled at what a battlefield it had become. Smoke rising, sparks flying. Flashes of white Patrons still being chased by fireworks, screams pitching high into the air. Daron covered his mouth with his sleeve against the swirling smoke. He knew this town well enough by now to walk through it with a blindfold and amused himself with the idea that when he'd first walked these streets, they didn't make sense to him. No street signs, no signs at all. Just buildings of different shapes sharing roads that only those who'd lived long enough in Glorian would know them.

It didn't take him long to quietly slink over to the entry gate of Glorian, the long stretch of road leading to the outside world.

"Daron?"

His heart clenched. He wondered if the Dire Woods had reached him already, before Aunt Cata limped into view a brief distance away. Between him and the gate, she somehow remained steadfast as ever in her pristine white uniform, marred with scorch marks and streaked with blood.

When she charged toward him, Daron ran.

It killed him, her crying out his name behind.

He did not look back. Not once.

His first steps out into the Dire Woods were hesitant, tentative.

He'd heard stories of what this forest could do to those alone and on foot. The only time he ever traveled through here was by horse carriage, and even that was enough to make him uneasy. The whispers still found him, even through the window.

They wrapped around him now like a snake coils around prey it intends to keep.

He didn't know where he was going, just walked forward. The mayor had given him no instructions or directions, just to go to the woods. And something about devils—

"Dare?"

His blood chilled at the figure approaching in the shadows passing. She wore her show costume, what she'd worn last time. "Eva?"

Her hands trailed from the trunk of one tree to the next as she moved. "Why haven't you found me yet, Dare?" she asked. "Are *you* lost, now?"

He turned around and could've sworn he'd taken just three steps from the gates of Glorian. But now, there was only a thick of dark trees behind him, Glorian nowhere in sight. As if he'd moved farther into the woods than he thought, or perhaps the woods had moved around him.

"Follow me," she said in the shadows.

"Why?" he asked, firm in the belief that this was not Eva. He was not so easily fooled. "Why should I?"

She didn't answer, but she got what she wanted because he followed either way. Afraid to lose sight of her for she was so obscured in the forest. A vision, a dream, leading him into the heart of a nightmare.

"Why did you stop looking for me?" she called over her shoulder. "Too busy looking for someone else, now?"

He was not answering it. He was not giving it the satisfaction of how deep the question sliced at his gut.

"You never tried this hard for me. I'm hurt." She sighed. "And I'm still lost. All because of you."

Daron couldn't even shut his eyes, so he stared down hard at his feet. "Shut up."

"You were supposed to find me," she whispered, the words touching his ears in a breeze. "And now you're too busy looking for her. It's like I'm nothing—"

"Stop it," he yelled, and she gave no reply. The entire woods quieted, in fact. Too quiet. Save for the splitting groan and crack of branches beyond him.

"DARON!"

His entire body seized. Aunt Cata.

Zarose, she'd followed him. Right into the Dire Woods. He took off running in the opposite direction, for she couldn't have been that far behind him. He heard her curse sharply, more branches breaking in the distance as though she were struggling to break free from them. "Get away from me!"

"Aunt Cata!" Daron yelled, both hands cupped around his mouth. "Keep talking, I'm—"

Lightning flashed around him, as though a storm hovered right over their heads. It was so bright, he caught nothing but the shadows of the spindly tree branches on the dirt ground before him, swaying in the wind. With each flash of lightning, longer than the next, it was like they formed a picture before his eyes.

"I told you not to, Daron," she said, coughing. "I told you not to go."

He followed the sound of her voice, grateful she was at least talking. "I'm sorry, but you wouldn't—"

His steps froze as another bout of lightning flashed, and something caught his eye in the shadowed branches across the ground. Not just branches, but something trapped within them. Branches vined around her wrists, holding them up while another entrapped her ankles and held her up like an offering.

Aunt Cata.

"*I* wouldn't listen?" Her form disappeared in the dark before another flash of lightning brought back her struggling form. "I'm trying to keep you safe."

"Where are you?" Daron shook his head, watching the shadows play against the ground. What was casting them? "Where are you?" he asked louder.

"I've always been trying to keep you safe. You're all I have left."

"Aunt Cata—" He tried running to the nearest trees, looking up to see if some illusion veiled what was really there.

"I can't lose you, too," she said weakly. In the next flash of light, he saw her form no longer thrashing, but sagging limply against the holds. "I can't—"

Her entire form bowed back as a branch brutally pierced through her gut. Another, through her chest. And another, and another.

The lightning was so blinding now, forcing him to see all of this.

He fell to his knees and covered his eyes, the wet seeping between his fingers. Blurring images and sounds he could not get out of his head.

Not real, he kept convincing himself. *Not real, not real, not real.*

"It's you."

Everything stilled at the voice. *Her* voice. The voice he'd been wanting to hear ever since she left. He almost didn't want to look up, afraid that, like everything, it was all a trick. An illusion.

A hand cupped his face and guided it up. His eyes devoured her as a breath broke from him. "Kallia."

"It's you." She smiled down at him sadly. "You found me."

She was all right. His heart pounded, taking her in. Every inch of her, moving, breathing, alive. Somehow the red of her lips shone brightly, matching a deep red gown that pooled behind her like scarlet moonlight. Like the jewels dripping off her neck, her gaze glittered. His heart was racing as he brought his hands to her waist, pressing his brow against her hip, unable to do more than just hold her tight. Keep her here with him.

Here. The word beat in time with his heart. Here, with me.

"But what if I didn't want to be found?"

One moment, he was holding her against him; and the next, there was nothing but air in his hands. His hands shook as his fingers curled into fists he pressed against the earth, anchoring himself to something, anything.

Whatever came next, he didn't know if he could take it. If what came next would be the thing to break him, entirely.

"Please," he whispered on a broken breath.

"You're wasting your time." Her voice carried on the wind. "What if I don't want you anymore, the way you still want me . . . the way you will *always* want me?"

Daron kept his focus on the ground, watching his own tears drip between his fingers.

"You did take my power, after all," she continued. "Why would I want you back?"

"He took mine, too." Eva's voice joined hers. "And he didn't even know."

"They never know." A collective disappointed sigh.

The sound of Aunt Cata's screams filled the air, of the wood breaking through her body and tearing her apart. Even as he covered his ears, he couldn't stop the sounds. The voices. All the questions he'd asked himself countless times, buried deep down even more, finding their way to the surface in these ghosts of his.

"Are you sure this is still what you want?"

When he looked up, Kallia sat high up in the tree, in a grotesque throne formed from its dying, blackened branches. Her dress draped over the trunk like dripping blood, rippling as she crossed her bare legs and straightened. She wore no crown, though she looked every bit a fearsome queen looking down upon him, her kneeling subject. "Only the willing and the wanting may enter."

It wasn't Kallia, he knew that now. Though his blood still scorched with hope every time he looked at her, painful as it was. "Enter where?"

She smiled, her red lips glaring. "The other side. It is a place below the surface, a place no one talks about," she said. "You're already halfway there."

That couldn't be. He hadn't walked more than a few yards, hadn't even been out here for that long. Though maybe that was the illusion. Maybe what had been mere steps to him had been miles, what had been seconds turned to hours.

The edges of his vision began to blacken from exhaustion, and he kept his hands against the ground to steady him. "Take me there."

"Even if she doesn't want you to come for her?" Her head cocked to the other side. "What could you do, anyway? Hardly any power, no friends, no idea what awaits you . . . those are not winning odds, Daron Demarco."

The Devils card in Ira's hand flashed in his mind.

He finally looked up at her, the false Kallia. "Please."

"Well." Her eyes gleamed. "Since you asked so nicely."

As his vision flickered and darkened, in and out, what he thought was exhaustion was actually shadows creeping in from the sides. They slithered in, eating the trees surrounding him and the moonlit sky above. Anything that marked this place to be the Dire Woods, for it didn't feel like the woods anymore. In fact, it didn't feel like a place he'd ever been in, where he was going now.

He tried to stand, but some invisible force kept him down, wary to let him go now that he'd given them so much.

Was this death, he wondered, as even the darkness began to darken, as he lost sight of everything but the vision before him.

The last thing that remained in his sight was Kallia, watching him from her throne without mercy in her eyes. Her lips held the barest hints of a smile, like watching a caged animal to see what it would do next.

The illusion collapsed as the edges of her vibrant red dress darkened to ash, the ground swallowing him up.

And with her name on his lips, everything went to black.

Vain had two rules when it came to dueling. In those few brutal hours, she drilled them into Kallia.

The first was to know the rules.

The second, to outsmart them.

And there were many ways to outsmart, as many as there were combinations of hands in a card game. The premise of the duel was so simple, but all the trappings around turned it into a complicated dance that demanded quick thinking.

The easiest rule was to stay in your circle. The tricky side came when determining which illusion came next, depending on the rule established at the start of the match.

"Let's go over another rule . . ." Jack was perched outside the window, legs hanging over the ledge. His voice, miraculously, clear as ever despite the street music that never ended. The ledge was now all the free space left in her room, since they returned to find it bursting with flowers and gift baskets and tokens for good luck. It turned the common room into a jungle of oddities and beauties and best wishes from the people of the city who would be watching tonight, knowing she had no chance of winning.

"Nothing airborne," Jack continued. "What can you do?"

"Water," Kallia readily answered from behind the changing screen.

"I turn that to ice."

"Then I make ice into iron."

"And if I melt that iron—"

"Burning tar." Kallia could see why Vain enjoyed that part of the duel the most. It was as much an exercise in concentration as it was a sharp mind game. Rules have ranged from nothing metal to everything must be the color yellow. Nothing repeated. And nothing was slow.

Vain barely pushed Kallia to use any power during their brief session, if only to save what she could for whichever Red Death Duke she'd soon be facing. Judging by her observation of them at their earlier meal, the fight would most likely resemble going up against a drunken bear.

Even then, according to Vain, those odds were still far better than hers.

"Just remember, they'll play by your rule but probably only on a technicality," Jack continued, the most focused she'd ever seen him. "Be ready for them to strike."

Once Vain had left them after training, Jack hadn't stopped quizzing her. And Kallia kept answering. She couldn't tell if it was cruel or kind of him to treat her like she stood any chance. But regardless of who he was, his advice was always valuable. It was just one of a few reasons why she could stand to let him into her room now while she prepared, in the first place.

"Let's say the rule is only things that could be found in a forest," he began, deep in thought. "And I start off with—"

"What did you think of Roth's plan?"

The weight of the meal had grown heavier and heavier on Kallia's shoulders as the day continued. It had to be the same for Jack. And as expected, the effect the words had was instant.

"Are you sure you want to talk about that now?" Jack glanced over his shoulder. "Especially before your—"

"The duel doesn't matter." She shook her head, knowing what a lie that was. If by some miracle she won, that would be all that mattered. But by and far, it was not the priority. "Roth is using tonight to announce his plans, and it's all going to burn like wildfire from there."

"He's adept at winning crowds, that's for sure. Even if it gets them cheering for their doom."

Kallia dabbed more rouge over her lips, slower this time. "You really think it could all happen again like last time?"

They both tensed at the idea. The secondhand account was warning enough for Kallia, but if Jack had seen what the devils did before, he knew that horror. And he knew exactly what Roth was capable of.

"I'm not sure, but I wouldn't put it past him," Jack said, a troubled note entering his voice. "It will take *a lot* of magic to saturate the air and blur those lines enough to reveal the gate in the first place."

"That won't take long." This Glorian was overflowing with power. Too much. She was surprised Zarose Gate wasn't already waiting just outside. "That's why I'm here in the first place."

"Why?"

"It's the only way someone like me can leave," she said. "The only way back."

That was, if she even made it. The gate's design was the perfect trap. A guaranteed tool to keep both sides separate, a way out with no way out. And only Roth would be the kind willing to risk one world for another.

"We'll . . ." A strained pause, as Jack pulled his legs back from over the ledge and turned. "We'll find another way."

He'd already said before there was no other way. To suggest otherwise was just foolish hope. "You're powerful, but even you have limits," she said. "However, you can also leave any time you'd like."

The reminder was for Jack as much as it was for her, but he said nothing. There was no reason he had to subject himself to a place he hated, where its people hated him in turn. He had a choice. And if their roles were reversed, she wouldn't hesitate.

If he decided the same for himself one day, where would that leave her?

Kallia glanced in the mirror, one last look at how she appeared in the outfit that had been laid out for her when she first strode back into the room. The shimmery, embroidered purple show jacket she wore now caught the light like jewels and sported a daring plunge. It was the flashiest piece of her attire, paired with dark pants and boots for easy movement. A surprisingly practical outfit for this world, but a duel warranted it.

Her eyes shut as she breathed, every inhale and exhale centering her more and more. Silencing all the world around her, clearing everything inside her. The routine grounded her now as it always had before every set.

So that when Kallia opened her eyes, she saw nothing but a dazzling magician in the reflection, ready to go out to perform.

It was so easy to feel powerful when you looked it, Kallia almost deceived herself.

"My friends," the Dealer's voice boomed from the center of the floor as he looked out into the crowd around him. "Welcome to a duel you'll never forget!"

Everyone in the Court of Mirrors roared and stomped their feet in such thunderous approval, Kallia worried the mirrors might shake off the walls. Their surfaces still glinted with glimpses of the true side— girls puckering their lips as they readied themselves for a night out, stolen kisses in some darkened bathroom, many figures rising for the start of the day or preparing for bed.

Tonight, nobody came to watch the mirrors.

"We have a *very* special announcement at the match's end," Roth teased, the spotlight following his steps across the empty ballroom floor. "Let's see a show of hands . . ." His grin widened. "Who will be staying until the end to hear it?"

The hint had everyone throwing their fists high into the air.

Kallia's eyes darted to Jack's, just as unsurprised by the reaction. Neither of them needed to stay until the end to know how the city would receive the show in the works. Roth already had them all firmly in the palm of his hands from the moment he opened the Court for a duel that night.

While Roth continued his opening statement, the Red Death Dukes formed a huddle as one giant red mass on the opposite end of the floor. They truly were an army, about six or seven magicians of similar brawny build, all looking nearly identical in their uniforms. By the time Kallia and Jack entered the arena, they'd already been practicing across the floor. Quick physical drills and exercises, interspersed with tricks to make for a sprawling preshow across the ballroom, keeping the early audience members satisfied.

"Zarose, all the ways I would drag them across the floor." Vain sighed, watching the huddled men through slitted eyes.

Kallia was nearly tempted to give her the slot, just to see it happen.

Not long after Jack and Kallia entered the Court of Mirrors, the Diamond Rings arrived by their side. More out of pity than support. Or necessity, when it came to Vain. Stone-cold as usual, she had no words of luck or assurances for Kallia.

"Truthfully, it'll be a miracle if you even make it past the first illusion," she said, clapping Kallia hard on the shoulder. "So aim for that."

Half-hearted applause came from Malice. "Inspiring words of encouragement."

"Seriously." Ruthless shook her head at them before patting the back of Kallia's hand. "Don't worry, darling. You'll be fabulous."

At least one person thought so.

"On this end, we have Filip d'Chane from our very own daredevils, the Red Death Dukes!" Roth grandly gestured over to the red team that had broken out of their huddle and whooped along with the spectators. They all thumped Filip in the back as he made his way to the front, grinning and waving in all the directions to catch all the applause he could.

"And now, we have a new contender in our midst . . ." With the low drop of his voice, the Court of Mirrors hushed. "You know her as the star of the mirrors, and now you'll see that shining star in action—let's welcome to the dueling grounds, Kallia Alastor!"

The applause was louder than any Kallia had ever received, but all she could hear was the name ringing in her head.

Kallia Alastor.

In one breath, she was given a family, a history, a past.

Everything her first name alone had none of.

"What are you waiting for?"

Vain's sniping question came with a small shove in the arm. "Just remember: no matter how horrendously you fail, it's not the worst thing that can happen to a magician."

"Is that supposed to be comforting?"

"It can be. But you have nothing to lose in losing tonight, since you already got your place here handed to you on a silver platter," she said. "Time to finally fight for it."

She pushed Kallia out onto the floor. Filip stretched out his arms in preparation, just outside his circle marked on the ground. A few paces apart, with the small anchor sitting in the middle, marked the distance where Kallia's circle awaited.

On the way, Roth intercepted her with a beaming smile. "Excellent turnout tonight, I must say!" He gave a warm press to her arm. "How is my star feeling tonight? Ready to fight?"

Kallia found herself preferring Vain's shoves over Roth's gentle touches. "I'm definitely ready for something," she said with a smile.

"Oh, don't be nervous. I know this is all very sudden, and your magic is not quite where we want it yet," he said. "But think of what an opportunity like this might do for you. It could be just the thing to spark something."

Every hope that hardened his voice was not for Kallia in the slightest. If launching her into the sky of devils was the instant trick to returning her powers back in full force, he would do so in a heartbeat without any remorse.

Whenever he looked at her, even now, all he would ever see was a power that could be.

"Maybe." Kallia fought back a grimace as the man kissed her on the cheek before coyly edging off the floor to find his seat. It took everything in her not to wipe off the touch imprinted with cologne and the rub of stubble with the back of her hand.

She still had a show to perform.

"Any day now, fancy meat," Filip called out from his circle, arms crossed. His fellow Red Death Dukes farther down on his end let out a round of *oob*s as if he'd just thrown out the best joke they'd ever heard in their lives.

On the off chance her powers did return tonight, Kallia knew exactly which magicians she'd be taking down first.

"What's the rule?"

"Oh that's precious, you even know how to play!" he exclaimed with mock-astonishment. "I'm a gentleman first, so I'll let the rule go to you. Don't think too hard, now."

Unsmiling, Kallia asked, "Are you going to keep talking, or are we going to establish a rule?"

"Pushy, pushy." Filip tutted. "I'm a gentleman first, so I'll let the rule go to you. Don't think too hard, now."

He was giving her the power. A pity move, more than anything. But still, likely the only upper hand she'd have in this duel.

Kallia shot a look over her shoulder. The Diamond Rings remained exactly where she'd sat before, with Ruthless gripping Malice's hands nervously while Vain took out a daggerlike file for her fingernails.

A thrum of panic went through her when she lost sight of Jack for a moment, but he stood off against the walls. Partly shadowed, most likely to stay out of her war path once the duel started.

If he so much as tried to interfere at any point, it would only make her look weaker.

From his subtle nod for luck, it became clear what rule she had to pick. Vain preferred rules that were more like riddles to confuse the opponent and play with their mind. Whereas Jack believed a good fighter knew when to use the weapon, or take it away.

"Nothing that'll draw blood," Kallia called out. "That's my rule."

A wave of loud boos erupted from the Red Death Dukes, joined by a few protests and groans scattered throughout the Court of Mirrors.

The signature brutality of the Red Death Dukes was clearly the crowd pleaser in any of their shows or duels. If they thrived on taking their opponents down painfully, she would not give them the satisfaction of seeing her bleed.

Filip scoffed, as if his favorite toy had just been taken away. "Shame. You'd look even better with a little more red on you."

"You have no idea." Kallia took her position, back turned until the dueling bell sounded. A smile curled at the corners of her lips as an old feeling coursed through her once she looked down at her boots over the marble floor. They reminded her of all the times she took one last moment to feel the stage beneath her feet.

Hellfire House had prepared her well for this.

Whenever she'd step off that chandelier and made contact with the dance floor, she saw all the patrons lined at the sides around her, watching and raising their glasses in cheer. Not like her acts in Spectaculore, a stage that raised its performers like gods giving a show for the mortals below.

The stage was more intimate because everyone stood upon it.

Kallia let that energy wash over her as more applause rained over them. She'd almost forgotten what it was like to hear her name chanted, hands clapping just for her. And from the looks of those around them, this had to be the most thrilling match to come by in a long time. A taste of something new, unpredictable.

The dueling bell rang again.

Kallia whirled around, her heart racing.

The anchor disappeared from the center.

Don't freeze.

She braced herself as Filip cast first, raising both arms high above his head like a bear about to attack. When he dropped them, a harsh gust of wind tore at her. If she hadn't planted her feet firmly before, the sheer force of it would've made her stumble backward. Out of her circle.

Kallia would not go down that easily.

Don't freeze.

The wind wrapped all around her, howling over the audience.

Pulling her down.

Don't freeze.

Kallia pushed back, astonished as the wind spun in her hand like threads she could pull.

Keep the illusion going, Vain's unrelenting voice barked in her ear as her own clock started. If the bell rang again, she would lose. She couldn't hesitate. She had to try.

Magic on the other side was a different beast. More reflex than thought, a storm without warning. Kallia gripped at those threads the wind had given her. Soon enough, they solidified in her palms, burning hot as a flame.

When she thrust them out, they shattered through the air over his head like fireworks.

The shower of light earned scattered cries of amazement. Even Kallia had to cover her mouth to keep the joyous shriek from bubbling out.

She hadn't frozen. She hadn't hesitated.

And her magic was finally answering her back.

The timer barely started for Filip as he rolled his eyes at the display, watching the sparks fall to the ground with his hand outstretched. They never fizzled out; they brightened and moved at his command, gathering in his palm like a long, sharp tail that grazed the ground.

Kallia barely had time to duck before he wielded the sparks like a whip—

A burn cracked against her face.

The cheers were deafening as Kallia fought to keep standing and cupped her throbbing cheek. Inside, she screamed at the excruciating bite of pain. All it left was a line of a scar on her skin, but no blood. Just the scalding mark of a burn.

There was barely time to recover before Filip thrust the fiery whip forward again. And again, and again. Kallia did all she could to stay within the ring, ducking and dodging as the sharp tongue sailed past her shoulder. She couldn't move far as he aimed lower.

When the whip struck at her leg, it tore through the fabric and seared straight into skin.

Her whole body tightened with a scream she pushed down. Even if she let it out, the roar of the audience would've drowned her out.

Filip cupped his ear to them, egging them on to holler even louder as he reared back the whip once more.

On shaky breath, Kallia saw it coming. The heat lanced right against her brow—another stab of fire—which she snatched before it retreated.

Her palms screamed at the burn as she yanked the whip out of his hands with a strength that surprised even her. The pain passed her nerves, numb to the adrenaline now as she ripped the blazing whip apart into different pieces.

As they hit the ground like limp pieces of rope, they reminded her of snakes.

So they slithered, lethal and swift, toward Filip.

Kallia planted her hands at her knees, a brief respite while he conjured next. Her breath grew more and more labored while her heart pounded as though it could smash right out of her chest. Sweat dripped down her neck. Her thoughts swirled.

Whatever magic she had left in her, she couldn't feel it anymore.

Couldn't feel anything.

When the next cold hit, it caught her hard in the jaw. She felt a crack in the bone, tasted blood against her teeth. It didn't stop once the next large rock struck her shoulder. Then the other.

The next slammed her gut.

Again and again, the rocks came at her. Relentless, never-ending, leaving no inch of her unbruised.

"Look how she bows," her opponent crowed. "How gracefully she accepts defeat!"

Kallia swayed, realizing the curves of her circle no longer surrounded her. They were far out of reach. Somehow, she'd staggered out and fallen to one knee.

The resounding laughter burned over her skin, but the disappointed frowns were worse. Thankfully the pain had reached a point beyond sensation, that she no longer felt anything. Not embarrassment or shame or humiliation. Nothing.

She fought for breath as she grew sleepier. And sleepier.

Get up, Kallia.

No matter how many times she begged, her body would not obey.

Because Kallia had gone deathly still the moment she looked up and saw Aaros.

He stood at the front of the sidelines, his dark eyes awash in pity as he shook his head slowly in disgust.

Kallia reached out a shaky hand, his name a hoarse whisper that died in her throat at the next hard blow to her ribs. It knocked her over onto the cold ground, sweeping relief across her body. She could rest. Finally.

She smiled at all the familiar faces she found across the floor.

Erasmus dressed all in red, pointing right at her in laughter.

A solemn Lottie, watching on with disinterest before throwing back her drink in one gulp.

Aaros appeared again. Juno. Canary. All of the Conquerors, by some miracle.

They were here.

Kallia's vision began to swirl as she looked for one more face, searching and searching and searching—

And found in the mirrors a glimpse of fire.

Glorian, burning to the ground. Before darkness stole her away.

Her eyes drifted open to the blur of night green and gentle white. Leaves and moonlight. The glow of the finest colors, soft as petals fallen.

"It's for you."

Kallia smiled, utterly boneless. The air was warm and sweet, just like a dream. "What?"

"It was supposed to be for you when you won."

Impossible. The duel had been blow after blow, the pain never-ending. Even when she'd stopped to take a breath, the breathing hurt from all the bruising. All the bones that had broken too fast to even feel it.

She could breathe now, seamless and easy.

"I didn't know what else I could give you."

Kallia went still.

Every thought, silent.

". . . until I stumbled upon this broken greenhouse one day."

His voice.

She waited to hear it again, searched for it in the dark. Soon enough, the room sharpened into focus, movement teasing at the corners of her eyes—belonging to the figure now stepping in from the dark. Shadowed and soft-eyed, just as she remembered.

Her heart ached to the start of the song, faint at first. Familiar as it thrummed through the old glass that formed the walls and ceiling.

What came next?

It felt like a dance itself, recalling the steps that kept it moving. That kept her in it.

Content, Kallia watched the tawny-skinned hand that hung at his side. So warm and close, real and alive.

The moment she reached for it was her first mistake.

Like ink thrown over the walls, the dream bled. It took the moon and the greenhouse, the music falling away on a cold wind.

The hand she reached for, gone.

Wake up, Kallia.

Another voice called as the glass walls crumbled and the warm air became ice.

Kallia flinched awake at the cold slicing her skin. Wind howling at her ears, blending into screams and laughter ever-present in the night. This wasn't the greenhouse, nor the Court of Mirrors where her opponent's taunts echoed at her from across. It had all been like a nightmare, like peering into a dirty, cracked reflection of one of the mirrors above her.

One that framed a Glorian, burning from within.

The image forced her up, her heart thrashing as she braced herself for that drowning wave of pain.

When it never arrived, Kallia blinked rapidly and pressed down all over her clothes. She found rips and tears from every hit the duel had left, but there was no pain. No scars, not even blood.

That couldn't be.

She'd felt *everything* in a way that made nightmares look like dreams.

The moment movement caught her eye, Kallia jerked. Over a short expanse of crumbled wall a few paces over, jagged as mountain edges, Jack paced furiously on the other side.

Something in her snapped at his presence. "Were you just in my head?"

At her voice, Jack's head whipped in her direction. Awash with relief, his face fell almost instantly at whatever he saw in hers. "What? No, I've been trying to help you."

Help. Whatever that entailed, whatever he had to do, Kallia didn't want to know. Not now. She shoved it all away with the hard shake of her head. "Never mind. I need to go back."

"Back?"

"To the Court of Mirrors. I saw something that looked like . . ." Her breath shook. She'd never felt this way, like every nerve in her could burst at once if she didn't go now. Whether it was panic or intuition, something wasn't right.

Alarm blazed in Jack's eyes as he studied her. "You fell under fast, Kallia." He stopped her gently, unsurely, by both shoulders. "Anything that seemed out of the ordinary, probably wasn't—"

"I *know* what I saw." Her teeth pressed hard into each other. "Just because you didn't doesn't mean it wasn't real."

Her imagination was nowhere near twisted enough to provide a glimpse such as that.

Until she remembered all the faces.

Those she'd seen at the match, ever since she'd arrived in this city. Faces of people in the same Glorian that burned, who couldn't possibly be anywhere near her at that moment.

But if mirrors reflected what was real, could they lie?

"Something's wrong." Some alarm had triggered, pulsing in the back of her head. She had to make sure; it wouldn't quiet until she did. "I don't know what, but they're in trouble. I have to go."

Kallia made it one step, when a hand suddenly latched onto her elbow.

"Who's in—wait, *what*?" A cord strained and beat against Jack's neck. "You can't be serious. You can't go back there after that duel. It's too dangerous."

Glaring down at his hand, Kallia threw it off and shouldered past him. "You're giving *me* orders now?"

"No, a warning." Jack kept steadily at her side. "I wouldn't be surprised if someone tried dragging you back into another match for the fun of it."

"Probably to make up for the one you pulled me out of," she fumed and twisted away from him, her skin burning. Blood, boiling. "I told you, Jack. Many times. You were not to interfere under any circumstances."

"Are you suggesting I should've just *left* you there?"

Irrational. That's how Kallia felt when it was phrased like that. There was no use arguing about it now. It was done, the duel was over, and she was alive. If anything, she should've been more grateful he'd decided to step in.

"You were hardly conscious, Kallia." His voice hardened behind her. "I couldn't just stand there and watch—"

"Yes, you could've, because I asked you to." Kallia whirled around in a rage that wouldn't let her go. "I told you, over and over again. The rules were clear."

"The *rules*?" Jack choked on the word. "The duel was already over and the idiot kept tearing you apart like a rag doll. You think the crowd was going to stop him? As your *guard*, I did what I was supposed to do."

"And as *my* guard, you're supposed to follow *my* orders." Every tense breath razed up her throat. "Not make me look even weaker and more powerless to this world."

"Why does it matter so much what strangers think?"

Her face burned at the quiet following his question, the way his gaze narrowed and lingered on her without any shame until she turned away. Whatever he was searching for, she didn't want him to see.

"The more you keep giving power to weakness, the faster it'll consume you," he said. "What others believe will never change that."

He wasn't wrong, but he would never understand. How could he, when he'd never know powerlessness or *anything* of the like? A magician molded purely from beings such as the devils, who cleared paths whenever he walked through crowds, couldn't comprehend such weakness as this. And all the ways it kept breaking a person, long after the fall.

"What others believe is how *we* look to the world." Kallia gestured sharply between them with shaking hands. "What others believe is the only reason we can even be like this. The moment you start acting rogue, how is that going to look to Roth? To everyone else?"

Theirs was a fragile balancing act that relied on remaining the picture of punishment and obedience. Concern was irrelevant. Emotions, too risky. One look at the wrong second was damning enough. If anyone realized Jack could break free from the leash she claimed to have around him, it was over. Her defeat against Filip was only made more humiliating with Jack swooping in to carry her to safety. But it would've been absolutely for nothing if someone began to question.

"I wasn't exactly thinking of them when you hit the ground," he said through gritted teeth. "You could hardly move, that's how bad the pain was."

The rage trickled back into her blood. Slow, and simmering.

"You don't get to decide how bad anything is for me, Jack. You don't know what I can handle," she said. "I'm not fragile. I can take pain. And as you've shown, even that can easily go away." She gestured down at her jacket, battered without any scars to prove it. "But suspicion stays. And in worst cases, it grows."

Not even he could deny it, and a tense muscle ticked along his jaw in realization. "Fine. But there's no reason for things to ever go that far again," he muttered. "You can't defend yourself in the sort of state you're in, and they *know* it. How weak you still—"

The drop to abrupt silence turned Kallia hard as ice.

Not once had he ever called her weak to her face. Nor made her feel lowlier than him in any regard, despite the power he possessed. Until now.

"Go on," she muttered. "You're not wrong."

"I didn't . . ." Jack dragged a hand down his face. "I didn't mean it like that."

Another lie, just like his others, though this one was harder to stomach.

Still, Kallia didn't cover her face, didn't hide. Didn't break. That, at least, she could control, and there was no time for it now. Not with Glorian burning in the back of her mind like an omen. "I have to go."

She needed to be alone, away from this.

And yet every time she moved forward, Jack moved, too. As she sidestepped him, he simply blocked her path. Boxing her in, as one would herd sheep.

"Jack, if you don't let me go," Kallia said hoarsely after a hard shove at his chest. "I swear, I'll—"

The threat died. There was nothing she could do, and he knew it. He *used* it, just like he always would.

Heat scalded the backs of her eyes at the knowledge, and she closed them. Dropped her hands to wrap them around herself. "If you won't let me leave . . . then please, just go."

"*Go?* And leave you out here alone like this?"

The subtle break in his voice tugged a cord in her. He knew very well what she meant. Without him in her sight, she heard what his face so often hid—an uncertainty tucked away in the corners of the most rare and powerful being to walk beside her. A piece of the magician, reigning over the illusion.

A piece wasn't enough to trust someone entirely.

"This isn't working." Kallia finally released a hard, steady breath. "I want you to—"

A thunderous blast cracked in the air.

She jerked back at the impact. The wind flared through her hair. A shower of splinters rained over her, and her alone.

Jack was gone. Nowhere around her.

"He'll materialize again just fine, don't worry."

Kallia snapped around at the drawl. Movement stirred from behind, within the tattered curtain hanging over an enormous torn canvas painting a few paces away. Large as a door, the drab portrait had long lost its face as it leaned against the remnants of wall like it hadn't moved in ages.

Not until the thornlike tips of green nails emerged from behind, before the whole frame fell over like the grand reveal in a stage show.

"Did you . . ." Kallia's wide eyes darted from where Jack once was to where Vain now stood, looking every bit like an illusion herself. "Did you just—"

"Catch your guard off guard?" The girl could not be more smug. "Didn't think that would work, but I do believe so."

"W-Why?" Kallia still couldn't fathom it. Since his fight with the devils, no one had raised a hand against Jack. For a while, Kallia wondered if anyone even could. That was, if anyone would ever dare try. "What are you even doing here?"

"This was *my* dump first," Vain deadpanned as she kicked away at whatever debris lay on her path. "And who are you to point fingers, mortal? When *I* just heard the most interesting conversation take place that's illuminated quite a bit."

Kallia tensed as the girl walked around her now the way crows circled the dead. From where Vain had hidden, it was the perfect vantage point. Well within earshot.

And her smile only grew more smug with the secrets it now knew. "You *really* should be more careful, mortal. I doubt Roth would find it as amusing to know his bright little star is running behind his back with her obliterated monster toy."

"I don't know what you mean."

Vain's sleek brow arched so high, the sheer mask she wore shifted. "Your lies could really use some work, mortal." She chuckled. "Don't waste your breath. I know everything."

Unwavering, Kallia tracked the Diamond Ring's slow, deliberate gait, her heart sinking with every step. Even at its furious pace, Kallia felt it drop like a rock, deeper in her chest, falling and falling and falling.

It was over.

Her one chance at the true side, gone in a moment. She didn't fool herself. One person knowing was all it took. The fact that that someone had to be Vain was an especially cruel form of torture.

At the explosive crack above, a trill of delight erupted from the girl, echoing the faraway shrieks from the streets. The sky went bright over their heads, streaming sparks that lit up the deviled night. An immense shape began taking form as more joined, though it was too early to tell. Not that Kallia could take in any of the revelry.

Vain had no such problem enjoying herself. "Lucky for you,

everyone's a bit too busy at the moment for me to call the cavalry on you." Her voice raised over the ghostly echoes of cheers, the lights still bursting overhead. "Nothing salvages a show cut short better than another party in the works."

The Show of Hands.

She'd known it was coming, and somehow, it was all still happening so fast. "And yet you chose to follow us instead?"

"Again, this is *my* spot." Vain bristled. "Technically, you intruded first."

Kallia couldn't understand what the girl was playing at. She should've been gleefully sounding the alarm, setting every magician on Kallia like the fresh meat she was to them. Perhaps it was overconfidence, or more time to gloat. Yet she didn't even indulge in *that*.

"The streets are so chaotic right now." Vain yawned despite the madness raging on around them. None of the usual aimless rhythm of celebration—this excitement was palpable. Alive and rare.

"One could practically go unnoticed in the crowds, if they weren't sloppy about it."

Kallia blinked hard.

Waited a breath. A beat.

"It won't take your devil long to return," Vain added, her face still tipped up to the sky to the lights swirling above. "So if you want to go find what you're looking for, now's your chance."

Now she *had* to be hallucinating. Or it was some kind of trap. Both flipped in her mind like a coin that wouldn't settle on one or the other. "What are you—"

By the time Kallia twisted around, Vain was gone.

Her figure retreated farther away to the burnt edges of the Ranza Estate, without so much as a threat or glare back to ensure Kallia followed.

She was letting her go. Just like that.

Whatever force drove Kallia next had to be stupidity, because she sprinted. Over wreckage and burnt wood, she staggered as quickly as she could to catch up.

"You're . . . helping me." Closing in, her frantic breaths made the question sound even more ludicrous. "Why are you helping me?"

"Why are you *following* me?" Grumbling, Vain charged on. "The streets won't be this insufferable forever, and I really don't want to be here when your clubkeeper regenerates. So just go to the Court of Mirrors and leave me be."

"Not until you tell me why." The more she tried to shake her off, the more Kallia refused to be shaken. A headliner who had shown her nothing but malice ever since she arrived had no reason to let anyone go unless she got something out of it.

"Zarose, do you ever stop?" When all else failed, Vain resorted to forcibly shoving her away until Kallia lost balance over a piece of wreckage. The ground shook before she even hit the ground. A violent, ominous rumble—met with Vain's harsh curse.

And Jack, standing right behind her.

"Answer." His hands wrapped around her neck. His eyes, positively murderous. "Because I'm curious to hear it, too."

"Great." Vain stiffened slightly. More in discomfort than paralyzed by fear as she threw a pointed glare Kallia's way as if to say, *I told you so.* "Would you mind calling off your brute?"

"So you can lead her to the wolves?" The warning was already poised on Kallia's tongue, but her mind had blanked entirely.

Jack.

Like his fight with the devils, seeing him again whole and alive as before, slammed the strangest relief against the sharpest dread. Especially when he and Vain looked about as placid as serpents battling for dominion in the pit.

"If you didn't notice, I wasn't bothering her," Vain sniped back at him. "I was actually trying to go my own way."

"Right." Jack scowled. "Because headliners are *so* well-known for their mercy."

"As if you're any different." Her scoff was a harsh sound. "At least I gave her a chance to go see her burning city or whatever delusion she's so worked up about. Something which *you* clearly couldn't—"

"I never mentioned seeing a burning city." Kallia's ears roared as every thought went slow. "How did you know when I never mentioned it at all?"

She was certain of it. Even more so in the silence that roared between them after, louder than the fireworks above. Lights ribboned over all of their faces. Except for the one whose bored gaze was fixed ahead as her shoulders dropped. "Just a guess."

"A very specific one." Kallia shivered as she rose back to her feet. Not even Jack had known, which was more than clear from the tightness of his expression.

"You're not the only one who can see, mortal." Vain shrugged. "We can all see whatever the mirrors show."

"And yet of all of them, you remembered *that* one?"

As she said it, there was something familiar about Vain's eyes, just then. The way they closed off and turned to stone, at will. Like someone she knew.

There was no talking her way out this time.

"Maybe I'll remember a little more without him around or his hands on me." Nodding her head back, Vain released a long, exasperated sigh. "I'm probably better company, anyway."

"Is this a joke to you?" Jack's sneer deepened. "Do you really think it's a good idea to try negotiating right now?"

"Even I have my lines and limits, guard," Vain shot back. "Your strings may be cut, but maybe that's an illusion, too. I'm not risking anything in case your devil brethren decide to call you back to the fold."

His brow hardened, his hold still around the girl's neck. "I can feel her pulse, racing at a liar's pace." He glanced at Kallia. "Don't listen to her."

"As if your lies weren't what brought her here in the—"

"Both of you, shut *up*." The throbbing at Kallia's temple sharpened at their voices, tugging at her back and forth, back and forth. One, she hardly knew. Another, she knew too well. Together, it was like playing catch with a double-edged sword, both ends equally lethal.

"Or I could find out exactly what she's hiding now . . ." Jack trailed off, deep in thought all of a sudden. "Then take her memory of tonight, and be done with this."

Kallia's blood went cold.

He wouldn't.

Only then did Vain's mask shatter as she began thrashing, kicking out wildly. "Don't you *fucking* dare—" She clawed at his grip, slashed at his skin. "Get off me!"

"*Jack,*" Kallia barked immediately, unthinking. Desperately sick to her stomach from Vain's cries, and the truth.

For the first time, she saw Jack as the others did. Any time he walked into a room or down the street, the people parted to escape his notice. Not for any horror he'd inflicted before, but the potential for it to come at any given moment should he snap. That unknown stood right before her: a magician with all the power and freedom to become a monster.

Blood roaring in her ears, Kallia couldn't unsee it. Not as Jack's hold persisted on Vain, as he ignored the call of his name.

Swallowing hard, she reached down for what she could. A rock, a brick, anything sharp—

Before hitting the ground as Vain fell against her.

Jack stood over them, his expression unreadable and thunderous beneath. The eye of a storm, keeping itself in place.

"If I find out you're lying, headliner," he said hoarsely. "Next time, I won't hesitate."

When he lingered, Kallia thought he might say more. She hoped to hear it, as he faltered a step back, blinking warily in her direction.

But in just another step, he was gone. Vanished into the night.

All so sudden, Kallia searched all around. She couldn't trust quiet completely. Couldn't believe he'd actually left her alone, for once.

"Despite what he claims, I'm *not* lying."

Standing up on her own, the headliner smoothed the swoop of her bang. "I'm not here to throw you in Roth's cage just because you don't want to be his personal power pet."

"Why?" Jack's suspicions were not unfounded, aligning with Kallia's from this city had shown her. No one in a world like this was ever kind or merciful without reason. "Because for someone who's a headliner, that doesn't exactly line up."

"I'm allowed to have opinions." A shrug. "Being a headliner doesn't make me a slave to the Dealer."

"Everyone here sure acts like it."

Vain held up a hand, baring the black triangles across her knuckles. "For a gig like this, yes. People would do a little dance and lick the bottom of every shoe he owns if it made him happy."

"Then why are you doing this?" Kallia demanded, tired. "*Any* of this?"

The tense pause went on a beat too long. "But anyone with a brain can see that the last thing we should ever do for both sides is summoning that gate. Zarose knows what fully breaking it open would do to the true side."

The blood rushed so forcefully to Kallia's head, she almost swayed. The Vain who'd spoken now clashed with the Vain she recalled delighting over the opposite. "You care about the true side? What for?"

"Do you think we all just randomly sprouted up from the ground?" Vain squared her with a puzzled look. "We were all called here from the true side to fall down the mirror. But the longer you stay, the more difficult it is to remember. The easier it becomes to not want to. I remember shit about my old life, but that doesn't mean those people deserve any of this coming through again."

"What do you mean *again*?"

"Any disaster that comes with that gate," Vain said. "Why do you think Zarose made one the first time like he did? To seal volatile magic in, or keep whatever caused it from ever getting out?"

The devils. The accusation was clear, every question a jolt to Kallia's pulse.

There was no logic there, either. A king that tore down his own kingdom was no king at all. Just an ordinary man, which Roth refused to be. "All Roth wanted was magic, and he got what he wanted. He wouldn't just destroy everything he built."

"Not unless it came with the terms of the deal," Vain said. "There's a reason only certain kinds of magicians get dropped here. Anyone without magic would probably feel like they're trying to breathe underwater. You can't just grow gills. Someone needs to give them to you first, and that someone would demand a price."

Never piss off a magician who's made deals with the devils . . .

It all brought Kallia back to that talk with Roth in his study. All those warnings Jack passed on. The devils rarely ever parted with their magic, and turning a man into a magician sounded like an impossible order. But making an illusion into one as well? The price of two impossibilities could only come at the cost of so much more.

"When the stories we're told have been twisted so many times, we rely on intuition," Vain said. "And the way I see it, there's a reason why these sides have been kept separate by that gate. We've already seen what reaches out from the cracks alone."

All Kallia could think of was her magic and Demarco's, and no doubt the other magicians scattered across Soltair whose powers turned into such an inexplicable force. She thought of the Dire Woods and its slow, conquering ruin over the land. All of the magicians who slipped into this world, disappeared without a trace in the other.

A tide of panic coursed through her at the thought of Glorian, burning in the mirror.

"You saw what I saw in the mirror," Kallia whispered, brow drawn. "Is that the work of the devils, too?"

A grim frown sealed over Vain's lips. "Possibly. I don't know. What's reflected isn't always as it seems," she said, looking up at the sky still streaming with lights. "But if we go now, perhaps you can find out."

"We?"

"We want the same thing, and you need my help for it," Vain asserted. "And you'd be damned foolish lying to yourself and pretending you don't need any help at all when clearly, you do."

With that, she strode off for the edge of the estate, taking the lead without hesitation. Kallia ran just to meet her pace, but something held her behind. A ringing in her ears that would not leave—

Until her steps stopped entirely.

A figure waited in the shadows a few paces past them. Faint in the dark, the sturdy set of his shoulders paired with the height was a familiar frame. One that followed and haunted, when she needed him gone most.

No, not now. Her heart lurched as she blinked hard. *Please just go.*

Or for once, be real.

"What is it?"

Vain's impatient huff snapped her eyes wide open. The headliner shot a questioning glance over her shoulder, oblivious to the shadow still waiting for Kallia to pass by, to haunt her alone.

Seeing him, *any* of them, it hurt too much—that pinprick of joy, with a cutting realization: it wasn't him. It would never *be* him.

Because he was in Glorian, the one burning in the mirror. And there was nothing they could do about it.

"Even if it's true, we can't stop it." Kallia's whisper had gone cold. "Not from here."

Vain crossed her arms, tapping her fingers restlessly. "So you're just going to give up without knowing? Hope everything is safe and fine over there?"

"I'm *not* giving up," Kallia fired back, that rage returning. The fact that they were on the other side meant they couldn't leave, couldn't warn, couldn't reach those they saw. "But we can't do anything from where we are. Unless you have any bright ideas, why the hell are you so—"

The next explosion high into the night cut her off, forcing their gazes up. The fireworks showered more light, the last of them from the resounding cheers at the shape taking final form: a spectacle of gold sparks dotting the dark into an ever-sharpening hand flashing four cards in the sky.

"Because my real name isn't Vain."

At the headliner's words, the air went still. Silent, amid the din of celebration.

"It's Eva."

Jack needed a drink.

As he sat on the ground, just outside the city gate, he brought the bottle to his lips. No glass this time; it wasn't necessary. Not even for the bright-green liquor, burning down his throat in a trail of emerald fire.

Not that it would do much. No warmth or numbness would ever arrive. At least, not at the rate that weakened most fools. A strangely disappointing discovery from the monumental first glass Jack had ever poured for himself. One he should've seen coming.

All taste, but nothing behind it. All expectation, without the true experience.

Still, it was nice to pretend. At the tables he frequented in Hellfire House, no one could tell. No one knew that on some nights, he could even pretend the act was real.

Not tonight, with the way she'd looked at him. Both of them.

Their eyes seared in his mind, fresh with fear.

Jack looked up at the sky, out into the barren darkness beyond. There were no shadows of the lost wandering in that fog, and no one dared even one step outside the gate to join them. As if they might be taken like a creature snatched by a hawk in flight. Once any magician found their way to the city, they never looked back. There was nowhere else to turn.

Which meant no chance of anyone stumbling by to bother him.

The way the city thrummed and crackled tonight was only a precursor to the main event. Far more would come, that much was clear from the glimpses of what Jack had seen of that night. Even from those faint recollections, he knew what was coming would light all the darkness surrounding them aflame.

I'm not risking anything in case your devil brethren decide to call you back to the fold.

His fingers tensed over the bottleneck, stopping his next swig.

It was as if she'd ripped it from his mind, the headliner who was all knife edges and malice. Jagged and sharp, especially toward him.

Your strings may look cut, but maybe that's an illusion, too.

They could agree on one thing, at least. One factor Jack wasn't even sure of, which could change everything if it were even a little true. If eventually strings would grow, held by the wrong hands.

He kept a steady, wary watch on the land ahead, waiting for that pull. That lure.

Something.

If the strings were growing, he didn't feel them.

Jack stayed out there, long after the bottle was finished. Long after the lights died from the sky, when the rowdiness of the streets finally dimmed.

He waited and listened, as he had before.

For some sign, a voice.

When he thought he heard a whisper, he wondered if it was real or just his imagination.

ACT II

Down in the world below, the magician could not escape.

Not without mystifying the gatekeepers within.

The darkness looked like home.

First, it was Daron's sun-streaked greenhouse library in Tar-
cana. Then his messy dorm in Valmonts when he was still just a school-
boy. One of his favorite quiet bars in New Crown he'd hide away in
when he wasn't in the mood to party with the other show magicians.

The dream pulled him here, there. Different places and different
homes.

As soon as the dirty bar floor beneath his feet shifted to clean carpet in that shade of burgundy he knew so well, he paused. The halls
of the Prima Hotel stretched out before him, with his room at the very
end. And one other.

It wasn't long before he reached his room, and turned to the door
across from his. A door he'd stared at far more than his own.

The hint of a shadow on the other side moved in the crease below.
A familiar laugh sounded, and his eyes closed as though the sun
had fallen over his skin. His pulse quickened and time slowed, as he
reached over to—

Daron woke up on a gasp to the hammering of metal.

His spine jolted upright, and the blankets slid right off him. At first,
there was nothing but noises. Jarring, clanging faraway noises that

made his ears ring. Nothing in this room but his own shaky breaths, and the bed underneath him dampened from the sweat on his back.

Bed?

Daron flinched at the low whistle, accompanied by the seedlike sounds of plinking glass. Wherever he was, he wasn't alone. The movement in the corner, the silhouette somehow familiar as he narrowed his eyes. "Eva?"

At the croak of his voice, the lights hanging from the ceiling illuminated after a clap from the other side of the room. Not Eva.

"Sorry to disappoint." A snort came from the dark-skinned young man Daron had never seen who continued sweeping a bit behind him. "I'm more of a Herald, actually. But that's neither here nor there."

"Herald?" Daron blinked at the remarkable colors of the stranger's casual shirt and pants, a hue Daron wasn't even sure he could define.

Dizziness. It had to be the dizziness.

"Yes, that is I. And *you're* alive." With a jaded breath of relief, Herald set his tools on the glass counter before hopping over the surface to reach the other side. "Now I can fully chastise you for nearly taking out an entire row of goods when I dragged your sorry ass in here. Don't even get me started on the state of my poor glass coach."

It was as though all of Daron's senses were returning in a slow crawl when he finally noticed his surroundings.

Mirrors.

So many in such tight quarters, the room was full to bursting with them. They lined every inch of the room in all shapes and sizes and frames, ranging from plain and stark to the most ornate and dazzling. Aside from the closed curtains draped in deep-violet velvet, nothing but mirrors and lights existed in sight. Like the emptiest art gallery he'd ever beheld, from the way all of the mirrors were racked against the walls like faceless portraits waiting to be purchased.

While Daron had long since stopped flinching at the sight of a mirror, an army of them still gave him pause. "Who *are* you?"

A series of soft clanking, a hiss of a curse before the smooth pour. "Just a friend of a friend of a friend's," came Herald's response as he walked over with a tray of steaming cups. "I don't often help strays who fall through the cracks, but you're the first one the Dire Woods has ever delivered. Can't really say no to that."

Daron's pulse raced. His entire throat knotted with thorns as sensation after sensation slammed back into him, the memory of the woods. The darkness, unending as night. A living nightmare he couldn't survive.

Had he?

"Where . . ." Daron coughed dryly, dislodging that knot. Forcing himself to breathe. "Where am I?"

He knew even as he asked the question. Kallia's voice slithered into his ears, a siren's whisper.

The true side. The place below the surface.

Herald gave a wry response Daron didn't hear. He pushed himself up on his elbows, bypassing the steaming cup offered to him even though his tongue felt drier than a dust-ridden floor. His knees nearly buckled when he stood, the blood rushing from his head to force him back down. By sheer determination, Daron staggered over to one of the curtained windows—careful not to crash into any more mirrors on his way, from the string of curses flung behind him—and peeled back the fabric.

Lights.

Flashing colors and sparks and all manner of—

"Need I remind you, this is a place of *mirrors*," Herald hissed. "If even one catches the light, they all will. And my vision is poor enough as it is."

The words went in one ear and out the other for Daron, even as his eyes burned from the intensity of the world below. It was unlike anything he'd ever seen, yet he'd seen it all before. He recognized those streets, bedazzled as they were. He knew the shapes of the buildings around him and the way they arched into the sky, dark as it was. A starless midnight of a sky, while the rest of the city was afire below.

Glorian.

Hell, the mayor had been right.

The curtain shut right in his face. Daron almost collapsed to the floor from the shock of darkness before he was yanked back by the elbow.

"So smiley for a mortal." With a shake of his head, Herald grunted as he hefted Daron's arm over his shoulder to guide him back. "I hope that look was worth it. You're probably going to be seeing fireworks for the next few hours."

Daron was too elated to care. His vision swirled as he lowered back down to the sweaty mattress, but he had never felt more alive. More awake.

Because for once, he wasn't dreaming. He'd *made* it.

Kallia. His pulse quickened.

"I have to go." He moved to rise again, shaky. "I have to find—"

"In *your* condition? You're not going to find anything but your face to the ground if you try going out there as you are now." Herald stopped him by thrusting the steaming cup into his hands. "Whatever you're looking for can wait."

It couldn't. Kallia couldn't.

Daron almost tossed the cup away, but wasn't petty enough for that yet. "I don't want to sit here and sip tea."

"All right, I may not brew the *best* tea in all worlds, but it's still good," Herald said defensively. "It's safe and won't hurt you. And better yet, it looks like you need it."

The temptation to throw the cup had Daron's head throbbing so painfully, he almost growled. As soon as the room stopped spinning and Herald had his back turned, Daron would be gone. "I didn't come all this way to wait."

"Why *did* you come here, then?" Herald sat close by with his back against the counter, taking a sip from his own mug. "Because if it took so much effort just to reach this place, then it's really not the wisest decision to fuck it up by being sloppy. Imagine if you took the wrong turn or landed in the wrong hands . . ." Another long sip. "Then it would all be for nothing."

All for nothing.

The worst words that could be strung together.

Daron stared down at the black glass mug warmed between his hands, a pleasant, flowery herbal scent he couldn't quite place rising from the steam. The stranger had a point. As much as Daron wanted to race out the door and take to the streets with his eyes wide open, these were not streets that he knew. And they were certainly not the streets of the Glorian he left behind.

All Daron knew was that a new world meant new rules. The practicality and common sense he lived by, frustrating as they were, told him he needed to think. He needed to get his bearings before walking out any door into the unknown.

Because he didn't get this far just to fuck it all up.

"Thank you." Daron raised his mug to Herald, feeling instantly like shit for how rude he'd been. To a stranger who clearly didn't have to show him any kindness at all. "I've just . . . been on my feet for so long, driving myself mad . . . I've forgotten how to sit still with myself."

The shop owner's brow arched, softer this time. "You don't need to be so harsh on yourself for taking a breath. Something tells me you're surprised to have even gotten this far. So if you want to keep running, you need to breathe." He shrugged before placing his empty cup beside him. "And you're welcome."

Daron inhaled deeply, the clench of his chest loosening slightly more since he woke up. He pressed the mug to his lips, and the first sip brought the sweetest relief. The most peculiar, delicious flavor of a minty flower burst on his tongue, tasting somehow, inexplicably, of the color white. "Sorry for breaking your mirrors. And your coach. If you need any help fixing things up around here, I'm handy with the proper tools." Daron gave a sheepish shrug. He looked around the quiet shop while the curtains rustled slightly to the beat of whatever music pounded from outside. "Maybe you could use the company."

It was a genuine offer, dovetailed by an ulterior motive that couldn't be helped. Daron was a stranger to this world, and in order for him to learn what he needed to know, it had to come from a stranger who wasn't.

A snort became a long, rueful sigh from Herald. "Shit, you really had to be a decent fellow."

Daron's brows drew together, before the warmth coating his throat turned into a numbness. It traveled gently down his body, before spiraling behind his eyes. Into his mind.

So relaxed, the cup fell from his hands.

"Who are—" The words slurred past his lips, warm and loose over the cold thrum of panic. "What the hell did you . . ."

"Don't worry." The other voice echoed like a song, a ring of sounds circling around him. "I did say it wasn't going to hurt you."

If Daron had a hard time standing before, his balance was nonexistent now. He tripped every step of the way to the curtain, and when he eventually met the ground, he crawled. Desperate.

Help.

If he could just break the window, yell for help.

With every bit of strength left, he reached for a fold of the curtain and yanked as hard as he could. He panted, unsure if the curtain's fabric was unnaturally strong or if he was simply weaker. He managed to open it just a crack, a slice of raging light pouring in.

Before fingers marked in black triangles grabbed it back, closing it completely.

"Careful, Demarco," the voice of the hand warned. "No one's supposed to see you just yet."

The first reel of ice stabbed clarity through the warmth.

How did he know his name?

"Everyone here knows your name."

That didn't make any sense. Did he hear his thoughts? *Were* those his thoughts? Everything swirled so violently, Daron wasn't sure what words were leaving his lips anymore. Just babbled nonsense, before a phantom weight drifted over him. All he could remember were the mirrors staring down at him from above.

In the frame of one, he could've sworn he saw Kallia dancing.

26

R oth refused to see her. Or at least, he didn't care to.

He'd sent no note, hadn't knocked on her door to check in after the duel. At first, Kallia wondered if this was his silent way of kicking her out of the Alastor Place. Becoming like a ghost, so he'd never have to dirty his hands with confrontation.

"You're not special, mortal. He'll vanish from time to time," Vain muttered alongside her. "When the Dealer has business, he takes care of it. That's all."

Annoyance spiked in her sly drawl, as if that's all she knew of it, too. The business he attended must've been serious if not even his headliners were involved.

"Regardless, he hates me." Kallia's eyes stayed hard on the ground. "They all do."

"Maybe that's not such a bad thing." With the barest shake of her head, Vain added, "To be loved by all is overrated, anyway. Especially in this town."

The mantra repeated in her head. None of this had ever mattered to Kallia before. She'd faced contempt throughout Spectaculore, even in Hellfire House from the most deplorable patrons. But scorn like that, born from the littleness of others, never hit her as hard as it rattled the others delivering it.

The judgement that met her that very morning was not amusing, as it was born from the littleness of *her*.

Sly whispers from headliners to the hungry stares of passing wait-staff followed her up and down the hall, some more discreet than others. To them, Kallia was the bleeding magician who'd lost. No amount of smiles or charm could convince anyone otherwise. Not with so many witnesses and spectators to keep the night alive.

Still, hiding out in her room was out of the question. It would've only given them more pleasure to push her further into the corner.

"You better look every single one of them in the eye, like you can see their secrets." Vain elbowed her sharply. "A good walk of shame will make everyone else squirm instead."

Kallia's brow jutted up. "Didn't peg you as the type to feel shame at all."

"I walk solely to shame *them*."

A small snort later, Kallia forced her gaze ahead, catching all the sneers. The sting of them lessened, after seeing just how much distance they needed to bite. Even more laughable among them were the looks of utter confusion upon recognizing her companion of choice.

No one was more surprised than Kallia to find Vain at her door when she awoke. After an impatient drumline of knocking, the head-liner stood waiting on the other side with her usual cool-eyed expression.

Kallia barely got a word out before a bundle of fabric hit her in the face.

"A gift from Ruthless," Vain said. "Now change, so we can go out."

Just like that, Kallia was walking down the stairs in a skin-tight lilac gown that stretched with ease, flaring out in a skirt that hung easy as feathers. It was similar to Vain's lightweight dress, in a shade and style slightly different. She more than enjoyed the puzzled reactions they received as they sauntered out of the Alastor Place to hail a carriage together. All that was missing to complete the odd picture was Jack following closely at their backs.

Every few steps, Kallia looked in every direction. A glance around, behind, then out the window of their moving carriage as if Jack might show himself in the crowd. She always found herself checking and always found nothing. Not after he vanished with those last words, that last look, at the Ranza Estate.

Only Kallia noticed the absence. Hard not to, when Jack had always left a trail of fear in her periphery.

Walking next to the Queen of the Diamond Rings, though, inspired fear of a different kind from onlookers.

The headliner now watched the city out the window, the lights washing over the sheer mask she donned today—a scrap of black mesh, studded with gold. If only Kallia could stop looking at the pieces of her face left exposed. A softer cut to her jaw, same eyes. Lips set in a perpetual curl with the tendency to frown when she thought no one else was looking. *That* frown.

Kallia knew it all too well, and it had been sitting in front of her all this time.

Eva.

Like a myth herself, she hardly seemed real. Not at all who she pictured as the lost sister from Demarco's stories; the girl across from her was another creature entirely.

You two would get along famously.

It felt almost cruel that they had found each other first when they were nothing but strangers. Two magicians now linked by each other's greatest secrets.

"Look . . ." Kallia cleared her throat. "Eva—"

"It's Vain."

The cut of her tone was like a dagger throw, yet her gaze never strayed from the window. "And you can stop looking like you know me, mortal. Anything you've heard before is irrelevant here. Names come with pasts, and pasts come with secrets. So if you tell a soul who I really am—who *any* of us are—I'll destroy you. No matter who you are to my brother."

Twisted as it was, the threat almost brought a smile to Kallia's lips.

Locking him away in the back of her mind for so long turned him into such a cruel illusion for her that just the mention of him now was an indulgence. It wasn't all just in her head anymore. What a luxury that was in a world like this.

"Fair enough, *Vain*." Kallia leaned back, still treading carefully. One wrong word, and the headliner would likely kick her right out of the carriage and into the traffic. "Though I'm not sure there's much damage you could inflict upon me that hasn't already been done."

"Don't underestimate me. There are so many ways to destroy a person if you're creative enough." She sized Kallia up as if plotting such ways now. "Stop your wallowing. You may not be in the best of places, but thank Zarose you're not in the worst."

"Which is?"

"Out beyond the gates, lost to nightmares until you and your magic waste away." Dread entered Vain's eyes. "Or back in the shadows, no hope of ever getting out of them any time soon."

They could agree on that. The past held shadows, and most weren't lucky enough to leave them unscathed, if at all. Those who never had to live in the dark, hidden and unseen, could never know. The light had always found them, so they'd never gone without.

No matter how Kallia and Vain bickered, they still shared shadows.

"Why offer up such information freely, then?" said Kallia, head tilted. "You really trust me that much?"

"If I'm not mistaken, you were the one refusing to trust *me*." Vain looked down at her nails, fluttering them out before her. "However, it had to be done. Now I know the secret to your downfall, and you know mine. I doubt either of us would be willing to double-cross the other the first chance we got, agreed?"

It was a strange logic both cutthroat and fair, though Kallia could really do with a better upper hand. This city knew too much about her, and she knew nothing really of the girl sitting across from her. Or where she was even taking her.

"Good. Now that's out of the way . . ." Vain straightened the chain around her neck, unmoved as the carriage halted to a stop as if on cue. "Ready to fly, mortal?"

The headliner's gymnasium had no right being such a marvel.

Light overwhelmed the cavernous atrium, assembled like a grandly tiered wedding cake with more windows than walls at every ascending level. According to Vain, one floor functioned as a wraparound trail that could shift from a stroll in the forest to a walk on the beach. Another was dedicated to strength training with various exercise instruments and devices, sitting just beneath the level constructed as a sinuous pool that snaked around in a loop.

Rubbing at her eyes, Kallia waited for her vision to even out. Never-ending nights had not prepared her for this an unnaturally bright trick of the mind.

"You get used to it." Inhaling, Vain straightened her mask. "We take our daylight where we can, even if it is all just an illusion."

Everything was an illusion, though that in no way deterred anyone else's enjoyment. Some magicians strolled between pillars with steam rolling off their bodies or lounging in lush robes. All relaxation in one area, clashing with the harsh shouts and orders from the main floor ahead. Performers executed series of stunts across the springy mats or jumping over the wide stretches of colorful trampolines.

Kallia couldn't help but watch. No matter how catty these headliners could be, there was no denying the talent on every floor of this gymnasium.

"We all used to get our own levels, believe it or not." Vain spared a bitter sideways glance. "Until Roth figured that dampened the competitive spirit. The man really loves shrinking his cages as much as he can."

"With all this space?"

"Tight quarters, more drama." At the wave of echoing hoots that rose from the Red Death Dukes, Vain's lips pinched tighter. "And practically no boundaries."

"Why crave boundaries when you get the best view in the city?"

At the low, posh voice, Vain turned and immediately gagged. Kallia blinked at the sight of the fit, purple-haired magician wearing nothing but a small towel at his waist.

"I should've brought a blindfold." Vain groaned.

"Please. I'm Jonny Triumph—you know you want this." The magician gave a saucy wink before noticing Kallia. "Oh . . . *you*."

It was remarkable, the poison of one syllable. She would've preferred it over the interest simmering in his eyes. "Another pretty bird to add to your little girl group, V? It's not like you to kiss ass while the Dealer's away."

Vain pursed her lips. "She's just training, Jonny. Maybe you should try it."

Chuckling, he raked his fingers through his long, dampened hair. "Geniuses don't *need* training. My music is *art* you can't train. Not like those adorable hoop tricks you all do."

He'd said a whole list of wrong things from the Diamond Ring's forced smile as she ripped off her necklace. "How about you take her for a ride, then?"

One would've thought Vain had brandished a knife when Jonny balked at the glittering charm dangling between them. "Sorry. I'll be late for my massage." He grinned, edging back a step. "Another time."

"Pity." Vain whipped forth the chained necklace—and the air burst in a loud fiery crack like the release of some fearsome creature.

Amidst the thin tendrils of smoke stood a large jewel-studded hoop, hooked to a seemingly endless snakelike chain.

Pale as a sheet, Jonny scampered off. The Diamond Ring snorted and hefted the chain's end skyward. The impossible length of it ran and ran and ran up to the ceiling, somehow finding purchase when the connecting links snapped into a taut, straight line above.

Kallia's jaw dropped as Vain stepped within the metal curve, one moment there.

Gone, the next.

A few headliners on the main floor paused their drills to watch

Vain soar high up with the grace of a pendulum, paired with the lethal precision of a bow taking aim.

Jonny had only just reached the end of the mat before a quick blur swooped in and snatched the towel right off his waist. Whistles and catcalls surged across the gymnasium. Vain's laughter rang loudest of all as the pale and unabashedly naked magician flipped both middle fingers at her.

"Oy mortal, catch!"

Heart pounding, Kallia looked all around. A warning whistle of wind was all the signal she got when she pivoted just in time to catch Vain's outstretched arm.

Before the ground vanished from under Kallia's feet.

"Hope you're not afraid of heights," the headliner shouted within her hoop, one hand overhead. "Just don't let go."

Kallia was only proud she didn't scream, though she wanted to. Not in fear. That strange flutter in her stomach at the weightlessness heightened like the warmth in her chest as they surged higher, farther and farther away from the small headliners below.

The edges of her lips curled, almost bursting out in a laugh. The rush of it all was joyous and breathless and terrifying. So overwhelming, she wanted to bottle the bliss for later.

For the first time in a long time, she'd never felt more alive, more awake.

More powerful without using even one ounce of magic.

The jarring stop nearly forced Kallia to let go, but she held tight. Her breath caught up to her, everything dizzy from the flow of constant motion to none while harsh voices piled around her.

"Come on, get her one!"

"Hold on—"

"Yes, before we both sink."

"Hold *on*." The sweet voice returned with a fury. "Oh, look at the poor darling. You just grabbed her without any warning."

When Kallia opened her bleary eyes, the Diamond Rings surrounded her. Malice, hanging upside down nearby by her knees, arms outstretched for catching. And Ruthless, sitting on her hoop across, tinkering with a shiny object in her lap. "Don't worry, almost done. Just hold on and don't look down."

"Or *do*," Malice suggested. "I personally love this view, everyone small and beneath me. It's how I usually see things, anyway."

"Any week now, Ruth." Vain huffed from above. "She can only hold us both for so much longer."

"Calm down. It'll take more than a few measly breaths before you drop."

"What!?" Legs still dangling, the fluttering in Kallia's stomach took a turn. She had descended on chandeliers plenty of times, but never from so high up. The kind of height that promised broken bones and more.

"Why are we up here?" The hoop lowered another stuttering inch, and her fingers tensed.

"To train you. What does it look like?" A yawn. "We usually start off at the ceiling so that anything lower will feel like groundwork—"

"Wait, train me for what?" Kallia hissed, arms trembling. "The duel is over."

"Not in this world." She cocked her hip from above. "And since you're working with the best, training you to become a Diamond Ring."

Kallia almost lost her hold entirely at Ruthless's loud squeal of delight close behind—before a thin, thread-light chain slid around her neck with the click of a clasp, the icy weight at her collarbone.

A diamond ring.

The small charm felt strangely heavier than it appeared when she'd first seen the performers wearing them. Though none of them wore theirs as jewelry, now. Hooked up by the large chains, the ladies wielded their hoops like armor. The wings they used to fly.

This had to be a trick. Eva or not, Vain played games as well as anyone in this world. And Kallia had walked into enough traps to recognize the walls. "Why are you giving me this?"

"You don't want it?"

After the duel, she couldn't understand why they would want *her*.

Since their first performance, she'd always known the Diamond Rings as an act to watch. To envy. Much like the Conquering Circus, but distinct as the seasons. Where the Conquerors arrived on the stage in a blaze of chaos and color, the Diamond Rings made their entrance like thrown knives that never missed. They exuded precision and power. Poise and poison. None of which Kallia possessed anymore.

At this point, she was just waiting for the joke. Some new cruelty to begin. "You all saw me last night. I *lost*."

"Just because you didn't win doesn't mean you don't show promise." Vain shrugged. "Given how little time you had to prepare, you were . . . definitely *not* terrible."

It had to be the closest thing to a compliment Kallia had ever received from her.

"Also, Filip's an asshole," Malice added. "A nasty dueler, like all of his idiots. Most of which, very predictably, are awful in bed."

Their laughter reeled over Kallia, which shook the chain and the hoop it held. It happened so fast, so sudden, there was no time to scream.

Her grip broke.

And she fell into nothing.

A storm of wind rushed through her hair. Her limbs flailed, grasping at the air. The Diamond Rings grew smaller and blurred as she plummeted to the bottom where pain awaited.

Nothing to catch her. No one to save her.

She was going to die with an audience.

Teeth clenched, Kallia braced herself for impact. The fine links of the necklace brushed her fingers like a shock of lightning.

Please.

She ripped the chain off. Threw it forward, as Vain had done.

A loud burst forced her back, her eardrums popping at a painful pace.

All noise and sensation and wind until the world stopped. Time froze, and the air stilled. Kallia clung to the only thing she could, shocked to find anything, much less the thick, curved metal, humming against her hand, steadying her.

Lifting her.

Her eyes flew open as she took in the large, long-chained hoop helping her ascend to the applauding Diamond Rings above.

Impossible. This was no magic Kallia had ever touched before. If she didn't know any better, she could've sworn that life flickered within the apparatus, rising on its own accord. Almost sentient. Even the long chain's end inexplicably disappeared through the ceiling as though encountering nothing but smoke, though clearly finding purchase within it.

"Works *every* time." Ruthless clapped her hands the instant Kallia rose within earshot. "The rings never fail."

"Are you serious?" Fuming, every furious breath raked up Kallia's throat. She wanted down. Or at the very least, to drag one of them down with her. "I could've—"

"You were in no danger." Draped in a sitting position, Vain kicked out her legs to swing back and forth. "To really fly, mortal, you first have to fall. Had to see if you could act quickly. Your ring, too."

Once she came to a full stop, Kallia blinked at the sleek metal framing her, keeping her afloat. "What is this thing?"

"That *thing* saved you." Ruthless pouted, giving her ring a gentle caress. "And now it's yours, so you better get used to it. It's going to become your new best friend with every show, every practice . . ."

On and on she went, until Kallia held up a hand. "This might come as a shock, but I don't want to be one of you," she bit out. "I don't want to be *anything* in this city."

She just wanted to go back to the one she knew.

To go back to a time when she wasn't like this.

"That is a shock." Malice sniffed. "*Everyone* wants to be us."

Vain sent the girl spinning with the kick at her hoop, sliding her narrowed stare back on Kallia. "So what will you do if you go off on your own, then? Think you have enough power to stop what's coming? What Roth has planned for you?"

Clearly *she* had plans for Kallia, which left a bitter taste in her mouth.

"And now that your trusty bodyguard is also no longer sulking by you, your shield is gone. People will talk," the headliner said pointedly. "Which means you need a new cover. A better one."

"As a Diamond Ring?" Kallia arched a brow. "As if no one will think *that's* odd?"

"I spin lies much better than you, mortal. I know what to say to get what I want. And if I want others to look away without raising too many eyebrows, then it'll happen." Legs crossed, the leader peered down at the main floor watching the headliners run about like ants in the dirt. "In games like these, there's power in numbers. And without your dark wild card, seems like you could use all the players you can get."

Those were too many odds stacked against her. Too many chances for betrayal. "Doesn't sound much like teamwork if you're cornering me into it."

"We all want the same thing. And we all know that if Roth wins, we all lose."

"That's not how it looks from here." Kallia glowered at the group sitting atop their hoops like glittering thrones. The whole gymnasium itself—no more than a kingdom for a few. "Forgive me if I can't believe any of you would risk your places at the top."

"Trust us, we are no strangers to performing at the bottom, darling. I can throw cards out in the streets with as much ease as I fall through the air here. The question is, which side is going to see you more?" Brows raised, Ruthless twirled a lock of hair between her fingers. "The true side wasn't ready for us then, probably doesn't even remember our names, not that it matters anymore. This is our side, our home, where anything is and should be possible for anyone. So *that* is what we're risking to protect."

"Hear, hear." Malice and Vain snapped their fingers, while Kallia turned to each Diamond Ring for a good look. No wonder they all banded together so seamlessly, when their stories reflected each other's. They were not competing against one another, not when they *formed* the competition together. They grew from the bottom to the top together. From nameless on the true side, to unforgettable on the other side. Lottie would have such a frenzy with this information if she ever found about her missing magicians, thriving on the stages beneath the surface.

"That's for sure." Malice pedaled her feet out softly, circling the group. "If you haven't noticed, life isn't perfect once you've reached the top. It only gets harder, because you can never be satisfied. Especially when you see so much more wrong in the world from there."

Kallia lifted an inquiring finger. "And you're only just thinking of changing it now?"

"Because everyone has always taken *you* seriously the moment you enter a room?" Vain sneered, her jaw set. "It's hard for a few to make change when there are so many keeping everything in place to their liking. If you can't strike fast, you strike smart at the right moment," she trailed off. "If this show of his succeeds, it'll be too late to do anything after. For our side, and theirs."

Kallia's throat tightened under a hard swallow. For once, it was a relief to not have magic on her side. "I highly doubt I'll be able to break the gate as he expects. My powers—"

"That won't stop Roth," she muttered. "He has it in his head that you're the answer to all of his problems, so it won't matter whether you're ready or not. Zarose Gate didn't have to break the first time around to destroy everything in its path."

That froze Kallia to the bone.

All it took was a crack. One night and one failed attempt on a city to leave the true side bleeding, long after the cut.

Perhaps that was what Jack had been trying to warn her about all along, except she wouldn't listen. She'd been too busy doubting every word he said and hearing lies where there were none. And still, he'd tried offering her hope where he could, no matter how the game was locked. A cornered victory.

There was no returning to the true side when it destroyed everything and everyone around it. All the people she knew, and the ones she didn't. The few places she'd called home, and the vast land she had yet to explore herself. A sea she'd never seen.

Somehow, all along, she'd known she was never going back.

"So there's no winning in this, is there?" she said, absently tracing the path of her ring from the cold humming metal to the smooth-cut diamonds studded outside.

"Now . . . I didn't say *that*."

Kallia lifted her head, her pulse thrumming. "You have a plan?"

A wicked smile curled Vain's lips. "I always have a plan."

There was light in those words. After wading through the dark, lost for so long, light was all that mattered. And she'd gone so long without.

For the first time since arriving in this city, Kallia felt certain of something. Of the three Diamond Rings glancing down at the main training floor while exchanging sly looks with one another. An unspoken order, a nod in response.

Before Ruthless let out a piercing howl, jumping straight off her hoop.

Malice quickly followed after.

Their screams shattered the air, echoing madly throughout the gymnasium. Heads below tilted up at the disturbance, all watching in fascination as the girls fell further and further.

Kallia's ears perked at the rapid clink of chains beside her that ran at top speed, dropping the rings like anchors that sank after them through the empty air.

"Well, what are you waiting for?"

At the suggestion in Vain's tone, Kallia clutched at her chest, the thundering beneath her palm.

"You need to loosen up, mortal." The headliner's laugh deepened. "Weren't you once a showgirl?"

"But—what about the plan?"

"Part of the plan *is* playing the part." Sighing, Vain eyed the figures below as the others resumed their drills across the mats. "One day, we won't have to."

The headliner led with hard-earned certainty that failure was not an option, nor a passing thought in the slightest. There was power in that belief that Kallia used to carry with her.

She wanted it back.

The Diamond Rings continued howling all the way down, disturbing all peace. Vain snuck another peek below. "Get your battle cry ready." She squared back her shoulders. "The longer we talk up here, the sooner they'll start talking down there."

The thought of falling again, on purpose, had Kallia's palms sweating. "When are we going to start actually training, though?"

She needed that at least, for some credibility. She couldn't stomach the thought of carrying a title she'd done hardly anything for, and she wasn't opposed to the work it would take.

This, she wanted more than anything. She wanted to be able to look down at the ground from the highest height without flinching, to jump with her eyes wide open and a fearless grin. She wanted that ability to turn falling into flying, that pressure to make her unbreakable as a diamond.

"Don't worry, mortal." Vain hefted herself up to full standing position, the lean muscles of her arms straining beneath golden-brown skin. "Training began long before your feet ever touched the mat."

With a salute and a high screech to join the others below.

Loyal as a soldier, her hoop followed. The endless, unbreakable rigging chain that disappeared up through the ceiling ran madly after her to keep up, stiffening into a taut line when it caught her at some point.

Kallia glanced up at her own chain that held her aloft, still wary to trust it wouldn't snap on her entirely. She had no idea how it was possible or what kind of magic made it so. Not that any of the answers mattered, soon after.

The only logical step forward was to jump.

Daron plotted his escape numerous times, but Herald was always one step ahead.

Every plan failed before it even started. The windows didn't even need curtains, for the iron screen bolted over the glass. Every time Herald's back was turned, Daron's eyes went straight for the door, which had a habit of moving all around the shop like a wandering cat. He even waited wordlessly for customers to walk through, though from the never-ending silence broken by Herald's unbothered whistling, it was clear nobody was strolling in any time soon. When he thought he'd started hallucinating the scribble of Lottie's pen, or saw a brief flash of Aunt Cata staring at him over the glass counter, Daron had had enough of the games.

The day Daron finally managed to catch Herald off guard with a swift punch in the face, the shop owner merely got back up and righted his nose with the efficient snap of a bone.

Fists raised, knuckles smarting, Daron readied himself for a fight. He thought about tearing off one of the mirrors as some shield when Herald reached around to grab something in his belt, a weapon, no doubt—

A grainy, light blue rag caught Daron in the face.

"If you're going to use your hands, Demarco, no use breaking them on little ol' me," he said. "Might as well put them to work, since you promised so nicely."

"Are you serious?" Daron fumed, close to tearing out his hair or punching the mirror closest to him. It would probably have more impact than the one he'd landed. "I'm *not* working for you."

"Look, I'm just trying to help you out." Herald shrugged. "Clearly you're bored."

"I'm trying to get out of here and away from *you*."

If anything could rival Daron's fury, it was Herald's utter and infuriating composure. "Trust me, nothing you do will get you out of this shop. I mean, just look at me." He snorted bitterly at himself. "Glorified mirror keeper, errand boy, and bounty hunter. Or in this case, nanny."

Daron crossed his arms. It was the first time they'd spoken more than a grunt at each other since he'd drugged Daron. Of course, Daron had no problem with silence—the quiet rarely ever bothered him.

Herald was the opposite, with every oddly cheery greeting he sent Daron's way or simply whistling if only to fill the room with some sort of sound.

When all else failed, it was the one thing Daron could use.

"I don't know *why* you're even looking after me," he said, tense. "If you don't like it any more than I do, then just let me go on my way."

"Do you really think it works like that here? Just because we don't want to do something, we can just choose not to? Maybe you had that freedom before over on the true side." Herald laughed, flashing his fingers in Daron's face. "But when you're here, and you've got *these*, there is no choice."

The black triangles across his fingers were so bold, no one could miss them. Just like the markings across Jack's fingers. "And what do those mean?"

"If you get a job, you do the job." With the smooth turn of his heel, Herald went toward the wall to straighten a few mirrors hanging slightly askew. "That's the deal with the Dealer of this city. And anyone who goes back on a deal can just go off on their own merry way."

That didn't sound so bad. "So you *can* choose?"

"If the other choice means being thrown far out of the city to find your way back to it, and essentially being left to the devils outside the gates who will siphon off your powers over time until you're nothing but a husk of a magician," Herald added cheerily. "No one ever really makes it back again the second time, but you know, anything is possible!"

Daron caught his face in one of the mirrors around him, where his mouth had fallen in abject horror. And disbelief. "Devils?"

"Ah, yes, your mortal side is sheltered from them. Lucky bastards." Herald rolled his eyes. "I genuinely don't know what's worse, living in an overly protected bubble or surviving out in the wilds." He paused to think about it for a moment. "Actually no, we may have devils, but at least we've got better food and clothes."

Daron still couldn't wrap his mind around the devils. It was as if he'd woken up in his home and suddenly discovered the morning sky was purple—only to be told it had been purple all this time. Except a different-colored sky never hurt anybody. Certainly not anyone's magic.

Go into the woods where the devils reach, and they'll welcome you with open arms.

It had sounded like nonsense, when the mayor said it. Though he should've known better, after walking through the Dire Woods. It preyed on the pieces of him no animal would take. The parts that fed a different kind of predator.

"Don't worry, Demarco. I'll save you from the big, scary devils here." Herald threw a wink over his shoulder. "Not that it'll ever come to that. You're safe, because you were brought here for a very specific purpose that involves—*don't* rip the rag, please, it's my favorite color!"

Daron hadn't realized how the sides of the rag had bunched tightly between his fingers until he looked down. His chest practically jumped from the way his heart beat heavily beneath it. "What do you mean I was brought here?"

He'd walked through that Dire Woods on his own. That hadn't been his imagination. He wished it could be, but that part of his journey had been very real.

"You don't think you got here all on your own, do you?" The shop owner moved toward the front glass counter before casually sliding up over the surface to the other side. He fixed himself a drink in a short glass from a vibrantly green crystal bottle, before glancing at Daron's face with a head tilt. "Oh, you do."

That fury coursed back into Daron's blood. "I walked through those woods," he bit out through gritted teeth. "For Zarose knows how long, I *walked* those woods until it brought me here."

He shivered, recalling the cold from the wind rustling through the trees, slicing at him with knifelike precision before the voices called.

"You did." Herald poured and nodded, not unkindly. "But who led you to those woods in the first place?"

I know only what they told me.

The words twisted in Daron's stomach, about to snap.

Aunt Cata had been right. Maybe to hide what the Patrons had concealed, but she'd never trusted the mayor because she never trusted coincidences. Whereas Daron was desperate to leap at the first hint to land at his feet.

"There's always someone pulling strings, somewhere, even if you can't see them," said Herald. "And those with enough influence, or devils on their side who can whisper sweet nothings in one's ears, can make anyone into a puppet."

Just like him.

Daron followed the bread crumbs through the Dire Woods, only to fall for the cage someone had planned for him all along. Whoever held the key must've been watching him all this time, waiting to spring the trap.

"But who would want *me* here?" he whispered. "And why?"

"You might think this is a lie, and I'm not sure if I should even be telling you this, but I don't know. Not the whole story, at least. The Dealer shows some of his cards, but not others." Herald made a hard tsking sound as he reached to open a bottom drawer in the counter. "I was merely tasked with keeping you safe, and getting you ready for—"

"I don't care." It felt like everything in Daron was sinking. Every bone, like rocks pulling him deeper under the water without letting up. He was tired of sinking. Of drowning. "Whatever game this is, I'm not fucking playing anymore. I came here—"

"Yes, I know why you're here." Herald brought up another empty glass, inspecting it for cracks. "We *all* do, remember?"

Daron pressed his lips hard together. He didn't have the stomach to even ask how. One more blow, and he might very well shatter.

"Which is *why* . . ." Herald dragged that last note out like a tune while topping off another drink with silken green liquid. "Your odds of getting what you want are much better with me than venturing out there on your own. You're not going to be able to just waltz in and take an Alastor home with you."

"Why would I want that?"

The magician paused over his drink before he burst out laughing. "Zarose, this is rich," he said. "Not sure if I envy or pity you for being so in the dark."

"Glad this brings you amusement," Daron grumbled.

"Oh, it truly does." He swished his drink a bit with a slow lift of his brow. "But the real question is, do you *really* want to know?"

He slid the other drink as one would a pawn across the board. Daron made no move to take it, immediately suspicious, which made Herald snicker.

"It's safe. I already know you won't be going anywhere," he said, raising his own glass. "There's much you don't know, and much more you probably should before I deliver you right at your showgirl's feet."

"Do you really believe I'm that gullible?" Daron knew a trap when he saw one.

"I swear on every mirror here, it's the truth. My job is to keep you out of harm's way, so that you and the diamond can reunite. It's pure selflessness on my part to ensure you don't walk in completely clueless." With a low chuckle, he gave the second glass another push closer. "Trust me, Demarco, you're probably going to want that before I start."

It was easier walking through the city wearing another face. No one watched him like a gun about to go off or veered out of his way like a ravenous wolf about to tear through the streets. Hardly anyone even paid any attention to him at all when he wore a servant's face, especially with the first night of the Show of Hands soon approaching. A new event promising a stage for all, which tore excitement through the city faster than a wildfire.

Fools. Roth picked his pawns too well. Powerful magicians, to be sure, but the kind that would pass a mirror on the wall and notice only their reflection—not the knife about to take them out from behind. Jack knew his place here, all too happy to hide in the background of it as magicians all over scrambled to solidify a feat and reserve a spot in the lineup. Hardly anyone hailed him over for assistance.

But when donning the fresh face and suit of waitstaff in the Alastor Place, not even Jack could get out of the work that accompanied it.

"Oy, window lad!"

Jack bit the inside of his cheeks, carrying on with his cleaning rag. He didn't mind the work; it gave one purpose in a world without. Though it also gave headliners all the more reason to act more boorish than usual. The usual suspects, in particular, treated servants like target practice to no consequence. From the lewdest compliments to outright insults, it wasn't as if true harm could *actually* be done to a legion of waitstaff comprised largely of illusions. They weren't real. Technically, *he* shouldn't even exist.

Regardless, all expectations to serve and please had to be met.

With a clenched smile, Jack paused his work. The ladder beneath him creaked as he turned, already inwardly cursing upon noticing the flashes of red that marked the group as those meat-brained oafs he'd love to launch outside the gate. Especially the leader of them. Filip. The dirty fighter from Kallia's duel. Once it registered, it took everything in Jack not to go break the boy's head between his hands like a ripe melon. "Yes, sir? Do you require assistance?"

"Just a question I'd like answered." Filip spoke with a king's disdain, his beady stare sliding far out of reach. It was the one thing Jack shared with the servants of this house—rarely anyone looked them in the eyes, for vastly different reasons. Jack maintained his empty, placid expression, trying not to look too interested in the opened leatherbound notebook that seemed far too academic for the Red Death Duke's hands. Scribbles and letters raced across the empty lines with a life of their own. All to keep pace with the suggestions the rest of the group behind him kept calling out.

". . . how about a feast, but where we eat the food off of naked bodies?"

"Or—" one of them piped up, raising a finger in a moment of brilliance. "We have a den where we get the Rings wrestling in pudding?"

Nothing pained Jack more than having to smile stiffly as they slapped hands with more suggestions. Each one more piggish and lewd than the last, the air turned greasier around them.

"Shut up," the leader hushed them with the wave of his hand. He stepped back before starting a slow, careful circle around Jack. "Tell me, were you designed to fight when you popped out of the factory? With fists or weaponry?"

An odd question, though Jack wished he could demonstrate how easy it would be to fold any of these boys like paper.

"Yes, if you wanted me to," he said in that practiced puppet voice.

"Would you be up for fighting another?"

The group chuckled as a chorus, watching on like vultures waiting for the scraps. It made Jack's blood boil more. These headliners had been in this house long enough to know his answer would always be the same. "Of course, sir. If you wanted me to."

"Same old song and dance." Exhaling an amused sigh, Filip once more took stock of his notes. "If Roth allows it, I hope you'd be willing to participate in a fun little attraction I'm pitching for the Show of Hands. *Obviously*, he won't say no to us."

"I'm sure he won't, sir."

Filip cocked his head in consideration. "Not sure we've ever seen illusions fight to the death, but could be fun."

When his other team members snorted, Jack mirrored them with an unnatural laugh as well. "Excellent idea, sir."

"Isn't it?" Patting Jack on the shoulder, the leader leaned in with a terrible grin. "Now, I'd like you to walk up to every room in this house. And then once you're done, jump out of the highest window."

Jack almost chose to break then and there. Already, the satisfaction alone was tempting—picturing their faces icing over in abject horror once his mask melted away.

If he gave in to pettiness now, he'd never be able to blend in again without them looking closer. "Happy to accommodate your request."

Thankfully, the Red Death Dukes grew bored as easily as they were amused, moving on from Jack's monotony with that same dismissal of spoiled children tiring of pets they'd only just received. No doubt to tease the next illusion unfortunate enough to cross their path, minding their own business. Unable to stop even if they wanted to.

Jack kept up the door-to-door act, even when the band of headliners had long since departed. Unbeknownst to them, they provided him with an opportunity.

The Alastor Place was known for its large pool of servants, real or conjured. Those who hoped to rise up the ladder would collect whatever gossip or questionable secret heard in passing, any offering they could toss their master's way for approval.

A servant randomly searching the Alastor Place, beyond his designated section, was a detail that could draw notice. An illusion marching to a ridiculous command, however, was not.

Door after door of nothing, Jack could only roll his eyes at himself. This was ridiculous.

He should've left this side a long time ago. No one would fight him on it. Kallia didn't want him here. Hell, *he* certainly didn't want to stay.

He also couldn't help himself as soon as he heard Roth had gone away on business.

The lie wasn't even a good one.

If running Hellfire House had taught Jack anything, it was that straight-laced men who relished the game of making bets and deals under the table were desperate for an escape. A puzzle that made even less sense, in a city like this. A paradise of escape.

Whatever he was hiding, it was something he could not share with the city. Something worse than even the worst behind its gates.

With every turned handle and twisted door knob, the Dealer was nowhere to be found. But he was here. Jack could practically smell that man's cologne from the sheer presence of his shadow servants, stalking slowly through the halls like phantoms.

Most kept out of their path. Even headliners shied away from the faces made of shadow.

Jack followed a safe distance behind, absently opening doors while keeping them in his line of vision. It wasn't natural, seeing them alone, without Roth toting them around like accessories. Others were more concerned with avoiding them altogether, but Jack had never been afraid of smoke. He was born in it, too, knew it led to the fire.

Then he would go.

If he could hold a secret of Roth's in his pocket, then he could leave this world happily and never look back.

A strange noise erupted further down the hall of abandoned rooms. Dead quiet, with no one around.

Until the noise came again. Clearer now, which only confused Jack more. Persistent, guttural coughing, harsh enough to break the lungs, came from one of the rooms.

On the true side, he would've thought nothing of it. Mortals fell sick so often in their world, a fragile place with fragile people and sensitivities.

On this side, no one fell ill. With so much power, there was no reason for such weakness.

When the pair of shadows stopped by one of the doors, Jack paused at the turn of the corner, breath held. If he made himself known too soon in a cemetery like this, there would be nowhere to hide. Even for an illusion.

He only had one chance. Suddenly, there was no more sickness in the air, only the cold, hard *thunk* of a door closing, and a lock clicking into place.

Jack checked both ways, exhaling at the sight of no devils anywhere. But they were somewhere, just like Roth. Behind one of the identical green doors that ran endlessly down the hall like a fun house trick.

Jack's ears perked up at the muffled laughter behind one door—

Before the sound was thrown to the door just behind him.

And another few doors down.

Jack cursed as he flew from the outside of one room to the next. Whichever door they were behind moved fast, but he caught a few threads every so often. Established two voices among them.

One hoarse, and one smooth.

"... please ... I can't ..."

Under another round of uncontrollable coughs, the whispers were entirely unintelligible. Soft and splintered with a mortal's fear. The other, the opposite.

"... *deal ... it's time* ..."

"Just wait ... of Hands, soon! ..."

Jack did not believe for one second those shadow servants had voices beneath the smoke of their faces. Devils had no need to speak, especially not in such a panicked voice accompanied by another vicious round of coughs. As the hacking subsided, the easy smooth drawl that came after.

A voice which sounded so much like—

The door flew open.

It slammed Jack backward until he fell hard on his back.

Frowning, Roth stood over him, his glare deep-set and blazing murderous. "You're not supposed to be here. Who sent you here?"

An odd feeling skittered down his spine for a moment. It remembered the way Roth shouted, even when he'd followed every instruction, every order. For the longest time, Jack didn't know what that feeling was, until the true side revealed its name. Fear.

He hated it, the way it never fully went away.

"Apologies, sir." Jack forced his expression into hollowness, his voice wooden. Unwavering. "I was given instructions—"

"*Fucking Zarose.*" The man hissed down at his clenched fist as if tempted to throw it at the nearest wall. "If I have to keep releasing illusions from idiotic—"

Jack rose with a start as Roth coughed even harder, harsher than before. The golden, warm tint of his face shined an angry red at the pressure as he brought his fist to his lips, coughing into the ink-stained white silk of a handkerchief peeking through his fingers.

The sight was more alarming than satisfying. Disturbing.

"*Please,*" Roth mumbled, as though his throat were thick with blood.

If sickness had no place on this side, then death was a stranger. Unlike on the true side, full of so many fragile lives. He'd witnessed enough death there to pity those who met its violent grip. Though he'd never seen it quite like this, had no idea what to do but wait for the shadow servants to finally emerge from the room before—

Don't forget that I made you, boy.

Jack stilled, cold in an instant.

Which means I can have you unmade just the same.

The stale threat reared its head back at him with a fury, and he scrambled to get the man back on his feet. Delirious, Roth groaned in pain, while Jack's insides twisted and rioted at every point of contact between them. There was no choice when desperation took over.

It all hit him in one staggering blow.

Like most illusions, Jack had died a thousand ways but came back every time. No blood, no bruises. All things must come to an end, even him. Even with acceptance, it was all still an ongoing guessing game with an extensive list.

Until now.

"We knew that would get you."

At Roth's drawl, Jack flinched away. The motion sent the man back down, falling into another fit of violent coughs as he clutched at the ground, peering up with a beseeching, bloodshot gaze.

And Jack ran.

As far and as fast as he could.

The act shattered. He wasn't even sure if he still wore the illusion's face or where he was going, but rapidly, he disappeared in bursts of distance between him and that scene. As much as possible, despite still hearing every heaving breath toll in his head.

He still saw them. Eyes so bloodshot, but there was something new to them. Something off and wrong and disturbingly familiar.

Because the moment Roth's eyes flashed to Jack, it was like being up on his roof. Looking right into the same night that watched down upon them every day.

The first night of the Show of Hands arrived with no grand announcement, but with notes.

Every magician in the city received one without explanation. Kallia
awoke that morning to find her own golden card perched on her pillow,
branded with an undeniable symbol: a flash of cards fanned out in
someone's grasp, with a devilish mask sitting underneath.

The sight left her cold. The Show of Hands would have its first celebration of many to lure the gate, according to Roth's plan.

Tonight started that ticking clock.

"I swear to Zarose, if I catch anyone scratching off a jewel
again . . ." With a threatening growl, Vain jabbed her slick brush
toward all of them. "I'm making them permanent."

"Bite me." Malice lounged on the bed, while Ruthless chuckled as
she admired her reflection in the wardrobe mirror. Their costumes
were every bit as show-worthy on their own as they were altogether—
long, rich gowns with sprawling jewel appliques that vined around
the bodice to the hem, with deceptively modest sleeves to offset the
devastating plunge in the front. The similarities ended mostly in colors,
a clashing rainbow of glittering purple to deep turquoise to metallic
black with veins of green.

Initially, Kallia had found her own silver-gold dress too bright for her usual taste, until she tried it on. The fit was impossibly sublime, she almost grieved the thought of taking it off. Like a star, she felt luminous and fallen, with bursts of rubies sweeping from her shoulder down to the hem. A dress that called too much attention for what tonight entailed.

"It's a shame these looks will go to waste tonight." Ruthless pouted at the elaborate beadwork along her champagne-purple gown. "Can we at least save our best looks for parties we don't intend on ruining?"

"And why are we going for these masks?" Kallia's neck was already stiff from sitting as still as a statue to receive the jewels across her cheekbone. "They hide nothing."

"Not true," Vain quipped while she worked. "I can hardly see those shadow bags under your eyes anymore."

"I wonder how those got there." It was the closest Kallia had ever come to a complaint since she started training with the Diamond Rings. No matter how many calluses grew on her palm or how violently her arms trembled at the slightest pressure, she quietly took on every challenge: Different lifts and presses to strengthen her muscles. Basic holds and stretches for balance. Spin training to stave off dizziness, which consisted of Kallia being spun while blindfolded for a session.

Being worked to the bone at least sold the story well. No one could deny Kallia's role among the Diamond Rings with the amount of training they put in during the peak and empty hours at the gymnasium. More often than not, while the entire city and the other headliners partied, the Diamond Rings practiced on hoops skilled enough to put on their own show.

"Just because the rings are charmed, doesn't mean we do absolutely nothing," Malice had huffed during one practice as they all stretched over the mats. "We know exactly how to use them, of course. But best to prepare for that, if they ever fail us, too."

Lifting her head, Ruthless glared. "Excuse you, but I learned everything from the marvel houses before joining this circus, so my rings are *flawlessly* loyal," she declared. "They sit on a chain by your heart all day, for Zarose sake. They'd follow you right into the bloody ocean if you so wished."

"What's the point in training like this, then?" asked Kallia.

"Precaution. You never know when a ring might go missing before showtime."

Her jaw hung at the thought. "People have stolen them from you?"

"Tried, failed, and gotten exactly what they deserved for it." Vain smirked, stretching out her other side. "Sabotage is part of show business, mortal. You should know. No one plays fair when we're all trying to win the same game. Some become desperate just to get ahead," she trailed off, growing more wistful. "But when it comes to wanting to watch the world burn, sounds a bit like fun."

That same troubling smile stared back at Kallia now when Vain gave a satisfied hum and finally set down her small brush. "There. Now we're all ready for war."

She cleared out of the mirror's way with a snort as Kallia grinned at her reflection. Her mask was as red as her lips, exquisite and bold. Delicately, she traced the swirls of tiny jewels that fell like art across her face before the others crowded around for a last look in the mirror and final fixes.

It was the strongest Kallia had felt in a long time, sparkling among the Diamond Rings.

"Now, let's see who's ready for the fire." With a toss of her coiled hair, Ruthless patted at the dramatic slit in her dress, framed with gleaming thick-beaded appliques running down the length. "Once these come off, hopefully it'll be enough to cut the power off early."

"As long as you don't accidentally set yourself on fire first," Vain said.

"I'll try my best." Ruthless absently snapped her fingers before Malice presented a crumpled booklet filled with text. "Mal got her hands on tonight's itinerary and there's *a lot*. We should go over positions, safe escape strategies, how to help the crowd if—"

"Help? We're helping by getting it done." Vain ticked her tongue. "What more do they need?"

"*I* need to know that we're only out to destroy this party. Not every-one in it."

Whatever they said next fell away from Kallia as a quick knock came from the door. No one else reacted or seemed to notice. Not even when the door creaked open behind them by the corner of the reflection—

"You ready, boss?"

Kallia stopped breathing when Aaros poked his head through the door's opening. He wore his pre-show conspiratorial grin that deep-ened as his eyes met hers in the mirror. "Now *that* is a look to help the guilty get away with murder."

No. She shut her eyes, and her pulse only thudded louder as the girls continued their chatter over her head while Aaros's voice trickled in between. So familiar and near, she longed to look again until he van-ished like the rest of them.

Not real.

"You all right there, mortal?"

Kallia's eyes snapped open, and three bejeweled faces stared back in worry.

"I'm fine." Her cheeks seared beneath the jewels. She didn't even need to check the corner of the mirror to know there was no one at the door. There never had been. "What, is something wrong?"

A rhythmic tapping answered, bold as heels striking marble floor, before the noise stopped. "Mal, Ruth, go ahead." Vain lifted her nails for inspection. "We'll catch up to you in the Court."

It wasn't so much a command as it was an unspoken agreement. Both girls sauntered off toward the door without hesitation, while Kallia resisted every urge to flee after them.

Being alone with Vain still felt like being cornered by a scorpion, somehow. Even with all their training. Kallia went along with all the hoop work and exercises and routines in the gymnasium, but rarely ever did they touch magic in their sessions. It was almost like an after-thought, doled out in the most underwhelming doses—summoning a spit of fire, conjuring a breeze to cool the sweat from their skin, slowing the pour of water into a glass. All simple, easy tricks that Kallia had learned as a child. Nothing to help her win a duel, as if Vain wanted her to fail.

"So, mortal, who was it?"

The question dropped so suddenly, Kallia blinked. "What?"

"Don't act like we don't know." Bent toward the mirror, she fixed a smudge of color on her lip while offering out a dark silk handkerchief with her free hand. "And your face doesn't hide a thing, so take this."

Kallia reflexively touched the corner of her right eye. No tears had fallen, but almost. And ever the watchful bird, Vain noticed. "Seriously, who was it?" When the cloth went ignored, it dissolved like mist in her hand. "A friend, a love? The opposite?"

Zarose. She didn't want to do this now.

At least Demarco hadn't visited just then. If he had, Kallia would've slid far beneath the vanity and never reemerge. The fact that Vain pried at all, though, was a first. She hardly ever brought up the past, walking around as though she had none.

While Kallia's followed her every day. In training, during meals, walking through the streets. Her body seized up every time, and she was tired of pretending like they were nothing. Like it didn't hurt, every time one of them appeared. "A friend."

The headliner gave a pensive nod. "A good memory, then."

"Does it matter?"

Good or bad, there was pain in looking back. In remembering.

Silence brewed in the room; the tension was so sharp, it slashed between them like claws.

"No. We need to focus." Vain let out a brusque cough and turned on her heel. "Tonight's too important and precarious enough as it is with just us four. Ruth practically threatened mutiny if this becomes a bloodbath."

"Can you blame her? That's not what any of you intended, going into this."

"Fate doesn't care about intention. Or who gets hurt." The headliner's lips pursed into a grim line. "No one has the power to save everyone."

The note of concern in her voice gave Kallia pause. "What if there was someone who did?"

Once the words rushed out, she regretted them. Jack hadn't shown his face in days. It was damn selfish offering him up after ordering him to leave. He certainly had no reason to stay for her sake, and his prolonged absence made that clear.

That still didn't stop her from leaving her golden card with the Show of Hands symbol on the roof, wondering what would come of it.

"No. Absolutely not." Vain's grimace of disgust was instant. "Your bodyguard stays off my team."

Her reaction was to be expected, yet it still pricked at Kallia. "You know he'd be the most powerful ally to have here."

"Someone with *that* much power can just as easily use it against you when it suits them. It's why we're even doing this in the first place."

Kallia gritted her teeth, keeping quiet. Jack was powerful, but he was no Roth. To those on this side, he was much worse. Whether out of fear or envy for a power that shouldn't be possible, it all grated on Kallia's nerves—how quick they were to judge a monster, as if they themselves weren't all monsters in some way.

"We'll be fine on our own." Shoulders squared back, Vain pushed away from the mirror. "As long as we stay focused tonight. *You*, especially."

"Why me?"

"Because your job is to stay in plain sight. It's all you can do, if Roth is watching. And since you're dueling tonight, he'll want to see a win. Or at the very least, improvement," she went on. "Which means if you get distracted because a ghost wandered by your fight and we have a repeat of last time, that'll be on *me*."

Unbelievable. As if she had *any* control over them. "Don't worry. With everything I've learned from the undefeated queen of dueling, there's no way I'll lose tonight."

"What's that supposed to mean?"

Kallia's laugh was a harsh scoff. "It means spinning on a hoop *won't* help me duel. Neither will conjuring a raindrop, or some other small, useless magic you keep throwing at me." Every bit of rage she'd kept bottled in rushed out, one after the other. "I agreed to become a Diamond Ring, but you also promised to make me into a magician who could actually win a fight."

The dark eyes behind the jeweled mask narrowed. "If that's what you think, then why not leave?"

Because she couldn't.

Kallia should've felt more shame. She hardly felt anything, for she had nothing. No power, not even Jack. If she lost the Diamond Rings, too, the way she had lost everyone and everything on a whole other side, then she stood no chance on her own in this city. Not as she was.

"If you're not going to leave, mortal, then listen." With a scathing breath, Vain forced Kallia up by the shoulders as though she were no more than a rag doll. "*I* can't make you into a magician. I was never going to be able to, because you already are."

"Don't patronize me." The inside of Kallia's cheek bled the harder she bit. "If magic makes the magician, what the hell does that make me?"

Roth's words were lodged so deep inside her, she couldn't get them out. She heard them every time she hesitated. Every time she imagined Zarose Gate arriving in a wave of destruction, she couldn't stop.

A snort erupted. "If that's true, then does a painting make a painter?" The headliner eased up her grip. "I've seen you perform, Kallia. In the mirrors, we've watched and gone over your acts."

"Torn apart, actually."

"It's *constructive*," she said, not missing a beat. "But even then, it shouldn't matter what I say. Not when you look so . . . *happy*. Every time you use magic. There's joy in it for yourself, that you share with others. As if everything you cast brings you to life, not just the applause—"

"What does that have to do with anything?" Kallia edged back with a scowl. She could barely remember the last time she felt that way toward magic. It sounded like a dream more than anything.

"You really need help figuring that one out?" Vain huffed while gathering a small bit of her gown's train. "Power is important, but

it's the magician who makes the magic. Not the other way around."
Just before reaching the door, she threw a coy look over her shoulder.
"And if that magician has the nerve to complain about performing the
smallest, most useless magic, then perhaps she should accept she's not
so powerless if she can do even that."

Oh.

"You were testing me."

"I'm always testing you." Vain smoothed back her hair one last time.
"When you do the work, you're not nearly as hopeless as you think you
are. But that's not for me to fix."

Kallia's jaw shut, and stayed that way as the headliner waltzed
through the door without looking back. Only her words stayed behind.

The magician makes the magic.

It rooted inside already, between every wound, as Kallia finally
moved to follow her out.

Of all things Daron thought he'd be preparing for in this world, a party was not one of them.

"You know, I always thought it would be fun to have a big doll to dress up." Tapping at his chin, Herald circled Daron on the pedestal surrounded by mirrors. "I just never thought it would be you."

"Shut up." Daron tugged at the sleek bow tie on his neck, suffocating under the weight of such clothes even though they fit him like a glove. He wasn't quite sure when Herald had the chance to even measure him, and yet the suit he provided had been tailored to perfection.

"Be nice. I could've given you a hideous reject the style houses threw out, but I'm too good for that." Herald chuckled, picking a piece of lint off the back of Daron's sleeve before stealing another look in the mirror. "And *damn*, I'm good."

Daron was hesitant to agree. It was not the kind of outfit he would've picked for himself, that was for sure. It was a sharp cut of a suit, with the jacket being an intimidating stark black to the right side, with the left sporting hundreds of bronze metal beads stitched like the intricate branches of a tree, flaring all the way to the left sleeve. It was the first time in a long time since he'd cleaned himself up like this, looking much taller and broad shouldered than he was used to.

He wondered what Kallia would think.

His pulse ran rapid.

Tonight, he would see her.

Tonight.

For some time, Daron had already been seeing her. A trick of the light, a figure leaping from mirror to mirror and landing soft as a melody. Dancing sinuously in the dark, until it was like wine hitting his veins. Like those games the Dire Woods played, but not half as cruel. These glimpses did not harm him; they were inviting, *tempting,* and for a moment, he wondered if maybe a devil had whispered these visions in his ear.

It was the truest proof of madness, how he welcomed the sight: the scarlet-lipped girl in the shadows he knew wasn't real. All in his imagination.

Tonight would be different.

"You keep smoothing your hair back and it's going to fall out," Herald warned, giving himself a once-over in the mirrors. He'd somehow managed to convert his spectacles into a bright-blue half-mask, matching the striking pinstripes and buttons of his suit.

"I'm fine."

"Then act like it." He clapped his hands over both of Daron's shoulders. "No one here ever enters a party like they're being sent to trial."

"How am I going to fit in with this?" Daron gestured at his outfit, met with a cackle.

"Your look is *tame* compared to what others will be showing up in," Herald insisted. "You've got a mask on, like everyone else will. So you'll slip right into the crowd like a raindrop to the sea. And besides, you've got other priorities besides blending in."

A strange silence dropped between them. From the moment they decided it was far easier to work together to get what they both wanted, a dysfunctional truce formed. Whenever Herald had to leave on some errand, Daron spent every second arguing with himself over why the hell he wasn't trying to break down every wall of the shop that kept him in.

Not that he would even know where to start, on the off chance he succeeded. Stumbling lost all over the streets would make someone easy prey in a city like this. Especially if they recognized him.

Daron still couldn't fathom it, cautiously watching the shop mirrors that surrounded him now. Herald assured him the mirrors here were not for viewing this side, but the true side. The mortal side. For how boring and dull Herald made Daron's world out to be, there was an undeniable fascination.

He was beyond thrilled to be getting out of the shop, but thinking of this world watching his every move, knowing him, speared more nausea into him that he stamped out.

If this entire ocean brought him to her, he would cross it without a thought.

"You're sure she'll be there?" Daron turned to step off the pedestal. "Unharmed?"

Herald gave an offended huff. "And here I thought we'd moved past this. *You're* the job, Demarco. And hurting your feelings is not beneficial to me. Not yet, anyway." His head cocked to the side. "I also don't waste my good liquor and delightful company on just anybody."

Daron couldn't help but cast his gaze up to the ceiling, trying not to laugh.

He wondered, if in another world, they could've been friends, and immediately took back the thought. Herald no doubt presented in the same way toward everyone—the kind of friend who could stab you in the front, and you still wouldn't see it coming.

"And yes, like I said before, your showgirl will not be harmed. You, on the other hand . . ." Despite Herald's carefree drawl, there was an off lilt to it. "I'm not sure."

"I know." Daron refused to dwell on the one gaping uncertainty, for there was no point in worrying. It only formed more of a looming shadow tonight.

"My orders don't go past tonight," Herald added. "So there's a good chance we'll be parting ways."

"Got it."

"Good. So glad you didn't get attached. That would've been an-noying." Without warning, he dove a hand in to scrunch up Daron's combed-back hair, taking every punch in the arm for it with a grin. "Easy, lover boy. You've got to at least look like you just came from a reasonably good time."

"Go to hell."

"Trust me, we're about to . . ." Herald strode over to one of the cur-tained windows. After a quick peek, he loped off toward the door. "I'll catch us a ride. *Don't* fix your hair."

Daron had already been reaching for his hair before the door slammed. He glanced at himself in one of the mirrors, his hair the only recognizable part about him now. Dark, disheveled mess that it was. Kallia always preferred it that way.

On a groan, he clenched the frame. Unable to look at himself, for the wave of silliness that crashed over him. "What are you doing?"

"What does it look like?"

With a start, he whirled around, nearly knocking the mirror over.

Kallia stood bent before him, taking off her boots with her hair tumbling past her shoulders. As soon as she felt his stare, she met it with a catlike smile as she stripped off her stockings—

Daron instinctively turned, then paused so abruptly his stomach twisted at the motion. At the memory, the song that played then, now weaving into his bones. This . . . this wasn't real.

But it was familiar.

"You don't have to turn away, Demarco," Kallia called behind him. "It's not like I'm naked. I'm only going to—"

He spun around, and in two large steps, stood in front of her. Bare feet and the hint of smooth calves peeked out from the sheer fall of her skirt. Every detail, just as he remembered from their days in the Ranza Estate.

But this was not that place. They were in the middle of a room full of mirrors, and when he forced himself to look up, he was alone in all of them.

"You're staring." With a knowing smile, Kallia kicked a bucket of water across the floor.

The water spread between them, touching the soles of his bronze-edged shoes.

So real, even if the mirrors could not see.

Kallia watched him intently, waiting for something as her eyes dropped to his lips for a second.

How had he not known, then?

Daron took a step toward her, playing along. "You're distracting," came his murmured response, as he lowered his hand to her hip. Letting it hover, when all he wanted was to touch her. To feel if the heat coming off her was real, or imagined.

"Demarco, what are you doing?"

Reality snapped back to him just as Herald walked in, perplexed.

Daron's hand still hovered in the air. "Nothing."

The briefest slice of suspicion crossed Herald's eyes, before mirth found its way back. "All right, if you say so, mortal. Now, stop admiring yourself in the mirror or else we're going to be far more than fashionably late."

Daron had been stuck in this shop for too long. It was clearly turning his head inside out. No vision of Kallia had ever been so vivid. So close, so real.

Not real. Just a memory.

"Come on, no frowning." Herald clapped him on the back. "I'm delivering you to your showgirl, after all. Not to your death."

Kallia knew she was in trouble once she entered the ballroom and found ghosts at every corner. She saw Lottie behind one mask, and Erasmus Rayne grabbing a wandering tray of drinks. The performers descending from the ceiling on golden silks became the Conquering Circus—and for a moment, she paused at the flash of Demarco somewhere in the crowd.

They were scattered throughout the party like a sea of ghosts and guests. Kallia drifted alone after Vain found herself stuck in conversation with a boisterous group of champagne-yielding magicians. She casually waved Kallia off with a teasing giggle and an icy nod. *Focus.*

Kallia swallowed hard, trying.

She had a role to play. And a face to find, if he decided to show up.

The Court of Mirrors had been transformed into a fever dream, much more extravagant than the last night of Spectaculore, but still a sight to behold. Everyone crossed the room in lush gowns and suits, more reminiscent of artwork than clothing, only the best the style houses had to offer. Many wore the most elaborate masks of animals and creatures not even Kallia could name, which made the ghosts more tolerable. All in a variety of costume props and designs sealed to faces, already lost in the revelry of tonight.

A spectacular night to remember, and the perfect stage for disaster.

Music swelled from every corner of the party as guests arrived and spread throughout the room for prime views of the festivities. From dueling headliners to style houses battling with their best looks, tonight's events bled together like a mess of colors in Kallia's mind. At best, she remembered the first few listed in the itinerary, one of which already kicked off the night in the form of a charmed dance floor that was quickly filling up.

As a light mist swirled between the dancers' feet, Kallia was unsure if that or the ground itself commanded their steps. They moved in such clean, orderly rows, pairs of guests facing each other before drawing dangerously close as one.

The song unfurled in a slow, steady stream of strings, rising in intensity with the steps. Partners lifted and circled as hands touched and legs grazed. The collection of movements seemed to change at every turn of the song, yet no one ever missed a beat or faltered out of line.

A game with no end as long as the music had no end.

Pacing along the sides, Kallia observed as guests fell prey to the floor at the experimental tap of their heel. Laughter rang over those voicing their wishes to stop, even louder as their pleas went unsatisfied. Once friends began pushing friends over the edges, Kallia drew back before—

A movement caught her eye.

So subtle, it would've slipped her notice were it not so familiar. And so strange to see, on an absolute stranger.

Along the edges stood an illusion servant from the Alastor Place. The crisp black-and-white uniforms were customary for Roth's waitstaff. And the fresh face of the young gentleman, blank as a canvas, was a customary feature for an illusion serving in his house. But while numerous servants wandered around with trays of drink and food, this one oversaw the dance floor. He could've been waiting on behalf of a guest nearby for all she knew, but it became clearer as the illusion brushed his knuckles with his thumb again.

The bastard thought he was tricky.

With his back still turned, Kallia moved in on the illusion. She hoped she was right, and *knew* she was as she pushed through the crowd. The chaos of the ball provided her all the cover she needed to sneak up on him for the first time in her life.

"Hello, Jack," she said close to his ear, satisfied by the slight hike in his shoulders.

The freckled face that turned toward her in no way resembled Jack's, but it carried shock similarly. Especially when outsmarted. "How did you—"

She answered by pushing him out onto the dance floor.

The music swept into her as her feet touched the ground after him. As if she'd practiced these movements for years, her body sang at the steps it was given. It was the soft warm pull of her leg forward, one after the other, sauntering toward Jack to the rhythm's lure.

One moment he looked down as the illusion before looking up with the face she knew. Seamless as a mask change. Out on the floor, it barely caused a stir with everyone lost in the dance. Kallia straightened almost instantly as they touched palms and circled slowly. After some time away, she found his noble eyes even more piercing as they regarded her now, deeply unamused.

"Was this really necessary?" he grumbled.

"What about pretending to be someone else?" Kallia countered at the switch of hands. "If you go through such ridiculous lengths to hide, I have to act fast."

"You *do* know I can walk off this floor any time I want." He chuckled when they drew apart, then back together. "I don't have to play along. Unlike you."

Kallia hadn't considered that. If devils could barely hold him, a dance floor certainly couldn't. "Then why are you still dancing with me?"

"Why did you leave the invitation on the roof?"

His voice struck a nerve, as if he'd asked it again and again, and still couldn't fathom why. It was an amusing sight: the magician who usually held all the answers, now in the dark.

She let him sit in it, for once. Just long enough to enjoy watching the question steep deeper in him as he bowed to one knee across from her, while she made her way to him at the song's whispered commands.

Circle him.

Trail your fingers across his shoulders.

As Kallia did, his back jerked in reaction. The muscles across his shoulders bunched as her fingers dragged across. "Haven't seen you in quite a while, Jack." Reaching one end, she started again on the other shoulder. "You're a horrible bodyguard."

A low laugh shook from him. "I was under the impression you no longer needed one. Your new group is more than capable, and I'm sure they don't mind my absence."

There was no further confirmation needed. Vain clearly led the charge with her dislike of Jack, though Malice and Ruthless never disagreed. No one understood their hesitation better than Kallia, but hesitation would hold them back if they ignored opportunity. Especially the one right beneath her fingertips.

"What's the point of being absent then?" she said, touching her chin to her shoulder as the song called for. "Why are you still here?"

In a snap, she was spun around hard until her back hit his chest.

"You tell me." His breath shook against her ear. His entire body, completely surrounding hers like a caged embrace. "I don't even know anymore."

She tensed. It had been so long since they'd been close like this, she almost felt dizzy from the force of the hold. The air was too stifling, too hot to even breathe; she wondered why he stayed. If he could defy the rules and pull away whenever he pleased, he could very well leave at any time.

Yet he stayed.

"You could help us." Her pulse thudded as she angled her head sideways. "We need help, and with someone like you on—"

In a single move, he twisted her to face him. Nearly brow to brow, breath against breath. So close, it was impossible to focus on anything other than what her gaze landed on first.

The pressed line of his lips broke in a cruel scoff. "*Someone like me? What the hell have you gotten into to need help from someone like me?*"

"The only way to actually stop the gate. And get rid of Roth." Her jaw clenched when he chuckled again. "There are plans in place, and one staged to go off some time tonight to cut—"

"You can't get rid of a magician with devils on his side, Kallia." Jack dropped his hands to her waist, squaring her with a look. "And on top of that, I didn't come here to help some headliners tear down this city so they can finally sit on the throne."

"It wouldn't be such a bad thing, all things considered." He could see so clearly through the Diamond Rings in just a few choice words, but his certainty regarding Roth chilled her. "But there's *so* much more to it than that."

It meant saving everyone she loved, saving *both* sides.

And saving her from failing to break a gate that would break her first.

"So much risk, you mean," Jack corrected. "If there are traitors in his ranks, Roth will find out. When he does, and if I entertain even a second of this madness, we all know who everyone would be throwing to the flames first."

"I wouldn't let that happen."

Kallia forgot the music entirely. She forgot that his hands were around her waist, that they were dancing, when the line blurted out of her.

What surprised her most was the truth of it; the viciousness, too. No matter what the Diamond Rings believed, Jack's help and his powers were too invaluable to ignore on the other side. Strategy would agree, and so would they.

But if someone was to ever deliver any punishing blow to Jack, it would be Kallia alone. And she'd need no help in doing so.

As if he could guess her thoughts exactly, his grin twisted to the side. "You'd be the only one, then."

She should've anticipated the lift from the squeeze at her waist.

Rising, Kallia took off from the ground, pressing her hands at Jack's shoulders for purchase.

And for a moment, she was weightless.

Soaring.

Not quite as high as the Diamond Rings took her, but the height took her back to a place before. She smelled the cold wooden floors of the practice room in Hellfire House, the slight chill that never lasted long whenever she moved.

She'd forgotten how memories were supposed to work when they haunted her everywhere. When remembered, they rose to the surface, unbidden, with small floating details. She'd often preferred practicing alone, but never turned Jack away in those rare times he'd stop for a moment to watch.

It was now that she realized it was the only time she ever willingly put herself in someone else's hands. Her entire self.

And not once had Jack dropped her. Not once had he ever gripped her hard enough to bruise.

He'd always held her with a gentleness that seemed stolen from a stranger. Not the master of Hellfire House or this servant to the Alastors, but someone she could trust when it was just like this.

Eventually the world came back as her feet returned to the ground.

The chatter of the party, the colors swirling around her, the music still guiding their movements.

And Jack. His hands were resting at his sides, thumb already pressed at the knuckles. If he remembered something as well, she couldn't tell. His expression was unreadable. Always unreadable when deep in thought.

"A lot of people could get hurt tonight," Kallia whispered. "Stay, and you could—"

"Become a Diamond Ring?" He cocked his head. "This city isn't worth saving, Kallia. It's best to let it burn."

"But don't you want to get rid of Roth?" she pressed. "You of all people should want him gone."

The song softened to a pause, with a resounding beat to begin the next round. Another chance to convince Jack.

When she bent toward her partner, there was only empty space.

Biting out a curse, she spotted Jack making his way off the floor. He was hard to miss, as he speared straight through rows of dancing guests without any collisions. Not held by the rules like the rest of them.

This Glorian of the other side was opposite to the one Daron knew in every way possible.

Not only were the streets packed to the sidewalks, they were alive. Every corner, performing magicians held court over crowds moving with the current. Every cobblestone, a different color. And those who walked upon them carried onward like a parade of dreams and nightmares hidden behind masks. After looking at the emptiness of mirrors for so long, the sudden dizziness of it all overwhelmed Daron. It wasn't long before his sight adjusted to the runaway chaos of this show, devouring every part of it. The fast-moving nature of this bizarre and beautiful world.

Once he got his bearings on the ride over, it was clear Daron's attire was far more subtle in comparison to the rest. Though he had to admit, he was grateful to Herald for selecting the outfit he did. After passing all of the towering top hats built like houses with windows, to the boots stacked with heels so high guests kept falling over others like chopped trees—Daron couldn't be more relieved to simply fit through the door as they disembarked from their carriage.

The air was hot with revelry, filled with screams lost in laughter and the ever-present melody pounding distantly along the breeze.

Head tipped back, Herald inhaled deeply as though standing before a sumptuous feast. "*Ah.* Love when the world feels wild as war," he said, grabbing Daron's arm before the crowd tore them apart. "There's always something in the air on the first night of anything."

Daron recalled the first night on any of his past tours when he'd performed with Eva, or the first night of Spectaculore even. There was a strange energy to them, an undercurrent of magic that couldn't be contained.

Most times for Daron, it was nervousness lighting the spark. He could never seem to shake it, no matter how often he stepped on the stage. That same force hit him when he looked up from the lit cobblestones, and found the Alastor Place staring back.

"Close your mouth." Herald elbowed him. "You're not fooling anyone if you keep gawking like a fish."

Daron elbowed back just as hard but gritted his teeth to keep his jaw shut all the same.

The thick current of guests moving along slowly made their way through the front doors. The Alastor Place gleamed under a darker light, not quite the same way it had on the last show of Spectaculore. Rather than triumph, there was an air of conquering. Not opulence, but indulgence to the most luxurious degree.

All along the hallway stood trees bearing green bottles instead of leaves, which passersby plucked to uncork or wield like scepters. The metal vines hugging the walls held candles overhead, lifting just out of reach when drunken guests tried touching the silver flames for a laugh.

Like a museum of marvels and delights, everywhere he turned was designed to enchant. They could've been in line for hours, and Daron wouldn't have noticed—were it not for the program suddenly shoved against his chest by the servant at the doors waving guests through.

The Court of Mirrors.

Like his jaw, Daron's stomach dropped as he entered, grateful for the surrounding sea moving him forward. The ballroom on the true side had been grand after renovations, but the Court of Mirrors on the other side was magnificent. The mirrors dominating the walls glowed with the faint images of faces and scenes from elsewhere splashed over the surfaces as he'd seen in Herald's shop. Though no one paid much attention to them when spectacle competed with spectacle from ceiling to floor: slow-spinning chandeliers throwing colors all over the room, descending rivers of golden silks rippling with dancers twisting down the lengths, regal magicians in the most ridiculous ballgowns strutting over tables with their glorious trains dripping over the edges.

As promised, the first night of the Show of Hands did not disappoint. Much tamer than the drunken partying out in the streets, it was a sprawling feast of feats. In the center of it all, the dance floor starred as the main centerpiece of the ballroom. A stage in and of itself, overtaken by a sea of masked magicians moving seamless as waves to the slow steps of a dance. The melody, soft and dark as smoke, found him like memory.

The last time he was on that floor, she'd taken it with him.

"Interesting."

Herald's narrowed gaze peered up from his opened program, the golden cover dominated by the inked symbol of a hand raising a grand draw of cards like the spread of a fan.

Daron cleared his throat. "What?"

"Never pegged you as a dancer, Demarco. The way you're gazing at that floor…" He sighed. "*I* don't even look at my own reflection that fondly."

"Shut up." When Herald proceeded to snort louder, Daron smacked his program to the floor, earning a scowl in return.

"I'm trying to help you strategize, lover boy. It's going to be a packed event, according to the itinerary." Herald bristled while crouching. "The music is charmed to guide the dance, so once that stops, it's duels—anyone versus headliners. Then the style houses have a pastel promenade planned, Red Death Dukes perform their usual death-defying bit, food and drink as far as the eye can see after." He released a deep breath. "Then it's all downhill as the sloppiness hits . . ."

The magician's words fell away as Daron glanced around and froze in place.

Aunt Cata, across the room.

His stomach dropped at the sight of her, sitting cross-legged on a table in a gauche scarlet dress with a crown of feathers atop her head. Unrecognizable in the getup, she held court over a group of men and women watching her with lust.

What the—

He flinched as someone nearly bowled him over with a slurred giggle. "Your hair is quite luscious."

Daron jerked away at the hands crawling up his jacket—hands with nails sharp as knives, and a face that almost had him falling over.

Aaros. Daron blinked rapidly at the man who tried reaching for him again. He was forged like a cabinet in his garish yellow attire. Not at all the assistant's build, yet the face behind the paint-splattered mask *was* Aaros's.

"He's not interested." Herald inserted himself firmly between them, when Daron continued gaping wordlessly. "Look, you're already giving him nightmares and he's not even sleeping yet."

A vulgar growl and belch erupted from Aaros before he stumbled away. Though when Daron's gaze flitted up for another look, there was no trace of the assistant on the harsh face of a glassy-eyed stranger.

Daron's pulse faltered. He searched for the red dress across the way—but the figure in it now was someone he'd never seen: a bright young face with tattooed roses sitting upon her cheeks. A different person entirely.

"Hello . . . ?"

The roar of blood in Daron's ears ceased at the rapid snapping of fingers. "Demarco?" Slightly alarmed, Herald poked him in the chest. "What the hell's the matter with you?"

If only he knew. Because as soon as Aunt Cata and Aaros appeared, more emerged. Familiar faces surfacing over guests like something out of a nightmare: Lottie, descending down from the ceiling on vast golden silks that wrapped around her ankles, stopping her in a split.

One girl strolled by, sporting shorter hair and jewels studded over a face that looked remarkably like Eva's. And then among the pool of dancers was Ira, in a lush, bouncing ballgown of frills with the Devils card thrust high above her head.

They were all around him. Vanishing, reappearing.

He was losing his damn mind.

"I see . . ." Daron shook. He needed a drink, and desperately began hunting for a tray. "I-I keep seeing things. People that shouldn't be here—"

When he thought he saw Eva again by the dance floor, joined by a couple other girls with jewels by their eyes, the nausea hit hard. He swayed, before a rough grip at his shoulders steadied him back firmly.

"Shit." Herald sighed with slight irritation before delivering a few smacks across Daron's cheeks. "Hey, you need to focus and get out there. There's nothing wrong, you're just seeing ghosts. It's normal."

Normal. A strained laugh bubbled up Daron's throat.

"It happens to everyone." With one last hard shake to the shoulder, Herald stepped back from Daron carefully. "The mortal life inevitably follows when you cross here. It's all illusion, unavoidable, but it passes."

Daron groaned as his head started to throb.

It was exactly what he needed, another reason to not trust anything around him. With a last deep breath, he dared one sweeping look around the room, relieved to find no ghosts teasing him from the crowd. For now. "Where's Kallia?" he bit out.

Find her.

The one anchor kept him from drifting away. She was here, and he was *so* close.

Just find her.

"I don't know." Herald appeared to be searching, but only to steal a delicate flute of some purple fizzy drink off the nearest table. "My job is essentially done. From here, it's all you."

"I thought you were supposed to deliver me to her?"

"I was supposed to deliver you to the party." The magician downed the entire flute in one gulp. "Though my advice is to get out on that floor. Because do you really believe the showgirl would be standing idyll around the room?"

The bastard was right, and he hated it. Kallia would never be waiting at the edges of a party; she would be right at the center of it. The eye of the storm.

And she'd be laughing in his face if she saw him right now. "I don't know the dance."

"Thank goodness for magic, then."

Daron barely fought Herald from guiding them both toward the edges overlooking the floor. Rows upon rows of people moved in lines to their partners at the strike of strings. An intricate collection of steps that everyone executed so perfectly in unison, Daron didn't doubt the magic guiding their feet. Once the song dropped to the grand chords of a piano, the dancers turned to switch partners— and the routine went on with newly paired couples, as orderly as clockwork.

"Come on, Demarco." Herald clapped a hand over the shoulder. "Time to fly."

Without warning, he pushed Daron onto the floor with such force, it nearly sent him toppling into a partnered couple. No doubt causing the start of the rows falling like dominoes.

Remarkably, once his feet rested fully on the floor, a thrum went through him and he straightened into position on the spot. It was like a drug entering his veins, his blood, wrapping them in some thrall. Every limb and muscle hummed as well, as though the song in the air somehow breathed through him, too.

At the first notes, a soft command fell over his thoughts. A spark of energy, waiting to be touched. He could refuse if he wanted to. But why would he?

Something in the start wanted him to bow one knee to the ground, so he did. The other partners in line with him bent down similarly, while the others across answered in a regal bow of their own. An ask and an answer.

Daron waited as his partner drew near, the picture to his frame.

He worried what awaited him upon lifting his gaze, relieved to find a face he didn't recognize behind a mask layered in copper lace that matched the fragile wirework of her gown. She gifted him a smile before circling him, walking her fingers across the backs of his shoulders before waiting for him to rise.

As the instruments switched, so did the direction; and as a result, the partners. Without the guidance of the floor, Daron imagined a battlefield of fallen bodies and pained cries with every graceless partner change.

The floor now, and the rows of dancers upon it, moved with an ocean's rhythm.

It was certainly a fantastic show of magic, easy to get lost in. Without doubt or exhaustion to hinder him, he felt compelled to stay for one more minute. An hour. Forever, if they'd let him.

Until his eyes caught a light.

Red jewels, red lips.

The cascade of full dark hair, curling at the ends.

Daron stilled as the floor disappeared for a moment. He jolted at the music's return to full volume. His body primed for the next steps, even as he craned his head over the sea. Searching. He hardly spared a glance at his partner until an annoyed, "ahem," huffed before him, the figure waiting for Daron to hit the next move. All muscle memory at this point, even if the strength behind his steps weakened. A halfhearted lift, a distracted bow.

He kept looking between every part of the routine for some other piece of her.

Her.

As he thought it, the ghosts came back as if to join his search. First, as one of his new partners—a slim-coated gentleman bearing Mayor Eilin's head, who, midturn, disturbingly dissolved into the face of Janette.

Then he spotted Erasmus Rayne a few heads over, partnered with Canary.

Aaros, executing an impressive leap toward the center.

Some left, others stayed. But they all kept coming, until Daron couldn't discern what was real anymore. It no longer mattered. The world blurred in this constant carousel of ghosts he might never see again. He didn't know whether to savor the glimpses or look away entirely.

The song came to an end, with a promise to start once more. It meant a breath, a momentary rest as he bowed down his knee. Sweat gathered at the back of his neck as he caught his breath and waited.

A glimmer caught at the corner of his eyes. A long silvery-gold hem with intricate beading trailed closer and closer to him. A new partner, another dance.

Lifting his gaze, Daron suddenly forgot every step.

His heart seized in his chest to one thought.

Her.

H*im.*

Despite the music, Kallia struggled to keep up with the steps.

Demarco stood before her, donning a striking suit and bronze armor across his eyes. The mask shielded most of his face, but she didn't need to see the rest. She'd know it anywhere.

The music surged her forward, and for a moment, she was almost afraid to begin. To get closer, to touch him.

Just a ghost. She repeated the words until they set her at ease as she stepped toward her partner.

The magician wearing Demarco's face watched her the whole time he kept his knee to the floor. Her stomach tightened at the careful way he followed her every step, even as she crossed behind him.

By the time her fingers finished trailing across the firm line of his shoulders, a stranger would be waiting when to meet her. But when she turned, it was still his face. Still a ghost.

And he wouldn't leave.

It was just what she needed after Jack's departure. Right before her duel, before Ruthless brought the night down.

Focus. Vain would rip into her if she didn't, now that the party had begun at the Dealer's entrance moments ago. When Roth's bellow of a laugh reached her, she tensed, relieved to be trapped on the floor away from him.

Until now.

The gems scattered over her cheekbones and forehead like additional armor she was grateful for. She needed it as she let the music take her. Losing herself to it.

Eventually, the command of the notes took them, and they fell into the steps. Just like before.

When their palms finally touched, her heart ached entirely. It remembered the hand that would reach for hers in secret, when they thought no one was looking as they walked along sidewalks. The hand that cupped the side of her face whenever the door closed behind them soon after.

Not real. He *wasn't* real.

Like everything else here.

When Demarco twisted her around, she focused directly on her palms braced at his chest. Her cheeks burned at how little it took to break her. How much worse it felt, to remember like this.

A friend, a love? The opposite?

Vain's words pecked in the back of her head like a taunt. Enough for Kallia to finally look up to Demarco watching her from behind the mask.

Kallia swallowed hard, resisting the urge to run. There was no need to fear him or any of the others who visited. But the power this pain held over her, carving deeper into her heart, was worth fearing. For an instant, a stranger's embrace made her forget. It made her remember, if she simply closed her eyes. And because she knew the truth but welcomed the hurt anyway, it made her weak.

The melody forced them away first. Every chord struck a new command in her bones, joining their hands while they circled each other. She kept finding him at every turn, meeting her step-by-step as the dance bound them together. A breath away, an almost embrace.

Until he lifted her up high when the notes swept upward, before lowering her slowly so that they were chest to chest, faces close. His heart pounding over hers.

They stood so still, as if the music had abandoned them entirely.

Though she wouldn't have noticed. Demarco kept haunting her, and he wouldn't stop until she let him go.

Let them *all* go.

They weren't going away. For Kallia, they were only growing stronger.

"Please," she managed, pushing at his arms. "Please just go—"

"Is this real?"

Kallia stopped breathing. "What?"

A new swell of strings swallowed the answer, snapping the floor into new formations swift as a twisting kaleidoscope. Couples parted ways, switching to their next partners. The melody urged her to do the same, but she fought it. Unsuccessfully, as the tide pulled her away to join the next row of dancers.

Frantically, Kallia searched over the heads and between shoulders, rushed through the motions while trying to pull herself from the song. Every time she caught him, she lost him.

The farther they grew apart, the more their gazes found each other's across the floor.

Until all trace of him was gone. No matter how many directions she turned for one last glimse.

Once her pounding heart returned to a steady beat, the voices and laughter slipped back into her ear. The party kept moving around her, even when the music had finally stopped. The floor cleared, the smoke swirling at her ankles gone. Under the dimming lights, the crowds gathering at the sides tittered in excitement as circles surfaced across the grounds. Dueling marks.

"Oy!"

Kallia startled at the loud clap in her face.

"Dancing's over." Malice strutted away with the toss of her hair and a wink. "It's showtime."

Clarity doused Kallia with much-needed cold water, and it still wasn't enough. Another duel. Any nerves for the occasion were long gone, crushed to ash as a sharp elbow threaded forcefully within hers. "Yes, try to redeem yourself tonight, mortal," Vain murmured, guiding them off to the sides of the dueling floor. "At the very least, don't embarrass me again."

"A true inspiration to us all." Malice sauntered beside them. Her smirk fell after a double take at Kallia. "Are... you all right?"

No. She was still trying to catch her own breath. Demarco *wasn't* here. She knew that. But no encounter with a ghost had ever left her so shaken.

Is this real?

"Oh, Zarose, not now." Vain drew them both to a stop and inspected Kallia's face with a spark of alarm, dropping quickly into a scowl. *"No stage fright. You're a Diamond Ring, which means you're better than that."*

Vain's worst thorns really only emerged when under pressure. Her one nervous tick. The last thing she'd want to hear was a strange ghost story about her own brother wandering about the party. "I'm fine," Kallia assured through clenched teeth, shaking off the nerves.

"Then prove it."

Like the changing of the stage, the enchanted dance floor from before had transformed into a grid of designated battlegrounds squared off to fit no more than a dozen duels at once. Attending illusions oversaw each corner. Some guests, especially those more elaborately and inconveniently dressed, opted to spectate from the sides and place their bets before anything began.

For the ones who wished to duel the headliners themselves, lines already formed around each prospective match.

Around the square reserved for the Diamond Rings, the line coiled like an unruly snake eating its own tail. Roth had yet to make his way to their square, but she'd seen glimpses of him with his devils not too far off. Attracting an audience of this size was sure to draw his attention soon.

"Would you look at that?" Malice nodded over her shoulder as they reached their side of the dueling board. "If we don't get any wins, at least we can claim popularity."

Kallia understood the true reason for the mob. Not so much due to popularity as it was the promise of a sure, quick win against her. After her last duel, the target on her back had only grown larger. Any magician hoping for an easy way to get noticed by the Dealer would take advantage of it.

"I'd rather claim victory." Kallia turned her back on the crowd.

"Likewise. It's a lot more satisfying." Vain paced, sweeping a furtive glance over the heads around them. "She should've been here by now."

Ruthless. The girl had slipped off on her own some time during the night, after making sure she was seen throughout the party. Whatever mayhem she'd forged into her gown, it would light the party up fast. And end the duels even faster, which seemed more and more unlikely as all of them inched closer to Kallia's starting place.

"Maybe she got caught," said Malice.

"Or decided she didn't want to do it," Kallia supplied, cracking her knuckles. "She was worried—"

"Both of you, shut up. She'll pull through." Pressing a finger to her temple, Vain took a moment to think before her features crinkled as if some terrible odor entered her nostrils. "Why is he back?"

Kallia looked up, and straightened as the hairs on the back of her neck rose.

Their sidelines were packed with onlookers, and Jack stood among them, stoic as ever. Already, a ring of space formed around him from those inching away, nervous to even catch his notice for a second.

Surprise fluttered up her spine, twisting at her insides, forming a strange smile she couldn't be buried across her lips. She hadn't . . . expected him to stay. When he left her on the dance floor, she assumed he'd be long gone by now. He had no further business here, nor any responsibility to her anymore.

Except he was still here. Refusing to meet her eye, which amused her all the more. "I invited him," Kallia said.

Vain's shriek was immediate. "After I told you not to?" Her expression flashed from annoyed to murderous in a blink. "Damn it, Kallia, what did you—"

The first bell rang, alerting magicians to assume their positions.

Fighters shuffled into place, while everyone else eagerly stepped back behind the lines.

"You better pray nothing backfires tonight, or else," Vain hissed, pointing a sharp-tipped nail at Kallia with a clear desire to stab. "Also, good luck."

Raising her chin, she stalked off. Malice followed, not without a thumbs-up and a wink for more luck that could very well go to waste if the duel was cut short. That alone should've been a relief, with Jack on the sidelines and the world watching her again. Waiting for yet another brutal loss.

But a different fire lit inside her tonight. One that wanted to win.

Her opponent waiting across was a magician she didn't recognize. A young grin on an older face, with sheared-short hair that faded to dusky rose. When he cleared his throat, all to cover a laugh, it felt all too familiar. Exactly how the contestants from Spectaculore had regarded her at first glance—a joke meant to be humored, then swiftly crushed.

If they wanted a laugh, she would give them one.

The rule decreed between them was nothing containing the color green. A simple enough rule for a first duel, and one she was confident she could follow.

When the attendant threw the anchor between them, Kallia's opponent acted first. The plain rubber ball between them stretched and exploded out into a boulder large as a table, which shattered into sharp pieces aimed at Kallia.

As the wave of needles and splinters surged for her, she breathed and fought back all reaction to hit back just as hard.

Focus.

Vain, clear in her ears.

Kallia's first instinct was to cast a grander trick. But grander wasn't always smarter. However loud or large an attack might be, what mattered most was its landing.

Instead, she split the pieces of rock further and melted them into rain.

The crowd vanished from her periphery; her hold on the rain was tenuous enough but not obscenely difficult to conjure. An illusion was fueled as much by imagination as it was by memory. She knew rain, and the way it could fall as she guided the storm over to her opponent's end. His move now.

Noise, Vain had emphasized. *Everyone attacks with a rhythm. Disrupt it.*

When the magician sent back shards of ice, Kallia widened the breadth of her hands, the ice forming bigger like blocks of glass. One by one, Kallia sent them down in bone-wrenching shatters.

His confused wince was as good as a winning point. He blinked rapidly, trick after trick flying fast behind his eyes. Just before glass crashed in front of his very feet, he managed to conjure something different out of the shatters.

A wave of sand emerged from the grains of ice, swirling toward Kallia as if on the path of a windstorm.

The magician makes the magic.

Kallia listened, gathering the sand to fuel the picture in her head as she pushed the stream back his way. Her opponent's features tightened in concentration, ready for any eruption.

Not the damp, chunky soil that splattered on his face.

Laughter rang, but she barely heard it. She only saw her opponent muttering a curse under his breath before a large plant erupted to the surface like a creature from the sea, a green, closed bud the size of a large dog opening its petals like jaws—

"Broken rule," the attendant announced with finality. And a salute toward the Diamond Rings' side. "Victory to Kallia."

Cheers exploded around her. Mouths hung in surprise, screams pierced the air.

But she heard nothing once she caught sight of Demarco again, watching on the sidelines of it all.

For the first time, she didn't care if she'd won or lost. It had all become noise, the moment she saw him.

Until more screams shattered the air all around her.

Kallia frowned at the smell of smoke before her mouth dropped at the ceiling lost in flames. They caught the hanging silks and ran rapidly down the cloths, sending aerialists jumping over magicians breaking their fall. The fire moved fast, unnaturally so, that it might have been mistaken as a spectacle on the itinerary were it not for the sheer panic breaking over the court as people ran once the ceiling began dripping flames over guests, setting costumes ablaze.

One moment, nothing. And the next, absolute chaos.

Malice ripped out a high-pitched wail, while Vain wore a convincing mask of fear as they stuck close together through the stampede. Headliners rose, throwing every force against the ceiling, but the fire would not die. And it could not be stopped.

Madness took over. The floors shook as magicians ducked for cover or ran for the doors in a large desperate, writhing mass trying to squeeze through the way out.

Kallia lost the others instantly. True panic set in with every elbow and shove that pushed her deeper into the fold, unable to see anything at all but smoke and tears and burnt fabrics smashed against her face. When she finally managed to squeeze through the doors leading out of the Alastor Place, she gulped in the fresh air, desperate for it.

Curses and cries were scattered over the gathering watching the Alastor Place fall. Some faces were frozen in shock, for nothing had ever touched their perfect little world like this. And more looked fascinated for that very same reason.

Kallia had to find the others. When she finally got her bearings, she stumbled away from the audience of this new show, down a quieter bit of street. She had to get away, plot her next move. Find the others without—

A hand grasped her arm and pulled her into the shadows between buildings. Someone. In the dark, her eyes adjusted. Her breaths panting against his as he leaned into her. Warm as the day, silent as a shadow.

Kallia pressed back into the wall. Her heart pounded deep in her chest at that glint of a bronze mask. And Demarco's face, still beneath it. "Who are you?" she demanded. "Why won't you just leave me alone?"

The words came out harsh and rough, ignoring that pain cutting her to the core.

She knew, without his answer.

Just because it couldn't be did not make it untrue.

Wasting no more time, he kissed her.

He had so much he wanted to say, so much he wanted to tell her. He meant to recite all the lines he'd practiced in his head for this exact moment.

And yet when she looked up at him, it was nothing like what he'd envisioned. No teary smiles or gasps of relief. No warmth of reunion. Just hard eyes and a sharp scowl, the mask hiding all her fears and doubts and secrets kept so closely guarded inside her.

It undid him completely.

This was real.

Finally.

His heartbeat thrummed with the word. With the feel of her against him, her scent surrounding him. He almost dropped to his knees from the relief, to sense something inside click back into place after so long.

Ice filled him when he realized she was not moving at all, stiff as a held breath.

Fuck.

He began pulling away, the adrenaline fading to embarrassment, but she dug her fingers painfully into his suit and crushed her lips back to his with the hitch of her breath. A happy sound, a sad one, as she slanted her lips over his and explored in deep, long strokes, absorbing the deep groan that rose in his throat, the moan in hers.

This couldn't be real. This couldn't be real.

This couldn't be real.

Just like the first time, how simply it had happened. No grand spectacles or desperate measures, but a moment where the world fell away, where it was just them. And it was real.

When he cupped the side of her face, it was wet. He drew back to look at her, the slide of tears over the red jewels pressed to her skin, framing her face like a constellation he couldn't stop tracing. The same red that matched her lips, smudged at the edges. No doubt, on his as well.

She fingered the edge of his mask, prying it off gently until his entire face was laid bare. A shudder went through her, through him, at the press of her fingers through his hair, trailing down to his jaw, stopping at the space beneath his mouth.

"Is this real?" she whispered, the exact words he'd said before. He closed his eyes at the sound of her voice, new words to his ears. Not from fragments of the past. Not from dreams.

Here.

"Wait," he bit out as he flinched back, burning inside.

How could he have forgotten?

"I shouldn't," he said, swallowing hard. That impulse driving him forward died in his veins. "My magic and yours . . ."

He couldn't.

Sorry would never be enough to undo all that had happened.

Her gaze fell, but her hand stayed right against his chest. His heart. "It's still not fully returned. I'm working on that," she said quietly. "But it will come back. Eventually."

Eventually. That hope in her voice, however small, lived. But he was the reason it had become so small in the first place, and nothing sickened him more.

"I'm sorry," Daron said, shaking. "For hurting you. For everything."

He didn't go on to say he didn't know. Or that it was some side effect of his powers he'd had no clue about. None of it made any difference now. The damage was done, and words would not fix them.

"You didn't know. I see that now, but it doesn't matter." She ended it, her tone soft yet detached. Never one to dwell on hurt, as she kept an alert watch on the opening of the alleyway behind them. "I don't know where to begin . . . what are you even doing here?"

Before he could answer, a curse flew under her breath.

And she grabbed him hard by the lapels, yanking him close. Reflex took over as his palm hit the wall, steadying them from crashing to the ground with little to no space between them.

The proximity left him dizzy. His eyelids drifted downward once he caught her gaze on his lips—before she craned a look past his shoulder. Movement. A few staggering shadows that passed from behind.

"No one can see us together." Her breath a mere whisper, she pushed him back slightly once the footsteps had faded. "*They* know too much."

Compared to when they first crashed into each other, the distance now struck like whiplash. His face remained hot. His lips were *still* raw from hers. And she couldn't even stare him in the eye for longer than a few seconds before letting go of his jacket with a curious expression. "How did you even get that outfit for tonight?"

Everything on him seemed to tighten instantly. He loosened the buttons by his neck. "I've had help."

It was a generous word to pair Herald with. Even Kallia raised a dubious brow. "You can't trust any help that's offered here. Nothing comes without strings."

"That, I know." Far too well. "Herald's been a bastard since the moment he—"

"*Herald?*" The cords of her neck popped out. "How the hell did you end up with the likes of him?"

Any warmth from before was gone. Just ice between them now. The longer it froze, the more it clawed inside Daron. This moment had been inevitable, and he still wasn't sure how to tell her the truth of it all, how his arrival came through the machinations of others. For her.

The shame still burned, that he'd played into it all too well. Ever the fool, falling for the breadcrumbs that guided him to the trap. They couldn't have selected a better target to beckon from this side of the mirror.

And now, there was no going back. No safe way of going *anywhere* from here. But he moved forward to finally find her, once and for all. So they could figure out that next step. Together.

None of this was unfolding how he'd hoped.

"How?" Kallia pressed harder. "You falling right into Herald's path seems a little too convenient, if you ask me."

"Convenient?" A harsh sound splintered off the back of his throat. "There's nothing convenient about the way I got here."

He still shivered every time he thought about the Dire Woods, those nightmares taking life behind his eyes. It felt like an eternity walking through it all, and he knew for the rest of his life he would never drive through its paths ever again without shaking. He'd remember what awaited him behind every tree, between every finger of those skeletal branches.

That was, if they were able to return at all.

"Then how?" Kallia leaned back into the wall, fingers pressed against the jewels lining her temples. "We all fall through the cracks of the mirror, that's norm–"

"I walked through the Dire Woods."

For you.

Her eyes fastened on him and stayed, unblinking. Either shining from the sliver of light hitting her lashes, or something glistening deep in her eyes.

His heart remained quiet as stone in his chest. "I walked through the Dire Woods. And saw things I will never forget. A darkness tailored specifically for me, nightmares each step of the way, until the world became—"

"No." Kallia shook her head, blinking furiously. "Those woods don't lead here. That can't . . . that's impossible."

"Why the hell would I lie about this, Kallia?" Rage tinted his vision red. He would've preferred her indifference to this—absolute distrust in everything he said. He'd been on this tightrope with her before, and returning was like meeting as strangers again. "I only ended up in those woods because we've all been searching for weeks, just for any sign of you. How could you think I would ever lie about that?"

Her hard silence stoked the flames even more in his blood. He'd searched too hard for this to be the end. They all had. "You think I would make up how *none* of us stopped looking for you ever since that night?"

"Stop," she croaked.

"Or how we all nearly set the whole city on fire, because it was our last resort? Aaros and Canary and Lottie, we all—"

"Demarco. *Stop.*" Her glare slitted to knives, stabbing deep. "I don't want to hear any more."

"And I don't want to fight with you anymore!" His voice cracked beneath every wasted word and breath raked in. This wasn't the first time they'd argued. Since he first met Kallia, they'd fought countless times. Behind closed doors and out in public, but always ending on an open note. The promise of more to come, the next time they met.

The girl before him was closed as a cage keeping all the world out. Though nothing troubled him more than the razor edge of her laugh that fell at the slow shake of her head.

"Zarose, *of course*. I should've known." Under a dark, seething breath, Kallia swore. Shot a quick glance over her shoulder, the opening clear of any stragglers. "I know exactly how Herald scooped you up, and why," she snarled. "*You're* the one who's here to help me."

Only she could make that sound like a bad thing. "Help you with what?"

"Opening the gate. Breaking it."

Everything inside went cold. Herald had failed to mention that. All of Aunt Cata's words about Zarose Gate that had long since quieted now surged back—the violence, the destruction, the uncertainty it delivered.

"Wait, why you?" he demanded, his pulse racing faster. "Kallia, you can't—"

"Apparently I can, because I'm an Alastor," she muttered unenthusiastically, squeezing the bridge of her nose. "There was never a guarantee before, as it's never been done and I could use that. But now . . ."

The confirmation of Kallia's family, straight from her own lips, shook him to the core. So Herald hadn't lied about it all.

A passing tidal wave of shouts and hollers drowned out whatever she'd meant to say next. No desperate screams from the party anymore, at the very least. Still, when Daron positioned himself subtly like a shield around her, that crumpled expression bordering on sickness stayed on her face. Until eventually, it seeped into him, too.

"I'm sorry," Daron whispered. The heaviness of the word carried all the apologies he owed her and every promise he'd made, to never hurt her again as he had in the past.

Already, he'd broken it. All in his attempt to fix what he could, to heal *this*.

Fingers curled against his shoulder, Kallia closed her eyes before firmly pushing him away. "I-I have to go."

"Why?" His chest seized, hollow all of a sudden as she turned. Until he tried taking her hand. "Please, wait."

The last thing he wanted was for her to leave, uncertain of when he would see her again.

Just as their fingers grazed, Kallia edged out of reach. "It's still not safe for us to be seen together," she said. "I'll . . . I'll try setting up somewhere for you, somewhere safe to stay, just until we can—"

"Stealing my tenant, showgirl?"

They jerked at the casual footsteps nearing them from the opposite direction down the alleyway. Nothing but shadow at first, before the broad outline of a figure drew closer—and Herald came fully into view, casually straightening his glasses over his nose. Oblivious to the tension, or possibly relishing it.

"Well aren't you two the picture of happiness," he noted sourly. "Found everything you were looking for, Demarco?"

The magician's presence struck a match in Kallia, who charged right up to him like a bull breathing fire. "I told you what would happen if you messed with me," she seethed. "I'm going to *destroy* you."

Whatever history these two had, it was not kind. Kallia rarely ever unleashed the full lash of her wrath; to his credit, Herald's sneer hardly faltered in the face of it. "You *could* do that," he drawled. "Or, you could take up my offer to Demarco instead, for another cozy stay in my shop—"

"And you just *happened* to be walking by at this exact moment to do so." Daron rolled his eyes. "What are you really on about? You finished your job, so we're done."

"Not yet, brother." Conjuring a silk cloth between his fingers, Herald began wiping at his flashy glasses. "The Dealer is not pleased with how tonight's festivities went. So outraged, I barely got a word in edgewise. His devils had to drag him away, just to cool off. Figure out what happened, how to make up for a lost night." He sighed. "So, alas. New orders, new job."

"What job?" Daron demanded, just as Kallia uttered, "What plan?"

"For now, that's between the Dealer and me." Herald smiled down at his cleaned glasses. "Not that there's any other option, showgirl. You've all got your plate full and more than enough spectators already."

The Show of Hands continuing on after chaos like tonight's didn't shock Daron in the slightest. This industry never changed, not even on different sides. First Spectaculore, now here. The world could be burning right at their feet—but as long as the stage stood, the show would go on. Disaster was no excuse, and certainly no reason to stop.

Kallia glowered. "Is that a threat?"

"Some friendly advice." Herald inspected his nails. "If it's Roth's word, it goes. Unless you want us all to take a walk outside this city together."

They all tensed. Despite himself, relief coursed through Daron.

Having no other option was sometimes easier when every step he made failed. Searching for Kallia had become the goal for so long, there was no seeing past it. Part of him hoped the rest could fall into place after, that he'd finally be able to breathe.

At least now, he could lick his wounds in the solitude of the mirror shop.

A disturbance sounded a short distance away. More hollering, growing rowdier. Herald shot a glance over his shoulder, taking stock with a groan of the sliver of the streets he could see. "Things will only grow messier out here to make up for a disappointing night." He nodded back at Daron, sparing a short bow to Kallia. "Counting on the next to fare much better. Though the bar is quite burned to the ground at this point."

As the magician advanced closer to the bright end of the alleyway, Daron turned to follow suit before the cool grasp of fingers stopped him.

"Come to the show," Kallia whispered, breath rushed.

"That depends." His pulse leapt at his wrist. "Do you actually want me there?"

His stomach coiled tighter. He was being an ass, which meant he needed to leave. Before he fucked this up even more. Every muscle in his body was charged to go, but he was unable to move. To stop himself from glancing down at the hand still holding his. Her palm felt different than he remembered, firmer with callouses that hadn't been there before in what felt like so little time since she disappeared. Eva always said the ways hands changed spoke volumes about a person. Daron wondered if she noticed his the way he felt hers.

"I don't hate you." His throat bobbed hard. Kallia, on the other hand, had made her feelings more than clear earlier, and he wished not to repeat it again. Especially to the backdrop of another night of empty revelry. "All things considered, with us . . . not sure that's the best idea."

But he didn't want to leave her. Didn't want her to go.

"No, I—I didn't . . ." Eyes closed, Kallia paused for a breath, and a soft shadow crossed over her face. "You need to come to the next show. There's someone you need to see."

What more? Every bone in him tensed as if ready to twist his body in half and break the rest. Daron recognized the pattern by now, the anxiety pulsing loud as a drum in his chest, in warning of the worst to come. He expected it. "Who?"

Until the glimmer of a first hopeful smile broke across her face. "Your sister . . . is here."

He was here.

Actually, truly here.

It didn't hit Kallia fully, not until she slipped off her heels and began wandering down the lit streets of Glorian. After everything, she needed to walk. A city loud enough to drown out all thought would be the only thing to clear her head.

Music blazed in the air without end or rest in between, trumpeting from every corner she walked. Some answered the call—those who swayed in place while standing in line into one of the packed dining manors, others running in pure delirium to form a dance floor where they could for themselves along the cobblestone.

The night raged on, as usual. Any trace of disaster that stemmed from the Court of Mirrors earlier vanished, forgotten by the majority who chose to lose themselves in other ways. It was a rule each side adhered to, true and other. The show must go on, and so must the party. An endless cycle that stopped at nothing, until it finally did.

The entrance into the Alastor Place was quieter than usual, the only sign tonight had any effect was the Court of Mirrors had been decreed off-limits. The fact that no one swarmed and interrogated her instantly meant no one suspected the Diamond Rings. If a scandal like that broke, she would've heard whispers on the streets, otherwise.

Status truly was the best sort of mask. Chin raised, Kallia forced herself up the first flight of the stairs without looking back. It was too soon, and Herald's mirror shop was too close.

All this time, Demarco had been so near. A mere building away, under Herald's watch. As much as Kallia wished to set Jack on the shifty bastard, Demarco didn't seem all too desperate to avoid the mirror shop or its owner. Not that she blamed him.

When panic took over, she snapped. Demarco was *here*, which meant he was trapped. No clear way out, unless she was able to do what Roth demanded.

Her jaw worked until it went numb as she ascended the stairs, barefoot and exhausted to the bone, avoiding the eyes that always followed. No headliners around to scoff at the sight of her, as they were no doubt partying outside when the Court of Mirrors fell. And no Roth, either.

Kallia wished she'd seen his rage, breaking all that polish he carefully laid over himself. Roth puppeteered this city like his own little doll house: nothing ever went awry without his knowing. No one would dare. Tonight, most likely, was the first time nothing went according to plan, or his favor.

And still, he had the last laugh. Behind every false smile, every claim of family and "dear" to sweeten the image, Roth had been working on a plan of his own long before the Diamond Rings had pulled them into theirs. As if he could already see right through Kallia like glass, before she'd ever stepped foot in his city.

"Oh, thank Zarose, she's here."

Kallia entered her bedroom alone and found three figures already lounging across her bed. Faces bare of makeup and jewels, out of the slick glittering gowns in favor of comfier silks. Ruthless and Malice sipped from dainty flutes of champagne, whereas Vain cradled an entire bottle in her arms like a newborn. All eyes lit up in relief at her arrival.

"Finally. We can now *properly* celebrate. . . ." Vain drawled with the cock of her head. "Unlike some people who were too thirsty for patience." She smoothly dodged a kick from Malice's satin-slippered foot. "Don't deny it."

"*I* took down the first night, so I'm allowed to indulge. Kallia understands." Ruthless wiggled her fingers over a decadent platter of glistening cherries, picking her share before offering to the others. "We were worried, darling. Even Jack wasn't sure where you went off to."

Another weight hit Kallia in the stomach. "He was looking for me?"

"Yes, well, he *is* your bodyguard." Using her teeth, Vain tore off the foil wrapped around the bottle's neck. "Not exactly a good look for the guard to lose the body. Especially when chaos is afoot."

The knots in her gut only tangled harder. The last she'd seen of Jack, he was drowning in a crowd that he'd been pulling to safety, those who regarded him as a monster. Devil-born. Asking for his help earlier had seemed silly at first, but when the moment arose, he sprang into action. As if he'd been waiting, ready, for a chance to do more. "Where is he?"

"Hell, if I know." Vain snorted, coaxing the cork free. "We were too busy trying to catch a peek at Roth before his shadow dogs dragged him away. He was practically soiling himself in rage over tonight. It was glorious."

"And far too brief." Malice tsked. "Such a shame."

At the thunderous pop, hoots erupted as sparkly fizz trickled down the bottle, which Vain proudly raised like a glass torch. "To a successful night." Taking a hearty sip before offering the rest to Kallia. "And your victory—the first of many!"

The Diamond Rings repeated the words while sipping heavily at their glasses and passing decadent trays of desserts among each other. Part of Kallia wanted to join in the celebration, to escape her thoughts for a second. She'd won a duel, humiliated the great Dealer at his own party, and they were walking free and feasting on treats too pretty to eat. Rewards of a battle won, a true victory.

Until Kallia's nausea reached its peak at the thought of indulging in any of it. "Demarco is here."

Someone spit out their drink as the room froze. A platter fell, dropping pastries and creams onto the carpet. Kallia didn't care, not even as cold champagne from the bottle she'd dropped fizzed by her feet, biting at her toes.

Vain jolted upright as if she'd been stabbed through the spine. "It's just a memory," she muttered. "You've been seeing ghosts and—"

"It's him." Something burst in her chest. Ghosts could not do the things Demarco had done to her. The kiss rushed back in flashes of heat and touch. Lips pressed against hers, trailing over her neck and her pulse point. Those familiar eyes devoured her from behind the mask, darkening even more as she took it off.

Is this real?

"*Shit*," Malice hissed, setting her emptied glass on the table. "Well, what does this mean now?"

All of their plans, all the training that went into this balancing act, had found the edge sooner than they'd anticipated. This was no mere complication or a hurdle to work around. This brought far too many unpredictable variables. Too many possibilities of everything going wrong.

"How did he even get here?" Vain snarled out the question. Her jaw clenched so painfully tight, it appeared broken.

I walked through the Dire Woods.

There had been something so sorrowful and changed in his voice, it made Kallia shiver. She hadn't had the sense to ask for the rest. To understand exactly what he'd been through, just to reach this point.

She wasn't ready to know it all, to hear who else was involved. She couldn't bear giving more life to the ghosts already haunting her.

Not when one had followed her here.

"Never mind. I know." A seething curse flew from Vain. She snatched another bottle from the foot of the bed. "It's Roth, isn't it?"

It was obvious even without Kallia's nod, and no one was more furious than she was at herself for not seeing it coming. True to form, this world would always be a show. Any player could be moved; any coincidence, orchestrated. Especially with a puppeteer like Roth watching all from above.

Vain kicked a tray out of her path with a harsh clang. "This doesn't change anything." Without looking back, she stormed off with the bottle still in hand. "Don't follow me. I'll be back."

"Please, Vain." Quiet panic radiated off her, the kind Kallia understood well. That need to lie through it. To run. "You have to see him. You have no idea how long he's—"

The door slammed shut with a force that shook the room. Like the shock of a gunshot, no one moved for a beat too long.

"Don't take it personally, darling." Ruthless gingerly propped herself up on her elbows over the messy bed. "She doesn't talk about him with anyone."

"She doesn't talk about the past in general, really." After a long sigh, Malice danced her fingers atop the empty bottles beside her. "We certainly popped these too early."

"And not nearly enough." The rosy glow in the other Diamond Ring's cheeks from before paled now. "Best to stock up on more. I think we'll need it."

Their voices drifted to a hush as Kallia went to the window, feeling no better with the weight of their eyes on her. She saw them in the reflection, brimming with sympathy from behind.

That was the last thing Kallia wanted to indulge in tonight. No doubt Vain fled for the same reason, but she wasn't the only one who could read silence. In the reflection, Ruthless and Malice both backed away, making a gentler exit through the door with every intent on returning in a bit.

But they gave her this moment. Sometimes closeness was a gift, but when needed, so was space. Silence.

Kallia couldn't have been more grateful to be able to breathe on her own for awhile. She needed to get out, to keep moving. Anything to get out of her head.

Hiking up the skirt of her dress, she pushed and climbed through the window, the warm candlelight shifting into cool night air. It was like shedding a second skin, venturing out where absolutely no eyes would follow. She made her way up to the flat of the roof that awaited, dark and undisturbed.

It was clear why Jack loved it so much. The one place one could think in a world filled with so much light, so much noise. So much everything.

The blank, black sky above allowed her eyes some rest from the wildness, a comfort in the nothingness. Until she remembered that Demarco was somewhere beneath that same darkness. The same devils, watching him from above.

Panic bolted through her. She couldn't believe how she'd let him go off, just like that. Her heart clamored against her chest to fucking *move*, find him. After all this time apart, why the hell was she still sitting here alone?

The question plagued her for moments, hours, however many it took—enough to no longer be alone, when another wordlessly sat beside her. Jack. She knew it was him before he even spoke. "Are you all right?"

Kallia stopped herself from outright guffawing. *No, she wasn't.* But if she closed her eyes, she could pretend. "Thank you."

"For?"

"Earlier. At the party, you—" She paused, with a small smile. "You helped. A lot."

"The most I did was save a few drunken idiots from tripping into the fire." Jack lifted a slightly insulted brow. "Are you truly *that* surprised?"

"Only that you changed your mind. You've made it very clear you wanted no part in this." That dance felt like years ago, when it was just hours earlier that the floor brought them together. The mere recollection raised bumps across her skin.

"I still don't." Blowing out a breath, Jack rested his elbows on his knees. "Though I guess being half-magician means being stupidly impulsive when the occasion calls."

He looked off toward the buildings in such a sheepish manner,

Kallia had to quell a laugh. Before, she wished for loneliness—but this, she didn't mind. Not at all. After his absence, a time spent wondering if he had simply gone for good, his presence brought the strangest relief. As if a missing diamond from her ring necklace had been found, finally set back in place where it belonged.

It was selfish to expect him to stay, just for her sake.

"What's wrong? You won tonight." His lips fell into a slight frown. "From your room alone, I couldn't tell if you all had only just started or finished the victory party."

Dread dropped back into her chest. The longer she avoided it, the deeper it dug. And this was no secret she wished to keep from him, not some tool to get her way.

This changed everything. "Demarco is here."

The air shifted, tensed.

As she stared down at her palms, she could still picture his face. The crease in his brow, like the crack of a mirror. "Are you sure? Not an illusion?"

Genuine curiosity. Kallia hadn't expected that. Neither he nor Demarco had even met each other, hardly spoken a handful of words, yet they knew too much. Too much to ever clasp hands as friends, or occupy the same room without setting fire to everything in it.

Her silence was as good an answer as any, but she couldn't leave it there. "Not an illusion."

The confirmation brewed in uncomfortable silence as the music blaring below faded to a dull murmur. Kallia worried where his thoughts might stray—whether that mask of ice would return on his face, or rage would shatter it. With Jack, it was hard to predict anything.

"Yet you don't sound too happy."

The tension ached in her chest. "I would *never* want anyone else to fall into a place like this with no way out. Least of all Demarco," she bit out. "He was never supposed to come here."

Regardless of what she wanted, she didn't want this. The only good to come out of losing her entire world the moment she arrived on this side was that she had nothing to lose. Nothing to dangle over her head.

Him. Of course it had to be him.

Kallia clutched at her necklace, rolling the small diamond ring between her fingers. "There has to be some way. . . ." To get him out, find a way back for him.

If his sole purpose in coming here was to be a pawn for Roth to move at his leisure, he would never be safe. He'd always be leverage.

Which meant she would never be free.

When her eyes watered, she didn't bother hiding, didn't care who saw. Pain demanded it. She thought she'd grown used to each lash like a muscle bearing more weight day by day. But pain like this felt new every time, because it always found new ways to hurt.

"Why aren't you with him now?"

Her stomach dropped. An unfair question, but a good one. One she asked herself every time she looked out into the city and felt her pulse thud back to life and her skin warm at the possibility. Demarco was near, waiting for her with so much to say. She'd cut him off in the alleyway, when there was so much she yearned to tell him, too.

Yet she remained perched on the roof, high above the city streets, where the hurt couldn't touch her.

He should've known to wake up as soon as the dream hit because he *never* dreamed.

No dream ever looked like this.

They were in his room, and he was holding her hand—a broken bloody mess from a fight in the club that melted away into smooth, soft skin at his touch.

Her smile lit up, always marveling at magic no matter what shape or form it came in. How big or small.

And then, she smiled at him, in a way that always made him feel like he'd done something right. Something good, for once.

That hand started trailing up the buttons of his shirt, and every muscle in his chest tightened. An ache unfurled along the line she drew. Once her fingers began playing with one button, about to slide free, he grasped her wrist.

If only she knew.

"Aren't you curious?"

Yes.

The word echoed around them, begging, as it did every time he saw her.

Yes, yes, yes.

But he was certain about what to do, the lines they never crossed. *Separate*. That answer sat on his lips, the one that played in his head when so many moments like this passed them by. It irritated her, every time they left.

"I want *more*."

With him.

The thought undid him so completely, it left an ache behind. A pain as she leaned into him and tipped her head up, waiting. Wanting.

Separate.

If only she knew why the lines were there in the first place.

As his hand slid to the back of her neck, he drew out this moment, taking stock of what he could: the warmth of her breath and the silk of her hair, the red of her smile that seemed to always hide a secret.

He knew what he should do. What came next.

Separate.

Lips at her ear, he was ready to give her a way out with a whisper.

It felt like falling into another dream, all over again.

Because this time, she turned her head, and kissed him instead.

He froze.

This had to be a trick. A lie.

When she breathed his name, the *way* she did, it made him lose sight of every line.

The next noise she made, and she drew out of him, obliterated them.

They were frantic as he pulled her closer, taking her in like a drug. She staggered for purchase somewhere, and he walked her back against the nearest surface. Her smile brushed over his skin, like patches of sunlight. Their breaths were heavy, the air crackling between them like a storm still on its way.

He cupped her face with both hands, took his time studying her the way she studied him.

The illusion and the magician.

At the voice, he jerked back slightly as another path laid out at their feet. Whispers welcomed him by name beneath a canvas of night, beckoning him to see the rest of the story unfold—a new story, now unbroken. Another chance, another path.

Only if he followed them. If he came back.

If he let them in.

You know she'll go to him.

You know she'll never forgive you.

You know you were never meant for more.

He shoved the voice out, buried it as far as he could. Except there was something different about the silence now when he looked down at her. Leaning close, she was still waiting for him, wanting more.

More.

It found him like a promise in the dark, opening its eyes, when he finally answered.

K allia didn't think this world would be able to top the splendor of the ball, but she was proven wrong when she woke the next day and saw a new world transformed seemingly overnight.

Lights were strung from every building, connecting everything like one large illuminated web. There were contraptions Kallia had never seen before—carousels large and small at every street corner, fashioned with impossible creatures riders could be seated on. Horses made of glass, wolves carved from ice, luminous velvet seats to make one feel as though they were lounging on a star.

So many other amusements in the making competed for attention, it was difficult walking through this Glorian without lingering on one street for too long. A fun house boasting about ghosts and hauntings to fuel the most thrilling nightmares, a slide so tall one had to tip their heads upward, then follow the steep downhill chute that disappeared Zarose knew how deep into the ground, and a small river that had somehow been carved out around the entire perimeter of the city with offered boat rides in contraptions that looked more like birds gliding across the surface.

After disaster struck the Court of Mirrors, Roth decided to move the festivities outdoors. Space was no issue, which meant no limits to what could be created and conjured. A promise that everyone took to heart. A few installations remained—construction hidden beneath swathes of tarp covering to guard the surprise or bursts of colorful smokes exploding through the openings. A genuine air of busyness pervaded every corner, once more bustling with magicians throwing themselves into their craft. The magicians with specialty acts practiced just as dutifully as if they managed to reserve stage time.

It had to be why Kallia received looks of surprise as she bypassed each site.

Like all of the headliners, the Diamond Rings secured a prime slot in the roster which would've landed them in the gymnasium for most of the day if their leader had anything to say about it. There was no sight of the girl at all that morning, a rarity for Vain who rose as if she still lived with the sun. The door to her room remained locked, and Kallia expected no less after last night. Just like she wouldn't be shocked at all if the girl still managed to burst through those doors hours later, looking fresh as a gem and ready to perform.

Still, it was early in the day. Showtime could wait.

Hunting down Roth could not.

When Kallia finally managed to reach the center of the city, she spotted him flanked by his devils overlooking the construction of one of the main stages scattered throughout Glorian. This one sat at the heart of it all.

Her hands balled into fists at the sight of him. The only satisfaction in his cheery wave was how diminished he appeared after the Court of Mirrors took such a hit. Like watching a man finally thrust out of a spotlight that's beamed down on him all his life.

"Ah, Kallia." At her approach, he wiped the sweat off his brow before leaning against the stage. "My dear, I heard a bit about your duel. A *vast* improvement, I've been told, which we love to hear."

Her victory was not hers to share with him, nor his to claim in any way. What grated on her nerves most was his tone, so damn pleased. As if everything were going according to plan.

". . . I'm sure you would've beat out the rest, were it not for the turn the night took." His mouth was a slash of annoyance. "No matter, such hijinks will never happen again. I'll make sure of it. Have you come to see the carnival early? I hear there's a charming champagne display that—"

"I'm not here for a pleasant chat." Her face had not shifted from the unwavering death glare. "You brought Demarco here."

Her delivery was cold, detached. Stronger than she felt when inside, she was breaking, shaking harder as Roth's smile bared teeth. "I thought you would be excited by the gift. What will help you—"

"Help me *how?*" With every coy tilt of his head, she resisted the urge to spit in his face. "You promised me no one I left behind would be harmed."

It only hit her then, at that sly turn of his smile, how they'd struck no such bargain. Not that she had any reason to anticipate this, with the rules so set in absolutes.

"And he hasn't." The man assured her. "He's been well taken care of, and will be for the duration of his stay, of course."

Her jaw ticked. "What do you mean 'duration?'"

"Oh, it's a temporary visit, my dear. You shouldn't work yourself up into such a worry since the boy will be going back in no time." Roth clasped his hands together. "We all will."

Her stomach plummeted under the weight of his hope that edged closer to certainty every day. Now, he had all the means to push from both sides, even without the gate.

"Doesn't sound like you have any need for me, then," she said through pressed lips. "If you had the power to break the rules and bring anyone from either side all along."

"Oh, if I had the power." Roth mused with a wistful expression. "Alas, I broke no rules. They change as the tides continue turning in our favor, and your boy tested the theory well by following the trail, finding his way here. . . ." He sighed. "I must say, even for one sour night, the Show of Hands is unmatched in making the impossible possible."

Cold shuddered down Kallia's spine, imagining what else could come. The thought of him luring anyone else from the true side— Aaros or Canary—simply because he could, or the Dire Woods sprawling farther across Soltair to find more victims to take below the surface . . . it all sent a spike of fear through her.

Especially when everything the Diamond Rings had done so far, to stop it all, changed nothing.

If this meant the show was working, then the gate was coming. And from the gleam in Roth's eyes, it was not slowing. The gentle pat he delivered on her shoulder was no comfort, but a seal of defeat.

"I do apologize if you did not enjoy my surprise," he said in a sunny tone, far removed from the sentiment. "But you can't deny, it can serve as a good motivation. And you've been showing progress with my Rings, but we need to up the ante. This gift was meant to push you further."

"A gift or a threat?"

She should've kept her mouth shut, with all the cards he held over her head. Those reasons kept her playing to get by, but she couldn't stand this role. Especially when it meant smiling for someone like him.

Roth laughed, as if delighted. "That all depends on what kind of man you think I am. We are family—"

"No." She seethed. "We're not."

He made a mockery of the word. However deep blood ran, it was no excuse for the past. And it certainly gave him no claim on her power.

Roth squared his shoulders and released a deep breath. "Careful." A strange gleam took hold in his eye, stranger than any she'd ever seen before, and it chilled her to the bone. "There are still so many strings I have yet to pull on you, Kallia. And you're not the only—"

His breath cut short at the cough that grew deep from his throat. Guttural and pained, constant as a murder crowing. Kallia paused in alarm, at the odd sound she hadn't heard in so long, when sickness rarely existed on the other side. They were beyond such trivial mortal plights in this city.

The man pressed a handkerchief to his mouth, catching his breath.

Just as the shadow gentlemen at his back gathered around him, no command given. With eerily quiet precision, they took their master by the arms and hauled him up.

Vanishing him without a word, a trace, only the damp, soiled handkerchief left on the brightly lit cobblestone.

Kallia didn't blink, unsure if it was a trick of the light, when the blood soaking the fabric turned black as ink.

36

Daron had gone to a few carnivals in his lifetime. He'd loved them as a young boy. The energy and constant laughter crackling in the air, the endless possibilities of amusements and games and rides at every corner.

The carnival that took over the streets of the city was unlike anything he'd ever experienced and probably ever would experience in his life. Far more extravagant than Spectaculore and the Conquering Circus combined.

Against the dark sky over their heads, strings of light drifted from the tops of every building, like veins within one body. The lights were all manner of colors, flashing in all manner of patterns. Beneath the luminous city-wide spiderweb, the carnival came alive.

Magicians sporting sparkling headpieces enticed guests down wide alleyways leading to an opulent chandelirium that glimmered a corner of the city like daylight, to a champagne garden where flutes of flowered flavors could be plucked from the ground. Game booths sat along street walks where one could toss daggers hitting the bull's-eye at every throw, or try on ocular devices rumored to feature spectacular views in the eye of the beholder. Smoke trailed from the food stands ensnared passersby with every scent and description heckled from behind. Cones of toasted nuts covered in spicy lovers' chocolate, mountains of marbled candies that promised confidence and luck, sizzling meats wrapped in dough, baked into any shape you can imagine.

Herald flicked a piece of popcorn in his face from the side. "You mortals make it so obvious," he said, scooping another handful from his serving cup. "Your delight is so endearing."

Daron's jaw snapped shut, only until they rounded a corner where the amusements grew even taller than the buildings neighboring them. A carousel of strange animals one could feed as they rode on their backs, from birds with fish scales to cats covered in flower petals. A seemingly endless roller coaster arched between fixtures, slithering up and down like a snake, throwing shadows over the guests.

It was almost too much. One marvel after another, each grander than the last.

Though none could hold his attention.

Daron straightened the mask across his nose for the hundredth time, searching through the chaos. An impossible hunt in a crowd like this. He wished only to rip off his mask, to be done with disguises, if there was any chance she might be looking out for him, too.

If. It didn't seem likely, after the way they'd left their last conversation. His face burned just thinking of it. All of it had gone so wrong, and all he could think of afterward was seeing her again to apologize. No matter who was right, who was wrong, he wasn't there to fight. He didn't want to waste any more words. Any more time.

"You won't find her among the commoners."

At Herald's remark, Daron shifted further away. It was as if the night before hadn't happened at all, waking up in the mirror shop hours later. He resumed his quips and light banter, all carefree and easy, but Daron had no patience for it.

"Come now, Demarco." Herald's eyes narrowed behind his spectacles. A dramatic whine of a sigh emerged. "Enough of your brooding. What will it take for you to stop being mad at me?"

"Tell me what the new job is." That was all. Whatever Roth's new plans had shifted into after last night, whatever secrets Herald held on his boss's behalf, Daron wanted to know. He *deserved* to know what piece he was meant to play. And if that information could be helpful to Kallia somehow, he had to figure it out. It was the least he could do when she never wanted him here in the first place.

Herald's mouth twisted in discomfort. "I can't."

The same answer every time. He shouldn't have been surprised. "You're that deep in the man's pockets?"

A harsh laugh snapped back. "In case you haven't noticed, we *all* are. Only a fool would pretend otherwise, or do something stupid to risk being kicked out altogether," he said through gritted teeth. "A fate which you, my friend, have been mercifully spared from knowing. Thanks to me."

Daron's fists tightened. "I'm *not* your friend."

"The fact that you're begging me to compromise *my* standing to give you answers means you actually believe part of me has the heart to consider it." Genuine amusement crossed his features. "It's rather sweet."

"Shut up."

"Testy." Wiping at his spectacles, Herald nodded ahead. "As your friend, I'm just saying, you won't find your girl out and about like you and me. She's a headliner, and headliners always get the spotlight. So follow it."

As he pointed forward, Daron was tempted to stalk off then. But he was not nearly proud enough for that, not in his position. He grumbled as they wound their way through the city to the main stages, one bursting with light and music and an overflowing audience at its feet; a sign high above, illuminated with glitter, as its crown.

The Diamond Rings.

The name rang in the back of his head from the night before, after Kallia had mentioned Eva in the same breath.

Daron's pulse sprinted. The entire back of the stage lit up in a hazy jade-green backdrop, so that whoever moved in front of it emerged like shadows. He followed the movement upward as a collection of hoops dropped against the screen, figures dangling off them. Some had their legs crossed, others lounged casually along the curve. Some even stood with their heels secured against the ring.

From afar, Daron counted about six hoops and six ladies, with a large fiery hoop descending in the center. The spotlight shined on the girl within it, standing fearless as a star in the middle of the hoop, somehow not burning from the fire licking along the metal curves.

With short hair sheared even shorter to one side, the girl who seized center stage wore a sheer mask that further emphasized the mischief behind. Rarely anyone could upstage Kallia, but this performer could compete with an entire firework display with just a smile.

Her name was a chant on everyone's lips.

Vain.

As lights washed over the rest of the Diamond Rings, the crowd went wild with hollers and whistles, growing louder as the ladies began circling their leader. Whoever worked the rigging chains that held them all aloft had their work cut out for them from the way their hoops swung with such force that gave them the illusion of birds soaring in flight.

"Is everyone having a good time out there?" Vain's voice boomed, and a roar of approval answered. At her raspy laugh in response, Daron felt something tug within him.

That laugh.

He knew that laugh.

"Don't let them catch you frowning." Herald clapped Daron over the shoulder as if to wake him up. "Unless you wish to become their next victim."

He was numbed to the screams erupting around him, could barely hear anything as the carnival echoed in his ears, as if the world had gone hollow.

It couldn't be.

Blinking, he studied the girl closer, picking apart all that he could and matching them with memory—until that laugh rose again, with a strained beat of his heart.

Eva?

When Kallia had brought her up, it sounded almost too good to be true—that he would find both of them here, and that they had found each other. As if he'd willed it all into being, when he told Lottie.

Emotion welled up deep in his throat as the show unfolded with Eva at the helm. She donned a different mask now than the one she'd wear during his shows, and this one suited her leagues better. Her entire face brightened beneath the jewels, matching her bold show outfit, while her lips kicked up in a sly, small smile that seemed to always hold a secret.

She looked happy.

The sight knocked the very breath out of him. His heart, hollow and full and racing until he felt nothing but the world turning on its axis, taking him with it.

Until one last performer descended.

And everything recentered, in one held breath.

Whistles and hollers shattered the air at Kallia's entrance as she floated down on her own sparkly hoop among the Diamond Rings. He couldn't tear his eyes away. Not from her joy, the smooth ease with which she leaned and swung within the hoop at a height that could break all her bones. Under the light, like the night before, her face was a mask of jewels, shining brighter as she smiled wickedly for the crowd.

A star in her element. Both of them, exactly where they belonged.

For the longest time, Daron hated himself for not just taking their magic, but this. The guilt gnawed at him so sharply, it made him sick. Every time that rose cloth came into view, its petals kept falling, like a fire slowly dying among the embers.

A smile touched Daron's lips for the first time since he'd arrived. How right it all felt, that even in a world so different from theirs, they would always find their way back to the stage.

The rest of the show passed in a blur. As part of their set, the Diamond Rings did choose a volunteer who they passed around from hoop to hoop in a way that would've made a sober man scared shitless, but their participant enjoyed the ride. They spun and twirled in the air, staged near-falls that had the audience screaming and actual falls with swift saves that had them cheering. Daron couldn't stop clapping, not even after they had all descended from their hoops—a few disappearing into thin air—while four stepped forward and took their bows at the end.

His gaze sought Kallia's from across the stage and locked on from a distance. She must've noticed him long ago from how quickly she found him, and the warmth fluttered up his spine when her lips curved. Sending him a small nod, her eyes never left him as she and the rest of the group hurried off the stage.

"What, you want an autograph?" Herald heckled after Daron, who already tore off through the crowd. His heart thundered, half-wondering if he'd fallen into one of his dreams that kept her in sight, but never within reach.

That dread died once he broke through the horde of spectators dispersing after the show. Breathing heavily, he treaded slowly near the back edge of the stage dotted with a rainbow of headliner tents.

At the burst of cackling from a gleaming pink tent, he stopped.

First Kallia exited, lost in a laugh at something said behind her before she froze at the sight of him only a few feet away, with a soft, breathless smile. "Hi."

Daron felt all of his senses leave him. "Hi."

He forgot everything—what they were fighting about, what they were doing, even forgot himself when he nearly leaned in to her. For what, he wasn't sure. He felt utterly helpless, especially when she was fresh off a show. Sweat glistened by her collarbone, at her brow along the jewels across her face, that thrill lighting her up like a fire stoked, wanting more.

He wanted more. His insides were twisting, and he could only wonder if she felt the same. If he hadn't entirely messed this up.

"Good job up there," he said, clearing his throat. "I've never seen you work a hoop, so . . . that's good. Expanding your skill set."

Who the *hell* says that?

Daron waited in agony for the ground to swallow him whole before Kallia burst out laughing. "What a glowing review."

The sound of her laugh drew him a step closer, then another, without even realizing. After weeks of remembering her in the dark, it was like walking toward a light.

And he wanted to close the distance, as he had in that alleyway. Raw instinct had taken over then, and nearly consumed him now when his gaze traced a path from her bare throat to her lips.

She was staring at his, too. Contemplating something before the warmth slitted past his shoulder with a growl. "Herald."

"Excellent show, showgirl." The magician's drawl was like a douse of cold water, especially when strolled right up alongside them, examining their faces smugly. "Though don't stop on my account. I'm no innocent."

Kallia scoffed, while Daron elbowed him squarely in the gut. "Can you *not*?"

Herald grunted. "I'm here to help you, lover boy," he whispered. "You can even have the mirror shop *all* to yourself tonight, if you know what I—"

"Go be gross somewhere else, mirror boy."

Everything went quiet at the voice from behind. It pricked like a thorn drawing blood, and Daron stopped breathing. Bumps rose across his skin as he twisted around to another set of glittering eyes above him.

Hers widened, just like his.

Eva.

The silence stretched on and on and on. Daron could barely form any other word or thought. He'd envisioned this reunion for so long, not once imagining it would feel like this.

Like two strangers meeting.

They might as well have been, when neither of them said anything. All he could do was take stock of her from head to toe, finding hardly a trace of Eva from her hair to her attire to her overall demeanor. So many changes and differences.

But no change in the eyes. Those were the eyes he'd catch across their stage to signal a turn in their act. Eyes so much like his own, that flashed with the same panic churning inside him now. He'd never been afraid to speak to Eva, not even in his own head.

Why now?

Herald's breath hitched in surprise. "Vain, too?" Impressed, he tilted his head at them both. "Damn, Demarco. Maybe you don't need my help after all."

The headliner set her dagger eyes on him. "*Leave.*"

At her fury, he fled to Daron's side immediately. "No can do, I have orders."

"Which are what? I'm fairly certain he's safer in our hands than yours, since you'd probably feed him to a python if Roth wanted it done."

Herald didn't deny it, but he also didn't proudly confirm it, which surprised Daron most of all. Not that he deserved any credit.

"Oh, Herald, there you are, darling!"

The tent flaps burst open as a soft-faced girl with silver-blond hair latched onto Herald's elbow, while his other was occupied by a brown-skinned girl decked out in a feather-lined fluffy robe. Both wore the same diamond ring necklaces hanging around Kallia and Eva's necks. "Yes, it's time to *finally* enjoy some piece of the night." The one in the robe pouted. "And it would be nice to have someone to hold our winnings when we play the booths."

"Lucky me," he muttered, his odds as one against four Diamond Rings clear. As they dragged him away, Herald shot one last look back. "Be gentle with him, ladies. I don't think the Dealer would be too pleased if either of you chewed him up and spat him out."

Eva smiled with hooded eyes. "We'll do our best."

"And don't get too destroyed, lover boy," he called out, eyebrows jutting upward.

"Remember, mirror shop's all yours tonight if you—" A yelp rose as one of the girls slapped the back of his head before they disappeared far within the crowd.

The tension burned and crackled even harder between the three of them.

"Oh, that reminds me." Kallia sheepishly shrugged her way back toward the tent. "Duels start up again on the main stage soon. So . . . I must prepare."

"You *just* remembered?" Eva looked unforgivably close to stabbing her, but Kallia had already scurried into the tent without another word.

Now, they were alone. The tension remained painful as ever, even when the carnival roared to life around them. He still couldn't look at her for more than a few seconds at a time. Still couldn't believe this.

"Let's walk," she ordered more than suggested, an Aunt Cata move from the way she firmly patted his shoulder after. "The whole world is scattered like rats in a cheese maze, but we'll be less noticeable if we—"

His arms locked around her in a hard embrace. Every emotion raced in his chest, straining each breath. "I'm sorry."

He wasn't sure where to begin, hadn't prepared anything. Nothing but the same word repeated over and over again under his breath. *Sorry.* Being able to say it to her, to say anything, hit him. It didn't even sting that she didn't immediately reciprocate his hold, he'd given her no warning. All that mattered was the feel of her alive. Found.

The force of it all thundered in his ears, muting her words. "What?"

"I said, *why* do keep saying that?" Eva calmly inched back, searching his face. Hers remained a hard mask, except for the slight glimmer in her eyes. Not even she could control that. "Sorry for what?"

For taking so long. For not trying harder.

"For everything." His brow furrowed at his answer, shaping it more into a question. Surely she knew he was at fault for it all. Her magic, and his. Just like his magic, and Kallia's.

Whatever they wanted, whatever it took to earn their forgiveness, he'd do it. Anything they asked, he was prepared.

"Let's keep moving." She gave a furtive nod back to the magicians walking by, somehow sensing the way they lingered at the sight of them. "If I have to live through any more disturbing rumors speculating about us ever again, I'm going to vomit."

Daron shuddered in agreement and kept steadily by her side as they walked down food stands of popcorn that could be seasoned with any flavor and cotton candy spun into glittering elaborate shapes and scenes atop a paper cone. Wonders met them at every corner, but his stare kept returning to Eva. So close, walking casually alongside him.

Zarose, the last time he saw her, her hair was much longer. Her eyes, less wily. Or perhaps they had always been wily, and he'd just never caught it.

He'd missed so much back then, but that didn't matter when she had it all now. As they moved through the streets lined in lights, adoring fans traced her movements and whispered as she passed. A notorious legend, strolling with some nameless masked stranger as her companion.

Oh, how the tables had turned.

"You've made quite a name for yourself," he noted.

The moving carousel lights glided over her face, illuminating her delight. Well-earned pride. "It wasn't easy, but I have."

It was a comfort, seeing her like this, after imagining only the worst in the years that had passed. "And I always knew you two would get along. You and Kallia."

That drew out a low laugh. "I had my reservations. . . . You can't be *too* sure of anybody here, so I gave her a hard time. And she took it. Still does." Eva stared up at the attractions and rides that glowed against the dark sky, shooting him a bemused sideways glance. "I never pegged you to go for someone like her, to be completely honest. Or for her to take to someone like you."

"I don't think either of us did." He grinned down at his feet, recalling those early days of Spectaculore when the world was much smaller. Simpler. Still broken, with all the bad surrounding them. That he had added to. "But . . . I took from her, too. Just like with you. And it's not right—"

"Dare, you don't have to keep bringing it up," she cut in. "It's in the past."

"That doesn't mean it didn't happen."

Eva withdrew from him, still walking but with sterner eyes. "Things have changed. You don't have to dwell on it."

Every curt response set him on edge. If she was angry, he wanted her to be angry. If she was hurt, he didn't want her to hold back. None of this could be so cleanly closed when it all remained so half-finished, half-answered. "And you don't have to avoid it."

Her gaze aimed straight ahead, narrowing on a burst of noise. A high-pitched yell. "I'm not avoiding anything."

"That's a lie." Just like him, she looked for distraction. Anything to escape a tough conversation. "Eva, please. Just let me—"

Daron's knees buckled as his legs became unsteady.

What the—

Screams burst around them when the ground shook again. The force of it was so violent, waves of people dropped to their knees. A few tall stands tipped and spilled over the cobblestone.

Daron gripped Eva to stop her fall just as she grasped onto his arm. The length of her nails almost bit into skin, but the ground was all he felt. The way it rumbled and thundered like a thrashing heart. "What's happening?"

Blinking rapidly, her eyes were near-black with alarm. "I don't know. This isn't us."

Whatever she meant by that soon didn't matter when they were shoved and pummeled from all sides. Cries filled their ears. Daron clung to Eva, holding on tight against the desperate stampede of guests nearly bowling them over. Running fast, despite the stillness of the ground.

A creak like a lightning strike cracked overhead.

And there were more and more, joining the screams below.

When Daron looked up, his entire chest seized.

Fissures veined along the sky-high slide as it snapped. The tense whistle of falling debris sent heavy pieces and chunks falling to the ground like rain, spearing through booths and stands. Derailed carts sped through booths and spun out of control through the crowds sprinting to safety.

Without even realizing it, they were running. Eva gripped his hand, shouted something in his ear, but there was so much noise. So many cries, he heard nothing but the ominous cracks like a wave about to crash, coming from the hulking shadow over them. The roller coaster's framework lost hold, its support beams snapping off its foundation.

Like an avalanche, it fell.

Piece by piece, all over the city.

Waiting for the tell-tale dueling bell, Kallia gave her appearance one last glance in the mirror before a force threw her right against the glass.

Desperate screams sounded outside the tent, even louder as the ground shook harder, vibrating beneath her feet. It shook their dressing tent into a war zone, sending costume racks and tall mirrors toppling over, makeup flying right off the vanity counters into a chaotic heap.

What was happening?

Malice had taken over serving tonight's disaster, but something felt off. It was too early, for one. And outside her tent, it seemed the world was breaking with every violent quake of the ground. Every time Kallia waited for the earth to still, she cringed at the sound of debris slamming outside of her tent, spearing through the fabric like arrows.

The worries ate into her as her thoughts went to everyone. Demarco. The Diamond Rings. Hell, even Jack. Imagining them all beyond this tent, caught in this storm wherever they were, forced her to her feet, reaching for the exit—

The air tightened for a second.

A moment of stillness before everything came crashing down beneath a sharp, heavy weight. With a start, Kallia fell back as she edged into some corner of a table—the entire pink covering of the tent coming down on her like a net.

She saw nothing past the tent's material. All she heard was the patters of those running outside, frantic to avoid whatever piece of the carnival came down hard next.

Whatever piece had fallen over her tent pinned everything down in place, trapping her.

Between heavy breaths, Kallia screamed and kicked her sharp heel through the material as hard as she could, but it wouldn't pierce through.

And she couldn't tear free.

Her heart thrashed in fear. It was a miracle the enormous, heavy object missed her body by a few feet. Had she been pacing around for a few moments more, any second earlier or later than she had, every bone of hers would've shattered as she crushed into the ground.

The thought sent bile up her throat. Only because there were no doubt worse sights right outside the tent from the cries of pain piercing the air.

Kallia hadn't realized the ground had fallen still for a while with the way her entire body trembled. The more she elbowed and thrashed beneath the covering, the more futile the effort. Even her magic felt paralyzed, frozen in shock, as her name echoed as if in a dream where someone was looking for her.

Please.

Please.

Please.

Whoever the word was for, she repeated it in her head over and over again, hoping someone would notice her gone, that she was still—

"KALLIA!"

At the roar of her name, her eyes flew open.

Demarco.

Her heart raced back to life as she heard a low series of curses between strained grunts and labored pants. He'd come alone, and he sounded furious. Frustrated.

And so, so close. Everything in her stirred into motion as she reached out and moved in any way she could with the limited range she had.

"I'm under here." Her voice cracked dry, eyes wet with relief. "Demarco, I'm—"

"I know, I'm right here," he sighed, his relief just as overwhelming. "I'm right here. Keep talking to me."

She did. As he dug his way through to her, she kept saying his name like a prayer, and more words slipped out without thought or reason. Words she would probably later regret. At one point, he suddenly went silent, spearing panic through her.

Before there was a rustle of movement—

And the trap gave way. Her heart pounded as the material's hold loosened, finally freeing enough for her to start wriggling out from underneath.

Until it all tore away in a sudden flash, the world returning to focus.

And all she saw was Demarco standing over her, his hand reaching out for hers.

He took them to the mirror shop, which seemed like the worst place to go when the world shook at a moment's notice.

"Safest, most unshakable place to be, according to Herald," Demarco reassured after shutting the door behind them. "See anything broken?"

Kallia paused to inspect the oddly clean aisles of the dead-quiet shop. After walking through the city once everything officially shut down, it seemed more like crossing through the aftermath of a battle lost. Buildings ruined with roofs caved in, booths and stalls smashed and toppled over in messes that spilled out into the street. There were many people they passed in wrecked gowns and suits, saddled with injuries requiring all manner of stitches and elaborate bandaging; by some miracle, no casualties accounted for yet. It shouldn't have come as a surprise, in a world filled with some of the most powerful, capable magicians.

Though Kallia couldn't help but wonder if maybe Jack had something to do with that, too.

"I can't believe you've been staying here," she muttered, her eyes drifting around as the lights dotting the walls slowly fired to life. "With Herald, of all people."

With a snort, Demarco made his way around the counter and began rifling behind the glass. "Certainly not my ideal roommate, but it could be worse," he said, emerging with two glasses and a vivid blue bottle that gleamed in the dark. "I suppose I can't be picky when there are no other options."

Her stomach twisted into knots, pulling tighter as he began pouring into one glass, then the other. The only sound in the whole shop, her heart thundered even louder.

What was she doing here? The first thing Kallia should've done was go back to find Vain and the others, make sure they were all right and figure out what the hell they were thinking, bringing down the night in such a blaze of horror. It was a sheer miracle the carnival hadn't turned into a blood bath, and that Glorian had taken the most hits. A life lost was lost for good, but a broken city could always be rebuilt.

If Demarco hadn't mentioned that Vain had gone to find the others, likely safer altogether if Vain was at the helm, then Kallia would've gone off in search of them. It felt strange to be split up from them, but there was no way around it once the night went to ruin. To cover more ground and find everyone, they chose the best course of action: Vain went for the booths while Demarco headed for the tents.

When they approached the Alastor Place on weary feet, that should've been her cue to head back to her room. The girls were all no doubt waiting to ambush her there. Perhaps Jack was even waiting on the roof, hoping she might show.

But Kallia let Demarco lead her to the shop, and she couldn't seem to leave. No matter how close she inched toward the door, she couldn't make herself go through it yet.

After topping off equal pours of the luminous blue liquor into each glass, Demarco pushed one in her direction with a clink against his own. "Cheers to making it out alive."

"Barely." With a small smile, Kallia reached for her drink, the glass surprisingly cool to the touch, even without ice. "Thank you."

"It's well-deserved, I think."

"No, I—" Her voice thickened under the knot in her throat. "Thank you for . . . for coming back for me."

His lips just barely touched his glass before he paused. The crease of his brow deepened. "You sound so shocked. Of course I would come back for you."

Zarose. He didn't have to say it like that.

Kallia shot another look toward the door, urging herself to go. Before she exposed herself further, her most vulnerable spots she guarded well. But not with Demarco. Without even trying, he knew just how to draw them out. "I was awful to you, the other night."

It was difficult to even look at him, when every time she thought of that alleyway, she remembered how his face fell. How it twisted and cut her up inside, imagining all it must've taken to find her, and how desperately she'd wanted to hear none of it. Shock aside, there was a meanness in those words, and they hit. With all the work it took to dig under Demarco's hard exterior, any time he showed emotion, he meant it. Deeply.

"Well, my being here probably didn't help as much as I'd hoped," he admitted after a brief, pensive sip. "Not sure what I expected, honestly. You, of course, which was more than enough for me."

Kallia tried not to smile, looking down at her finger tracing the rim of her glass. "And your sister," she added. "Were you able to talk with her, at least for a bit?"

Selfish as it was, that was all she wanted for them both: a chance to say what hadn't been said before. Not that she had any business inserting herself in the first place. She would never know a bond like theirs, the thorniness of having a sibling—and a lost one, at that. What she did know was how deeply she cared for them, and all the ways she saw regret hurting them. Vain couldn't stand to talk about her past as if she had none, whereas Demarco carried his like a punishing weight on his back every day.

Damage had been done, but not beyond repair. If there was any light in coming to this other side without any way to leave, then at least it could be a place where some wounds could finally heal.

"Yes, we did indeed." Demarco pursed his lips into a tense line, holding in some deep thought, that gradually curved with a glimmer of warmth. "But I don't want to talk about that. I'd rather talk about what you said to me tonight. Under the tent."

Kallia tipped her gaze back up at the ceiling with an inward groan. Hell, she could've said anything. Everything in that moment had become one frantic blur, fueled more by panic and adrenaline than logic. And from the looks of his lopsided grin, whatever she'd babbled on about had made him all too pleased, which was most certainly a sign of trouble.

With deliberate slowness, Kallia took a leisurely sip of her drink. "I'd rather not."

"You'd rather not?"

He was just toying with her, at this point. "Clearly I wasn't in my right mind. I could've been crushed at any moment. What more do you want?" she bit out. "It's bad enough that my final words could've been absolute nonsense."

Demarco cocked his head. "Absolute nonsense?"

"Are you going to keep repeating everything I say?"

"Just until you remember, maybe." His voice went soft as he came around the counter, stopping just a few steps away. His shirt remained damp in patches with sweat over his front and back, torn in a few places. Still far more presentable that what she could say for her show costume. Many of the jewels on her face had fallen off in the fray, until they appeared more like specks than a mask.

Now, more than ever, she needed her mask. He'd seen too much, and she couldn't bear the way he looked at her: like he was certain of something, every time he saw her.

As if they were still in Glorian and nothing between them had changed.

The cold shard running down her spine sent Kallia back a step. *Go.* The instinct to run gripped her tight, burning deep in her bones.

Go, before it hurts even more.

Almost instantly, his brow creased. "What's wrong?"

That he even had to ask, when it was so clear nothing would ever make this madness all right. In the end, it only gave Roth more power over her, over him. "I have to go."

"Wait, *what?*"

She twisted around to leave, finally, but Demarco blocked her path, stopping her with a gentle press of her shoulders. "What happened? Was it something I said?"

A laugh choked out of her, a pained sound. "You need to stop taking the blame for everything, for once. Some things aren't anyone's fault, they just . . . are. And we have to live with them, even if it's not what we would've chosen."

Demarco shook his head slowly. "I don't understand where this is coming from."

"I have to go now," she said under a hard swallow. "But you have to go *back*."

Y*ou have to go* back.

There was a ringing in his ears, a spike in his heart.

At first Daron wondered if the drink had something to do with it, but after one glass, he was still completely sober. "There . . . *is* no way back. I thought that was the point."

"I'll figure something out," Kallia said, prying his hands off her. All controlled composure. "There's always a way, but—"

"If that's true, then why just me?" Every muscle tightened in his body. "You said I have to go back."

Not us. Not we.

Somewhere in between, she'd decided that no longer existed.

Daron wasn't sure what happened in the space of that one breath, but it sent his head spinning, how fast the discussion turned. His knees felt like water holding him up, so that he had to lean against the counter for the support.

"Only one can go through Zarose Gate. It's volatile enough as it is, but it can be done." She sighed and raked her fingers through her hair, all soft waves tangling at the ends. "If this gate comes, they want me to break it to see what happens."

"I *know* what will happen." Clearly she did too, from her solemn acceptance. His teeth clenched so forcefully, they nearly cracked. "You can't actually consider throwing yourself in front of that."

"What other choice is there?" Kallia's eyes flashed on him. "If you don't go, then he will use you against me. Push you to push me. He already has. That's not a sustainable arrangement, Demarco, and you know it."

"So *this* is your impossible solution?" His voice raked against his throat. "You're willing to risk your life for an outcome that has no chance of succeeding?"

"Isn't that what you did, when you walked through the Dire Woods?"

Heat flew to his cheeks. "It's not the same."

"Isn't it?" She couldn't look at him for the longest time, just her feet. As if there was some safety in it. "You're able to risk a lot the way you did, but I can't?"

"There was slightly more to back up my chances." Manipulation, for the most part. But at the very least, something guided him with a certainty that he would make it to the other side intact. "Whereas this . . . there's nothing to back it up, whatever this plan is. I'm not even sure *you* know what it is."

"Maybe, but there's time to plan." A slight waver ruined the steadiness of her voice. "At the very least, I can try."

He needed to breathe. He needed to stare at the wall until his thoughts reset and regained order. Agitated, Daron paced deeper into the shop, letting the cool air wash over him. To his surprise, she didn't immediately run for the door—she followed until the mirrors captured her reflection, one bouncing off the other, until Kallia was everywhere. Everywhere he looked, she stood just behind him. Waiting for him to turn and face her.

It felt like the cruelest trick of all. Not even all the ways she'd come to him as an illusion pricked as sharp as this. The longer the silence stretched between them, the more he bled.

"Please don't do this," he rasped out. "No one is powerful enough to rewrite rules like that, Kallia. If you find a way for one, then why not another person?"

"We shouldn't think so idealistically." Her lips fell to a grim frown. "It's hard enough to see what allows *one* magician through. Hoping for two would be pushing that luck."

"Then don't waste it on me."

The air tightened before a sound resembling a snarl emerged. "Why not?"

Daron swallowed hard, looking down at his hands, the scrapes they'd taken after pulling and heaving chunks of debris off the tent earlier. The memory of her words—desperate and breathless—found him in the chaos. Back then, they'd made him smile. Now, they crushed deep in his chest. "Do you want to know what you said to me?" he asked, finally turning around. "Earlier tonight?"

"No."

He snorted at the bite in her response, before he let the words go. *Take me home.*

Kallia went rigid, weighing the thought in her head. "I never said that."

"You did. It's probably something you would never admit out loud, but that is what you said. And that is why if this plan all magically works out the way you want, I'm not going," he said through gritted teeth. "*Please* don't choose me over yourself. You keep telling me I have a chance to get out of here. But you deserve a life, too, Kallia. A life beyond illusions."

"You won't change my mind about this. Don't make this any harder."

"I don't think I could, honestly." He scoffed, the sound harsh and biting. "You've made your choice. To stop exploring others."

"Don't you dare shame me. You don't know what I've been through here, what I've had to force myself to let go of. What I've had to make the best of, just to stay sane." Shit. The tears were already gathering in her eyes without permission. "I was only just starting to accept all of this, and then you had to come."

The words were like knives leaving her mouth. They hurt him, far more than he would dare admit. But his face probably said it all, the deepness of his breath. "I'm sorry I came here, thinking for one second you might want to come back with me given the chance."

Her reply cut short to an odd silence.

Daron glanced at her, her face drenched with jewels and made up for war, and she looked entirely stunned, her lips parted and eyes wide as she took in the room. He followed, and his heart stopped entirely.

Gone were the cold shadows of the mirror shop. It vanished under bright greens and glowing leaves, fiery petals that rose in the soft dark all around them. The moon shone gently through the ceiling above, the starry night sky appearing just a bit blurry through the musty glass encasing the entire room. If Daron closed his eyes to focus, he would probably be able to pick up on the sweet humidity. But he didn't want to close his eyes, for fear the illusion might disappear.

"Do you see it, too?"

Kallia instinctively backed up, her shoulder touching his. Her fingers brushing his, until they held on. Done so without thinking, for her eyes remained fixed on the new room that had come to life around them. Her fingers trembled slightly, so he held on to them tighter.

"Yes," he rasped out, his voice thick as the room grew clearer and clearer around them. But he didn't need everything to come into focus to know where he was. He'd been in this room so often, he could walk through it blindfolded.

The greenhouse at the Ranza Estate.

Music thrummed against the glass, a slow, muffled beat from the Conquering Circus performing at the heart of Glorian. The same as it did that night, which felt like years ago.

"How . . . ," she whispered, finally lowering her gaze to trace the long leaves with glowing veins above their heads, before meeting Daron's. "How is this possible?"

"I don't know. The memories usually find me alone." They'd tease him until he met the edge of madness before retreating back into reality. For so long, he'd found escape in them. Then dread, like the first taste of sweetness before it became too much. But this one felt different, if it found them both. And transported them back to a time, to a place where his heart last felt full.

"Same," she said, the wonder in her voice fading. Like someone who's been burned one too many times. "But it's gotten better for me."

"Better?"

"Less frequent," she clarified. "The more time you spend in the haunted house, the less ghosts haunt you."

"You mean the more a ghost you become, in turn." His teeth clenched. "And then what, you forget your life?"

"I've really only been in two places my whole life, so there's not much to forget in the grand scheme of things," she said. "Though I know what it's like to start over again and again. For memories to shift, and life to change. It's easier when the slate is clean."

She said that now, but the way she looked at her surroundings . . . it was as if she wanted to remember everything about it. Every sight, every detail. This was a good memory for her, too. For them.

"What do you do when you see them, then?"

"I ignore them," Kallia said on a shrug. "Why, what do you do?"

Flashes of illusions played in the back of his mind. Kallia and Eva. No surprise they haunted him the most. At first when he saw them, he thought it might be something of a punishment for the way things had gone between them. How wrong he'd been, for what his own memory had taught him.

"All I've ever wanted to do is go back and change everything," he said softly. "This world only gives half of that wish, so it's best to take what I can from it. I let them play out to see what it's trying to tell me. So I can remember every bit of what I might've missed before."

"Even if it hurts?"

Daron nodded. "Especially if it hurts."

Kallia slipped her hand from his, walked a few steps deeper into the greenhouse. The glow of the plants and haze of moonlight hit her in such a way, he wondered if she might be an illusion. When she turned, her face was full of jewels, her eyes sparkling. Glistening. "You and me," she said. "I wish it didn't have to hurt."

Mess was an understatement. A mess could be cleaned; it could be fixed. Nothing about what would come next after this felt like a fix to the problem. Maybe to one, but not everything. And Zarose, he wished he could have everything. He wished they could have more time.

As she looked back at him, she seemed to be memorizing him the same way he was remembering her. Re-created, in this moment. "Demarco?"

His throat tightened at the soft way she said his name. "Yes?"

"I don't want to fight anymore."

Something gave way in him. A little pull that released all the steel in his bones and muscles, around his heart, the armor he'd donned since he'd arrived. How heavy it had been, how much it had worn him down. "I don't want to, either."

At that, Kallia offered her truce in a smile. One he would remember for the rest of his life, as she lifted her hand out to him. "Dance with me?"

The question caught him so off guard, he nearly choked on a laugh. "Wait, what?"

"That's how the rest of this goes, isn't it?" She gestured at the moment all around them. "I asked you to dance."

His heart thumped faster as she crooked her finger at him. Waiting. "Come on. Who knows how much longer this will last."

He didn't need to be told twice after that. He went to her, took her offered hand, knowing he would have to let go eventually, but right now, being given a moment felt like more than he'd ever had.

The room echoed with music from the outside, hitting the glass in slow, descending notes. Kallia straightened her spine, already moving one hand to sit atop his shoulder. Daron gave a quiet, low chuckle as he slid her hand right to the nape of his neck, and pressed his temple against hers. "Closer," he whispered, right against her ear.

Now was not the time for proper holds or any space in between. No more distance. He'd felt enough of it, and so had she, for she dropped her hand against his chest, and he covered it with his own. If she couldn't hear his heartbeat before, he was sure she could feel it now. The nervous, desperate rhythm that wanted nothing more than to stay in one place.

The last time he'd danced with her at the ball, it had been a series of steps at the music's command. Brief touches and moments of closeness. This dance was all closeness, all-consuming. Heart to heart, swaying slower and slower until there was hardly any movement at all. Just holding, just standing in one place. In this moment.

At some point, as the music began to fade from their ears, the brilliance of the greenhouse growing fainter by the second, everything inside him began to lock up. Her body tensed against his, as he felt her face lift from his chest, staring over his shoulder, her expression somber. Unsurprised.

Like an act in a show, the moment was drawing to an end. No matter how much they played into it, hoping to prolong it.

"You were right," she said. "This does hurt."

Daron nodded, inhaling deeply. "It's a good memory, though. They're rarely kind like that."

As Kallia watched the greenhouse vanish around them and the mirror shop reappear beneath, she wondered when the next illusion of memory might find her. If they would even come back at all. At what point did she completely lose the pieces of her old life still clinging to her?

Did she want them to?

At the thought, Kallia stepped back from his hold, noticing almost instantly, the greenhouse disappeared. She couldn't be swayed this easily. Not by a memory that felt too good. By the one right in front of her who, just moments ago, would do anything to change her mind.

"Nothing has changed, Demarco," she said, resolute. "Not you, not this."

He glanced over his shoulder, at the mirrors he'd become so familiar with over the past few days, that suddenly felt like they didn't belong there. "I know."

"I'm still staying. And you're going."

Why did she have to keep saying it? He knew he would not be able to change her mind. He never could.

Daron closed his eyes for a hard second. "I know."

As his heart thumped, a waiting silence stretched between them. As though she hadn't expected him to bend so easily. "All right, then," she said in a clipped tone, squaring back her shoulders as she began turning for the door. "It's time for me to finally—"

She'd barely had time to turn before he took her wrist again and pulled her back. Not harshly or forcefully, as were the grips she'd become used to in this world, but just firm enough that should she want to break free, she could. Even as he brought her close against him, faces breaths apart.

"You said you were staying," he said. "So stay."

His eyes seared into hers so quietly, so intensely, she had to look down for a moment. "Please. Don't make this any harder."

"It's already hard, Kallia." Sorrow carved into the lines of his brow. "One day, a long time from now, you might even forget me." As he said it, he brought his hand to the side of her face, fingers in her hair. "You will move on."

It was true. The way the Diamond Rings rarely dwelled on the past, as if it were a fleeting dream. Just ships passing as you moved further than the sea itself, off the map onto somewhere uncharted. Everything about the true side would become like that for her, in time. When time no longer felt like a measure of anything anymore.

"Then why do you want me to stay?" she asked, her nerves jumping as his touch skated down her neck. "You won't forget as easily. It's cruel to you."

"I want you to stay because I don't want to forget. I *want* memories. And I don't have nearly enough with you," he rasped out. "I don't want to waste any more time."

Not on fighting. Not on searching. Their time on this side of the world would be even briefer than their time on the other. He didn't want to think of it, but it was the truth. She would not be leaving with him, even though she should. Even though she deserved a way out more than anyone he knew. He felt that deep inside.

One moment she was just looking at him, memorizing him as though she would find some way to hold this moment in her mind with all that she could.

The next, she was kissing him.

At first, all he felt was pain. The ache in his chest unfurled like a fan of a knife, scraping beneath his collarbones. And then her hand speared into his hair and tugged him closer, though not an inch of space existed between them. Every hurt melted into warmth, gathering all around him.

"Wait, Herald." She spoke against his lips, breathless. "Won't he be coming bac—"

"Not tonight." Daron couldn't be more grateful that all remained around them were darkened mirrors, the city lights flashing in slivers through their windows.

Through his daze, he hitched her legs against him, carrying her to his makeshift room. He pulled back the curtain, for that's all that separated him from the rest of the shop, baring the small cot of a mattress and a gathering of blankets. The sight instantly stilled him, doused him in cold water.

"I'm sorry," he said, looking away. Cheeks flaring. She'd lived in the Alastor Place, a palace of a home where she no doubt rested on silks and satins. He never could offer her any of those riches she so deserved. "I know it's not much—"

"Demarco, shut up and just put me down." Her lips found his again, restless and frantic.

He spoke no more as he closed the curtain behind him.

No more memories came to life around them, though Daron swore he felt exactly as he did when they were back in Glorian in the Ranza Estate they knew, on the floor with his jacket spread out beneath them. They hadn't waited then. He had asked again and again—*are you sure, is this okay, tell me if*—until she pulled him to her, laughing against his lips before they found another rhythm. So impatient, they were, anytime they were together. Careful, but impatient.

Tonight, he was determined to go slow. So he could remember.

The arch of her back. The fall of her lips. The bite of her grip when their breaths stilled. The way she urged him to go where she wanted him, spoke to him as he spoke to her. Whispers into kisses, gasps against skin. Each sensation, a memory worth keeping.

He stopped trying to track every moment.

He knew, without even trying anymore, that he would remember all of this.

She wasn't sleeping. Neither could he. Against his chest, she felt his breath rise and fall, calm yet intentional. It had been a while before their hearts slowed to a normal rhythm, though if she were being honest with herself, her pulse still raced. As if it refused to be complacent, when all she wished to do was rest like this.

"I have a question."

She lifted her head almost immediately, her eyes sleepy and warm. "What?"

"Why do you call me Demarco?" he asked. "You rarely use my first name, and I've always wondered why."

"I called you Daron tonight. Many times."

He squared her with a look, heat slicing through her. "I'm serious."

Kallia's hand slid up to his jaw, to the side of his face, her fingers thumbing the strands of rough dark hair that curled by his ears. "I don't know. Habit, I guess," she said. "You were such a strange puzzle to me from the start that I didn't want to look any closer."

"Now *that's* a lie."

"Maybe." She smirked. "Daron still feels like a rare name to me. I can't just throw it anywhere. But Demarco, I can toss wherever. I've walked with Demarco, fought with him, performed with him—"

"Hated him."

Kallia ignored him, shaking her head. "I'm happy to use both, but I met Demarco first. So I'll always know that name best," she said. "And I did not hate you. I just didn't know you."

The answer had not disappointed, from the way his brow curved in amusement.

"Also, you're one to talk," she countered. "You weren't exactly happy to see me every time I walked into the room."

Demarco remained silent for too long, and when she looked up at his evasive expression, she smacked him in the arm. "Now I know you're lying."

"Maybe *happy* isn't the word," he relented. "But part of me always looked forward to seeing you. Even when we fought."

Kallia enjoyed the idea of him lighting up inside every time she walked by. She'd been so focused on winning Spectaculore, she'd hardly noticed the finer details of those around her. Though deep down, she'd always been hyperaware of Demarco whenever he was in the same room as her. She didn't know when it had started, but as soon as it did, that feeling never went away.

Never. Always. She had to stop thinking in absolutes. It would only make everything harder.

She laced her fingers within his, memorizing the look of them. The warmth.

"Demarco?"

"Yes, Kallia?"

The way he said her name, the only one he knew her by, touched every nerve inside her. "I'm happy you're here," she whispered. "Thank you for coming back for me."

He shifted so that she was pressed even more snugly against him. "You don't need to thank me. I really didn't do it alone." He shrugged, his lips on the edge of a sly smile. "I . . . I had some help from a few friends."

"Friends, you say?" She remembered what she'd seen in the mirror, the people she'd never imagine banding together all sitting in the café at the Prima. Aaros, Lottie, Canary, and the Conquering Circus. Even Ira. She'd seen enough of them in illusions, and out of survival, done her best, not sparing anyone a thought. What use was there, when she had no option to return to any of it?

"Kallia," he said softly, noting the shift in the air. "Do you want to talk about it, now?"

His heart beat in her ears, a slow and steady thumping. The most at peace she'd felt in a long time. "Will you tell me everything?"

"Only if you will, too."

They talked to stretch the night into many more, until their voices were half-gone, their eyes heavy. But their stories kept them awake, and they told them to each other until the end.

40

A sharp rustle shook Daron awake.

His eyes shot open, and he nearly braced himself for the glaring morning sunlight, but this world held none of that. Only slivers of city light, peeking through the windows. Through the half-opened curtain partitioning off his space, he noticed her standing by a mirror, combing her fingers through her hair.

"You're already up?" And dressed. Which meant she would not be staying. He tamped down the surge of disappointment and sat up.

"I need to get back to the others. They're probably worried sick about me."

He ran a hand down his face, forcing himself to wake up. To stand up. He didn't want her leaving without getting a good look at her. She continued fixing her hair as he approached her and noticed the top button of her dress had been left undone. Without another thought, he came up right against her, slipping the tiny button through the loop before dropping a kiss to the back of her neck.

Her gaze finally met his in the mirror. In time, his arms wound their way around her, and she leaned back slightly, settling against him. They didn't speak. As if falling into this comfortable silence would be enough. He didn't want to fight with her or make matters worse, not in this peace.

On a deep exhale, Kallia tilted back toward the mirror for one last look before stepping away from her reflection. "I have to go," she said. "Herald will probably be here any moment now."

It was bad of Daron, but he hadn't spared Herald one thought since they'd arrived in the shop. He could've walked right in, and Daron wouldn't have noticed. "When will I see you again?"

As if she could sense his apprehension, she squared him with an amused look before pulling his face down. "Tonight," she said against his lips. "I'll come back."

"I'll check my schedule." He angled his mouth over hers, deepening what was meant to be a brief brush. A small peck. No more half-measures.

He could feel her smile, her shudder of a breath as he pressed his lips down the slope of her neck, her laugh as she finally tore from him. Reluctantly. Her cheeks were flushed as she made her way to the door, looking back every so often with that reprimanding glint in her eye.

Zarose.

His breath locked in his chest, trapping his heart until she finally closed the door behind her.

He immediately changed back into his day clothes, fixing his appearance should Herald wander back in. He was almost hoping for it.

There had to be another way.

Countless times, Daron had been told finding Kallia would be impossible. That coming here would be impossible. Journeying through the Dire Woods had been impossible. Hell, long ago, he'd thought coming to Glorian would be next to impossible. He didn't know what Kallia knew of this world. She'd been here longer, known its rules longer, was told those rules could never be bent. But from experience, he knew there was always another way. There had to be another way.

Everything that's now possible was once deemed impossible.

Why not this?

He wasn't leaving. Not yet.

The heaviness lifted from his bones as he peeked through the curtains at the bustling streets, people still recovering or staggering from
the revelry of the night before. Herald wasn't among them, but Daron
hoped to catch him in the crowd soon. Before seeing Kallia again tonight, he needed a plan. He couldn't just boldly march without direction as he'd done before. It had gotten him this far, but not without
trouble. He needed to know more about this world before trying to
bend the rules of it, and Herald would no doubt offer any bit of knowledge if it might—

At the abrupt sound of the door opening, Daron all but leapt to the
front of the store. He hadn't felt this much energy in ages, and it only
heightened as he recognized Herald standing right at the threshold.
"Finally, you're back!" he said, waiting for him to shut the door before
coming any closer. "Where have you . . ."

The question drifted off Daron's lips as he realized Herald wasn't
making any effort to shut the door to the outside, for he wasn't alone.
Another figure loomed behind, and Daron instinctively took a step
back, his heart slowing as the other magician shoved Herald inside the
shop before giving the place a predatory look over.

"Demarco," Jack said by way of cold greeting. He looked just as he
had on the night of Spectaculore. Polished as a pistol, ready to shoot in
the suit as dark as the triangles upon his hands. And his eyes were now
a storm at night, all darkness. Nothing human at all. Unlike him, Herald was a mess. The sleeve of his shirt torn, hair in disarray, the hint
of swelling by his eye. Most of all, the look in his eye was different. A
quiet panic that seemed ill-fitting on the magician he'd come to know.

"What do you want?" Daron demanded, pulse racing. "Are you all
right, Herald?"

At that, Jack laughed. "Oh, that's sweet. An unlikely friendship."

The world began shrinking around Daron, and anytime it did that,
it meant something was wrong. Something was off. And it was far too
late to fix any of it.

The way Kallia had spoken of Jack, with grudging respect and a
softness he couldn't understand, made Daron think he could be more

or less trusted. Maybe not with everything, but where Kallia's best interests were, at least. Daron should've trusted that doubt spiraling in his gut, the one that foresaw the cold smug smile on the man in front of him who looked as though he'd stumbled upon a hunt he'd been looking forward to for the longest time.

"Alas, I am here under orders," Jack continued, snapping his fingers. Two devils walked through the door and took Daron by the elbows. "There's a dangerous magician out on the loose, causing all this chaos and mayhem. Roth's out for her blood, and I hear you're connected to her."

Daron's stomach dropped.

"You all made it almost too easy," Jack said as the shadows gripped Daron by the wrists, the ankles—the coldest smoke slithering over him like a chain, before one wrapped its claws around his eyes.

And all went dark.

41

Kallia walked the streets of Glorian, her heart feeling lighter than it had in a long time. The dreamlike state consumed her as she walked back to her room to the amused looks of servants taking in her bedraggled appearance, and took off all her makeup and show clothes with a loose grin she couldn't shake. For so long, she'd kept herself wrapped tight as a fist, hardened in survival mode. It had been so long since she felt like she could rest. Like she could take comfort in the light again.

It would make everything that much harder. It hurt now, to think of Demarco's face hovering over hers in the dark, knowing their time was far too limited. That one day, she would forget that face in the dark, smiling over hers, and this ache in her heart would fade in time, too.

Today, she would shove it all out of mind. It was tomorrow's problem.

For now, she would allow herself to smile.

When she made her way to the ruins of the Ranza Estate, her grin widened as relieved gasps burst from inside the burnt house.

"Holy shit, you're alive!" Malice gave her a tight hug before shooting her a smug look. "And looking extremely well-rested."

Ruthless slapped the girl in the arm. "Don't make fun!"

"Yes, shut up. Please," Vain interjected, folding her arms as she got a better look at Kallia. "Glad you found the note. When you didn't answer your door, I got worried."

"I'm sure you did." Malice cackled, for which Ruthless slapped her in the back of the head.

For the life of her, Kallia did not want to meet Vain's eye, possibly ever again. Though when the headliner nudged her foot to look up, Vain only shook her head with a hint of a smile. "No details, or I *will* kill you."

At that, the two other Diamond Rings whined while Kallia returned the smile. "Deal."

The last thing she wanted was to talk to Vain about her brother. And yet, Kallia was still curious about what sort of conversation they'd had together, and if they were able to mend the distance. Demarco had been very tight-lipped about it, as he often was, but that still didn't hinder her curiosity in the slightest.

Still, it could be a conversation for another time.

"Why are we here today?" Kallia looked around them. It had been so long since they'd last stepped foot on these grounds, back when she could hardly freeze an illusion from slamming right into her face.

So much had changed in so little time.

"Gymnasium's undergoing some repairs after last night," Vain stated. "So we are spared from some of the more intensive equipment training for a brief time—"

Malice and Ruthless cheered with such intensity, Kallia couldn't help but join.

"You all would be useless without me." Vain *tsk*ed and rolled her eyes. "Just because the gym is in shambles does not mean there's absolutely nothing left to do."

She couldn't hide the smugness in her tone as they let out a series of groans.

"I thought we were going to hold back on the destruction moving forward," Kallia muttered under her breath. "What happened?"

"That wasn't us."

"Really?" Her eyes widened, breath stalled. "What was it?"

"Divine intervention?" Malice offered. "It was my night, and I didn't even have to lift a bloody finger."

"There are such things as accidents." Vain arched a sharp brow, a quiet blaze of triumph in her eyes. "The fact that accidents can happen is a promising sign that Roth is losing his hold on the city. And if the devils are not pleased by that, all the fucking better."

The Diamond Rings let out a wild series of howls, as if they were falling right through the sky for all the world to see.

It wasn't long before Vain got them back to order and back to practicing.

Like the first time they crossed this area in the city, they dueled in the dirt and rubble. Kallia was relieved for the repetition, to feel in control of her power. To feel her magic coursing through her like a fire.

With everything Vain threw at her, Kallia met her with an ease that had Ruthless and Malice hooting from the sides as they watched. They were throwing all manner of illusions against the broken wall of the Ranza Estate, from gusts of winds strong enough to shake the foundations to large vines that stretched over the cracked surface until it began breaking apart even further. Such tricks Kallia hadn't even felt capable of doing when they had first begun practicing, but now they felt like challenges she just wanted to conquer.

"Good," Vain said approvingly when the last of the wall had finally broken down. "You're getting stronger."

It was perhaps the best compliment Kallia could have received.

"Well, *that's* a relief, I'll say."

Kallia blinked at the new voice, and they all turned to find Roth observing them with two devils at his side. He looked absolutely terrible. Dark shadows beneath reddened eyes, a sallowness to his skin as if he'd been up all night. And the anger. There was an anger radiating off him, boiling beneath his skin. And something more sinister Kallia couldn't quite put her finger on.

Kallia exchanged glances with Vain, and the other Diamond Rings stood at attention.

"It's truly wonderful to see you've been taking your practices so seriously, Kallia," Roth said. "I couldn't be prouder. And the results speak for themselves. Seem like you are ready to face the gate after all. And the timing could not be more perfect."

Kallia swallowed the lump of dread in her throat. As much as she wanted to get stronger for her own self, she hated what that made her in the eyes of Roth. "How so?" she asked stiffly. "Did you want a demonstration?"

"Nice of you to offer, but why waste time on a demonstration when we could just skip to the real thing?"

Her entire world narrowed in one blink, one breath. Surely he had to be joking.

She wasn't sure if it was a comfort or an omen that the other Diamond Rings appeared just as confused. She certainly felt more uneasy when Roth clasped his hands together. "Oh, isn't this exciting?" he trilled. "Last night's turn of events was actually quite the blessing in disguise. At first, I thought surely we could not have an accident *again*. That would be too . . . coincidental."

Kallia gulped, keeping her face as neutral as the others'.

"It definitely feels like an orchestrated attacker." Frowning, Vain folded her arms. "We were worried what this would mean. To break the gate."

"That was my concern as well." His voice was all light, soft as a feather. "Which is why I'm so grateful you took my Kallia under your wing so diligently. Even when chaos ran rampant, you kept at the training and have made her into a better, stronger magician."

A slight sting of heat flew to Kallia's face.

"You wanted the best from the best." Vain shrugged. "And I don't disappoint."

The magician makes magic.

How easily Vain flew from one lie to the next. The skill was as impressive as it was unnerving.

"You certainly don't." Roth nodded, letting out a deep breath. "But you have disappointed me."

Muttering under his breath, Roth pointed to Vain, and almost instantly, the devils appeared at her side and were upon her.

"What the *hell*—" For the first time, fear flew into her eyes as she snarled, struggling. "Get off me!"

Ruthless and Malice rushed to Vain's side, but the devils shifted forms to bar them away. Even Kallia tried using it to pry them off Vain, but it was useless against them.

"What's going on?" Kallia set her glare on Roth. "Call them off."

Her heart sank even deeper as the man ignored her. "I'm very disappointed in you, Vain," he said calmly. "You were one of my most trusted. Though I guess that should've been the first cause for suspicion from the beginning."

Vain's curses were muffled behind the devils' hold, more like a wall of smoke that covered her entirely.

"I gave you a stage, your very own show night—and this is how you repay me?" With a slow *tsk* of his tongue, he only shook his head. "I made you what you are. So now I can unmake you."

Kallia drew in a breath of horror at Vain's screams. She'd heard those words before, thrown at Jack like acid.

Where was Jack?

Her pulse drummed hard as the Dealer's hands came together in a final clap and the devils vanished—taking Vain with them.

Kallia's blood turned cold at the silence, at how suddenly it came.

"Where did you take her?"

"None of your concern," Roth said, already turning. "You just focus on your practicing—"

"She didn't do it alone." She stopped him in his path, her fists clenched at her sides. "I helped her. If you're going to take her, you'll need to take us, too."

With Ruthless and Malice standing behind her, there was no need to put on an act anymore. She couldn't tell how long Roth knew it had all been false, but there was no point in her pretending. She wouldn't let Vain face punishment alone.

She expected Roth to express disappointment. Disapproval.

Instead, his laugh sent a chill down her spine.

"Honorable of you, my dear, to shoulder some of the blame if only to help your friend," he murmured. "Jack told me you would spin lies like that."

Her heart gave a hollow thump as she froze. Behind her back, Malice and Ruthless gripped her hands, but the comfort lasted no more than a second and Roth chuckled at what her expression must've shown.

"I did warn you, I've got strings on everyone, my dear. Just like the devils do." On a whistled note, he turned with a wink over his shoulder. "You might want to practice a bit more. The gate arrived only just last night, so the clock starts *now*."

ACT III

Satisfied as the gatekeepers were of the magician's feat,

they demanded one more spectacle.

One last test.

42

Daron woke up to darkness. To cold.

The ground was ice hard against his face as he stirred with a groan. His muscles spasmed with every movement, no matter how slight. He couldn't recall where the pain had come from, but it would go away. If he could only just get up.

Get up.

"Dare?"

The pain vanished at the firm jostle at his side.

"You have to wake up. *Please.*"

Eva? Even in darkness, he knew her, and the panic chipping at her voice drew him up instantly. "Eva," he gasped. "What are you—"

"Oh, thank Zarose." Her head hung as she exhaled, crouched just over him. Her short black hair flared out like thorns, and he couldn't help but marvel at the way the style opened her face, sharpened every-thing on it.

Especially fear.

As he looked beyond her, he blinked at pure darkness staring back. Everywhere he turned his head—nothing. As if they'd been dropped inside of a shadow, a night with no stars. No lights or colors or music pulsing everywhere from the world before.

This world went entirely without.

"Nice of him to punish us together, I guess." Eva half-shrugged, rising to her feet. "Or cruel. Can't tell which."

"Why are you—and I—" His heart stuttered. He could barely speak through the relief breaking him inside. Seeing Eva—so near and alive, talking, *breathing*—would never stop feeling like a dream. Even in a nightmare. "Where *are* we?"

She drew out a long, grim sigh. "We're outside the gate. Far from the city."

The way she said it, they might as well have been shackled to the ground and left for dead. But all they had was each other and the wind for company, able to move about as they pleased with nothing stopping them.

A warning bell rang in his head, throbbed at his temple. It was too easy, freedom like this. No restraints or anyone around to hold them in place.

Whatever was coming, running wouldn't stop it from finding them.

"Has anyone ever made it back?" Daron's throat dried, already hearing Herald's sardonic chuckle in answer. Nowhere to hide, only darkness where no rules applied. Roth never forced anyone to live in his city, but he could certainly force anyone he wanted out of it. And everyone knew that beyond those gates, the devils waited.

Daron saw his odds in the endless dark ahead. This land breathed over his skin like the Dire Woods had, sweeping through his hair, staking its claim before he'd even taken a step.

Harsh hands yanked him by both arms.

"Come on, we have to keep moving," Eva said, hefting him up to his feet with surprising force. "And keep your eyes down."

Alarm pierced his bones as he followed her lead and jogged to catch up. "Wait, why are you here? When did—" His vision spun so violently, he stopped. *"Kallia."*

Something in him snapped. The last face he remembered before losing consciousness was Jack's—carved more cold-eyed than usual, like darkening glass from the smoke trapped inside. Whatever it was,

it had led him to Daron. And it was only a matter of time before he
went for Kallia next.

He *needed* to go back. "Which way do we go?"

"No need to turn into a raging white knight, Dare. Kallia has been
taking care of herself longer than you know. And she's too important
to Roth now to dispose of—unlike us," Eva pointed out with a huff.
"So for once, put yourself first. And for fuck's sake, just keep walking."

His mouth dropped slightly when she threw her shoulders back
and strode forward. She'd reprimanded him in his thoughts so often,
hearing it aloud brought a bite of whiplash.

"Now, forward." She nudged him brusquely in the shoulder. "And
eyes down."

"What the hell for?" he muttered with a hard nudge back. "Yours
aren't."

"That's because you don't know what to look for." Something
snapped in Eva as she whirled around fast, eyes ablaze. "You're not
keeping watch for the city lights, I am. Because I have more power
and training than you. Because when *I* first fell here, I had to walk this
land alone. And I made it."

All the wrath of the Queen of the Diamond Rings couldn't hide
that splinter of terror in her voice. Herald had spared Daron from
knowing it by bringing him safely through the gates. A mercy he
shouldn't have taken for granted, Daron now realized, squeezing his
fists by his sides. "How did you survive it before?"

The wind hissed sinuously between them, around them.

"Zarose knows how any of us gets through it." Eva pushed on.
"Anything that shows you what you want to see is smart enough to
take what it wants in return. And I wasn't going to let them take
what little I had left. What made me a magician."

Power.

The guilt daggered through him, twisted as the breeze carried its
own words. Voices, at every step. Stilted laughter and distant glee,
broken joy from faraway. All of them, lost magicians. Imagining Eva
among them made Daron want to crawl out of his skin.

"You look down." With firmer steps, he hastened. "We'll take turns."

"This isn't a game, Dare. We can't make things fair here."

"Then let's both look and lose." He trained his eyes as much on her as he did on the path before them. "Because I'm not letting you put *me* first before yourself."

He could practically hear the cogs whirring in Eva's head, resentment dimming her eyes as she finally lowered them to the ground. "But I'm older."

"And? I'm your brother." Even in an impossible world, she still wanted to do the most for him. After everything. "If it takes me, you run. And if it takes you, I'll run." His pulse faltered a beat. "And if either of us sees those lights, we both go. But this is how it's going to be."

In the absence of certainty, Daron planned. Even if strategy was only the illusion of control, it helped to run through their options in any game: how they could lose, how they might win.

If only he knew what card they would draw.

"So intimidating." Eva's amused drawl rose to a laugh, as if she could hear every thought firing off in his head. "I almost forgot what it was like taking the stage with the great Daring Demarco."

The joke sank heavy as a stone inside him, slowed his steps. His breath. "I'm sorry."

"What for?"

"Two years." He hated that he couldn't look her in the eyes. Wished more than anything to be anywhere else, talking to his sister as he used to back when they had more time. "I'd thought you were gone for . . ."

He buried the knot down his throat like a lit coal, bracing himself as Eva finally lifted her gaze. In the sliver of light, her eyes grew shadowed. "We shouldn't do this now."

"Then when?" He wasn't going to pretend. Not again. "Eva, we *need* to talk about it some time. While we still can—"

"We *need* to keep going." Her jawline tensed to an icy edge. "And it's your turn to look down."

Lips pinched together, Daron felt the blood rush to his face as he turned to the ground, the dirt dark as everything around them. "I really am sorry."

"Again, for what?" Begrudgingly, Eva edged closer to his side. "You keep saying that."

The moment she acknowledged it, the words were all gone.

For everything.

Everything he missed, everything he took from her. Everything she refused to talk about during the night carnival all came bubbling back up to the surface, rushing against whatever time was left between them.

"Lottie told me everything. I never realized I . . . " Daron stopped. Excuses changed nothing. He needed to stop hiding behind them. "No, I should've known. Something was wrong, and I didn't—"

"*Lottie?* Figures." She barked out a fond laugh. "Sharpest bitch I ever met. Glad to see you two finally made nice without me."

"How can you be so cavalier about this?" His breaths cut cold through his lungs as he dug a hand through his hair, unable to make sense of any of it. "I-I had been taking your power. I made you sick."

Eva. Kallia. And Zarose knew who else.

He was worse than a devil. Just as toxic.

A groan rose regardless, steeped in irritation. "Yes, I know what happened. Trust me, I was there." Eva stopped them with the turn of her heel, arms crossed. "But why the hell does any of that matter now?"

"What do you mean?"

"What do you *actually* want from me, Dare? My eternal loathing, a punch in the face?" She gave a wild wave of her hands, sweeping an anxious glance around. "Doesn't seem like the best use of our time right now."

"I don't understand." His face burned. She was right, as always. The past was trivial out here. He felt like a fool for even digging it up. Yet he couldn't ignore how easily she did away with it all, as if he'd committed a simple mistake. "I'm your brother. And I . . . I hurt you. Couldn't find you, for the longest time—"

"What if I didn't want to be found?"

A stabbing silence struck the air. The kind from a duel finally at its end, because she shot first. Perfect aim, from the pain blossoming in his chest.

Averting his gaze, his sister darted another hurried look on either side of them as if hoping devils would show. "Just so we're clear, I haven't spent my time here plotting my revenge or waiting to be saved, Dare. But I'm not entirely heartless," she said. "When I saw this place for what it was, I embraced it. Had to. If you don't, you sink. And it's not every day you get a second chance to start a new story in a new world." Her nostrils flared. "But we all come with ghosts."

From the way her glare hardened, Daron could've been the only one haunting her. A ghost to her as she'd been to him, long before he ever stepped foot on this side.

"When those faded, I searched for you all in the mirrors. Like most do. Just to see everyone alive and whole, that's all." Eva kicked at the ground before tipping her head back skyward. "But you . . . I couldn't find you for the longest time."

In an instant, his thoughts quieted. And the words echoed. "You were looking for *me*?"

There was something so unbelievable to it. Years of guilt had run him ragged. Every failed attempt to locate her gutted him. Yet in all that time, it never once occurred to him that she might've been searching for him, all the same.

"Of course I did, you idiot," she snapped, voice thick. When her stare dropped to her feet, and stayed, Daron couldn't watch her. Didn't reach for her, knowing she would only dodge kindness to keep that mask from breaking.

Instead, he forced his gaze up to guide their path, feeling his chest cave in more and more with each breath. "I wasn't around mirrors much. I just couldn't, after . . ."

There was no need to spell it out again. He knew better now.

Strangely, a hint of a smile broke over her lips. "You neglected *this* dashing face?" From the side, she flicked at his chin before mussing up his hair. "No wonder all of this became so unkempt, then."

"Shut up." Daron swatted her away, shielding his face. Almost normal, for a moment.

"You shouldn't have kept away. It nearly drove me mad." Her grin soon slipped back into the cracks as her frown gradually resurfaced. "I could only imagine it was how you felt when I'd gone. As if you had disappeared."

It wasn't the first time he'd heard it. He'd broken so easily, like the mirror he'd pushed her through that night. And once she disappeared, so much else followed. Without her, without the stage or his magic, every constant in his life had vanished. Every anchor to steady him and pillar to lean on, shattered to pieces. It was no wonder how hard he'd fallen.

If only he could stop.

"Eventually, I did find you. Among other things." Eva claimed the watch back, her gaze narrowed straight ahead. "When everyone forgot about me, you never could. You never stopped believing I was somewhere out there, even when the world had moved on," she said quietly. "And yet, you'd look so broken. It was like seeing you in pieces sometimes."

A pinch of hot shame scalded around his neck. She'd witnessed him at his lowest. His loneliest. "Maybe deep down, I always knew you would never come back. Even if you had a way out."

Head shaking, she sucked in a breath through her teeth. "You act like the only thing this place can ever be is one big cage—as if the true side is any better off." Her brow jutted up. "If it's my choice to stay, is that really so bad?"

"But to be without your friends? Your family?" His throat tightened. "How can you choose what is all just illusion, Eva? None of this is real."

A faint alarm rang in his ears when her spine went ramrod straight. Tense as a hawk. Her wrath doused the air as she stepped right in his path, glowering with eyes dark as a snake's waiting to strike. "It may not be real to *you*—but what I've been able to build here, for myself, is plenty real to me," she bit out. "Here, I can live. Let go. Rise higher than anything the real world has to offer."

The thrill lighting that fire was all Vain. The main headliner, leader of the Diamond Rings. Watching her perform within her hoop the other night left him in awe of the stranger wearing his sister's face. No longer Eva, but Vain.

Though perhaps the performer had never been the stranger to begin with. Perhaps her true side was this—the very stage she made for herself.

"All I've ever wanted to do is find you and make things right." His voice became even smaller at the drop in the air. "To fix this."

The mantra that had carved through his thoughts for years hushed at the surprise bite of nails. A hand that so rarely reached out for others, taking his now. "Some things break for a reason. And some things just . . . break," she said. "You pushed me through the mirror, but I chose to fall." And if *I* have no regrets over it, you shouldn't . . ." She trailed off slowly with troubled eyes sliding past his shoulder. "Do you . . . hear that?"

Daron froze.

The devils. They were coming.

His heart slammed in his chest, thundering so loudly in his ears he begged it to stop.

Run. They had to run now.

"No," he stammered, pulling her into a sprint with him. "I don't hear anything, we have—"

Eva refused to budge. Still as a statue, carved with ever-widening eyes and an eerie ghost of a smile. "That applause means it's show time . . ."

Daron dropped his hand from her.

Eva?" Panic tore through him the longer she stared through him like glass, unblinking. He fought every urge to turn, simply whispered her name again. Took her by the shoulders with a pleading shake. "Please, wake up. You have to—"

Pain burst everywhere from the burning force that slammed him to the ground. Daron lost his breath for a moment, tasting blood as he coughed. Eva's laughter fell over him as she walked on, talking to herself and whatever waited for her.

If it takes me, you run.

Daron gritted his teeth, eyes tearing as he forced himself up.

And if it takes you, I'll run.

Without hesitation, he ran for Eva and threw her behind him. Her screams pierced at an unnatural pitch as she scratched at his arms, drawing blood with her claws.

Daron felt nothing at all when he welcomed the illusion stretching over him like a net.

Go on, he dared. *Take everything.*

As he gave himself up to the darkness, only then did he see light.

43

Kallia didn't cry. She didn't resist. In silence like this, she wasn't sure what to do. Getting ready in the way she did, without the usual chatter and laughter and cursing that volleyed among the Diamond Rings over her head, was more hollow than she could've ever imagined. Without the others by her, without even knowing where they were, she felt so small. So alone.

So unprepared.

She squeezed the diamond ring on her necklace, wishing she could just rip it off and fly away.

Only there was nowhere to fly to. Nowhere to run, except back into the cage.

Her heart cracked a little, but she stopped it at that. If she gave in to thoughts that would sink her to the floor, she would never get up.

She welcomed the deep rouge she brushed over her lips, the bold lines she painted along her eyelids. The blush that livened up her face like a lie. The jewel bowl stared at her from the edge of her vanity, the last piece of her mask. The most complicated one to put on.

It felt silly to put on makeup before she was brought to the gate, but she would take any power she could get. Anything to hide behind.

Soft footsteps sounded behind her, falling quiet as shadow on the carpeted ground.

Her body tensed, knowing those steps. Freezing the moment he came into the frame of the mirror, at her back. She focused only on the path of buttons of his suit by her ear, the one hand that almost dared touch her shoulder.

"Can I have a moment?"

His voice breathed more winter than usual. So calm, so controlled, it only stoked the rage in her more.

Before he could touch her, she whirled around with her fist flying hard—

Jack caught it in his ice-cold grip.

And eyes, black as the night above, stared back at her.

"Jack?" She faltered, fear digging into her when he kept his hold on her like a shackle.

Despite the terror, the dimmest hope sparked inside her. She knew Jack well enough at this point to know that this was not him. He was there, behind those eyes, with his own thoughts and wants and concerns.

He was simply unable to break free.

"Jack, wake up." She forced iron into her voice, pulling back her fist with everything she had. "Let me go—"

He obeyed. The force sent her falling back onto her chair, facing the mirror with his hands over her shoulders. Keeping her there.

"You could never hurt me, Kallia," he said. "But I could always hurt you."

The tension in her jaw could split her skull in half. Despite gritting her teeth, they still chattered. Still shook. "Jack. Please. Wake up."

"I am awake," he said, dipping his head into frame of the reflection. His dark eyes, shining through. "We all are."

She shuddered as he continued gliding his cold fingers up and down her shoulders, the length of her throat, before reaching the chain.

She flinched.

Jack smiled. "I won't harm you. I would never," he said. "Besides, I wasn't given orders to hurt you."

The specificity set her on edge. Meant to taunt her, like bait. "What did you do?"

"Nothing too worrisome. Just sent two on a walk outside." His fingers danced by her necklace. "Roth's orders."

Her heart stopped cold. He wasn't joking. Without even asking, she knew who had been sent. The wounds to press to get her to scream the most.

"The gate is just outside," he said, skimming the thin chain. "It's waiting for you."

"Why the hell would I help now?" she bit out, ducking out from under his touch. Easily, Jack snapped her back into place, her back to his front.

"Because your cooperation determines when the torture ends," he whispered in her ear. "If I were you, I wouldn't wait too long. The devils are ravenous. And they love a good hunt."

Her heart became a crushing weight in her chest. Everything it touched hurt. Every breath brought an ache of pain. She was only glad she wasn't crying. This Jack would relish the sight, breaking her down without even breaking a bone.

"Where's the gate?" she seethed. Her insides tensed, the realization hitting her with a numbing force. The gate was here. It had brought its own wave of destruction to the city the night before, and now she would meet it.

She would face it.

"Just outside our gates." Jack sounded pleased to answer. "Roth will be watching."

"And you?" When his hand trailed beneath her jaw, she stopped him by the wrist and gazed up at him.

Please.

Those dark eyes narrowed on her grasp like a candleflame, curious. The first emotion to emerge from him aside from cruelty. When he didn't pull away, she felt something coil tightly inside.

Closely, she studied his face as her thumb stroked the tops of his knuckles.

Jack.

Every soft press of her finger to his, she waited for him to show. For a piece of him to soften and warm, his lips to—

There was a hard yank, and the sound of a delicate break reached her ears.

Her heart echoed, feeling nothing but numbness, waiting for the pain to rush in a scalding wave.

Except he hadn't snapped or twisted any bone.

With a hypnotist's grace, he dangled her torn necklace before her eyes, letting it swing slowly as a pendulum while pieces of broken chain plinked against the table.

Kallia finally felt the edges of her eyes water.

Jack observed her with an accomplished smirk and whispered close to her ear, "I'm here to make sure you can't escape."

Kallia walked out through the city gates with her eyes closed. Her teeth chattered. She didn't even care to wipe away the tears streaking down her face.

Jack had already watched her cry long enough. The fact that she couldn't stop seemed to please him all the more.

"You'll have to open those eyes eventually, my dear . . ."

The voice was Roth's, but there was so much more inside it. More monster than magician. All along, he'd been exactly so.

Coward, too. If he wanted her to open her eyes, he'd have to force them open himself.

As she walked forward, it was the one thing she could choose.

One last choice, made out of terror.

Shame should've poured over her, covering her like hot oil before the drop of a lit match. She waited for the flames to devour her completely, to burn where she stood.

For each step after the other, to be her last.

The tears poured freely as the music met her ears. There were those who still celebrated in the Glorian behind her, completely unaware that death was just outside their gates. That death had been coming for them, every night.

If she didn't get this right.

The thought filled Kallia with bile, before her fingers brushed cold glass.

She froze.

Open your eyes.

Her heart thundered hard against her chest, it pained every breath.

There were no more steps to take, no more time to think. Only one thing left to do.

Open your eyes.

They only shut tighter, even as tears fell. She was sure if she looked, she'd see only the picture of fear staring back at her.

It was the last thing she wanted to remember about herself.

"What are you waiting for?"

Roth's roar from whatever safe pedestal he stood upon to watch was a sound of rage. Of demand and force. She knew what would happen if she didn't obey. She heard what he would do to them, just in his voice.

Kallia hadn't even given herself a moment to fear where they might be, what he might be doing to them despite what she was doing now.

At least they weren't here to see her. To see this.

Open your eyes.

Her fingers shook as she lifted her hand once more, buying whatever time she could before the time came for her to see.

In all her dreams of this moment, she never thought it would feel quite like this. The worry had eaten away at her, when Vain told her not to worry at all. They'd been so confident, too sure, that it would never come to this.

Once here, she was even less ready than before.

She didn't feel any more powerful than she did, first walking through the gates of this Glorian. Terror turned her back into that weak magician, grasping at whatever magic she could to feel powerful again. Whatever power she had gained would still never be enough.

Because when her fingers brushed at the cold surface again, she felt more power than she could ever hope to destroy.

The sort of power she'd always wished for, that she'd always dreamed of.

That it would be her end was not at all what she'd expected.

The hellish cries that rose around her drowned out the music that surged from the city behind her. A language she could not understand that sounded more like the growls and snarls of predators on the hunt. All of the devils that awaited in that darkness, that took up the sky, reveled and readied as one.

They would wait no more.

Shakily, Kallia dragged her finger over the smooth surface, reaching the web of broken lines in—

A scream.

It pierced through her like a knife and twisted as more followed.

Cries for help, in agony, for the end.

Names desperately shouted. Names she'd never heard before, the last word for some.

Kallia wanted to cover her ears, tear them off to silence this nightmare of noise. A sob caught in her throat, bile rising at the evil she felt in just those cracks. They stabbed more pain, more sorrow, than anything she'd ever felt.

It was the mirror's promise, burning through every vein and every thought beneath the fractured surface—

Kallia . . .

She paused, stilling her touch over the crack at the weak whisper that rose from it. The crushed sound of someone's last word.

Her name.

It almost sent Kallia to her knees, hearing that voice die. That final moment of a woman this mirror remembered. That this mirror had seen.

These weren't promises, nor a future she heard.

The past remained in the scars of the mirror. Every break she felt held the screams of those from before, the last sight of the surface before.

Death, to all of those forced to face it.

The pain was overwhelming, and the mirror remembered it all.

Every life it took, marked in every crack left over like a wound. An infection.

Kallia knew why Roth thought it would be easier this time, to break the mirror once and for all. One more blow, and it would shatter to pieces. A gate so powerful was just a fragile mirror, after all. Even the weakest magician, brave enough to go up to it, could easily make it shatter.

Kallia.

She held on to the voice it gave her. It could've been a mother. A sister. Someone who loved her enough to make her their final thought once that mirror took them.

For the first time, the tears fell for them. These strangers who would forever be at a distance. She would never know them. And they would never know her.

And they would live on only in the pain of this mirror.

Open your eyes.

Break it.

Kallia wanted to. She wanted to pull away and run, if only to get the screams out of her head. To find silence.

Her breath shook as she pressed her brow to the glass. The web of veins and cracks, so sharp against her skin, she wouldn't be surprised if they cut at her. A parting gift from one broken thing to another.

This would be Kallia's.

The screams still went on in her head, where they would probably remain for the rest of her days. So much pain remembered, but never forgotten. She never wanted to forget this, or silence them.

She poured what she could into the scars. She didn't have enough power to break, but this, she could do.

Slowly, the breaks in the glass softened under her brow, as did the voices in her head. The screams that would forever be remembered.

As her name rose for one last time, Kallia dropped to her knees.

Her muscles trembled from so much loss, she could hardly stand. Could hardly breathe.

As the world came back in a storm of noise, she found she had no choice when someone gripped her by the neck and yanked her up.

And stared straight into Jack's fathomless eyes.

"Where did it go?" he growled, crushing her throat. "What the *hell* did you do?"

Roth's voice flowed through him, and she smiled. If they were angry, then she must've done something right.

Through her blurred vision, Zarose Gate was gone. She saw it from the ground as he threw her down. She could barely feel the pain. She felt utterly boneless with bliss. Light and floating.

She lifted her head as someone approached. Roth, looking down at her, seething. He was a nightmare of shadows now, his face was hardly even recognizable. They'd been careful to place her away, far out of reach from the mirror. Roth glanced coldly at it from where he stood. "Why must you make this harder, Kallia? Harder than it should be?"

With his shoe, he kicked her over so that her back was to the ground. So that she had no choice but to watch him circle her from above.

"It can't be broken," she slurred. "It's gone."

"Don't you know I can smell lies now, Kallia?" He laughed. "And yours taste so sweet. You thought you really did something with that poetic little act of rebellion."

Doubt. He was trying to make her doubt.

She knew his games, the way he twisted minds without reaching into them.

"And all for what—waste your powers fixing a mirror that will only be broken again? Sending it away?" He laughed. "I thought I'd feel bad ordering Jack to throw your friends out there anyway, but now I'm glad I had the foresight."

The light feeling dimmed as a sound rolled in the back of her throat.

"Oh, what was that? I can't hear you." He crouched down over her. "Yes, the trap Jack laid out for them is quite the hell for them both. They seem like they're enjoying their time."

He smiled as if he could see it now, and that made Kallia act.

If he could still see it, it was still happening.

"If you get to them, you might be able to pull them out of it," he said with a sigh. "That is, if you can find them out there. You'll just have to tell us where the mirror is."

Kallia tried throwing him off, but he drifted away in a puff of smoke instead—materializing before her in corporeal form as she staggered to her feet. The darkness beyond the gate was endless and vast, but the devils stood in their orderly line, like soldiers waiting for the war to start. The first shot to fire.

Demarco.

Vain.

The thought of them set her off through the maze of devils, the darkness beyond—

A hand dragged her by the back of her outfit, forcefully enough that she heard a tear.

"I hoped it wouldn't have come to this, but you leave me no choice, my dear." Arms crossed, Roth stood aside to watch Jack hold her back up by the neck. "Find out where it is or force her."

Fear lashed through Kallia.

Jack smiled at the sight. "Easily."

No. She clawed at his grip on her, surprised he hadn't crushed her throat at this point. He could've stabbed her right through the heart, and the overwhelming panic would've masked that pain. "No, please—"

"*Please?*" Roth laughed. "That's sweet. I'm sure you wished you hadn't just wasted whatever meager power you worked so hard to get back. Because you know what's easier to break than a mirror?"

A sob knifed up her throat as she felt the telltale press of thorns.

"The mind is far more malleable than glass, after all."

Kallia thrashed, kicking her legs out, but Jack easily held her aloft. Every time she stared in his face, there was nothing. His eyes were as shadowed as Roth's. Whatever part of him cared for her was long gone to the devils. They'd destroyed that part of him.

If it had even ever been real.

Kallia pushed.

Jack.

Her mind screamed the name as she pushed back with everything she had. There was no way to stop him from coming into her head; she had to go into his head first.

Jack.

She didn't know why she thought she could stop him, but she had to try. There was no effort on his face as the thorns came into her head. Overpowering her, as they always did.

Her eyes closed as she waited for the darkness to come and take what it wanted. She couldn't fight him. She never could.

"Don't you dare close your eyes, Kallia," he ordered. "Look at me."

She didn't know what called her to obey, but when she did, her eyes widened with a start.

This isn't real.

This is an illusion.

When she glanced down for a brief moment, in the darkness at his side, she caught the movement from the fingers of his free hand.

The slide of his thumb across knuckles.

Only when she dragged her gaze up to his did she find the smallest blink of noble eyes staring back.

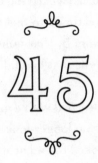

45

Kallia's eyes shot wide open.

There were still shadows in Jack's, endless shadows that took away the eyes she'd known. Noble eyes. And a proud smile.

"What's wrong?" Roth asked, annoyed. "Just do it already."

"She's . . . ," Jack said in a convincing show of frustration. "She's putting up a fight."

"Then end it."

Kallia's heart was racing the hardest it ever had as her feet hit the ground. Jack's clutch on her neck loosened. The fever of panic broke over her, and it was like she could finally see everything.

And she felt *it*.

Something she'd gone so long without. It filled every hollowed crack and crevice inside her. She'd almost forgotten what such a sensation felt like. That heat in the flame, that cold in the ice. She felt like a storm, with lightning in her blood and thunder in her bones.

Power.

She felt it the way she knew she was alive. With absolute certainty.

"Get down!"

Kallia threw herself out of the way as Jack launched himself on Roth. The two struggled against each other—Jack's flung fist burning with fire, stopped by Roth's wrapped in smoke. Shadows flared angrily like snakes all about them, a fight of silent orders met without compliance.

Roth spat in his face. "You stupid bo—"

With a merciless snap, Jack twisted the man's arm into a shape that was all wrong. Roth, who claimed to feel no pain, howled out loud. Even louder as Jack lifted him by that same arm and threw Roth far, far over the heads of the devils that had fallen from the sky and gathered out in the distance.

Breathing heavily, Jack turned with a gaze still shadowed and terrifying as ever, but his face no longer looked like a mask. A touch of warmth to the cold as he looked out all around them.

"How?" Kallia dared another step toward him, breathless. "How did you . . . what did you do to me?"

The words echoed between them now, one glimpse in his head was all it took. And she saw him now. Not an illusion, not a devil. Beneath those shadows, Jack waited.

She almost reached out a hand to touch his face, just to make sure.

"I didn't do anything." A ghost of a smile graced his lips before he turned so that his back was against hers. "He won't be gone for long. I can feel it. He'll be back, but the devils are there, all around him, so it's only a matter of—"

All of the shadow servants stationed out in the distance began to charge.

So many, they looked like one moving mass of black.

"There's too many of them." And even then, they would be able to just multiply. Kallia's power was the strongest she'd ever felt it, but still nowhere near Jack's. And even Jack's alone wouldn't be able to handle the incoming horde. "Do you have a plan?"

"Maybe." He looked all around them as if searching for something in the skies. An answer. "I thought I did. I truly didn't think this far ahead."

"What?"

"There were no guarantees with what you would do, Kallia," he sniped behind her. "There was just banking on hope, and I sure didn't think you'd get rid of Zarose Gate."

Her pulse thrummed as the devils raced, getting closer and closer. To them.

And Zarose Gate.

"They can't get near it," Kallia said. "If it breaks again—"

She didn't even want to imagine it. The break would be the start of everything all over again. The city behind them, powerful as it was, would be in ruins. Roth before would never risk it, but now, he was more than just a magician. He would risk anyone in his way.

With the thrust of his hand, Jack took out the first line of devils with a cutting gust of wind. Like cutting a sliver off of the mass rapidly approaching.

Kallia barely thought, she just threw what she had.

Everything she could.

Fire shot, ice spears. Roses with thorns and stems as sharp as daggers. It was like a rapid-fire duel in her mind, one illusion after another she conjured, stabbing the devils one after the other.

It slowed them, but it didn't stop them.

Jack cursed as he breathed heavily with a skyward gaze. Her mind was torn in every direction, her powers divided. She didn't want to leave him to fight them off alone.

Until a glimmer of light caught the corner of her eye.

It trailed across the ground before one found the devil.

Not even her illusions impaling them made it scream the way that flicker of light did.

"Fucking *finally*." Jack sighed as his head tipped up. Not in exhaustion, as he shouted, "Down here—"

Kallia whirled around and caught the barest shape of a hoop.

A blinding flash of light.

Before someone crashed into them from the sky.

"Please say that worked." A blindfolded Ruthless fell on top of them, her head turning frantically. "Also, who am I on?"

Kallia could barely contain the happy sob that rose from her before Malice dropped on them with a pained hiss, blindfolded as well.

"This is so stupid," she grumbled. "Is it safe to look? How the hell are we supposed to—"

Kallia ripped off both of their blindfolds, to which they screamed with their eyes closed.

"The gate, it's gone," she said, throwing her arms over them both. "You both can look."

Her heart swelled to have them back, but a hollowness still remained at the gaping absence of those missing.

Vain, Demarco. Their names raced in time with her pulse, frantic.

Kallia turned to Jack. She wanted to believe him, but at the same time, she was terrified to do so. "Where are they?"

"Finally showing up." He cursed, getting back to his feet. "We *really* don't have time for this."

"How the hell are we supposed to trust you?" Ruthless shot at him. "Where's Vain?"

"And where's Roth—" Malice's eyes went wide at the devil horde coming at them. "Oh, *shit.*"

Kallia's breath seized as they took in the horde heading toward them. Kallia feared that Roth would be in there, charging behind the devils. He would return, Jack said, and she felt that force already coming back.

The first person he would go for was Kallia.

Just to get back the mirror.

An impossible flash of light erupted from the distance. Kallia feared it might be Roth, blasting his way through the army to get to the front.

The last thing she expected to see was a horseless carriage speeding through the devils, running over everything in its path. The devils hissed and scampered away from the carriage's path, even beyond that for how it shone so brightly, even Kallia had to squint her eyes. The same sort of light that reflected off Malice and Ruthless from the cuffs around their arms.

"What is that? What's wrong with the light?"

The devils didn't normally shy away from light. They preferred darkness, but it never actually hurt them.

"It's a reflection of light, in a reflection of a world," Jack said, eyes narrowed, glancing down at the girls' contraption. "Mirror light."

"Turns out, the mirror boy is good at something," Malice noted, admiring her armored cuffs. "Imagine that."

For the first time, he looked genuinely impressed. Relieved. Until he caught what was coming right behind the carriage. Not just a devil, but Roth chasing the speeding vehicle. Unlike the devils, he wasn't shying away from the mirrored carriage. It didn't debilitate him the same way it did to the others.

"I know our plan now," Jack said. "I'll throw him off. But we need to take him down, and all the rest will fall. That's our plan."

Just as he was about to rush off, Kallia grabbed his arm. "Wait, but what about you?"

"I'll be fine. You just have to figure out how—"

"No, what about you?" she repeated harder. "We can't get rid of Roth and the devils without . . ."

Destroying Jack.

From the tic in his jaw, he knew, all along, it would come to this.

"No," she said, shaking her head. "We need to find another way."

"Sometimes the only way is the only way."

Without another word, he pressed his hand over hers, before pulling it off and running in Roth's direction. Before Kallia could even say goodbye.

She didn't want to say goodbye. To any of them.

Somehow Jack vanished into thin air, before an explosion went off like a powder keg high into the sky, releasing the carriage. It came speeding toward them by the city gate, bruised and battered by the beating it had taken from Roth.

It was a miracle that the passengers who staggered out of the door even made it out alive. First Vain, taking dizzy steps, her short hair disheveled and standing on all ends. "Where's the fighting?"

"Other way, darling." Ruthless and Malice took her by both arms, steadying her.

For a moment, the headliner looked close to being sick, until she caught a glimpse of Kallia's face and something broke over hers. It could've been joy. "You good, mortal?"

Kallia could only muster a teary smile as the two other passengers came out of the glass carriage. "Pull your weight, Demarco. I'm not some groom carrying you over the threshold."

"Zarose, I'm never riding in one of those ever again." Demarco panted, his arm slung over Herald's shoulder for support.

"Too fucking bad. I need cover, and you can't exactly—"

Demarco stilled the moment he saw her.

The moment she saw him.

"Oh," Herald scoffed, "*now* you're up on your feet."

Kallia was on hers, too, running as he limped forward. She tried to be gentle, but she threw her arms over Demarco and he gripped her back just as tightly, shaking.

"You're all right," he said, swallowing hard as he cupped her face. His eyes traced over every part of her. "You're all right."

He repeated it again and again, against her hair.

"What about you?" She pressed her cheek to his chest, his heartbeat steady. Alive.

But there was something so different about him now. Something she couldn't quite explain when he didn't answer.

"They're coming back."

Everyone turned at the fear in Ruthless's whisper.

Whatever Jack had done to buy them time had fallen through. The devil horde was back and coming for them. More, from the looks of it, flying down from the sky.

"There are too many," Vain said, already trying to strategize and finding no clear solution in the odds before them.

"We just have to take one down." Kallia looked for Roth in the horde of them, but he was no longer in sight. Neither was Jack.

The fact that the devils were still charging at them meant that their leader was still about.

So they didn't think. Didn't pause. They ran toward the war, with mirror light in hand.

Every blow from Roth, Jack served it back even harder.

The fight was only even when he had his devils pull him by the limbs.

Only to materialize, moments after.

Every damned way Jack could die, he returned with a vengeance. It was the one time he was truly grateful for the ability. To die again and again, only to come back to haunt the living.

The barely living.

"We could go at this all night." Roth laughed, his teeth glistening with black blood. The process of watching a magician become a devil was every bit as terrible as one would think. The human form was not enough to contain a devil—and as many as Roth held in him now, he was surprised to still see the familiar face in there.

"You can keep punching me down all you like, and I can keep tearing you apart all I like," the man continued. "But you all will always be outnumbered."

Jack gritted his teeth as he fought, pushing against Roth. If only he could tire out the king, the rest would fall. But he was still up. Still fighting.

Which meant his devils would continue as well.

"There's no point to your plan anyway," Jack bit out. "The gate is gone."

"The gate doesn't just disappear. The party is still going on, which means it's somewhere. And that bitch knows where."

Sharpening his elbow, Jack threw back a jab, but Roth was quicker. Without any effort, he grabbed hold of Jack's elbow and twisted.

Gritting his teeth, Jack grunted. He hardly felt pain from anyone else, but there was something to a devil fighting him that no magician could ever make him feel.

Jack kicked Roth back and righted his arm back into place. He was tempted to throw all the magic he could at him, but it would only further feed him. As it did with all devils.

A twinkle of light caught the corner of his eye.

There, right before the glowing city, flashes like lightning tore through the army of devils. The one with the mirrored carriage drove through most of them, taking out a large chunk while the others on the ground fought with a combination of mirror light and magic as they soared through the air on their hoops.

A valiant effort, but they were still too few against too many.

"They won't last." The man's voice slithered all around him. "Not like us, Jack. We will always be here, at the end of it. You and me. And without me, you go, too."

Jack edged back, and the two predators began circling again.

"You think I fear the end? It would be refreshing, honestly."

"Martyr talk won't impress her, you know."

The taunt stilled him for a brief moment, long enough to earn a derisive sigh. "This isn't about her."

"It's not?" Roth continued, "You're an absolute waste. Perhaps the most powerful being in both worlds, and you would throw it all away for someone who chose a powerless magician! Such humiliation. Such shame."

"Oh, trust me, I know what that feels like," Jack seethed. That shame had burned when he'd been nothing but the Dealer's servant.

Every order, obeyed.

Every command, answered.

Jack was never born with a choice; he'd found it. He knew how precious it was, more so now than ever. "You can't make me do anything, ever again."

"No, maybe not." Roth frowned. "But I can make sure you watch everything happen."

With that, he raised his hands to the sky.

And the devils fell. They rained like dark shooting stars and rose from the ground.

So many, even Jack stepped back.

All of a sudden, he felt that distance like a block in his chest. He'd been drawn out so far, far away from everyone else. And now he was surrounded.

"And there's more where that came from." With a snap of his fingers, the devils swarmed Jack, more and more rushing like a wave taking him under, writhing all over him.

Too many covered him, until he saw nothing but black.

Nothing but Roth's back as he walked toward the city.

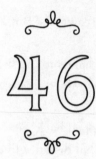

There was only so much they could do for the city behind them. Nothing would stop the devils from breaking down the gates into the city and feasting on those with magic. They were drawn to it, and no one inside would be the wiser.

Kallia tried to concentrate, but the sound of a crash pulled her out of her thoughts.

She frantically looked for the carriage zooming through the devils, and found it completely tipped over on its side.

No, no, no. Her heart lurched. The mirror light it blazed with slowly disappeared as more devils began swarming it.

From behind, Vain snatched Kallia's hand tightly in hers, stopping her in place.

"We can't, we need to get out of here." Vain's breath hitched, something inside her breaking. "Hold on."

They watched in horror as the carriage disappeared under the pile altogether, before her feet flew off the ground entirely, rising higher and higher.

As high as Malice's hoop would take them.

"Too heavy." Malice gasped, holding on to Vain's arm. "Ruth, take Kallia."

Vain started to swing Kallia's arm toward the other hoop next to hers. Ruthless's hand was outstretched, desperately reaching to grab as Kallia let go.

Midair, their fingers brushed—

"Where do you think *you're* going?"

The hand that yanked Kallia's leg dragged her down to the ground.

Her vision blacked out from the force against her skull. She had enough lucidity to cover her face, waiting for the devils to trample her like beasts.

The utter stillness chilled her more, as Roth stood before her.

"It's just you and me, my dear. Away from the noise. It's about to get ugly."

When he gazed past her shoulder, Kallia whirled around.

The city was impossibly far now, a mere blaze of light. She saw the Diamond Rings, holding on to Vain over the surge of devils overtaking the gates of Glorian. They still gathered over the carriage like bugs piling on to each other to feed on a scrap.

"Where is the mirror, Kallia?"

His voice was so close to her ear, she shuddered and threw a blast in his face.

She ran as fast as she could to the city. As fast as her feet could take her.

"You could run for days, and you still wouldn't reach them."

Roth pulled her back by the scruff of her neck, throwing her to the ground.

When Kallia pushed herself back up, she saw how far the city still was. As if she hadn't moved more than a step forward.

"It didn't have to come to this. Not even all the magicians in the city could take this on. Your sad bunch of friends are just ants in comparison. Even Jack is rather occupied."

Kallia backed away from Roth's shadow rising over her.

The monster in her nightmare. The monster all along.

"Tell me where the mirror is, Kallia," he said. "And I can call them off the city, off your friends. You can stop this so very simply."

She didn't believe him. Roth lied. He always lied.

Just as she lied, too.

"Where is the gate, Kallia?"

"I don't know," she screamed.

A displeased sigh. "If you're going to lie to me, at least say the lie to my face."

Kallia rose from the ground with a force that straightened her suddenly until she felt the bones down her spine crack in response. She looked down at the ground where her feet hovered above, before Roth forced her to face him.

The moment he touched her, she threw her hands up and felt the sun blast out of them.

It pushed Roth back, just a bit. Like an errant wind. A minor inconvenience.

"I was expecting a lot more from a born magician." He laughed. "I thought you would at least put up more of a fight."

Kallia's heart sank.

Her power was her power. Nothing special, nothing huge. Nothing but hers.

She'd been hoping for something more to come, but this was all she would get.

Power, but not enough.

Against him, it was an impossible duel.

"I was wrong about you. *We* were wrong," he seethed in her face. "That power you want . . . it's not power. It's spotlight, it's applause. Not the kind of power that would put you on top of the world."

He watched the tears fall from her eyes. One of his cold fingers followed the track, swiping off the tear. Looked at it curiously.

"We thought you could be someone great," he said, flicking the tear away. "You could've set us all free, but you're just another foolish little girl who wants to be a star. Nothing special."

"Nothing special." Her voice trembled. It hurt to give him that, because it was what he wanted to hear. And she had nothing left.

"You're right," she said weakly. "But I still got you exactly where I wanted."

She relished the way his smile dropped hard like a brick when that last hold she kept finally released.

And the mirror appeared beneath their feet.

Without hesitation, Kallia sent a blast of light downward.

And closed her eyes to the sound of his screams.

It was by luck that when the carriage turned over, it was on the other side of the door. That left only one side with the window vulnerable.

"Demarco." Herald huffed out a breath beside him. "It won't hold much longer."

When they tipped over, Daron was more than certain he'd twisted something. Herald sported a bloody nose that gushed in the beginning, but there was no time to stop it when the devils began banging on the window.

The last mirror Herald had packed was a large one, inconveniently so. Not practical enough to use or carry as a shield, but large enough to barricade the other side of the carriage.

Which was how Herald ended up on the ground with both feet pressed up to the back of a mirror on one side, while Daron's shoulders supported the other.

Without a stream of light to refresh the surface, it died.

Soon, the scratching began to break the mirror.

And when the frame itself started to crack under the frenzy of movement on the other side, Daron began to panic.

"It's going to break. Soon," Herald said, wincing at a particularly rough shove. His legs were no doubt trembling as much as Daron's by now. "And when it does—"

"You have to go," Daron said. "You have to leave me, because I won't be able to fight them off."

Herald huffed out a warning breath. "Now is really not the time to be a martyr, Demarco."

"Just like it's not the time to be honorable," Daron bit out. "You know I would only slow you down. Don't pretend I can fight them like you can."

Daron thought the truth would weigh on him more heavily.

The moment his magic left him completely was like the ropes that had bound him had finally fallen free. In that trap, it was either Eva's or Daron's, and the choice was easy. All he could think about was her. And Kallia. And all the power he'd taken without knowing.

It was no longer his.

The chance to give it all away was a chance he never thought he'd get, and he'd taken it. No matter how vulnerable it left him.

Swallowing hard, Herald just gave a shake of his head. "You can't ask me to do that. I'm not just going to leave you behind like that."

The fact that he sounded so insulted was the most amusing part of all. "You're a good friend, Herald. I hope you know that."

Herald grimaced, his jaw set. "There was never any new job."

"What?" It hardly seemed relevant at a time like this.

"You kept asking, so here's your answer: I was lying," he snapped. "After the ball, I just wanted to see what would happen."

A splitting pain tore through his chest when he felt a laugh rise from him. Still, there was a special kind of irony to it all, for Daron couldn't help but think of the card Ira had pulled for him. He'd known the ending for a while, he supposed.

This place, this other side, was a world for magicians.

Anyone else who didn't fit did not belong here.

Daron felt it in his bones. As if the air he was breathing now was not the air his body needed. Like a fish on land, with the ocean far, far away from him.

It would've been slow, if that were the case. With the devils clawing away at the other side, it might be quick. Merciless, but quick.

The mirror cracked further, until a dark hand broke through and shattered the glass.

No more cover. No more shield.

"Go now!" Daron shouted, throwing himself back at the hands swarming in, shielding his face from the glass. "Please, you need to go—"

The hands stilled.

Before they dissolved into smoke.

Stillness. Silence.

Herald blinked long and hard when suddenly, a beam of daylight streamed in through the smashed window.

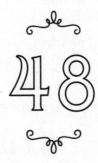

48

Somehow, Kallia could see the light even with her eyes closed.

Every morning in the Glorian she knew, she'd wake up just like this. An early air of silence. The soft light outside, peeking through the curtains to pull her from the dream, coaxing her from sleep.

For a moment, she wondered if this was just that.

A dream.

One so elaborate, she was still standing.

Open your eyes.

For the first time, Kallia trusted herself enough to do so.

Her heart stilled at the sight.

The sky was as gray-white as a Glorian morning all around her. No clouds or sun, but it was a beautiful shade she knew well. Not a devil in sight, neither above nor below.

The barren desert surrounding her was utterly still, untouched as soil packed flat.

And on the ground lay the mirror, reflecting the sky it now faced.

Kallia didn't feel the need to hide from it. It was never fear of looking at the mirror, but what the mirror would see in you. It was a part of the story Roth got wrong.

She wondered what else they'd been wrong about.

The warmth of seeing no devils, no Roth, no darkness abruptly went cold when she realized Jack was gone.

The more she waited, the more silence.

She called his name one last time. Gave one last look behind her.

Before she beckoned the mirror to follow as she turned around and walked back toward the city of lights.

Daron almost fell to his knees when he saw Kallia walking toward him.

Please be real.

When he actually did fall, she ran for him.

You better tell her, Eva had told him. Not a ghost's whisper, but an order followed by a punch in the arm.

How he wanted her to come back with him.

How he wanted them all to return.

The others had left him alone, gone into the city to see the aftermath, to give him this moment to tell her himself.

When Kallia finally made it, she fell to his side. "I can't believe it." Her breathing became erratic. The feel of her hands tracing over him, as if to ensure he was all solid and in one piece, was sublime. "What's wrong?"

He couldn't stop looking at her. There was so much he wanted to tell her, so many things he'd thought he'd never get to say to her when he'd been trapped in that carriage with Herald. But it would be selfish to give her those without giving her this first.

Daron reached out to cup her cheek, noticing the way her eyes closed a second too long, as if she wanted to capture this moment as well.

"I have to tell you something," he said, stroking her cheek one last time before letting his hand fall to the ground. "But first, I want to ask if you wish to stay here?"

"What?" Her brow furrowed. "Why would you ask that?"

"Because this place . . . this place is not the trap everyone needs to be rescued from. It's truly the place for stars to thrive. There's so much freedom, power, and opportunity. So many things most aren't afforded back home," he said, swallowing hard. He would never fault Eva for choosing to stay. For her, this was home, the place where she was most in her element. He would never fault her choice to choose the best for herself. He was not the judge of that; she was. "You've always deserved the best, Kallia."

"Where is this coming from?" she asked, trying to get them both up. "Come on, I think we should go in—"

Daron hissed sharply, startling her as she took them both up. The physical pains were one thing, but his insides felt entirely bruised. Kallia looked him up and down, her frown deepening. "Demarco, what is going on?"

He closed his eyes in a slow, hard blink. "When Eva and I were stuck in one of the devils' traps, they took it all from me."

He didn't have to elaborate; the silence was all he needed to know she'd gathered his meaning. He was new to this world, but she wasn't. The devils could take what no one else could. A fear for most, but a relief for others.

"I'm not a magician anymore, Kallia." He sighed, too nervous to look at her face. See her reaction. "It wouldn't be fair to kiss you until you knew that."

If she even still wanted that.

He was not the same, and they would not be the same again even if they tried.

"*That's* what you're worried about—are you fucking kidding me?"

He'd never seen so much rage in her eyes. It was confusing as hell when she pulled his face to hers and kissed him hard.

"You're an idiot, Demarco," she said against his lips. "You lose your magic and look like you're on death's door, and you worry about what *I* want?"

Herald probably would've clinked a drink with her over that. He'd tell Daron exactly how melodramatic it all was. And the way she said it like that, it was rather ridiculous.

Just like the first time he told her about his magic. The first time she realized he was Daron Demarco. Kallia never cared about any of that, and she looked downright insulted that he'd ever imagine her starting now.

He exhaled deeply. "You deserve so much more. You would never be happy without magic."

"That's different. What magic is to me is not what it is to you." Kallia took his hand, squeezing tight. "And it doesn't matter what I think. You need to ask yourself this—without magic, are *you* happy?"

Daron blinked. There was certainly relief, but it was still too early to tell. Too soon to know entirely. "I don't know yet," he said. "But I think I could be."

Her eyes narrowed, as though she could read his thoughts all too well. "If you're happy, then I'm happy." She laced her fingers within his. "That's how this works."

This.

He didn't understand how a word so simple could fill him with so much light.

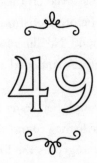

An illusion was always tied to its magician.

With Roth gone, the city fell.

Slowly, gently, the way color bled off a soaked painting, leaving glimmers of what once was. A shame, when the devils' night no longer shadowed the streets.

The rare brightness overhead exposed the city without its mask of flashing spectacle. Under the light, the world appeared less vibrant, less alive. Music that once roared now pulsed at a softer beat. Buildings and cobblestones carried less of the shine and boldness that marked them apart. No performances occupied the sidewalks and street curbs. The people were much too busy peering up, slack-jawed and mesmerized by their world fading under an unfamiliar sun.

Kallia darted past every figure, shielding her eyes the entire way. With every step, she felt a heart beating slower. The dream, lifting.

This city of Glorian, finally going to rest.

She ran faster. Demarco had insisted he didn't mind waiting, but she knew better. Without magic, he stood as good a chance of surviving as this city without its magician. And Zarose Gate would not stay forever, however long it would take for the high of the Show of Hands to wear off.

This was her last chance to find it.

As Kallia burst through the grand doors of the Alastor Place, her jaw hung instantly at the emptiness on the other side. Colorless walls held framed paintings that dissolved off the canvas. Portraits of figures and idyllic scenes flickered before vanishing completely.

And there was no one around. No illusions or waitstaff milling about, no herds of headliners in sight. Abandoned as a house without its dolls.

She hoped she wasn't too late.

Adrenaline pumped through her veins as she took the stairs two steps at a time. It was a miracle the ground still held as she reached her room's level, desolate and changed as the first floor. Until she walked through her door.

Everything remained right where she had left it. Every shade of red was vibrant as ever. Even her bed was the same rumpled mess from when she'd last slept in it. The only sign of wear was in the lush carpets, slowly losing brilliance. It was subtle enough that Kallia caught herself casually fixing up the blankets and pillows a bit before realizing how silly the effort was. That was not what she had gone back for.

Inhaling deeply, she reached under her bed. She grasped and stretched before her fingers brushed cold—

A jolt went through her at the touch on her neck. A whisper, a breeze.

Kallia jerked up, certain she was alone. When the breeze came again, she hardly completed a turn before stilling in place.

The window was cracked open.

Leave. Her heart started thudding. *Just take them and leave.*

One moment she stood staring at the window, and the next she was climbing through it. No fear as she balanced on the outer ledge, hefted herself up in the way he'd taught her. A twinge of soreness finally spasmed through the adrenaline. The ache settled in her muscles once she met the top of the roof, but the pain left instantly.

A figure stood at the edge of the roof, overlooking the world.

Same height, same sinewy frame beneath an untucked shirt with the sleeves pushed to the forearms.

He stilled at her first step and turned at her second.

Kallia froze. "You're here."

Any uncertainty in Jack's eyes cleared the moment a familiar, slow smile tugged at his lips. "Disappointed?"

Her mind blanked and raced in every direction at his voice. He looked and sounded just as he did in her memory. Only this time, there was light all around them.

"It's a shame to lose all of this." His lips drew into a wry smile, before he pivoted back to take in the view. "I always wondered what it might look like in the light."

She had no response. Every emotion and wound—all the words she wanted to shout in his face for all he'd done—ripped inside her. For every cruelty, each lie. For vanishing without a trace as though he were truly gone for good, after everything.

"You say that as if it's beautiful," she bit out. "It's half a city."

If she hadn't gone back, would he have simply stayed away?

None of this seemed to bother Jack half as much as he exhaled, looking down. He seemed almost pleased. "Not for long."

From their vantage point, the roofs of smaller marvel and style houses scattered about appeared as transparent as the beginnings of a mirage. The stunned silence had broken as faint protests and curses scattered over the streets, demanding answers. Any authority. The weight of it all fell over her shoulders for a moment as she envisioned that chaos, claimed by the Diamond Rings.

There would be so much to put back together once there was nothing left standing.

"Why are you here?"

Jack's quiet question came out of nowhere. It took some time before his stare lifted to hers. That he could even ask it, after everything, astounded her.

"Why are *you* here?" Kallia sounded remarkably calm for how much she wished to scream. "And . . . *how*?"

A smile cracked through his hard expression. "I guess we can cross Zarose Gate off the death list."

"This isn't funny, Jack," she said flatly.

"I'm not joking." When it was clear she wouldn't play along, his face dropped a fraction. "Roth didn't make me, no matter how much he claimed it. Took me long enough to realize my ties are not actually to him."

"The devils?" She didn't know which was worse, being at the mercy of a weak-willed magician or a force of terrible power. All this earned was a casual shrug from him.

"That *can't* be, they're gone." Kallia blinked rapidly at the brightness above. "This proves—"

"Even the sun has to set eventually." Jack shoved his hands into his pockets. His lips drew into a resigned line. "This won't last forever. Where there's light, there will always be shadows. No matter how diminished, power like that can't just vanish entirely."

"What are you saying?" Frantic, she studied him even closer for any signs of weakness. "Are you all right?"

"I am still here," he said in answer. "Which means so are they." His gaze drifted over to the disappearing gate where those vast, empty lands awaited. "Hopefully not for a while, though."

Optimism was not the card to play with such uncertainties. Unable to tell when the light would run out, when darkness would fall once more, turned even balance into a cruel joke—what had to be for something to stay. It was the only reason Jack still stood now. As long as darkness existed, so did he.

"How does that affect *you*, though?" Gritting her teeth, she looked him over. Closer. "What of your power and—"

"You really don't have to worry about that."

Her eyes narrowed to sharp points. She had no patience for his jokes, even less for evasiveness. "So why won't you tell me, then?"

"Why are you even still *here*?" His nostrils flared with his raised voice. He still didn't look at her directly, only took little sips of her in glimpses. "You both have your chance to finally go, so *go*."

Not like this, when it felt like they were still crossing a tightrope about to snap.

"It's not that simple," she bit out. "Especially when . . . we don't even know if it'll work—"

"It will," he said without hesitation. "Still, there's no excuse not to try. Don't waste a second chance when this world so rarely offers them."

So how had he known that this time, it would? Kallia refused to accept any of it as coincidence. There was no such thing anymore, not with how the cards had fallen precisely into place. Such an impossible outcome was not the result of a miracle dropping from the sky. There were always strings attached, and there was no puppeteer more skilled than Jack. He never acted without intention, which meant he'd always *known* Zarose Gate would arrive, and Kallia would face it. Just as he'd known what would happen once he sent Demarco and Vain out to those devils.

Why?

The simple question stilled on her tongue. It haunted her more than the answer, something Jack would only lace with lies. True to form, a magician never revealed his secrets. No matter how much she wanted them. How much she fought.

"I don't want to fight with you anymore, Jack." Kallia let out a breath of defeat, closing her eyes. There was too little time and there weren't enough words left to justify wasting them. "I just want—" Her throat bobbed with a hard swallow under Jack's unflinching gaze.

"You just want . . . ?" He lifted an expectant brow at her, waiting.

It irked her, but she would miss it. She would miss him. "I wanted to say goodbye. Properly," she said, lifting her chin. "I'm glad you're still around, Jack."

And she meant it.

Even though he released a bitter laugh in response. "You don't have to be polite and say that for my sake."

Kallia frowned. "I'm not."

"Then you'd be the only one." He shrugged his steady shoulders. "Everyone in this world probably thinks I'm gone with all the monsters. Maybe I'll let them believe it."

Something rose deep inside her chest, different from when the Diamond Rings had embraced her hard enough to crush bones. Jack wasn't even touching her, and every word he said threatened to snap her in half.

Jaw clenched, Kallia gripped the warmed metal at her side like an anchor. The weight was much lighter than she remembered, more familiar.

It was time to give them back.

"Do you want to know why I returned here?"

Before Kallia could stop herself, she pulled Jack forward and forced his hand out of his pocket. A noise of surprise broke from him, an intake of breath when she pressed the black brass knuckles into his palm.

Everything about his face transformed at the sight. Softened at the edges.

"It was because I didn't want to leave something of yours behind." Heart pounding, Kallia firmly closed her fingers over his, over the brass knuckles. "Because these belong to you."

His hands stilled beneath hers, just as hers had done when he'd given them to her on this roof not long ago. She never should've kept them. There was no reason to hold memories she could not remember, along with ones she'd rather not. Answers she didn't need, and questions long past the point of asking. Because of that, they'd always been more his than hers. She felt it with every brush of his thumb across his knuckles, the endearing way his large palm cradled the object now as she began withdrawing.

Jack pulled her back, and she gasped at the abrupt motion. The feel of his cold, hard chest against hers. Uncertainty fluttered straight down her spine, waiting.

Waiting.

Waiting until a quiet fell over them, and nothing more. Not even words. As Kallia lifted her face up, Jack's stare dropped and lingered on their hands; hers, covering his like armor. An embrace.

"Thank you," he rasped out, before finally stepping back.

Kallia blinked as the world drew back into focus, with time snapping back into place. It made her want more.

More time, more words.

"It's been strange, not having these. I had a feeling you'd pick up on it." He slipped on the brass knuckles in one smooth motion and grinned down at them as if greeting an old friend. "Now you know my tell."

Warmth pooled in her chest. One secret was enough.

"Maybe I can properly punch you in the face with them one day."

A small laugh left him, trailed by a deep, wry exhale. "You know that's not how this works."

"What do you mean?"

Just as sudden as the warmth had come, cold dropped at the grim line of his lips. "Second chances are rare. Third, nonexistent. We're lucky to be able to bend the rules once."

"But . . . weren't you made to cross over whenever you'd like?"

"Back then." He shrugged. "Not quite sure when I'll have enough power for it again, but certainly not at the moment."

The contented beat of her pulse skipped to a confused rhythm. He had to be lying. Jack never claimed anything unless it served him.

Then again, he'd never claimed weakness at all. Not in front of her.

"If this is a joke, it's not a good one."

His eyes remained firm on hers as he shook his head slowly. "I was never meant to stay there for long anyway," he said. "And like many here, that world is not to me what it is to you."

Kallia didn't know how to react. It frustrated her, how after years of knowing him, she could read him well but not enough to be sure. To know his lies from truths, when his face remained a mask not even she could take off entirely.

"So what are you saying?" Blood thundered in her ears at the crack in her voice. Leaving meant losing everything and everyone here, that was a given. As much as she hated that, there was comfort in know-ing that at least she wouldn't lose everything. There would always be Jack, because Jack was that bridge between both worlds. He could pass along messages and updates, visit wherever he'd like without the threat of Roth watching.

To be cut off from it all was painful. A pain she was sure she'd never felt before. "Will we see *any* of you ever again?"

She couldn't ask about him specifically, was not ready to cross that line. Either way, his breath stopped and his jaw tensed. "Maybe one day."

No, Kallia. You won't.

She wished he'd just say what he meant. The truth.

Even though she knew it already.

"Why are you crying?"

His intense expression had contorted in such surprise, Kallia had to roll her eyes. "I'm not heartless." She sniffled. "I wish it wasn't like this . . . losing so much, at every turn. I just want—"

Everything. Just like she always did.

But she didn't want this. This choice felt like a punishment. Limiting instead of empowering. She didn't want to have to choose between sides and people like right and wrong. She didn't want regret to always make her wonder or look back to where the other way would've led. Regardless of her choice, those were the ghosts that would follow. No matter where she went.

"You're losing nothing, Kallia."

A scoff sliced through her lips. "I thought we were past lies."

If Jack truly believed that, then he was just as naive as she was. Just as she was about to turn from him, he stopped her. Not with force, but with the gentle lift of her chin in his fingers. "I'm *not* lying to you."

Kallia resisted the urge to shut her eyes. His were too much, this close. Stormy and regal, like lightning contained. They hadn't stood this close since she'd pushed him through the mirror, since their last dance.

This, too, would be a last.

"You know this isn't a true life." Jack waved his free hand all around them. "Most forget that, because most are fools who don't ever wish to look back. But there is *so* much more than this out there."

She couldn't deny a word of it, couldn't help but feel so immensely small, all at once. Apart from Demarco, her friends, and the people she'd met—the home she'd found in them all—the true side was a stranger. After all, she knew one house, one city. Nothing else. It struck a fearful chord in her, all that she wasn't prepared for. "More what, exactly?"

"That will be for you to decide," Jack said quietly, deep in thought as he searched her face. "Finally."

The Court of Mirrors was still intact for the most part when Kallia stood before Zarose Gate. This monster from legend, a beast that carried so many shadows.

Nothing more than an ordinary mirror.

This one would not hurt her.

"What's the matter?"

Kallia startled at the brush against her elbow when there was no one else in the reflection but her. Outside of it, Demarco stood beside her, taking in his lack of a reflection with curiosity. "Oh."

It only saw magicians. This was all the proof she needed.

To move forward.

To go back.

Take me home.

"What's the matter?" He cupped her face, lifting it up. "I thought you wanted this, too."

"I want it too much."

She always had, always would.

Confusion creased his brow deeper. "Is that a problem?"

Not now, but later. Losing over and over again had left that mark, the kind of terror as bone-deep as certainty. Even with Demarco's hand in hers, she could feel him slipping away again already, so easily, if fate wanted to play another game. She could see everything she'd ever wanted in her grasp, falling through her fingers just as she'd reached them. Just like before.

There was hardly any hope when she faced the mirror. When she looked, she saw only a cautionary tale. A trap, baiting her with every impossibility offered on a platter: for two to go through, for that freedom to go back, to return to everything she'd lost.

There was simply no way. Luck like that was like looking a devil's trap in the face, and she didn't trust it. Not after everything.

Demarco didn't settle for just holding her hand. He pulled her close and held her for so long she was tempted to close her eyes.

"It's okay to be afraid," he whispered against her hair, "of not knowing what comes next."

The knot in Kallia's stomach tightened, growing more tangled with every thought. "I'm more worried about what I'll lose next," she said.

"Then you're worrying about something that hasn't happened yet. That may not happen at all."

Kallia stared at her reflection, the one she'd healed with her very own hands.

The one that beckoned her through, warm as a welcome. Inviting as trust.

Take me home.

There was a reason she'd said those words to him before, and that those words did not apply to this side.

Whatever happened next, at least she would be home.

It was hardest to say goodbye, but somehow, they managed.

Kallia was showered in tight embraces, kisses on cheeks.

When she reached Vain, who'd simply held on to Demarco for as long as she could, only then did a breath begin to choke her.

It was the hardest goodbye yet, so she didn't say it at all as they held on to one another. Once more, before it was time.

"Thank you," Kallia said, pulling back with a shaking breath. It was nowhere near an adequate thanks for everything, but somehow she knew Vain could hear it all in two words.

"Be sure to pass it on," Vain responded with a sly smile of her own.

Demarco had already taken her hand before she could take his. The warm, coarse feel of his palm against hers steadied her as the nerves started up again when they stepped up to the mirror.

She took her fill of the scene, the Court of Mirrors falling and fading, patches of the walls fully formed and painted while others had become translucent as ice.

Her heart seized for a moment.

A figure leaning against the half-translucent wall caught her eye, far back enough he could be mistaken as a shadow in the corner.

But she knew that form, the sharp cut of the suit even at a distance.

Take it, and don't look back.

She nodded softly and stepped through the mirror with Demarco as though it were air.

Somewhere in the dark, they'd begun to walk. The path found their feet with each step, not quite solid ground. But with each step, the path grew firmer.

It was a long road, and neither of them spoke. They talked in the squeezes of hands, to make sure the other was okay, to keep from disturbing whatever fragile balance of a road they were on now.

Kallia couldn't imagine walking this road alone, and was glad she didn't have to.

For the silent dark was the best home for doubt. The last thing either of them needed to move forward.

She fought to recall the faces of her friends on the other side, and found it was much harder than before. Time away had faded their features in her head. Nothing frightened her more than forgetting the ones she loved. As if by sheer will, she concentrated, digging deep into her memory to see Aaros and Canary and the Conquerors, to remember Glorian as it used to be and the way she felt upon its stage.

Remember.

Her temple throbbed at the effort.

Remember.

The squeeze at her fingers sent a jolt through her. When she pried her eyes open, there was light. A speck, as far away as a star.

For some reason, some mirrors had remained when everything else had fallen. There was no apparent reason for it, but Jack didn't trust it.

Without drawing notice, he'd collected them all in one room, in case they might tempt anyone to start looking at them again.

The more separate each side remained, the safer all would be.

It was the most he could do with all that he'd lost, but at least it was something.

Until one mirror remained, and he couldn't bring himself to break it just yet.

Just in case.

"I thought I smelled a monster."

He glanced at the mirror's edge, and there was a figure leaning against the door, filing her sharp nails like tending to knives.

She'd snuck up on him.

How the hell had she done that?

"What are you doing here?" He turned back to the mirror with a glare.

"What are *you* doing here?" Vain shot back, raising a brow. "Thought you were supposed to be dead."

The fact that she displayed no shock, at least not her usual amount, meant she'd known for a while that he wasn't.

"If you won't tell anyone, I won't," he said, hoping she'd leave it at that. If they didn't want anything to do with him, then he wanted nothing in return.

His head lifted in slight surprise at the sound of a cold heel taking one step in.

"I didn't say you could come in."

"You see, that's the thing." Another click of her heel. "You don't make the rules around here. I do now."

Jack snorted. "And why would I ever follow them?"

"Because I know how hard it is." Behind him, Vain crossed her arms, tracing the golden frame. "Because I know it's not all just breaking glass."

At least they could agree on that. Breaking glass like this was severing something real. A connection.

Strong yet still fragile, for how easily it could be lost in a fractured surface.

"Think they made it?"

His eyes found hers in the mirror, and for once, she didn't turn away. She held on with unwavering command, as if willing him to be the first to fold in this game.

"I don't know," Jack finally answered. Maybe they never would. Maybe it was better that way. "I haven't looked to see, but if something were wrong, I'd like to think I'd feel some way about it. Some pang in my chest or alarm in my mind."

After Kallia had left Hellfire House, there was nothing but wrongness the moment it happened. As soon as they'd left through the mirror, he'd felt no different. Still felt that way. At first it had worried him, though perhaps it was a silent blessing. A way to move on.

"I guess it's not such a bad thing, to feel no worry. We don't want it for them, and they wouldn't want it for us," she said, still watching him though she'd already won the game, before her piercing stare drifted away. "There's only one thing left to do, then."

Jack blinked down at the brass knuckles encircling his fingers before looking back up. Vain had disappeared on a different note than before. Still icier than winter, but on the cusp of spring. Though the next time she saw him, the expectation in her eyes would be clear.

It had to be done.

With one last inhale, he threw his fist against the mirror.

Quicker than a second.

Harsher than a stab.

Fragments of the mirror broke off and fell, joining the shards sprinkled across the ground. Large chunks of the mirror still remained, cracks webbing in jagged shapes against the frame. Just moments ago, Jack stood there whole as ever, but now there was barely half of him left. His face was cut in half by a thick slab of glass still hanging on.

He was a story half-told. Half-truth, half-lie.

He pressed his knuckles against the remaining piece until it crushed even more. He was glad to no longer see his face, nor himself, in the mirror anymore. Just an empty frame with a plain wooden backing, waiting to be filled with something different.

Something that could be.

He had seen it long before the city fell. He saw it now in the broken pieces of mirror scattered everywhere on the ground, in the headliner who walked around as if she wore a crown too heavy for her head already.

Jack didn't care for crowns or what would come next, though he could see it all unfold with perfect clarity.

A broken land needed to be rebuilt.

Which meant it was time to raise another kingdom.

EPILOGUE

The star stood at her mirror, waiting for the show to begin.

It had been a while since she'd prepared like this. Her face painted and bolder than usual. Glitter dusted over her collar and bare shoulders. The neckline of her costume plunged into a scarlet confection of studded gems and feathered tassels that flounced whenever she twirled into a step.

The last time she'd worn an outfit like this, it was for another show that belonged in something of a dream. A dream far, far away.

That's what she told the world when they asked her where she'd been. Why she'd gone, and how they had returned.

Were you abducted, miss?

Was it some powerful trick gone wrong, or were the Patrons involved in yet another scandalous cover-up?

Is it true you ran away with a second lover and decided the harlot's life just wasn't for you?

The press was a delightful beast. Hardly ever slept when it was hungry for a scandal. And she had all the knowledge to feed it. She could go on and on about a land dominated by endless night, full of parties and power games between all of its players. The best show magicians in the business whom the world would never know.

Surprisingly, no reporters came knocking at her dressing room door. They'd hounded her at rare outings with friends, or dining with her assistant, who was more than ready to punch any nosy stranger who got too close.

With the star's grand return to the stage tonight after a year away, everyone wanted the story.

To the world's displeasure, it was a story she would never tell. A star was entitled to her secrets, after all. Those memories were hers, and they were all she had of those who stayed behind the glass.

"I can't believe this." An annoyed scoff rose over the crinkle of a newspaper from the corner of her dressing room. "They're *still* writing about him?"

"And you're *still* reading in here?" The star could've laughed at the way he claimed to loathe the papers, yet always carried some issue to peruse while she primped. It helped that the press had at least stopped hailing him as "the powerless magician." Some outlets had even graciously phased out labeling him as "fraud" and "liar."

Chagrined, he peeked over the top of newspaper. Beneath dark, disheveled hair, his expression was the odd combination of charmingly boyish and stoic as stone. A handsome face no one could hate, especially when the star had returned with his hand in hers.

It was a magic trick, in and of itself. All the vitriol flung at him before, vanished. Every glare and seething rumor, gone in a blink. Yet somehow, with every issue, he managed to dig up the thorns instead of the roses.

"Why must you read those if they make you so angry?" She swiveled her chair toward the mirror once more, studying his reactions in the reflection. There couldn't have been anything staining their names in recent articles. Once the press caught whiff of a new show in the works, it had been a feeding frenzy the moment the story broke. But soon after, it was total silence. A temporary peace from the media, perhaps the best present their friend with the poisonous pen could've given them.

"I'm not angry," he bristled, flipping to the next section and read aloud. "Just listen to this . . . *Erasmus Rayne, of the formerly known Conquer-*

ing Circus, has been taken into custody after a dispute in the casino rings of New Crown when the man was found soliciting and propositioning young servers, maids, and footmen to join in his new entertainment venture he has repeatedly promised will make 'everything that came before look like quiet afternoon tea.'" An aggravated grunt cut his next breath. "Why would *anyone* find that enticing?"

She fluffed her hair over her shoulders, amused as she watched him. "How is it that in a battle between paper and man, it's the paper that's winning right now?"

He chose to ignore that by reading on after a few skimming whispers. "Ah, yes—*Rayne, who oversaw the disastrous run of Spectaculore that gripped all of Soltair, also recently came under fire due to claims of mistreatment of his performers—one of whom had been found unconscious and unresponsive during a troubling period of accidents, only to wake up weeks later to the proprietor's demanding tour schedule. All members of Rayne's Conquering Circus unanimously disbanded to form their own independent troupe, soon to start their first—*"

"*I* could've told you that in less than a blink," she scoffed.

"This was published today," he said, scratching his head. "And we only just met up with them last night."

"You vastly underestimate the power of a few stolen hours with a bottle of wine." She chuckled, catching his stormy expression in the mirror. "*You* chose to skip last night's gathering."

"My partying days are over." He folded up the newspaper before tossing it on the table. "I'm a changed and *very* exhausted man."

"That last bit sounds either boring or promising, depending on how you hear it."

The assistant's ever-grinning face poked in through the door, narrowly ducking to avoid a small pillow thrown at his head. "*Rude.*"

"Says the one who strolls in without knocking," came the thorny response from across the room.

"Don't worry, if I ever catch you two in a compromising position again, I now know to avert my innocent eyes immediately," the assistant quipped, dodging a small plush toy that bounced off the door instead.

"No fighting." The star's eyes darted between both of them as she leaned by the door frame. "How's the crowd?"

"Show is starting soon, so . . ." The assistant's conspiratorial grin mirrored hers. "The house is packed."

"Excellent." That's what she loved to hear. "And what of the academies? Did the girls show up?"

"Queen Casine's practically filled up the front rows. I think even some Valmonts boys are in the audience."

It was more than she'd expected. Most spectators figured the first leg of her tour with the Conquerors would start in New Crown, kicking off where most shows launched in the heart of Soltair's entertainment capitol.

No one expected a quiet strip of land between the academies in the southern region to be their first choice of stage. An odd one, but perfect, in the star's eyes.

She made sure to send her assistant invitations by the cartload for every student curious to enough to come see the show.

Curiosity would be the first step to her greatest trick yet.

The setup began like the sky when dusk hits, that moment just before night breaks where the stars remain hidden in the wings, waiting for the first to appear.

Because once one star stepped forward, another would follow.

And more would come.

"Flirting time is over, kids. No more distractions." The assistant crooked his finger. "She's on in ten to open with Canary, so get your ass in the front row. It's a sea of lovely and lovesick schoolgirls. You'll fit right in."

The star caught the next projectile—a velvet box of chocolates—before it slammed against the swiftly closed door. "If you throw one more thing in any of my dressing rooms these next few weeks, I'll throw *you* out."

He slowly rose toward her with a grin before plucking the box right of her hand. "No you won't."

The box clattered to the ground as he deftly spun her until her back hit the door.

His face hovered over hers. *"Am* I a distraction?"

It was unfair how close he was. The way his eyes grew hazy and flitted to her lips, too. "Now you are."

"Good. Now you know how I feel after seeing you in this dress." When his grip tightened over her hips, every fingertip burned through the fabric. She wanted more. Eyes heavy, she arched her neck up, lips catching the edge of his jaw.

"Your makeup." He drew more firmly back, landing a swift kiss over her brow. "I'll try not to be *too* distracting from the audience."

"You're such a liar." Twisting the fabric of his shirt, she dragged his face down to hers and kissed him hard on the mouth. Every time he watched her perform, even during a casual practice where he walked past the doors, he always stopped to watch. If the house were burning, if she were conjuring the same exact illusion seven times over, his gaze would stay. As if she were crossing that stage for the first time.

He didn't leave for some time, mostly to fix his face as thoroughly as she redid hers.

He left her soon after to find his seat in the front row. Best seat in the house, which he had happily claimed for tonight. Along with every show after.

Alone, for the first time all day, she closed her eyes and breathed. She counted every inhale and exhale, until all went quiet in her mind. That place she loved to go, just before she took the stage.

She imagined the descent of a chandelier from the ceiling.

The rise and fall of a slow-swaying hoop.

And the first real stage to touch her feet.

Her last ritual was the reflection. Every time she stared in the mirror, she couldn't help wondering if someone was on the other side. If someone pressed luck to her fingers every time she brushed the cool, smooth surface before leaving her dressing room.

Now, she was ready.

ACKNOWLEDGMENTS

If you're reading this page, you've either reached the end or chosen it as your starting place. Either way, thank you for arriving here. And most importantly, thank you for picking up this book—my duology—in the first place. I've often talked about how writing *Where Dreams Descend* was pure joy. *When Night Breaks*, however, was entirely the opposite experience. Amongst authors, writing the dreaded Book 2 is a difficulty all on its own; that, on top of it being the end of a duology during a pandemic, amongst other life, mental health, and debut book curveballs, made for a truly dark and crushing time. For so long, I felt like this book had broken me as many times as I'd broken it, that it scared every other story left inside me. At one point, I feared I would never be able to finish *When Night Breaks* no matter how many times I tried.

While I viewed the first book as a dream and hoped the next would follow suit, I ultimately realized this sequel was a mirror. *My* mirror. A broken reflection created when I was not my best self, riddled with cracks on every page, scars I'd rather not remember, reminders of every delay and extension I was so desperate for and thankful to get, and every pain I had to push aside to work through. Although this experience is not uncommon amongst authors and creatives, this is what *When Night Breaks* will always look like to me.

Because writing this book often felt like writing in the dark, readers might sense that. And I'm truly sorry if you do. This book was made in dark times I'm still healing from, but being on that journey in the first place is what led me to this finale and all of its broken paths. A finale I never thought would happen. And the only reason that feat was even possible was 1000 percent due to the phenomenal people I'm lucky to have in my life, who kept me going all the way to that finish line.

Thank you so much to my brilliant agent, Thao Le, who first opened the door for me and never hesitated to hold my hand through all the good times and the bad. You *always* go above and beyond in ways I never knew an agent could, and I would not have been able to complete this series and feel that spark in writing again without you. I'm truly honored to be working with you after all these years. Thank you for all you have done, and all that you do.

Thank you so much to my incredible editor, Vicki Lame, who gave this writer a chance (many, in fact), gave a showgirl a spotlight, and gave us both a stage to tell our story from beginning to end. I can't express how grateful I am to you for never once giving up on me or this book. For the endless support, patience, and understanding that kept Kallia and me afloat. And most importantly, thank you for this unforgettable journey. An author could not have asked for a better guide and champion at her side.

I don't even know how to properly convey my deep gratitude and love for everyone at Wednesday Books who helped bring my books to life, but especially those who paved the way for this tricky book during such tricky times. Thank you to Jennie Conway, Angelica Chong, and Sara Goodman. Thank you so much to those in my wonderful marketing corner, DJ DeSmyter, Alexis Neuville, and Brant Janeway; thank you to my amazing publicist, Meghan Harrington; thank you to my immensely talented cover art design team, Kerri Resnick and Micaela Alcaino, and Rhys Davies for the stunning map. And a huge thank you—*so*, so much—to the remarkable production department at Wednesday Books who tirelessly move mountains behind the scenes and truly went above and beyond to give me the

ACKNOWLEDGMENTS ∽ 469

time and space to write and heal. Thank you to Devan Norman, Elizabeth R. Curione, Elizabeth Catalano, Lena Shekhter, Jessica Katz, Carla Benton, Lauren Riebs, Melanie Sanders, and NaNá V. Stoelzle.

Every stage of this book felt like an uphill battle, and nothing about it was easy. Thank you all for braving that journey with me and supporting me when I needed it most. I'm proud to work with you all, and to have you all on my beloved Dreams team.

No journey is ever complete without a buddy system, and mine is without doubt the greatest. Thank you so much to my talented, tireless, Shrek-tastic cult for being the best kind of strangers to meet online. Thank you Maddy Colis, Akshaya Raman, Meg Kohlmann, Kat Cho, Christine Lynn Herman, Amanda Foody, Claribel Ortega, Tara Sim, Katy Rose Pool, Ashley Burdin, Melody Simpson, Alexis Castellanos, and Erin Bay. Thank you to Mara Fitzgerald, my Joseph, Hellmo, and Shrek buddy—I truly don't know how I would've survived the doomed debut year without you, but I'm glad we can always suffer together. Thank you to Axie Oh, who never lets me blast off at the speed of light alone. *Stitch and robot noises* And an epic thank you to Amanda Haas, the cleverest fox I know who gave this book its True Name. So many hugs and thanks to Diana Urban, Julie C. Dao, Ashley Schumacher, Sara Raasch, Andrea Tang, Mei Lin Barral, Ellie Moreton, Roshani Chokshi, Hannah Reynolds, Susan Dennard, and Erin Bowman. Thank you for your endless kindness, wisdom, check-ins, support, and friendships over the years—and most of all, thank you for always being there. And to my fellow resilient Roaring '20s debuts, thank you for all the strength, love, and tears shared online. Publishing is said to throw the lowest of lows and the highest of highs at authors who stay in the game long enough, and I truly hope things are only looking up for every person in our class. Now, let's get those jerseys, because we definitely deserve them.

To every member within the vast bookish community—from book twitter to booktube to bookstagram to booktok to book blogging and beyond—thank you for championing stories and for lifting mine up so graciously for new readers to discover. A huge thank-you to Alexa at (@AlexaLovesBooks), Bethany (@BeautifullyBookishBethany), all the Writers Block Party lovelies (@WritersParty), Kate (@YourTitaKate), Shealea (@shutupshealea), the members of WDD Nation: @dearcresswell, @wonderousmel, and @alizaydnasir. And a big shout-out to the folks at OwlCrate for giving WDD and WNB the incredible opportunity to reach so many readers with such stunning editions of this duology. Naked hardcovers for the win.

I'm so thankful every day for my family, and I truly would not be writing today without them. Thank you so much, Mama and Papa—for always believing in me, for laughing with me, and for loving me. The love I have for you two can only be accurately measured in all the messes I leave behind. Thank you to my ultimate constants in life, my siblings: Lia, Michael, Chino, Nina, and Joseph. And to the true lights of my life: Michael, Sophia, and yes, Luke/Master Skywalker—thank you for being my main sources of serotonin. Thank you so much to the best Daydreamer I know—for holding my hand through it all, for answering every call, and for being by my side in life in so many ways, like Happy and Ramen. Last but not least, thank you, Norma Angeles—my grandmother, my Loli. The true first writer in the family, who encouraged me and was so proud to see me on my way. Whenever I dreamed of my first book launch party, your face was *always* the one I wanted to see most in the crowd, and it breaks my heart knowing that will never happen. I miss you and am thankful you're still somewhere over my shoulder, making sure I'm writing.

And finally, thank *you*, readers. Thank you so much for being on this journey with me, for embracing Kallia and the gang, for every lovely book review and wonderful book post created, for all the reader emails that have made me tear up, for every librarian and bookseller who's ever recommended or ordered copies, for every person who has ever flailed over musicals with me. You, readers, are what make this road worthwhile when the days are hard and the words don't come easy. Thank you so much for helping me get to this finale. And as always, I hope you enjoy the show.